NORTHERN LIGHTS

NATURAL WONDERS
BOOK 1

B.J. HILL

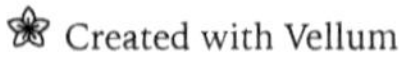
Created with Vellum

DEDICATION

To Sunny, for believing in me.
To Stacey, for guiding me.
To Nick, for loving me.

PROLOGUE

IS *this what death feels like? Because I'm completely numb.* I'm sitting here in the hospital, waiting on news about my sister and brother-in-law.

Mom called me screaming in the middle of a study night, telling me I had to get to Grant Medical Center as soon as possible because Belle and her husband, Alex, were in a car accident. Their nine-month-old daughter, Sunny, was in the car with them.

And now they're in the hospital.

My sister and brother-in-law are both in surgery and have been for hours. I have no idea how long I've been sitting here. One hour? Two?

It doesn't matter. I can't feel anything.

I feel like if she was alive, I would know it. I feel like if she wasn't alive, I would know it. Aren't you supposed to feel a soul-deep connection to the people you love? I've read about people feeling a tug on their souls when something terrible happens to their spouses or families.

That didn't happen for me. While my sister was experiencing hell on wheels — *dammit, Alis, now is not the time for puns* — I was over-stuffing my mouth with pizza, bopping my head and feet to Taylor

Swift, and reading through my paper about the symbolic anthropo-morphism of *The Raven* for my American Lit seminar.

And now? I can't think. I can't feel. I can't do anything. I'm just staring at the wall, looking at this ridiculous framed print of a pelican.

Who the fuck thought a painting of a pelican sitting on a jette would be a comforting scene to look at while waiting for a loved one to get out of surgery? Pelicans are giant sea birds with the largest double chins in the history of double chins. They aren't pretty. They aren't serene. This picture isn't at all relaxing to look at. It has no purpose.

I take that back. I'm annoyed with the pelican painting. Annoy-ance is a feeling. The pelican serves a purpose.

Glancing away from the bird, I look over at my parents, huddled together near the waiting room door.

This kind of stuff happens in movies, but not in real life. Right?

Dad said the guy who hit them died on impact. He was drunk, veered into their lane, and hit them head-on when they were on their way home from dinner.

That's something I loved about my sister.

LOVE. Not loved. She's alive. Past tense has no place here.

I love that, even with a nine-month-old baby, she and Alex still go out to dinner. They live full lives and include Sunny in their fun. Belle never hibernated or complained about being too tired to take a crying infant into public places. I hope that, if I ever become a mom, I'll be like her, and will see my children as whole people from the moment they are born.

Our family has never subscribed to the "children should be seen but not heard" mentality. I'm thankful that Belle and Alex followed in our parents' footsteps.

Gosh, what is taking so long? I swear she has been in there forever.

Alex too. Alex has been in surgery for hours.

Sunny seems fine. The doctors looked her over and thankfully she didn't have any internal bleeding. She's bruised from the car seat straps and I'm sure she was shaken up during the collision, but other than that she's fine. They're keeping her overnight for observation, and my aunt is sitting with her in her hospital room.

Note to self: Post a five-star review for Britax on Amazon. The Uber-expensive car seat saved my niece's life tonight.

I'm still staring at my parents. It looks like they're slow dancing, hugging each other and swaying as mom cries silent tears. Every so often they still, breathing heavily, until more tears come, and their bodies sob and sway once again.

Watching them together is the most beautiful, heartbreaking thing I've ever witnessed. It should warm or break my numb heart. But the thought just appears in my brain, beautiful words devoid of emotion.

My parents hugged me when I arrived, but I couldn't stay in their embrace. My body repelled any physical contact. I needed space. Silence. A bench to myself. A wall to stare at. And then the stupid fucking pelican showed up. I guess the pelican didn't show up; I did. The bird was here first.

Shouldn't I have some underlying feeling of hope or dread? Am I in shock? Is this what shock feels like?

Jarred from my thoughts, I look up as the double doors swing open. A doctor in scrubs walks in. "Alex Donnelly? Alex Donnelly's family?"

That's us.

I stand and meet my parents as they signal to the doctor that we are Alex's family.

My sister met her husband while studying abroad in Ireland. They fell in love, eloped, and then he followed her back to America. They now reside in the same small town our family has lived in for three generations. So. Exciting.

I've never understood their decision to return to America. It seems backward to me. I figure if you're going to marry a hot Irishman, you should … you know, live in the Highlands or something. Wait, the Highlands are in Scotland, not Ireland. Whatever.

Damn, my wandering thoughts. The doctor is speaking, for Christ's sake.

"Mr. and Mrs. —"

"Gilmore," Mom interjects. "We are Alex's in-laws. We're his only family here."

"Yes, Mr. and Mrs. Gilmore. I'm so sorry. We did everything we could, but Alex wasn't able to pull through. We lost him in surgery."

What?! Alex is gone? Dead? No longer breathing?

Mom's knees buckle and she sobs into Dad's chest, gripping onto him for dear life.

I blink. And blink. And blink some more.

My brother-in-law is gone. My sister just became a single parent.

My sister just lost the love of her life and became a single parent. They've only been married three years. They were just starting their life together. And now. Now he's gone.

I try to inhale. My vision is blurry. I can hear my heartbeat in my head. I close my eyes, trying to get a grip on myself.

Alex is dead. My sister has to raise her baby girl without her dad. My thoughts are officially looping.

Belle deserves everything happy and wonderful in life. She is the kindest person. She loves with every piece of herself. And now she has to live without her lover and raise her daughter without a father.

I feel a piece of my heart break. Physical pain throbs in my chest and my heartbeat continues to grow louder in my ears. This is not happening. *Am I having a panic attack?*

I sit back down on the bench, head in my hands. *Breathe in. Breathe out.* When I finally glance up, I'm once again staring at the pelican. That fucking pelican. Stupid fucking double-chinned bird. My brother is dead and my sister is alone and WHO THE HELL PUT THIS BIRD ON THE WALL?!

My inability to process the current situation has me focusing any and all emotions on a picture of a bird. *God help me.*

I wish my anger had a proper target. If the drunken idiot who smashed into the front of my sister's car was still alive, I'd probably kill him. He got lucky and died on impact — thereby avoiding my wrath. Stupid asshole deserved to suffer a longer, more fitting death.

I sit there, stewing in anger — a step up from numbness —

staring at the pelican for what seems like another few hours. For all I know I've only been sitting here for a few minutes.

The doors swing open once again, and another surgeon donning scrubs asks for "Donnelly? Isabelle Donnelly's family?"

Dad lifts his hand, "That's us."

"She's out of surgery and stable. But we're not out of the woods yet. We've put her into a medically-induced coma for the time being to help her body heal. She has a lot of swelling in her brain, and her brain scan didn't show much, if any, activity. She had internal bleeding, four broken ribs — basically the entire left side of her body was crushed. We'd like to monitor her for the next twenty-four hours to see if her swelling reduces and the brain scans show signs of recovery."

"So, we wait? Can we see her?" Mom asks, looking hopefully at the doctor.

"Once we get Isabelle settled into her room in the intensive care unit, you'll be able to sit with her."

***

I WALK into Belle's hospital room. Seeing my sister hooked up to machines, a breathing tube coming out of her mouth — I have no words.

Mom walks over to her bed and presses a soft kiss to Belle's head. "I love you, baby girl," she whispers. Dad stands on Belle's other side, caressing the back of her hand with his thumb.

I'm frozen at the threshold, frozen in place, and not sure where to go from here. Eventually, I move into the room and sit in a chair, glancing back and forth between my parents and my unconscious sister.

Is she going to wake up? Is the swelling in her brain going to subside? How long until she wakes from the coma?

Now that I'm finally starting to regain feeling in my limbs and clarity in my thoughts, the doctor is gone and I'm left sitting here without answers to my million and one questions.

"Julia," my dad breaks the silence after what seems like an hour. "We should check on Sunny and your sister, and then get some rest before the doctor does his rounds tomorrow morning. We won't know anything more until then."

Ah, my dad. Ever the pragmatic one. At least he's functioning. Mom looks like she'll collapse any minute — either from physical or emotional exhaustion. Probably a combination of the two.

"But, my baby," she whimpers, sadness and worry coating her words.

"I know, honey. She's my baby, too. We still need to think of Sunny, and we need to sleep. You can barely stand as it is. There's nothing we can do tonight, and we need to rest before talking to the doctor tomorrow."

She nods, squeezing Belle's hand one last time before taking a step back from the hospital bed and walking to meet Dad at the other side.

"Alis?" Dad asks, looking at me to see if I'll follow.

"I'm going to stay with Belle tonight. Give my love to Sunny." I pull my feet into the chair, bending my knees and holding them close to my body.

"Alright. Try and rest. We'll see you in the morning." He walks to me and plants a kiss on top of my head.

"See you in the morning." He turns, sliding his hand into Mom's, and gently leads her out of the room.

I stand and push the chair closer to the bed, hoping I can recline the chair and still comfortably hold my sister's hand. Nope. Not happening.

I return the chair to its upright position, curling back into it with my knees once again up against my chest.

I stroke Belle's hand and lean my head back against the chair.

"I love you," I whisper. I don't know if she can hear me. "You won't be alone, ever. Alex may not be here, but I'll always be here to help with Sunny. You and me — we're a team. We'll figure this out, together."

I sit next to my sister, silently holding her hand, and eventually fall into a dream-filled sleep in my chair.

"Alis! Look! The purple ones are back!" A seven-year-old Belle looks behind her right before kneeling in the meadow to pick a purple flower. I run until I catch up with her, but instead of kneeling gracefully, I trip over my own feet, tumbling into the tall grass and wildflowers.

Umph. That's going to leave a grass stain on my overalls. "No, silly, those are blue," I tell her, touching the petals of my favorite wildflowers.

"I still think they're more purple than blue," Belle retorts, spinning the flower between her fingers. I guess she has a point; the one she's holding is a mixed shade of blue and purple.

"No matter which color they are, they're still my favorite," I say, picking a few more to bundle into a bouquet for Grandma. "Mine, too," Belle says while starting her own bouquet.

Summer in Colorado is my favorite time of year. Belle and I spend a month at our grandma's house every June — running through the meadow, painting on grandma's back porch, helping in her garden. I love my parents, but Grandma has always and will always be my favorite person. Well, besides Belle of course. She's my best friend. She'll always be my best friend.

We walk back toward Grandma's house, flowers in hand, and as soon as she sees us from the kitchen window Grandma meets us outside with two vases filled with water.

"Myosotis scorpioidis! They're lovely, girls. We'll put one vase in the living room and the other on the breakfast table. How does that sound?" Grandma smiles down at us while we each set a flower bouquet in a readied vase and then carry them into the house.

"Sunny, why don't you take yours to the living room. Don't forget to set it near a window so they get enough sunlight." Belle nods in affirmation and skips to the living room to find the perfect perch for her flowers. I walk with grandma to the breakfast table and set my vase on the doily sitting perfectly centered on the round table for four.

"I thought they were called forget-me-nots, not myoso — what did you call them?" I look up at Grandma with a confused expression.

"Myosotis scorpioidis. That's the genus name for the flower that grows wild here in Colorado."

"Myo-so-tis scor-pioi-dis," I sound out slowly, committing the name to memory. "So why did mommy tell me they are called forget-me-nots? Did she forget the real name?"

Grandma chuckles, "No, dear. They are also called forget-me-nots. Remember when we learned about the northern lights and I told you they are also called the aurora borealis?"

My face lights up at my nickname. "Yeah! Like my name! Alis!"

"That's right, dear. Just like your name." Grandma smiles down at me just as Belle enters the kitchen.

"I put my vase right next to the window with the stained glass butterfly!" Belle beams, clearly excited to place her flowers next to the hanging glass artwork we made last summer during our visit.

"I knew you'd find the perfect place," Grandma smiles at her as she walks toward the oven to pull out a slider filled with chocolate chip cookies. Belle retrieves the milk from the fridge to pour each of us a glass while I gather paper plates and napkins for our cookies. Once our glasses are filled and the serving tray is overflowing with cookies, the three of us sit at the breakfast table for our afternoon snack.

I open my mouth to speak, but I can't pronounce anything properly with a mouth full of cookie. I like to avoid misbehaving at all costs, so I swallow my cookie before saying, "Belle, did you know these flowers are called myotosis scorpioidis?"

"Myosotis, dear," Grandma corrects. I nod. "Yeah, myosotis scorpioidis!"

Belle looks confused. "I thought they were forget-me-nots?" Suddenly I'm filled with pride that I know something my sister doesn't. As much as I wish I was, I am not smarter than a second grader.

"It's both! Like the northern lights and aurora borealis!" I beam.

"Oh, cool! I'm going to keep calling them forget-me-nots because that science name sounds weird and I won't remember it." Belle shrugs her shoulders and picks up another cookie.

"Me, too," I nod in agreement. If Belle calls them forget-me-nots then I'll do the same because she's my big sister and my best friend and I'll never forget that.

ONE

Alis

IT'S BEEN *years since I've inhaled this much smoke. It's irritating my eyes and making it difficult to breathe. Whose idea was it to put smoke machines in clubs, anyway? Why does this smoke hover near the ground instead of rising? Is it because it's cool instead of warm? I should look up the science behind smoke machines. Also, why again did I agree to come tonight?*

I can't believe I let her talk me into this. And by "this" I don't just mean a night out at a club. When (after incessant begging) I gave Skye carte blanche on tonight's look I didn't expect her to replace my glasses with contacts. I *loathe* contact lenses. Not just because my astigmatism hates them, but because a night without glasses is a night without any buffer between myself and the rest of the world.

Skye? Are you sure you want me to go out in public without my security blanket? That's the quickest way for me to go from hero to zero, just like that. (If you missed the reference, please re-read that last line with the appropriate Hercules tune and z snap.)

"Alis! Get your sexy ass on the dance floor!" My best friend Skye yells, sandwiched between two men with gelled hair.

That's seriously disgusting. If your hair is glistening before your skin joins the wet and sweaty club, I don't want to be anywhere near you — much less close enough to have your cock rubbing up against my ass and your hair brushing against my neck. No thanks.

I've never understood the appeal of dance clubs. If you want to hump someone, do it in the privacy of your own home. Not in a room full of people watching — or worse, wanting in on your action. Dance clubs are a waste of space with shitty lighting and overpriced drinks.

I guess there was that one club on the cruise ship that holds some pretty great memories ...

I digress.

Let's back up to how I got here in the first place.

Skye, one of my two wild and crazy best friends, recently moved to the city with my daughter and me so I could finish school and so she could get out of her "rut" or whatever she's calling it. Basically, she hates small-town America and wants some adventure. I didn't want to venture so far from home on my own with Sunny in tow — single parenting is scary enough *with* help — so, when I was accepted into Middle Peak University to finish my master's in English, Skye jumped at the opportunity to tag along.

Gosh, I love her so much. A best friend who willingly uproots her life to gallivant across the state with you and your daughter to start a new life is a rare find.

That's why I'm here tonight. In this club. Inhaling smoke and trying not to let the loud music take over my senses and throw me into a tailspin of a headache. It's because of Skye. She wanted a ladies' night out before my mom returns to her housewife life tomorrow. We don't know anyone here — yet — and there's no way in hell I'd leave Sunny with some teenager from a babysitting app. This is our one night, according to Skye, to "let loose and party before our new life becomes real life."

I'm ready for my new life to be my real life. I feel like life was put on pause nine years ago when my world fell apart. My path didn't just take a turn — it exploded right before my eyes, leaving me clueless as to what the future would hold. Without part of that explosion, I wouldn't have my daughter, so it's safe to say beauty came from those deadly ashes.

I miss Belle. She'd be happy I'm out tonight. She always told me I needed to get out more.

Out. I am out. At a club. And I need to get out of my head. I'm supposed to be having fun, letting loose, and yet I'm still sitting here watching Skye and her sweaty man meat bumping and grinding while I hide in a booth, lost in my thoughts, as usual.

Okay, here we go. I'm getting up.

I'm up. Damn, these heels. Skye might've picked a hot dress, but these shoes are ridiculous. Who needs to be five inches taller than their natural height? NO ONE. The dress by itself is stunning — long sleeves with a high neckline and deep back, black and shimmery, hits at mid-thigh. It's sexy but not too revealing. Thank God I'm sporting a B cup and nothing more, otherwise this dress wouldn't work for me. The open back is mostly hidden by my long, wavy blonde hair — another reason why I refuse to dance and drench myself in sweat. The heels take this dress from sexy and classy to "Hey man, wanna look at my vag when I inevitably twist my ankle and fall spread eagle onto the floor in front of everyone?!"

That would be my luck. Hence, the booth hiding.

Scooting out of the bench seat, I slowly rise to my feet, careful to hold onto the back of the booth to make sure I'm stable on these fuck-me stilts before I take one step forward.

What do you know? The smoke isn't as bad up here. *It has to be the smoke temperature keeping it so low to the ground.* These five-inch monstrosities just became air quality control supports. I'll keep telling myself that until my brain stops worrying that I look like a five-dollar hooker in a room full of twenty-something cover models.

Something about being thirty and spending an evening in a nightclub depresses me. I love to dance but I feel incredibly out of place. At least we didn't go to a club on the other side of the city near campus. Ha! If I feel out of place here, I can't imagine how uncomfortable I'd be dancing in a room full of young college coeds, bumping and grinding the night away before the new semester begins.

I take my first few steps toward the dance floor and decide better of it. Nope, not dancing in these stilts — I mean, air quality control supports. I pivot to the bar instead. I won't hide in a booth like a hermit — I'll sit at the bar and maybe even talk to people.

Pfft. Probably not. I look good tonight, and I know it, but I haven't stretched my flirting muscles in years. I'm not very peopley. Knowing me, I'll say something incredibly awkward trying to ignite chemistry with a man and end up getting the deer-in-the-headlights WTF look.

It's probably best not to chance it, but I'm already on my feet and walking that direction so I might as well commit to at least one drink at the bar. *Here we go.*

I approach the bar and sit down with an empty stool on either side of my new post. Shimmying into the seat and making sure my dress doesn't ride up my thighs, I lift my eyes to the bartender and signal for a drink.

"Whatcha having, honey?" the man in too-tight jeans asks. He's cute, but I'm fairly certain those pants are cutting off circulation to his goods and therefore he's sterile. Not that I'm here for breeding, but seriously, those pants are grossly tight on him. And his perfectly coiffed pompadour and bright pink nail polish tell me he probably bats for the other team. So, even if his pants fit him like a normal person, he's still not an option. At least I can be comforted knowing he won't hit on me.

"Vodka soda, please. Belvedere, if you have it."

He snorts as if I'm an idiot for thinking he wouldn't have it. It's been ages since I've been to a bar. I'm clearly out of practice.

So many strikes against me tonight. Can't remember how to flirt, sounded like an idiot to the bartender, can't walk in these stupid fucking shoes — who knows what will come next?

This isn't so bad, really. I may not be interacting with others or dancing myself into a sweaty mess, but I'm no longer hiding in a shadowy booth in the corner. This feels good. Dare I say, comfortable? I chuckle to myself. *Comfortable. Not by a long shot.* But that's okay. All things considered, this night out isn't terrible. I hope the arrival of my drink will trigger the departure of my lingering nerves.

The seat to my right scrapes across the floor. I'm surprised I could even hear it over the music, but I glance to my right and, for the first time tonight, I don't smell smoke. I smell sandalwood mixed with some sort of spruce. Sheesh, that smells amazing, and I feel my shoulders relax a bit.

Glimpsing over, I see thick, wavy dark brown hair neatly tied in a man bun. Oh my. Something about a man confident enough to wear his hair that way stirs something inside of me. The hair frames a face with olive-toned skin that looks like it has tales to tell. I quietly will him to turn my way, eager to get a better look.

And then, there's the beard. Not the scruffy kind that feels like sandpaper, nor the overly long one that can be a mouthful. No, it's that perfect two-week growth, just right for running fingers through during a lingering kiss.

He takes a slow, thoughtful sip from his beer bottle. How it must feel to be that close to those lips, nestled between the beard and...

Hold on. When did I become this person? One enticing scent, one fleeting look, and I'm this lost? Well, it's been a while.

His gaze shifts to mine, a warm, inviting half-smile playing on his lips. It's genuine and absolutely heart-stopping.

"Hello," he purrs, eyes locked onto mine. They're deep, brown pools of intrigue. Warm. Knowing.

"Hi," I breathe out, realizing it's my turn. Why is this suddenly so hard?

"I'm Dexter."

"Alis."

"Fitting, seeing as I first caught your reflection through the looking glass," he says with a sly nod to the bar's mirrored backdrop.

"Literary foreplay. Impressive. Definitely beats the usual wonderland line."

A moment of surprised delight and... was that a mutual spark?

Let's hope I keep this momentum going. *Ten points to Gryffindor!* God, please tell me I didn't say that part out loud.

"To assume we'd journey to Wonderland tonight might be a bit presumptuous, given our fresh acquaintance," he observes with a playful tone.

"Well, you're right. We won't be venturing into any fairytales this evening. Especially not any unsuitable for work," I smirk. Yet, something tells me I might have misstepped with the dashing Mr. Dexter, complete with a sultry man bun and beard.

His grin widens, revealing a set of teeth that are enticingly uneven. I've always had an odd fascination with smiles. While many are drawn to hair color or eye hue, a captivating smile cripples me. Dexter's is splendidly flawed — nature's own design. Oddly, perfectly aligned teeth make me think of a boob job. Nothing against them — boobs or braces — but finding a natural smile with its own charm? It's incomparable.

"You've hardly thrown a wrench into the evening," he comments, leaning in closer. "I'm quite keen on a spirited discourse with an enchanting lady. Care to indulge me?"

Attempting to play it cool, I lower my gaze and murmur, "I'd be delighted."

Just then the bartender sets my vodka soda down in front of me and as I reach into my clutch to pull out some bills and pay the man, Dexter pipes up. "Put her drinks on my tab."

The bartender nods and walks off to take orders at the other end of the bar.

"Drinks, plural? Expecting a long chat, are we?" I quip, trying to keep the conversation light.

"If the pages should turn so easily." He quirks his lips in that irresistible semi-smile.

With a playful raise of his brow, he inquires, "Now, who, pray tell, is Alis?"

"You're diving right into the prologue, aren't you? Any particular chapter you're keen on?"

"The full volume."

I chuckle, feeling a bit more at ease. "Well, I'm a recent addition to Grand River, having moved here two days ago. My profession? For now, editing. Freelance. I majored in English, with a sprinkling of creative writing courses. Life led me on a detour for a while, but I'm hoping to reclaim my narrative."

Seeing his engaged expression, I wince slightly, "Sorry, I'm not very interesting."

He offers a comforting grin, "It sounds like a tale I'd be engrossed in."

"Hardly," I demur. "Though, if Lewis Carroll had penned about one of my wilder college nights, I might be more compelling. But I doubt Alice's escapades align with mine."

His laughter is hearty, and the atmosphere between us grows even more magnetic.

He chuckles, the warmth in his voice palpable. "You wear many hats: an editor, a writer, and a reader. Too many more and you might go mad. Tell me more."

His gaze deepens, a spark of genuine interest flashing as he sips his beer. I can feel him hanging on to every word I'm about to say.

"I wish I had more tales to spin, but honestly, I'm a pretty open book. How about you, Dexter? Have any tales of adventure? Save many damsels in their time of distress?" I pose the question as I take a refreshing sip of my vodka soda.

His grin widens, those teeth again making my heart race. "Adventure? I guess that depends on your definition of the term. As for damsels, I can't say I've ever had the pleasure of saving anyone, and I'm fairly certain that even if you were in distress, you wouldn't require my assistance. My life is tame at the moment. I teach. Outside the classroom, you'll either find me engrossed in a novel, watching my dog chase its tail at the park, or doing something related to hockey."

I let out a short laugh. "For a moment there I genuinely thought you only spoke in literary prose. I'm happy to learn I don't have to think too hard to keep up."

His smile is disarming. I lean closer; I can't help it. "I love books.

I love words. But I'm also a modern man."

"Fascinating," I comment, struggling to keep the enthusiasm from my voice and failing miserably. "A modern man, with the soul of Austen's heroes. I've won the lottery, having captured your attention."

He leans in, a playful glint in his eyes. "I'm no Darcy. And clearly, I've read Carroll, given our literary banter. But in the realm of classics, Dumas is my muse. Which brings me to the reason why I'm sitting here."

Intrigued, I raise an eyebrow, "Dumas drew you to me?"

He nods, painting a scene with his words. "Tonight, I was the unwilling tagalong of friends on the prowl. The noise, the crowd — it's all a bit much for me. But then, amid the clamor, I spotted you, a beacon in this cacophony. This night was deepest darkness till you appeared and illuminated it all."

Marguerite de Valois. The man knows his French lit.

"It's a bit too early to think of me as your sun by day or star by night," I quip.

His laughter is infectious. "Maybe so, but you've added a much-needed spark to my evening, making my stay worthwhile."

Flattered, I confess, "I'm glad you chose to stay."

As I prepare to enjoy another mouthful of Belvedere, an unexpected jolt spills my drink, sloshing liquid from my glass and down my dress.

"Allllliiiiiisssssssssss, why aren't you dancing with me?!" Skye whines. "Shit, did I just spill your drink? Shit, shit, shit. Sorry!"

"It's fine," I say, giving her a slightly annoyed look while dabbing at my dress and legs with the tiny bar napkin. "Ugh, this isn't going to work. I need some paper towels from the ladies' room."

"It's packed. Line out the door," Skye reports. I roll my eyes.

"I'll grab some from the men's. Be right back," Dexter says, touching my arm as he slides off his barstool and then heads toward the washroom before I can protest.

"Who is THAT tall glass of water?!" Skye leans in and whisper-yells as her eyes follow him toward the back corridor.

"His name is Dexter. Honestly, I think he's the one guy on this planet who could get me into bed on night one," I reveal, a sly grin playing on my lips.

Skye snorts. "No fucking way. You? The prude? I'd pay good money to see that happen."

"He has this enchanting way of quoting classics as though they're whispers between old friends. Essentially, he's fluent in my love language. He may yet hold the key that unlocks my chastity belt," I reply with a smirk.

She blinks, eyes locked with mine and moving from one to the other, but doesn't say anything.

"What?" I ask.

"I'm sorry. One, you're doing that thing again where you speak like an old book and in my head that just doesn't compute. Second, my best friend hasn't even been on a date since college and now she's telling me she wants a one-night romp fest with a bearded man bun named Dexter. Who are you?!"

I shake my head and laugh. "Right now, I honestly have no idea. I was Alis in the booth, Alis at the bar, and then somehow I channeled my inner Skye and started flirting with the gorgeous man who sat down next to me."

Skye smiles wider than she has all night. "I dare you to go home with him."

"What are we, twelve? You aren't daring me to do anything." I shrug and let loose another smile. "I want to keep talking to him, and we'll see where it goes. Besides, I already told him I won't be going home with him tonight and he was fine with that. Said he just wanted to talk."

She snort-laughs again. "Yeah, okay. He's fine with that as long as the conversation ends with you naked and spread out across his bed."

I swat her stomach and nod toward the mob of dancing people. "Go dance, hussy. You're the one who wanted to go to a club tonight and I'm pretty sure the grease twins you've been dry-humping all night miss you."

Twiddling her fingers, Skye spins and saunters back to the dance floor. She disappears into the crowd of bodies before I see whether or not she found her two slices of bread. Nothing like a Skye sandwich to make her night magical. I've never been into the two-guys-at-once thing. Not that I've ever tried it, but considering my sexual roster is a mere two guys deep and hasn't been added to since age twenty-one, I can't even think of attempting anything close to that right now. *Ew*. No. I'll leave the crazy sexcapades to Skye.

And crazy sexcapades include one-night stands in Alis's world. Dexter is gorgeous, no doubt, but I've been talking to him for what, five minutes? I don't know if I'd forgive myself for ending a nine-year dry spell with a man I've literally just met. Nope. Not happening.

I'm shaken out of my runaway thought train when the smell of cedarwood and spruce reappears next to me. "Here; these should work better than that three-by-three-inch excuse for a napkin," Dexter says as he slides back onto his bar stool.

"Thanks," I breathe out, taking the paper towels and dabbing them on my chest and dress. "That was my more exciting and adventurous half. She has trouble balancing on two feet."

"Well, don't the two of you make a cute couple," Dexter says through a smile.

"Pfft," I shake my head in exasperation. "Friends is as far as I'll ever go with that tornado. Or any woman, for that matter."

"I see," he laughs. "So, where were we? I believe you were thanking me for staying." That half smile has officially turned into a smirk. So he is a bit cocky. Or confident. Either way, that smile/smirk is driving me insane.

"I don't know that I was thanking you, per se. But I am glad you're here." I smile at him and rest my chin on my hand.

"So, Alis —" My phone goes off, Stewy from Family Guy yelling, "Mom! Mommy! Mommy! Mama! Mom!" on repeat until I answer the damn thing. I open my clutch, pulling out the phone to silence the ridiculous ringtone, and read the text from my mom.

I exhale. "I'm so sorry; I'd typically ignore my phone but I need to check this."

"No worries," he smiles, motioning for the bartender to get him another beer and replace my spilled vodka soda.

> Mom: Sunny woke up running a fever of 101.2. I can take care of her, but she's crying and asking for you.

> Me: Did you give her anything for the fever?

> Mom: Some cold water and a cool washcloth. I'm not sure where to find her medicine in all these boxes.

> Me: Ugh. I have no idea either. I'll swing by a drugstore on my way home. Be home in 30.

"I swear that wasn't a 'save me' text, but I do have to leave," I say, looking up at Dexter as he takes a swig of his new beer.

"That's a shame; I was enjoying learning about Alis and wanted to hear more about her adventures in Wonderland."

"Like I said," I point to myself and let out a breathy chuckle, "boring. I was enjoying getting to know you, too," I say, looking down at my crossed legs. "Would you —"

"Could I have your number?" he asks, right as I was about to ask if he wanted that very same thing.

"Sure," I squeak, my face lighting up at his request. Seriously, I have lost all cool. I'm like a puppy — giving my affection freely and looking like I want to hump his leg. *Oh God, now I'm thinking about rubbing up against his leg.*

Shaking myself out of my ridiculous and perverted thoughts, I ask, "Do you have a pen?"

"You could just plug it into my phone."

"True," I laugh, fumbling to take his phone off the bartop in front of him.

"Don't think you can get in without the passcode," he quips. Gosh, I am such an idiot. I was doing SO WELL and then Skye screwed up our conversation and I never got the chance to get back into my flirtatious groove before Mom sent me that text.

He puts his hand next to mine on the bartop, sliding the phone away and unlocking it before handing it to me.

"Thanks," I say, opening his messages. I smirk, regaining my flirtatious momentum and sending myself a text. *Let's see if the man knows his Tolstoy.*

> Unknown Number: Nothing is so necessary for a young man as the company of intelligent women. Namely, Alis.

I push the side button, blacking out the screen so he can't immediately read the text.

"There you go." I hand the phone back to him, then turn to see if Skye is anywhere near the edge of the dance floor or if I'm going to have to squeeze through the masses to find my friend.

We stand at the same time, our bodies closer than they have been all night. He's tall. Like, perfectly tall. At least six feet and all kinds of manly deliciousness.

"Whoa there," he chuckles, gripping my waist as I adjust to the stupid shoes yet again.

I look up at him, my senses overwhelmed with his scent, the feel of him against me, the sound of the music pumping around us.

One hand still on my waist, Dexter lifts his other hand to my jaw, skimming his thumb over my bottom lip.

"I'd really like to kiss you."

My brain short circuits. I blink. Blink again. *What?*

"Alis?" he asks, raising an eyebrow.

"Um, what? I mean, yes. Yes, I'd like that." I'm a bumbling idiot who can't keep her shit together for more than a few minutes.

He leans his face down, closer to mine, dropping his thumb from my lip and tilting my chin up with his index finger.

I breathe in. I haven't been kissed in so long, I don't know if I'll be any good at it. And will this be a peck? Tongue involvement? I don't remember how first kisses work.

My thoughts are cut off as his lips gently press against mine. His hand on my waist wraps around to the small of my back and he draws me closer to him, deepening the kiss and sliding the tip of his tongue between my lips, coaxing them open. My tongue meets his and I melt into him, never wanting this kiss to end.

I'm not one for sloppy, mouth fucking, too-much-tongue kisses. This isn't that. This kiss is — perfection. Our lips move in sync like we've done this before. Like a perfectly choreographed dance of lips and tongues and hands and bodies. My hands slide up his chest and wrap around his neck, grazing the loose hairs at the base of his hairline.

Also, I was right. I was *SO* right. His beard is the perfect length for making out. No wiry hairs tickling my nose. So good. So so so good. I wonder if the inside of my thighs would enjoy his beard this much.

Whoa now. Getting ahead of myself. Simmer down.

He slowly pulls away, pressing his closed lips against mine one more time before whispering, "Goodnight, Alis."

I swallow, staring up at him with wide eyes that want nothing more than to keep looking at him all night. "Goodnight, Dexter."

I untangle my hands from around his neck, grazing his shoulder with my nails before pressing my hands to my stomach and looking over my shoulder toward the dance floor. I glance up at him one last time, smile softly, and then take a few steps away from the bar, looking toward the mess of sweaty bodies to find Skye.

"Oh thank God," I exhale, seeing Skye laughing at her Kenicki doppelgänger dance partner as they walk — nay, stumble — toward the bar. The other guy is MIA. Guess he lost interest in sharing?

"Skye!" I yell, hoping she can hear me over the music and her raucous laughter. Thankfully, she does.

"What's up, babe? Ready to dance?" Hasn't she had enough dancing for one night? She's dripping with sweat.

Please don't hug me. Please don't hug me.

She hugs me. "This is the BEST night!" She plasters her sweaty cheek against mine.

"Yep. No doubt. But we gotta run," I tell her, thankful I don't have to yell since she's still stuck to my face. She pulls away and I wipe away her sweat, trying not to show how annoyed I am by her current lack of awareness concerning personal space.

"What?! No!" First I had loud Skye, then laughing Skye, and now whiny Skye. This woman gives me whiplash.

"Sunny's running a fever and Mom can't find the ibuprofen."

She drops the moping act, standing up straight and nodding her head once. "Gotcha. Ok, no prob." *Hello, responsible Skye.* She turns to her man friend, blows him a kiss, wiggles her fingers goodbye, and starts pulling me through the crowd to the exit.

I stumble after her, thankful she's holding onto me so I don't faceplant from the shoes. "That was abrupt."

She shrugs. "He was fun to dance with, but conversation was not his strong suit."

"You expected to converse with him out there? Could you even hear each other over the music?"

"Oh yes. And rather than asking my name, he kept moaning and grunting into my ear every time I rubbed my ass against his crotch."

"Ah, I see. Well at least you know he enjoyed himself."

"If he didn't, it's only because I didn't slide my hand into his pants and rub him off in the middle of the dance floor."

"That's disgusting," I say, crinkling my face and shaking it side to side. "Dammit, Skye, now I can't get that image out of my head."

She laughs. "Stop being such a prude."

We finally make it to the door, and just before stepping out, I turn to look over my shoulder toward the bar, hoping for one last glance at Dexter before I leave.

He's there. Right where I left him. Elbow resting on the bar, eyes fixed on me, half smile firmly in place. Goodness gracious he's beautiful.

Smiling, I turn back to Skye and follow her through the door and into the humid summer night.

I pull out my phone from my clutch and find more than my personally-sent text from Dexter.

Unknown Number: Not one word, not one gesture of
yours should I, could I, ever forget.

TWO

I WAKE up in the hospital chair the next morning at 7 a.m., just as my parents walk into the room. They don't look much better than they had the night before, Mom's eyes nearly swollen shut from crying.

My restless night hadn't been much better. I woke with a knot in my neck, compliments of my pretzel-twisted sleeping position.

"Hey," I croak.

"Morning." Mom doesn't sound rested. I wonder if she was able to sleep at all last night. She walks to Belle's bed, brushing her matted hair aside and kissing her forehead.

"Has the doctor begun his rounds yet?" Dad leans out the door, looking side to side down the hallway.

"I'm not sure. I only just woke up when you walked through the door."

"Right. Of course. I'll check with the nurse's station to see if they can give me a time frame on when we'll see him." Dad turns and walks into the fluorescent-lighted hallway in search of Belle's nurse.

"How was she last night?" Her question is quiet, heavy with

grief. She never looks away from Belle's sleeping face and continues to stroke her hair.

I stretch, trying but failing to loosen the twisted muscles in my body. "No change." My yawn muffles my words. "I sat with her and talked to her for a bit, and then fell asleep in this chair."

"I'm glad you got some rest." Mom's soft eyes are now fixed on me, a small smile on her lips. As soon as it appears her lips begin to tremble, tears filling her eyes. "I don't know how we're supposed to tell her Alex is gone." She chokes on a sob, covering her mouth with her hand and closing her eyes to keep the tears at bay.

"I don't know that she heard me, but I tried to tell her last night. I told her she won't be alone, that we will be there for her and raise Sunny together."

Mom cries quietly, her shoulders shaking as she nods her head in agreement.

A knock sounds on the doorframe, signaling the arrival of Belle's doctor and my dad's return.

"Good morning, Mrs. Gilmore. Miss Gilmore.

"I'd like to run another scan to check Isabelle's brain activity. Last night the activity was minimal at best. But we did not want to let her go until the swelling in her brain subsided. If she shows no sign of improvement today, we can discuss your options moving forward. Namely, whether we give her more time or remove her from the ventilator and let her go in her own time."

Let her go? LET HER GO?! I want to lash out, to tell this doctor my sister will not be 'let go' if my life depends on it. I will not just 'let go' of my Belle. Thankfully, I still maintain some semblance of self-control, and keep my mouth shut.

The walls are starting to close in around me. I need some space. Air. Distance.

Without saying a word, I pick up my purse, squeeze Dad's hand, and leave Belle's hospital room.

I look around for any sign of the exit, walking toward the red glowing sign before stopping at the nurse's station.

The curly-haired nurse is immersed in her work and I don't think she heard me approach. "Could you tell me where to find the pediatric ward? Or, better yet, can you give me a room number for a specific patient? She's my niece." She startles as she looks up at me. I was right, she had no idea I was standing here.

"Sure thing. Name?"

"Sunny Donnelly." My fingers tap, tap, tap on the countertop. My palms are starting to sweat. I need to get out of here. Leaving Belle's room didn't do much in the way of stopping the walls from suffocating me. First I'm numb, then I'm angry, then I'm exhausted, and now I'm claustrophobic. I must be overwhelmed.

No shit, Sherlock.

"Miss Donnelly is in room 4201. The pediatric ward is on the fourth floor, and if you turn right out of the elevator you'll see a sign directing you toward in-patient rooms."

I smile, thank her, and walk toward the elevators located just outside the ICU.

I look to the elevators, then left to the doors leading to the stairs. Which is the lesser of two evils? Either way, I'm closed in.

I choose the tiny metal box because the risk of twisting an ankle is significantly less on a flat surface.

I press the signal, calling for the elevator, and thankfully it doesn't take long to arrive. As the doors open I thank God the thing is empty. I'm introverted by nature and being surrounded by strangers is the last thing I need when I'm overwhelmed.

I let out a deep exhale as I enter the elevator and press the number 4, followed by the closing button to prevent any other travelers from hopping on board. The walls don't feel suffocating to me. This is good. This is very good. *Breathe in. Breathe out.*

"Give her more time or remove her from the machines and let her go in her own time." What the hell is that doctor thinking? If she wasn't going to make it, why did they hook her up to the machines in the first place? I'm not a doctor but, dammit, even I know ripping the bandage off is preferable to prolonging someone's agony.

She's going to be fine. I know it. Belle is strong, determined. She loves her life and I know she'll fight for it. *But how do you fight without brain activity?* That's a stupid thought. I don't fucking know but I'm sure she'll figure it out.

She has to. Sunny needs her. *I* need her. I'm selfish. Standing here thinking about myself and how my life will crumble without my sister, meanwhile, a nine-month-old baby girl is lying in a hospital bed, about to face a world without her father and possibly without her mother. I can't imagine my life without Mom and Dad. They're my rock. My biggest fans. The best parents in the world. The thought of losing them does not compute.

The elevator finally arrives at the pediatric floor and I step out, turning toward the in-patient rooms as instructed by the nurse downstairs. The sign tells me 4201 is to the left, so I turn in that direction and read the numbers on each door until, finally, I reach 4201 at the end of the hall.

"KNOCK, KNOCK," I whisper, slowly opening the door and hoping I'm not disturbing Sunny or Aunt Melody if they're asleep.

"Alis, honey, I'm so glad you're here." Melody stands from her recliner near the window and walks toward me for a hug. "She's still sleeping. Poor thing was up most of the night. I can't imagine that crib contraption is at all comfortable."

"No doubt. Plus she's still nursing and sleeps with Alex and Belle most nights."

"Ah, I see. No wonder she didn't sleep well. I'd wake up every few minutes as well if my bedmates disappeared."

Disappeared. Is that what happened? Did Alex disappear? Will Belle disappear?

I give my aunt a small smile and walk toward the crib to find Sunny, chestnut curls splayed everywhere around her head like a lion's mane. She sleeps like a starfish and her blanket is wrapped around one leg and tucked behind her back.

I stifle a laugh. "The kid sure knows how to take up space. I can't imagine sleeping with her arms and legs spread eagle and poking into my side all night."

"She is adorable." Melody comes closer, placing her hand on the small of my back and resting her chin on my shoulder as we both watch her sleep.

"What's the update on Belle? Everything going well in the ICU?"

I exhale. "I honestly don't know. The doctor said something about swelling and a lack of brain activity, but they're keeping an eye on her today and I think they'll run the test again this evening? He said we'll know more after the next brain scan."

"So, is that good or bad?" Melody lifts her chin from my shoulder and looks at my profile. I can't turn my face and look her in the eye or I'll lose it and start crying.

"Either? Neither? I don't know. He didn't sound particularly somber, but he also didn't sound encouraging or hopeful."

"What is he, a robot with no bedside manner?"

A small smile pulls at my lips. "No, he's kind and actually gentle in his delivery. I think he's just an expert at walking the line when it comes to these types of injuries. He doesn't want to give us false hope, nor does he want to throw Mom into a deeper pit of despair than she's already wallowing in."

"I see. So your mom isn't handling it well? I saw her last night before your parents headed to the hotel across the street to get some rest. I think she wanted to stay with Sunny but Jim vetoed that plan and took her to the hotel."

I sigh. "She seems to be holding herself together pretty well. She cries a lot but she's not screaming or fainting or anything. I think Dad is helping to hold her together during this limbo stage. Who knows what will happen after the next brain scan? I don't even want to think about that right now."

"You don't have to, dear. Are you going to be here for a while?"

"Yeah. I slept alright in the recliner next to Belle's bed last night so I'm good. That ICU room has no windows and I started feeling claustrophobic with Belle, Mom, Dad, the doctor, and myself in that room together. I needed a change of scenery, and I haven't seen Sunny since the accident so I figured I'd hang out here for a bit."

Melody walks toward a side table and picks up her handbag. "Sounds good. Do you have to leave for work or anything later?"

Still watching Sunny sleep, I reply, "No. We're on fall break right now so Dr. Ryan doesn't have classes." My head snaps up. "Shit. I need to email him to reschedule our meeting later this week. He wants me to teach three of his classes next week and there's no way I'm going to be able to do much of anything after last night. Assuming Belle pulls through, I'll need to be with her and Sunny."

"Try not to stress about it. If you need to reach out to your professor you can use my laptop. It's in the bag in the corner." Melody lifts her chin toward the messenger bag near the couch. I nod.

"I'm going to grab some coffee and something to eat. Want anything?" she asks.

Food. Do I want food? I'm not hungry, but who knows how I'll feel in an hour. "Sure. Just whatever you're having. I'm not picky."

"Sounds good. Text me if you need anything." She squeezes my arm before turning and leaving the room.

Sunny shifts in her crib, trying to move her legs even though the one is pinned by the blanket wrapped around her. She stills and continues to breathe steadily as she sleeps.

I reach down and finger one of her curls. They must have bathed her before putting her to bed because she smells like soap, not gasoline or soot.

"Sleep well, baby girl," I whisper, then turn and fetch Aunt Melody's laptop from her bag so I can email Dr. Ryan.

I sit and open the computer, remembering I didn't ask Melody for her password. Thankfully she has a guest user option.

I log into my school email account and find a slew of emails from students. I swear, college students are idiots. I've worked as Dr. Ryan's TA since my first year of grad school, and I absolutely love it. I don't, however, love it when students email stupid questions that are answered in the syllabus.

I glance over the unread student emails and find the last message from Dr. Ryan.

Alis,

I know we discussed meeting this Thursday morning to go over next week's teaching schedule, but I need to shuffle appointments and meet with you in the afternoon instead. Does 2 p.m. work for you?

Best,

Dr. Ryan

Thursday. That's two days from now. Nope. Won't work for me. *How am I supposed to tell him I can't work for a while? Will he need to find a new TA?* I'm not his only grad student, so I'm sure he can easily find a fill-in, but if I'm gone too long he'll have to find a permanent replacement. *Ugh. Please, no.*

Working as Dr. Ryan's right hand is the most coveted student position in the English department. I spent my entire four years of undergrad working my ass off to maintain a 4.0 GPA and never missed an opportunity to establish myself as Dr. Ryan's favorite student.

I'm kind of a fan girl. Not like a creepy or inappropriate fan girl. I've just followed Dr. Ryan's work since high school. I've read every journal article, book, essay, etc. he has ever published. His expertise in eighteenth and nineteenth-century French literature absolutely blows my mind.

I'm captivated by novels. The ability to escape reality and venture into imaginary worlds or even transcend time is the most fascinating thing I've ever experienced. I knew from a young age that I wanted to major in English or literature and eventually become a writer. That desire cemented in my soul when fifteen-year-old me toured Grant University's campus and sat in on a lecture by Dr. Jonathan Ryan about Gustave Flaubert's debut novel, *Madame Bovary*, and its contribution to literary realism.

The rest, as they say, is history. After graduating with my bachelor's I entered into the master's program, studying under Dr. Ryan, and eventually secured my place as his TA.

No one, and I mean NO ONE, would ever walk away from this job.

Except me, it seems. Maybe not. Maybe I can step away for a week or two and then pick up where I left off. I can help him find another student to fill in for the few classes next week and then I'll be good to return after that.

> Dr. Ryan,
>
> I'm so sorry, but Thursday isn't going to work. I had a family emergency last night and I won't be available for the rest of this week. Also, I don't think I'll be able to teach next week either.
>
> It's a lot to explain over email, but if you're free to talk on the phone sometime today I can give you the details.
>
> As for next week, I'm happy to reach out to Brad or Michelle to see if they are available to teach. Let me know how I can help, and when you're free to talk.
>
> Thanks,
>
> Alis

Right. That takes care of that. I close the laptop and lay my head back on the chair, staring at the ceiling.

One. Two. Three. Four. I count, making my way across the first row of tiles, skipping over the light, and then resuming my tally as I work toward the wall. *Seven. Eight.* Pivot. I count down the next row, then the next, moving my eyes from tile to tile. Why do hospitals have tiles in their ceilings? And why do they use fluorescent lighting when everyone hates it?

I finish my count — 52 tiles, not counting lights, in case anyone was wondering — and move to stand as the door opens and Aunt Melody reappears with sustenance.

"Smells good," I say, walking toward her to relieve some of the burden from her arms.

Melody's smile shows excitement — something I haven't seen or felt in the last twenty-four hours. "The cafeteria here is awesome! They serve Starbucks coffee and cook food to order, so I was able to get fresh breakfast burritos and some cut-up fruit."

"Perfect." And it does sound perfect. Good thing I didn't decline her offer for breakfast. I set the drink tray on the side table and work free the cups.

Sitting down on the couch next to Aunt Melody, I hand over her coffee before taking a sip of my own. I'm not a huge coffee drinker — I prefer tea — but warm, liquidy, caffeinated heaven is in this cup. We eat in silence, hoping Sunny will continue sleeping as long as possible. Poor kid needs it after what her body went through yesterday.

After finishing our meal, Melody collects the empty trays and wrappers, setting them aside to be discarded later. A tranquil calm settles over the room, only broken by Sunny's soft breathing. The ambient light filtering through the window casts a warm glow, bathing everything in a gentle, comforting light. It seems at odds with the turmoil roiling in my mind, the storm of worries, fears, and uncertainty regarding Belle's condition.

As we sit there, side by side, the reality of the situation descends upon me yet again, knotting my stomach and clenching my heart. This room, with Sunny sleeping innocently, unaware of the gravity of the situation, feels like a refuge, a pocket of normalcy amid a sea of chaos and despair.

I see Aunt Melody silently wiping away a tear that escapes her control, and it reminds me of the tightrope we are all walking on — trying to maintain a brave face, to be strong for each other while grappling with our own personal turmoil.

It feels like we're in the eye of the hurricane; the quiet room a stark contrast to the whirlpool of medical terms, scans, and the painful back-and-forth of hope and despair that circulates the ICU.

A soft knock on the door breaks the silence, and the door opens to reveal a nurse with a kind, empathetic face. She comes in, steps quiet, and nods towards us before going over to check on Sunny.

"I hope I am not intruding. I just came to check on the little one.

How is she doing?" The nurse asks, her voice a whisper that carries the weight of understanding, as she peeks into the crib.

"She's sleeping soundly, thankfully," I reply, matching her hushed tone.

The nurse smiles a sad but warm smile and nods. "That's good to hear. Sleep is the best medicine at this age. It helps in healing." She checks Sunny's vitals quickly, expert hands moving with a tenderness that speaks of years of caring for the little ones. "Everything looks fine. Call us if you need anything."

"Thank you," Melody and I murmur almost in unison as she retreats, leaving us to the peace of the room once again.

My gaze drifts back to Sunny, her chest rising and falling with even, deep breaths, the peaceful expression on her little face bringing an ache to my heart. It's both a blessing and a curse, this innocence. Shielded from the fear and uncertainty clouding the hearts of the adults around her, yet blissfully unaware of the gravity of her mother's condition.

I reach out, letting my hand find a place in Aunt Melody's, seeking the warm, grounding connection of another human being, another heart that is beating with the same rhythmic pulse of fear and hope.

We sit there, holding onto each other, the silence thick with unspoken words, yet full of understanding and shared pain. We both know we are in the waiting game, a cruel and torturous passage of time where we grasp at straws of hope, preparing ourselves for both miracles and heartaches.

It's a moment frozen in time, yet it feels like an eternity, a slow tick-tock echoing in the recesses of our minds, a constant reminder of the delicate thread that life hangs by.

"Melody..." I find myself whispering, breaking the silent pact we seemed to have formed. "Do you believe in miracles?"

She squeezes my hand tighter, her eyes welling up with tears as she tries to find words, any words that could encapsulate the tempestuous sea of emotions swirling within us.

"Yes, Alis. I have to believe in miracles," she whispers back, her voice choked with emotion. "Sometimes, it's all we have left to hold on to."

Her words linger in the air, a fragile thread of hope, woven from love, resilience, and a desperate plea for God or the universe or fate to be kind. A whisper of faith that miracles can happen, that Belle will wake up, that our family will be whole again. A desperate grasp onto hope, because sometimes, hope is the only thing stronger than fear. It's a bridge to tomorrow, an anchor in the storm, a beacon in the darkness.

We hold onto each other, a pillar of support in a trembling world, holding onto the glimmer of hope that flickers in the shadowy corners of the room, praying for the miracle that will bring light back into our lives.

THREE

Alis

"SKYE! STOP IIIIIIIIIIT!" The giggling protests of my almost ten-year-old echo down the hall and through my closed bedroom door. It's 7:45 a.m., which means I should be awake. Too bad I was up working on book edits until 2 a.m. and I have no plans to get out of bed any time before 9. It's Sunday. I can afford to sleep in one day per week, right?

Wrong.

Skye and Sunny's annoyingly loud banter refuses to let the hard-working adult of this household sleep another moment. Looks like I'm getting up.

I throw off my comforter and try to swing my legs over the side of my mattress. However, the top sheet is wrapped around my ankles so now I do the sheet-untangle-jiggle-wiggle until finally, my feet come loose and the top sheet gets shoved to the bottom of the bed. For the life of me, I do not know why people still sleep with top sheets. The fitted sheet and the comforter work just fine, and provide a free range of movement, tangle-free. Mom set up my bed while she was here last week and made sure both my and Sunny's bed had all the requisite accessories — including bed skirts, top sheets, and throw pillows (i.e., the three most useless items on any bed). I'm glad she was here to help and spend time with us before starting our new city life, but I'll never be thankful for her insistence on the necessity of the top sheet.

I pat over to the master bath and splash water on my face to help me wake up before facing the crazy in the kitchen. The bags under my eyes do nothing to hide my late-night work routine, but I'm not going anywhere important today so it doesn't really matter. I brush my teeth and then flip down my hair to tie a messy knot on top of my head. No use brushing this mop.

"I'd ask what you're bickering about, but it's Sunday so I assume you're painting each other with pancake batter," I say as I walk to the kitchen bar, sliding out a stool and plopping myself down on it.

Both Skye and Sunny turn to face me, pancake batter splattered on their faces and clothes. "You betcha!" Skye slaps Sunny on the butt with her spatula.

"Will you stop it!" Sunny grumbles, or pretends to grumble, while laughing and twisting away to press her backside against the cabinet.

"You know it helps to get the batter onto the pan instead of your shirts." They both roll their eyes in unison, laughing and turning to flip the pancakes that actually made it to the griddle.

I live for moments like this. Our family may be unconventional, but it's perfect. The aunt-mom, the adopted niece, and the funky friend-aunt. Three peas in a pod. I thought it'd be weird living so far away from Tori, but considering she's been married for a decade it wasn't like I left my roommate behind.

"Is there coffee?" I yawn.

"Yeah — but not the fancy kind." Sunny pulls my *friends don't let friends live uncaffeinated* mug from the cabinet and pours me a cup. "Thanks, Sunshine," I smile at her and reach over the bartop to grab the creamer.

I couldn't care less about fancy coffee. Give me Maxwell House with a hefty dose of vanilla creamer and I'm good to go.

I take a sip, sigh happily, and look to Skye who's weighing her whole-bean coffee on a food scale. "Enjoy your sludge. I'm making *real* coffee," Skye says over her shoulder.

"You can keep your fancy snob coffee. I don't have time to weigh beans and grind them and then conduct a massive science experiment just for a cup of joe."

Skye snorts. "You don't know what you're missing. Brewing coffee is —"

"*An art, only mastered by those with sophisticated taste,*" Sunny and I mock in unison. Skye watched some documentary about a barista competition a few years back and since then she's taken up coffee as a hobby and part-time job. Who knew you could make a living from being a pretentious hipster?

Skye rolls her eyes and turns back to her gadgets.

"Is there bacon?" I ask as I take another swig from my mug.

"What is breakfast without bacon?" Sunny crows, looking at me like I've lost my mind. I've raised her well, it seems.

"Good point. Can I help with anything? Eggs?"

"Nope. I think we're good," Sunny says, following that with a report of today's menu. "Bacon should be ready in three minutes, pancakes are done, fruit is washed. We're out of eggs since we made the pancake batter from scratch this time, so some of your protein is hidden in your carbs." Protein hidden in carbs? My girl is ridiculous. Or a genius? TBD.

"You know that's not how it works, right?" I raise an eyebrow at Sunny as she bends to pull the bacon out of the oven.

"Maybe not, but it makes you feel a little less guilty for eating pan-fried cake for breakfast." Sunny looks over her shoulder and smirks at me.

"You're not even ten yet and you're already a smartass."

"I'm your favorite smartass." Her grin stretches wide across her face.

"Language, young lady," I remind her. I walk a fine line between mom and cool aunt when it comes to Sunny. I legally adopted her after her parents died so I'm technically her mother, but I still feel like just her aunt in so many ways.

She's so much like Belle, sometimes it feels like I'm hanging out with my sister as a kid. As if her spontaneous and extroverted personality wasn't enough, she's the spitting image of my sister. Athletic build, average height, chestnut brown wavy hair, and an infectious smile that lights up a room. She got her freckles and blue eyes from Alex, but that's it. Everything else is Belle to a T.

Skye finishes setting up her French press and walks around the bar to sit next to me. Sunny assembles the breakfast plates and hands them to us, placing her own plate on the counter and standing to eat while facing us.

I grab the syrup and start to pour it over my pancakes. "We have to get you some school shoes today, so let's head out after breakfast so we beat the crowds, yeah?"

"Monty, I hate shoe shopping!" Sunny whines and tilts her head back like shoe shopping is akin to torture. I do not understand this child. What female does not enjoy shoe shopping?! I hate crowds but even I'll brave the masses for new shoes.

"Tell your feet to stop growing and then we can stop buying shoes every three months." I give her a flat, this-is-not-my-fault smile, and then shove a bite of pancake into my mouth.

"Um, I want new shoes!" Skye chimes in. "Do I get to come with?"

"Sure. I don't care. But I'm not paying for yours, too. I don't care if your birthday is next week."

"Never mind, then. I guess I don't NEED new shoes. I could use a new top, though. I have two interviews this week and I'm sure they'd like to see my professional side rather than my typical crazy."

"You? Crazy? But leopard print has never looked so classy!" I poke fun at Skye and her eccentric sense of style.

"Yeah, Skye." Sunny's talking with a mouth full of food. "I'm sure a new top won't matter once they spend an hour with your calm and professional personality." I try not to spit out my food while laughing.

"You both suck." Skye slaps me on the arm before pressing her coffee and pouring it into her mug.

"I'm with you on needing new professional attire. I think I'm good on shoes, but I need something more business casual for my new job with Dr. Matthews. I'm pretty sure yoga pants and cropped sweaters aren't in the dress code."

Dr. Abigail Matthews — my new supervising professor and boss at Middle Peak University. When I started looking into master's programs to finally finish my graduate degree, I wasn't sure where to start since I wasn't seeking out a specific professor as a mentor. I would have gone anywhere to study with Dr. Ryan, but when that relationship went to shit and I dropped out of my first master's program, I didn't think through what I'd do in the future if I wanted to go back and finish. Working with him again was never an option, and I haven't spent any time in academic circles these past nine years so I had no idea where to begin.

My priorities are also a bit different this go-round. My first foray into graduate studies came with scholarships and the hope of an eventual fellowship and PhD. This time, however, scholarships aren't really an option. My budget is tight, and I'm no longer responsible for only myself. I also didn't want to move Sunny too far away from her grandparents, so my best option was MPU.

A bit later we're headed to the holy grail of retail stores: Target. Nothing like a one-stop shop for clothing, home decor, groceries, and toiletries.

"Oooooh, Monty! Look at all the glitter!" Sunny is practically salivating at the pink, sparkly high tops on the shelf. One problem — they're $35. There's no way in hell I'm paying that much for a pair of high-tops she's going to grow out of in a few months.

"Sunny, babe, that's way too much money for a pair of shoes." The look she gives me is pleading. I hate saying no to that sweet face.

"Nope. Not too much. Check the app." Skye pushes her phone in front of my face and sure enough, today is 20 percent off shoes for the family.

"Can I, can I, can I?" Sunny's pleading is adorably annoying. Especially when she starts running in place like she has to pee.

"Sure, kid. Go for it." She squeals her delight, clapping her hands and hopping up and down. I chuckle and roll my eyes before walking toward the women's department to find myself an outfit for meeting Dr. Andrews.

Two hours and $375 later (*shoot me*), Sunny's wardrobe is officially school ready and I won't look like a teenage hobo when I meet my new advisor. And even though I could have made do with my current selection, I saw an adorable pair of yellow flats and decided they would come home with me. I know I'm thirty and shouldn't be nervous, but the thought of returning to school and meeting a ton of new people makes my skin crawl. I'm not very peopley, to state it mildly.

We're walking out to the car when my phone goes off. It's not Mom's ringtone, so I ignore it.

"You gonna get that?" Skye looks at me like I'm insane for ignoring my cell.

"Um, no? I'll check it later." She rolls her eyes at me and clicks the fob to open the trunk.

"What if it's Mr. Tall, Dark, and Bearded?" She smirks and lifts an eyebrow. I blush and look at my feet. Thankfully, Sunny's already climbing into the car and buckling her seatbelt, so she can't hear our conversation.

"I've been thinking about that, and as swoon-worthy as he was, I don't think now is the right time to get involved with anyone. We've been here less than a week, I'm about to start a new program, and I also have Sunny. There's no way I'm bringing a man into her life right now."

"Who said anything about introducing him to Sunny?! Or getting serious, for that matter. You haven't even gone on a real date in years. What's the harm in having some fun?" Skye may be able to simply have fun with a man, but I'm not built that way. At least, I haven't been that way since the accident.

"You know I'm not a casual girl." I give her an exasperated look. She's not deterred.

"Maybe you should be," she shrugs. "Not everything has to be so serious all the time."

"Serious? How can I not be serious?! I have a nine-year-old and I'm not living with my parents for the first time in a decade. For the first time since becoming a parent, I'm paying my own rent and utilities, going to school full-time, adjusting to a new city, not to mention helping my daughter adjust to being away from her grandparents and friends for the first time in her life. Excuse me for being a responsible adult." I slam the trunk and turn to walk toward the driver-side door.

Skye's staring at me, mouth agape. "What the fuck was that?"

I look up from the door handle and see Skye, still standing by the trunk. "I'm sorry. I'm just stressed out and I keep all these fears and thoughts bottled up in my head because I'm afraid if I let them out around Sunny she won't transition well. It's hard enough on the kid as it is."

"I get it, but at some point, you have to stop freaking out about everything and remember that you have needs just like any other woman."

I snort. "Needs. You mean sex?"

"I'm not a nympho, Alis. I don't *only* think about sex. I'm talking about the need to relax, take a breath, have some fun, enjoy some more-than-platonic companionship." Sometimes Skye can be an adult.

I let out a breath and look up at the sky. "I know. And I will." I once again make eye contact with Skye, my face and tone pleading with her to drop it. "Just not right now, okay? Give me a few months to get through this transition period and then, maybe, eventually, I'll think about meeting someone."

"I'm going to hold you to that." And I know she will.

Skye walks to the passenger door and slides in, putting the keys in the ignition and starting the air conditioning for Sunny. I turn my back to the door and lean against the car, grabbing the phone from my handbag and checking the notifications. Sure enough, it's a text from — *Sexy Dexy?! What the hell?* Skye.

Sexy Dexy: Hi Alis, I had a great time with you
Friday and I'd really like to see you again. Are you
free next weekend? Dinner?

Do I respond or do I ghost him? I'm not a child. I shouldn't ghost him. I also don't know how to tell a guy I like that I don't want to see him again. Scratch that — it's not that I don't *want* to see him again, but right now is not a good time for me to even consider exploring a relationship. I probably should have thought about this before I gave him my number and kissed him at the club. I need to respond. I can't ignore him. I'm just not that person.

Me: Hey, Dexter, I had a great time as well. I'm really
sorry, but I've thought about this and right now is
not a good time for me to get involved with anyone.
Maybe I'll see you around at some point.

Sexy Dexy: No worries, I understand. Let me know if
you change your mind. I'd love to show you around,
grab coffee and whatnot.

Yeah, that won't be happening any time soon. I don't respond. I do, however, update his contact information to Dexter instead of Sexy Dexy. *I really need to change my passcode.*

I'm sure by the time I'm ready to explore a romantic relationship, some other woman will have snatched him up. And if I keep in touch with him and stick him in the friend zone I'll have to watch him eventually fall for someone else.

Nope. Not happening.

FOUR

I'VE BEEN SITTING with Aunt Melody for a while now, and I need a shower. I smell like hospital, stale pizza, body odor, and breakfast. That's a disgusting combination, and considering I can smell myself, I don't want to know how rank I smell to everyone else.

"I should head out. I need to take a shower and make some phone calls, and I'll come back in a few hours. Do you need anything before I leave?"

Aunt Melody looks as tired as I am. She doesn't stink, but now I feel selfish because she's been here longer than I have.

"I'm good, honey. Your uncle will be here shortly to sit with Sunny while I go freshen up and take a nap at your parents' hotel room."

Ah, right. The hotel. "Don't forget to have him bring you a change of clothes. Or if you've already told him, don't forget to remind him."

Melody chuckles. "Good point. I'll send him a reminder because he will definitely forget. That man would lose his head if it wasn't attached."

"I'll see you later," I say, kissing her on the cheek before I grab my purse and phone and head out of the hospital.

Once in my car I take a few minutes to close my eyes and try to process the last seventeen hours. Just yesterday morning I was text bantering back and forth with Belle about a date I went on last weekend.

And now. Now she's hooked up to machines and may not make it. She may very well die. And she'll be gone. And I'll never hear her voice again or wrap my arms around her middle for a hug.

Thoughts about yesterday's texting conversation, the accident, Alex dying, Belle in limbo, and Sunny's uncertain future all flood my head at once. I'm going to lose it.

I throw open my driver side door and spew every bit of my breakfast onto the parking garage pavement. Tears pour out of my eyes as I sob and gag at the same time, trying my best to empty my body of every bit of food and drink in the hope that emptying my stomach will somehow also empty my brain of everything.

I can't do this. I can't lose Belle. Thank God nobody seems to be in this part of the parking garage right now because I can't handle someone checking on me to make sure I'm OK.

No, I'm not fucking OK.

Turning on my seat so the bottom half of my body faces outside the door, I wipe my face with my t-shirt and try to take a deep breath. My stomach is hollow, my throat stings, and my mouth tastes like eggs and stomach bile. Lovely.

I'm starting to hyperventilate from crying. And, dammit, I can't control my bladder when I puke. *Fuck my life.* Tears, vomit, and piss. A trifecta.

A few minutes later the sobbing subsides and I'm able to calm myself enough to breathe normally. *In, two, three, four. Out, two, three, four.*

Righting myself in my car, I reach into my purse and pull out my phone, turning it on for the first time since I arrived at the hospital last night. Skye's probably freaking out that she couldn't get ahold of me after I left her house. It's not that I didn't want to keep her updated; I just knew feeling my phone vibrate every five minutes would stress me out even more than I already was.

Sure enough, as soon as my phone receives signal it goes off about twenty times.

Skye, 8:12 p.m.: Did you make it to the hospital?

Skye, 8:15 p.m.: Are they OK?

Skye, 8:16 p.m.: I tried calling and it went straight to voicemail. Do you not have signal in the hospital?

Skye, 9:04 p.m.: OMG the accident is on the nine o'clock news.

Skye, 9:04 p.m.: Holy fuck the cars are smashed.

Skye, 9:05 p.m.: The man that hit them was drunk?! What the hell?!

Skye, 9:05 p.m.: The driver died at the scene. Did you know that? OMG the accident was bad enough to kill people.

Skye, 9:05 p.m.: ARE THEY OK?!!!!

Skye, 9:43 p.m.: I'm wondering if I should come up to the hospital and sit with you.

Skye, 9:45 p.m.: I'm assuming since you aren't answering me that you aren't reading my texts and if I showed up at the hospital without invitation you wouldn't be happy about it.

Skye, 9:46 p.m.: I hope they are OK. I hope you are OK.

Skye, 9:46 p.m.: I love you.

Skye, 11:22 p.m.: Are you still at the hospital? Or are you asleep? Or are you asleep at the hospital?

Skye, 11:24 p.m.: Alis I'm worried sick and you aren't answering my texts!

Skye, 11:24 p.m.: Sorry. Typed before I thought. I'm sorry.

Skye, 11:25 p.m.: Call me in the morning. PLEASE.

Skye, 11:25 p.m.: I love you.

Yep. I'm glad I turned off my phone. Skye is amazing, but I couldn't have handled her extroverted rapid-fire texting last night.

I open my contacts and tap Skye's name in my favorites list.

"OH MY GOD ALIS IS EVERYTHING OK?!"

Did the phone even ring? Cheese and rice, she's loud.

"Hey. Sorry my phone was off."

"YOU TURNED OFF YOUR PHONE?! WHILE I WAS HERE FRE—"

I cut her off. "Skye. Stop yelling. Gah."

"Sorry. I've just been freaking out all night and haven't heard a peep from you. You bolted right after that call from your mom saying Belle was in an accident and I didn't know anything else until the news showed the wreckage and said the drunk fuck died. You had your phone off and so I have no idea what's happened to Belle and I just want to make sure everything and everyone are ok."

"I know. Too much is happening right now. A lot is still uncertain. I just tried to process some of it and ended up vomiting next to my car."

"Oh, shit."

"Yeah. I — I —" My eyes fill with tears and I choke out the horrifying truth of last night.

"Alex and Sunny were in the car, too."

"WHAT?!"

"Yeah. They were coming home from dinner and the guy crossed over into their lane and hit them head on."

"Oh my gosh."

"Sunny is fine. She got banged up a bit and they kept her overnight, but she seems ok."

"Thank God. And Belle and Alex?"

I swallow. "Alex — Alex didn't make it. And Belle is in a coma and hooked up to a bunch of machines."

Skye lets out a deep breath. "I am so, so sorry, Alis."

We're quiet for the next minute. I can't respond.

"Hey, I'm sorry but I need to go. I need to head home and take a shower and then get back up here."

"Yeah. Ok. Can I do anything? Do you want me to meet you up there? What about Tori?"

"No. Not right now. And no, I haven't called Tori. I'll let you fill her in. The entire situation is overwhelming and I don't think it'd help anything for you to be here with us. Thanks, though."

"Definitely."

"I'll keep my phone on, but do me a favor?"

"Slow my roll."

I chuckle. "Yeah. And tell Tori not to text me either. I promise I'll update you as soon as I know something, OK?"

"Yeah. OK. Love you."

"Love you."

The call ends and I sit there for another few minutes, staring blankly out my windshield.

***

TOO BAD SHOWERS can't wash off emotional turmoil. My body is clean and the hot water worked wonders on my headache, but as I step foot back into the hospital every ounce of despair settles right back onto my shoulders. If this nightmare doesn't end soon I'm going to become a permanent emotional Quasimodo.

It's nearly 7 p.m. and I haven't eaten since emptying my stomach in the parking garage around noon, so I swing by the hospital cafeteria to grab sustenance before returning to my sister's room. I'm not actually hungry but I'm afraid if I don't eat something I'll pass out — either from happiness or grief — when we meet with the doctor about Belle's brain activity.

Chicken? Soup? Burger? Sandwich? Apple? Oreos? Ugh. None of this sounds appealing. Instead I walk over to the coffee shop and order the largest latte available and a croissant. Pastry never hurt anyone after puking. I'm playing it safe.

As I leave the cafeteria and head toward the elevators, I spot my dad waiting in the hall for a lift.

"Hey, dad." He turns to me as I enter the waiting area and offers me a warm, exhausted smile and a squeeze on my arm.

"Hey kiddo. You look refreshed. Did you take advantage of the hotel shower?"

"Nah. I drove to my apartment so I could change clothes and grab my laptop and books. I figure if we're going to spend another night here I could use a productive distraction." I shrug my shoulders, only then remembering the backpack weighing down my shoulders.

"I wish your mother had something to occupy her while we wait. She's still sitting next to Belle's bed, holding her hand and watching her sleep."

"Well, hopefully the doctor will have good news for us in the next few hours, yeah?"

"I hope so, kiddo. I really hope so."

When we walk through the door to my sister's room, my mother is exactly where dad said she'd be, but thankfully with her head laid on the bed, sound asleep. I'm glad she's resting — I'm pretty sure she's cried enough for the entire family these last twenty-four hours.

Just as I'm about to set my pack down, the doctor knocks on the doorframe quietly and steps inside.

Thankfully, he sees mom's sleeping figure and keeps his voice to a whisper. "We're at the twenty-four hour mark since the accident, and now is the time for her second brain scan. We won't need to relocate her for the scan; the machine is brought into this room to avoid complications that can arise when moving an intensive care patient."

"Alright." Dad rubs his chin as he speaks with the doctor. "Do we stay in the room or do we need to leave for the testing?"

"It'd be best if you stepped out for the time being, simply because we'll need to move her bed some to accommodate the fMRI. You won't need to go far, though. Just into the ICU waiting room on this floor. We'll let you know when the testing is complete."

"Thanks, doctor." My dad rubs mom's shoulder to wake her, and whispers in her ear that it's time for testing and we need to relocate for a bit.

Nearly an hour passes before a nurse comes to retrieve us, and I don't know why but I'm nauseated at the thought of hearing Belle's test results.

What if she has no brain activity? Will we really let my sister die? What happens to Sunny if she loses both of her parents? Too many questions flood my brain as worry grips my heart tighter and tighter by the second.

Once we've resettled in Belle's room, the doctor enters with a soft smile on his face. Seriously, this guy has the best poker face I've ever seen. His demeanor gives nothing away. *Come on dude. Give me something.* Another doctor enters behind him, and she's just as calm.

"Mr. and Mrs. Gilmore, Miss Gilmore. After studying the results from Isabelle's fMRI scans, I'm so sorry to report that she is not showing any signs of improvement. She shows no signs of brain activity, and without any activity after twenty-four hours, I do believe now is the time for you all to say your final goodbyes."

I'm suddenly underwater. Or at least that's what this feels like. Sounds around me are muffled at best, distant. I know my eyes are still open but all I see is my sister's face, laughing at something I've said while trying not to shoot soda out of her nose. I can't hear her, and the memory runs in slow motion, but her face is clear as day. I have no peripheral memory — the room around us is a blur, as is the bed we're sitting on. Belle rubs her eyes to prevent tears from falling as she continues to laugh uncontrollably. *Why is this the vision I see when I've just learned my sister is never coming back? This is no laughing matter. What the heck, brain?*

"Miss Gilmore, can I get you anything?" I shake out of my stupor as a hand grips my shoulder and suddenly I'm looking into the face of the unknown second doctor.

"Um, what?" I blink a few times to clear my vision, coming back to the present.

"Can I get you anything? Some water, perhaps? Why don't you have a seat." The doctor tries to lead me to a chair but I shake her hand off my shoulder.

"Um, no, thank you. I'll be alright." I try to give her a reassuring smile but I'm sure she can sense every bit of effort it takes for me to force that one facial expression.

I see my dad continues to provide strength to mom as she falls apart in his arms. *How does he do it?* This entire time he's been so calm, collected, acting as our rock while blow after blow smashes against us. The doctor is talking with them but I can't make out what he's saying.

"I'll leave you all to talk through your next steps, and I'll return shortly to answer any more questions you have." Both doctors nod politely and sympathetically toward my parents and then me, and turn to leave my family to the most difficult conversation we'll ever experience.

The smell of the hospital room wraps around me like a heavy cloak, the lights above burning too bright as they flicker against the sterile white surroundings. The mechanical hum of the machines tethered to Belle, to my sister, is deafening in the somber silence that follows the doctor's departure. The empty chair next to her bed seems so forlorn, silently begging for someone to occupy it and hold Belle's hand once again, to whisper words of love, to hope, to pray.

But as I gaze upon my sister's pale, inert form, I know deep down in that abyss of despair curling in the pit of my stomach that all the prayers in the world can't undo this reality. I want to scream, to rage against the unfairness of it all, to shake Belle until she wakes up, until she laughs and jokes and lights up the room just like she always used to.

Yet I find myself moving mechanically, inching closer to the bed, drawn to her silent presence as though pulled by some invisible thread of sisterhood that refuses to be severed, even now. My hands tremble as I reach out, hovering over her still form before finally settling down to take her cool hand in mine.

She's so still. Not the lively, vibrant force of nature that I know and love, but a quiet echo of herself, lying motionless beneath the crisp hospital sheets. Her face, usually animated with emotion, is tranquil now, a peacefulness that belies the turmoil surging like a tempest in the hearts of those left behind.

The tears come unbidden, a torrent of grief cascading down my face as I squeeze her hand, my other hand reaching out to touch her hair, her face, tracing the familiar yet unfamiliar lines and contours with a sort of detached wonder.

My parents stand there, a pair of statues carved from pain and loss, their faces crumpled, their bodies shaking with silent sobs. I can see the questions in their eyes, the shattered dreams and crushed hopes reflecting in their tears as they clutch onto each other, their grasp a lifeline.

I keep waiting to feel Belle's presence in the room, grasping at any gentle reminder that her spirit, the joyous, irrepressible force of nature that was my sister, is still here.

FIVE

Alis

"ARE YOU NERVOUS?" I glide my hand slowly down Sunny's ponytail as she looks out the passenger side window.

"Kind of." She shrugs her shoulders and looks back at me, her soft smile not reaching her eyes. "What if no one talks to me? What if they hate me?"

"Hate you? That's not possible. You're a ray of sunshine — even your name says it." I wink and tug her hair, and she responds in true Sunny fashion with an exaggerated eye roll.

"Whatever."

"I'm serious. You have nothing to worry about. You're fun and pretty, smarter than any other kid I know. And with your quick wit, bullies don't stand a chance. Anyone who comes at you will get a verbal lashing of epic proportion." I slide my hand around her shoulder and squeeze lightly.

Sunny's looking down at her lap, ringing her hands together. "I know. I just miss my friends and my school. I miss home."

"I know, hun. I miss home, too. Try not to be nervous about making new friends — just be yourself. Your first few days might be a little uncomfortable, but you'll get the hang of things. Do you want me to walk in with you?"

Suddenly she snaps her head up and glares at me. "Not a chance. I'm nine, not five." I laugh at her sass.

"I know, goof. You remember where your class is? That tour we took Friday was seriously information overload." Sunny laughs. There's that smile.

"Yeah, Monty. I know where to go."

"Alright, kiddo. Skidaddle. You're going to make me late for *my* first day if I don't head that way now."

Sunny grabs her backpack from between her legs, opens the car door, and slings the pack over her shoulder before turning to look at me. "Love you, Monty."

"Love you, Sunshine. See you after school. I'll be the crazy one yelling obscenities because I can't figure out the carpool line. Can't miss me."

Sunny shakes her head as she turns and walks toward the school building.

I wish you could see how grown up she is, sis. She looks just like you and she's just as awesome.

When I pull into the campus parking lot I'm pleased to find a handful of open parking spots near the sidewalk. Hopefully this lack of overfill is the norm. I step out into the perfect August weather and make my way to meet Dr. Matthews.

Clothes still wrinkle-free? Check.

Teeth still white post-coffee? Check.

Messenger bag with laptop? Check.

Matching shoes? Check. Yes, I have been known to walk out of the house wearing two different shoes. Come at me.

Taking a deep breath, I open the door to the faculty office building and quietly make my way to the directory. Dr. Matthews is on the second floor, Pod C. Got it.

The building has an elevator, but I prefer the open stairs so I turn to walk up them. This building is silent, except the echoes of people walking on the hardwood floor. I opted for my new flats today. No sense in trying to look sexy-chic when surrounded by English nerds, am I right? I'd probably break my ankle anyway.

Once I make it up the stairs, I head toward Pod C.

"Hi, I'm Alis Gilmore, here to see Dr. Matthews." The secretary looks up at me with a warm smile. She looks so much like my grandma, I'd be concerned they were long lost sisters if my grandmother wasn't about the same age as this woman when she died fifteen years ago. Her name plate reads Amelia Murphy.

Amelia, that's a pretty name. Grandma's name was Analise, so they both start with an A. God, I miss that woman.

"Hello, dear. Dr. Matthews is expecting you. You're a bit early, so why don't you have a seat. Would you like some coffee or tea while you wait? I'll let her know you've arrived." She's as sweet as Grandma, too. This lady might be my new best friend.

"Nothing to drink, thank you. I'm fine."

"Alright, dear. You just let me know if you change your mind." She gives me one last smile, then adjusts her glasses and looks back to her computer monitor to continue working. This gives me a few minutes to study her features.

Her gray hair is styled in a twist, and her round face is soft. I can see lines near her eyes and mouth, a sure sign of a joy-filled life. I wonder if any of the picture frames on her L-shaped desk are of her children and grandchildren? Her pearl earrings are small and dainty, and complement her delicate, gold-rimmed glasses. Oh, and would you look at that — her wedding ring has a pearl center stone instead of the traditional diamond. Stunning. This woman is simply stunning.

A door opens to the left and out walks Dr. Abigail Matthews, senior professor of English and American Literature. Her straight dark blonde bob, flowing silk blouse, and wide-legged trousers give her a professional, yet approachable look—but the bold red lipstick screams powerhouse. She's a woman effortlessly in charge, and she's not afraid to show it.

Meanwhile, Dorky McDorkson here looks more like an elementary school librarian with my low chignon (read: messy bun), glasses, light gray blouse, dark blue and white polka dot skirt, and yellow flats.

Please, please, please, can I be like her when I grow up?

"Aurora, it's so nice to finally meet you face to face." I stand as she extends her hand for me to shake.

"Hi, Dr. Matthews, it's great to meet you, too. And please, call me Alis. The only person who calls me Aurora is my mother, and that's only when I've done something to upset her." Dr. Matthews laughs, and tilts her head toward her office.

"Right, Alis, then. Come with me. Let's chat."

I follow her into a large office streaming with natural light. The furniture is modern and sleek, light woods and gray leather. Everything has sharp angles, but the wall of white built-in bookshelves filled with books and framed quotes gives the room a grounded, cozy feel. The entire back wall is floor-to-ceiling windows and the view of the mountains from this vantage point is breathtaking.

"Wow," I say under my breath. She hears me and says, "I know, right? I never imagined having an office with this view."

"It's incredible. I love your office, also. It's beautiful."

"Thank you. I figure if I'm going to spend seventy hours a week holed up in here I better decorate it to feel like home."

"That makes sense."

"Please, have a seat." Dr. Matthews gestures toward one of two gray lounge chairs, and I set my bag next to it before sitting down.

"Did relocating go well? Any hiccups?"

"No, thankfully, everything went smoothly. Our apartment is furnished, so we didn't have to move anything heavy. My mom drove up to help us get settled. I don't think things would have gone so smoothly without her."

"Our?"

"Yes. My daughter and my best friend moved here with me. We're renting a three-bedroom apartment about fifteen minutes from here, closer to the suburbs."

"Oh, that sounds wonderful! Now that you say it, I remember

you mentioning that you are a single parent. How old is your daughter?"

"She's nine. Going on nineteen." I roll my eyes and Dr. Matthews chuckles.

"Strong willed?"

"Not so much. She's funny and kind. She's also quick-witted and sarcastic, which she gets from spending too much time around my roommate and me. She's a lot like her mom was — full of life and always looking to take care of the people around her."

Dr. Matthews quirks an eyebrow, confusion filling her expression. "Her mom?"

Whoops. I'm not used to talking to people who don't know our history, so I forgot to provide context. "Yeah, sorry, I should have explained that. Sunny is my biological niece, but when my sister and her husband died they named me as her guardian, and I adopted her a few years later. Legally becoming her mother made doctor visits, school paperwork, and such a heck of a lot easier."

Dr. Matthews is taken back by our story. "Wow. That's … wow. She sounds like a lovely girl. I hope to meet her someday."

I smile, hoping to ease any heartbreak my voice revealed while explaining the loss of my sister and the resulting mother/daughter relationship. "I'll try to bring her to campus sometime. I'm sure she'd love to meet you as well."

Dr. Matthews leans forward, elbows on her desk. "So, let's get down to business. We have a busy semester ahead of us, and we've had some shuffling in this department so your responsibilities have changed a bit from the last time we spoke."

"Changed, how?"

"Nothing too drastic. You are still mainly my teaching assistant and grader. You'll teach my undergraduate English composition classes — that class meets Tuesday and Wednesday at 9 a.m. You'll teach, but I'm still listed as the professor of record. Fall classes begin next week, and I already emailed you the syllabi for my five classes. The one syllabus you don't have is for a fall break intensive, and I'll need you in that class from

8 a.m. to 5 p.m. the entire week to help students, and to handle assignment turn-ins, and grading while I lecture. The students in that class have book reviews due at the beginning of the course, and a research paper due two weeks after class ends. The only other grades in that class are for participation and daily reading quizzes. It's the only other undergraduate course I teach, and it was added to my plate at the last minute."

"Okay. An extra class and a week in the classroom doesn't sound like too much to add on." Dr. Matthews smiles, a tinge of nervousness present. I guess there's more?

"You'll have a few other things as well. I'm sorry to toss this on you, but with budget cuts we weren't able to hire on more help, so we've redistributed the workload among the remaining professors and teaching assistants instead of fighting the board for more funding. They only let us know about the budget changes three weeks ago, so we've had to scramble to sort everything out."

My eyes go wide. "That sounds intense."

Dr. Matthews chuckles and shakes her head, rubbing her forehead. "A bit, yes. So, part of redistributing is that you'll serve as grader for two other professors for the next two semesters. You won't have any lecturing responsibilities for them, but you will grade all papers, quizzes, tests, etc. Both professors mainly teach undergraduate courses and have a much lighter class load. Dr. Miller is an adjunct, and she teaches three basic English comp classes online. Dr. Belanger is a crossover professor from the foreign languages department. He has three classes this semester, I believe? One is a graduate-level course and the other two are undergrad. He teaches French language, French lit, and an English comp class. Originally I had planned to only add Dr. Miller to your workload, but you are the only TA in our department who speaks French, so you're the only person capable of grading for Dr. Belanger."

I'm writing the class list down as quickly as possible, tallying the ever-growing workload coming my way. Yes, I speak French, but I don't use it very often so I'm a bit rusty.

"Ok, six classes for you, two for Dr. Miller, and three for Dr. Belanger — so eleven total."

"Yes, but you're only responsible for teaching the one English comp class we discussed and you'll lecture on an as-needed basis for my other five. You won't have to sub in for Miller or Belanger. Online students are a pain, but most of their questions you can pawn off on IT as they aren't course related. Dr. Belanger is pretty hands-on with his students, so you shouldn't have to field questions from them."

"Sounds doable." I think. Please, God, don't let me drown my first semester here!

She looks at me with confidence in her eyes. "I know it's a lot but we're stretched thin this year. We were supposed to get one new professor and three new TAs, but the board thinks engineering is more important than English, so they got the padded budget this year. Amelia and I are working on a few grant proposals due this spring, so hopefully we can get more funding from those instead of fighting the board."

I nod in understanding. "I'm vaguely aware of how university budgets work from my time in my previous program, but Dr. Ryan wasn't much of an administrator so he didn't handle any of the numbers. He was the consummate absent-minded professor. Super smart, very passionate about his work, not great with details outside his field of study."

Dr. Matthews' face lights up at the mention of Dr. Ryan. "I remember your application stating that you studied with Dr. Ryan for a few years. I've met him a few times and I can definitely see him as a one-track mind kind of man. And you're spot on about the passion — that man has charisma."

I smile, but it doesn't reach my eyes. I don't want to get into a conversation about Dr. Ryan. But I also don't want to let on that I'm no longer his biggest fan. That man went from maven to moron in one conversation, and if I never see him again I'll be perfectly happy.

"Am I assuming correctly that you becoming Sunny's guardian had something to do with you leaving his program?"

Shit, I *really* don't want to talk about this. "Yes. I had a lot on my plate at that time — grieving my sister, learning to be a parent, working and studying, moving in with my parents. Working for Dr.

Ryan was more than a typical full-time teaching assistant position. I worked on a lot of research projects with him and also took a full course load. I was trying to finish my master's in two years even though it's set up as a three-year program, so I was pretty slammed."

"I've heard working with Dr. Ryan is quite the experience, to say the least."

Ha — understatement. She has *no* idea. And that experience went far beyond what I signed up for.

"It was. And crazy competitive. The students at Grant are like sharks, always circling and looking for any opportunity to strike."

She shrugs. "Well, when you have the celebrity status he has in our world of academia, that's to be expected."

"Yeah, I guess," I say, pushing my glasses up and attempting to hide my disdain for Jonathan Ryan behind a fake as fuck smile.

"I don't mean to pry, but given the work it takes to become Dr. Ryan's right hand and the competitive nature of his program, why didn't you just slow down? Why did you decide to leave the program entirely? It seems like a lot of effort to walk away from, and Dr. Ryan is so selective with his students I'm sure convincing him to let you go wasn't easy." Ha. Let *me* go? That bastard let a lot of things go — like the truth.

I let out a sharp breath and shake my head, looking down at my lap. *Why can't she stop asking questions I don't want to answer?*

I reestablish eye contact, professional smile in place, and answer her as best I can without flat out lying. "You are not the first person to ask me that question. I wish I had a cut-and-dry answer, but the truth is complicated. A lot happened around the time my sister died, both with my family and in my school life. I was overwhelmed and something had to give. I weighed all my options and Dr. Ryan was willing to work with me to slow down and hand off some of my teaching responsibilities to other students."

I look back down at my notebook, unable to hide the pain in my eyes for much longer. I swallow. "Some unfortunate things happened during that time, and I decided it was best to leave school and focus on raising Sunny."

Look up, confident posture and smile back in place. And, go. "I always planned to finish, and that's why I'm here now." There. Not a lie. She doesn't need to know the details.

She smiles, warmly. "I'm sure you are an incredible mother to that little girl. I'm glad you're here."

"Me, too. And thank you. I've certainly had a lot of help with Sunny. There's no way that kid would be half as awesome if she only had me raising her."

Dr. Matthews laughs. "What is it they say? It takes a village?"

"It certainly does." I nod in agreement.

"Right then. Amelia has a packet for you at her desk with your employment paperwork and the extra syllabus for the intensive. She should have contacted IT this morning to get your school login credentials. Once you log in you'll see the courses divided by professor, in addition to the classes you're taking. How many are you taking this semester?"

"Just one. I haven't been in school for nearly a decade, and when I got the job as your TA I decided to ease my way back into being a student instead of taking on a full load from the start."

"Smart. Especially with the extra work I've tossed at you."

I laugh. "No doubt."

"I want to introduce you to Dr. Belanger while you're here. I think he's on campus today — hold on a sec." She stands and walks to her office door, opening it slightly. "Amelia, can you call Deborah in languages and find out if Dr. Belanger is in his office? Thank you."

She turns and walks back toward her desk chair. "If he's in today we'll walk downstairs and you can meet him."

"Same building? That's convenient. I guess it makes sense to keep all the languages together."

Dr. Matthews nods her head. "Especially when you have crossover professors." Amelia says something from her desk, and Dr. Matthews turns back toward the door. "Feel free to leave your things here. We'll come back up afterward so you can grab your employment packet and such."

I stand and follow her out of the office. Her heels don't make that high-pitched *click* as she walks — a sure sign of expensive footwear — and standing next to her I hope I don't look like a child. She's 5'10" of sexy, professional boss lady, and here I am, 5'5" on a good day, with my Peter Pan collared blouse and, in case you forgot, *yellow* shoes. I thought I looked sophisticated when I left the apartment this morning, but now I feel more like Ms. Frizzle.

Hold on, let me overthink this. The blouse is fine, but I should have worn a pencil skirt and heels. At least then I'd look more sexy librarian than nerd. Eh, but then it'd set a precedent that I consider myself somewhere in the same league as Dr. Matthews — the boss lady major league. *Pfft. Yeah right.* It's better that I showed up looking like myself. Professional, cute, and quirky. *Take a deep breath, Alis.*

I run my hands down the front of my blouse and skirt, smoothing any wrinkles that developed while sitting. Everything seems nice and smooth, so I stop fretting over my outfit and walk next to Dr. Matthews down the hall, down the stairs, and then to Pod A: Languages on the first floor.

"Deborah, it's so nice to see you." Dr. Matthews smiles at the faculty secretary, who looks a heck of a lot more frazzled than the calm and sweet Amelia.

"Hi, Dr. Matthews. Dr. Belanger just got off a call so you should be good to head in."

"Thanks." She motions for me to follow her and heads toward the last office on the right, which has "D. Belanger, French" carved into the nameplate on the wall next to the door.

She knocks and pokes her head in, checking to make sure he's ready for visitors. I stand behind her a few feet, waiting to be welcomed in. The professors greet each other and then Dr. Matthews pushes the door the rest of the way open and tilts her head inside. I walk in behind her.

"Dr. Belanger, this is Aurora Gilmore, my new TA who will be grading for your classes this year."

I step out from behind Dr. Matthews as a tall man wearing tailored trousers and a button-down shirt with rolled-up sleeves walks around his desk. His long hair hides his face as he cleans his glasses with a cloth and puts them back on.

"I apologize for the clutter. Hi, Aurora —" Dr. Belanger looks up and we make eye contact. He freezes. My eyes go wide.

No, no, noooooo freaking way. No way is this happening.

Dr. Belanger and I have met once before.

Last Friday night, to be exact.

At a club.

Sitting at the bar.

Where we exchanged phone numbers and kissed and he made me all tingly in my lady bits.

Up until this point, however, I only knew him as Sexy Dexy.

SIX

MY INNER MONOLOGUE is getting a kick out of this. *Plot twist!* If I could punch my inner self in the face, I would. This is *not* happening.

He coughs and continues his introduction. "Hi, I'm Dexter Belanger." He extends his hand and I take it, lady bits reigniting when we touch. *Cool it, vag. Now is not the time.*

I plaster my most professional smile onto my face. "Hi, Dr. Belanger. Please, call me Alis."

"Right. Alis." He nods and releases my hand, his eyes full of confusion. "Is that a middle name?"

I swallow and shake my head. "No, not a middle name. Alis is the nickname my grandmother gave me as a child. It stuck. Aurora is a mouthful and growing up in the age of *Gilmore Girls*, I wasn't about to let people call me Rory."

Dr. Matthews laughs at this revelation. "How did I miss that?! Rory Gilmore. I love that show! Watched it religiously in college."

Dexter looks between us, completely lost. "Never seen it," he interjects.

Dr. Matthews smirks at him, playfully. "Well, considering you weren't a high school or college-aged girl when it aired, I wouldn't think so." Dexter just nods.

Not skipping a beat, Dexter diverts from TV talk and gets straight to business. "Dr. Matthews, thank you so much for bringing Alis down to meet me. Would it be alright for me to sit down with her for a bit? I'd like to walk her through my syllabi and better prepare her for the semester." *Nope, nope, nope. Don't leave me here alone. Please, don't leave me here.*

"Sure thing," she says to him. "Alis, come back to my office when you're done. I'll put your paperwork with your bag."

I nod, trying to act as normal as possible while internally I am FREAKING OUT. I'm about to be in an office, alone, with the *one* man I've felt attracted to in nine years who is now completely off limits. This. Is. Awesome. *I'm not sweating; you're sweating. Is it too hot in here? Why doesn't my top have buttons? I need to undo some buttons.*

"Will do. Thanks, Dr. Matthews."

She turns and walks toward the door, Dexter following close behind. He bids her farewell and gently closes the door, turning back to face me.

He scans me top to bottom and then looks at me expectantly. *Yeah right, buddy. I'm not leading off in this conversation.*

"So, this is ... unexpected," he says. I nod. "You didn't tell me your name was Aurora."

I shrug, feigning nonchalance. "Nobody calls me that, so I don't normally introduce myself by that name."

I'm trying not to sound like a smartass, but I don't think it's working. I turned him down; told him that now is not a good time for me. But seeing him again makes me want him so much more. *No, Alis, you cannot have a cookie before dinner.* Cookie being Dexter and dinner being school, responsibilities, my freaking JOB.

"Of course. That makes sense. You explained that already." He lifts both hands to his hair, pushing it back and away from his face. That hair. Gahhhhh! I want to run my hands through it as I press my body against his and never let go. And those glasses — I can only imagine how sexy he looks in the morning, sitting at the kitchen table with a cup of coffee, hair falling loose around his face, glasses on while he reads the news. Of course he reads the news in the morning — he's too scholarly and mature for a morning trope through Facebook or a quick round of Two Dots. *This man is delicious.*

"You wear glasses." I say, pointing out the obvious.

"As do you." He gives me that smirky half-smile. Dammit, I don't want to be attracted to him now that he's my boss. *Well then stop picturing him shirtless while reading the news.* Ha — easier said than done.

"I guess it's a good thing I said 'no' to dinner, considering I work for you now." He gives me a puzzled look, like he's confused by the statement I just made.

"And why would that be a problem?"

He can't seriously be that dense. Are the glasses a lie? Is he actually stupid?

"I can think of a handful of reasons why that would be a problem, most notably: I'm your employee, I'm a student at the university where you're a professor, Dr. Matthews would crap a brick if she found out her teaching assistant was dating a professor…" I look up from my finger counting to his face. "Should I go on?"

He laughs and shakes his head. "Yeah, okay. We'll agree to disagree on that. When we met, I didn't realize you were young enough to be my student. How old are you, anyway?"

He now thinks I'm a child. Frustration builds, but I bite back the snark and answer simply: "Thirty."

He nods. "That's what I would have guessed when we met. You don't look early twenties." I don't respond.

"So you're thirty and just now going to grad school?" *You condescending asshat.* Maybe it won't be so difficult not to be attracted to him.

He leans against his desk, hands in his trouser pockets. My eyes trail down his shoulders to his biceps and forearms, across to his abdomen and down, slowly, to his … *Dammit. Stop it, Alis.*

I snap my eyes back up to meet his. "Yes. Is there a problem with a woman my age going to grad school?" I cross my arms over my chest. Now I look like a defiant child. Great.

"No, it's just not the norm. Most students in our grad programs are twenty-two, twenty-three, just out of undergrad. I've only been teaching here for three years now, and maybe other programs have students of all ages. I just haven't had any. Maybe we have some in the online programs, but not on campus." His face takes on a quizzical look, as if he's only now considering people of all ages go to college. "So, Alis, why go back to get your master's now?"

"I told you the other night — life happened and put my plans on hold. Now I'm in a better place and it's the right time to finish my degree."

"Finish? So you started once before?"

"Yes." I say plainly. I've already had this conversation once today and I don't have the energy to do it again.

"Care to expound on that?"

"Nope." I look at him blankly, hoping my face effectively communicates: *drop it.*

"Alright, then. Let's talk shop. Have a seat." He gestures to a seat in front of his desk as he stands and circles back to his desk chair. I need the barrier between us, if only to keep my eyes on his face and not all over his body. *Whyyyyyyy is this happening?*

"You speak French?" he asks, lifting an eyebrow in question.

"Oui, je parle français." (Yes, I speak French.)

"Vous parlez couramment ou vous apprenez toujours?" (Are you fluent or are you still learning?)

"Je parle couramment, mais ça fait longtemps que je n'ai pas parlé français." (I speak fluently, but it's been a while since I spoke French.)

"Et vous vous sentez à l'aise de corriger des devoirs en français?" (And you feel comfortable grading homework in French?)

"Oui." (Yes.)

He nods. "Wonderful. This should work out nicely, eh?" Eh? Is he Canadian? Belanger is French. He's probably Canadian. Why does that make me want him even more?

"Looks like it." I give him a stiff smile. *I need to get out of this office.*

"Right. Well, my class assignments are pretty straight forward. I teach Intro to French Language at the undergrad level. Those students don't write any papers, but they are quizzed in each class and have a midterm and a final exam. The exams include an oral component, and depending on the class size I may need you to attend that day to proctor while I administer the oral exam in the next room."

"That shouldn't be a problem. Do you have a notepad I could use? I'd like to write everything down and I left mine in Dr. Matthews' office." He looks around his cluttered desk for a notepad, to no avail. "How do you find anything in here? I've seen teenagers' rooms cleaner than your office."

Dexter looks at me incredulously. "You're kidding, right? I know where everything is in my office. It may look chaotic to an outsider, but I have a system."

"And does your system include a spot for notepads?" I lift an eyebrow in question.

"Apparently … not today." He lifts his hands in defeat. "We'll just talk and I'll send an email with all the information and the syllabi. Sound good?"

"Sure." Time to exercise my nonexistent mental note-taking abilities. I'm sure I'll forget half of what he says, and he'll forget the other half. Hopefully between the two of us we can remember all the pieces to this conversation.

"Okay, so, we've covered Intro. Then I have another undergrad course — English Comp — and a graduate level French Lit. English Comp is basic, and since you're teaching one of Dr. Matthews' comp classes you shouldn't have any issues grading for mine. All syllabi are approved by Matthews before finalization to ensure continuity, so we're covering the same stuff."

I nod. "Yeah, I don't foresee any issues there."

He continues. "My grad students have to pass French 1, 2, and 3 before they can take Lit because I require all texts to be read in the original language. The assignments in that class are mainly essays, but they don't write assignments in French. Read in French, respond in English. I want my students to understand the meaning of the text in the original language, especially because the English translations often miss the true depth of feeling or meaning."

I listen intently. I can tell by his animated speech that he loves teaching. He's gorgeous no matter the setting, but if he lights up like this just talking about teaching, I can't wait to see him in action. I bet he's breathtaking.

Is there anything sexier than a man who is fully alive? I doubt it. I'm a textbook introvert, filled with social anxiety and preferring solitude, but when I'm lecturing about something I love, my anxiety melts away and I'm fully in the zone. I bet Dexter operates similarly.

As the minutes tick by and I listen to him talk, I find myself wanting to draw closer and touch him. Seriously, thank God for this desk in between us or I would be tempted to climb into his lap. This entire room smells of him; it's intoxicating.

Snap out of it, Alis. You CANNOT have anything more than a professor/employee relationship with this man.

Or, maybe I could? He didn't seem to think it was a bad idea.

No! He's a professor. I'm a student. And everything that went down with Dr. Ryan, I know how easy it is for someone to misconstrue the nature of the professor/student relationship.

"Alis?" *Whoops.*

"Sorry, my thoughts trailed off for a second. Could you repeat that?"

He smirks as if he knows I was fantasizing about him. Leaning his forearms on the desk, he repeats whatever I just missed. "I said I think it'd be best for us to meet once a week to go over upcoming assignments. It's important that we communicate regularly since you're handling the grading for my classes."

"Weekly meetings? Is that really necessary? Seems like an email report of weekly assignments would suffice. And you should get a notification whenever I post grades in the student portal." I know what he's doing, and I'm not having it. I'm hanging on by a thread of self control as it is; I don't need any motivation to cross the line.

"Why send an email when you can drink coffee and enjoy friendly company?" He leans back in his chair, trying to look nonchalant as he imposes weekly coffee dates.

"Look, Dr. Belanger —"

"Dexter. Call me Dexter."

I flit my hand at him, annoyed. "Fine, whatever, Dexter. We had one flirty conversation and an incredible kiss, but I already told you I can't date you. Now is really not a good time for me. And even if it was, you're still a professor and I'm still a student."

"Incredible, eh?" Thank the good Lord this man has a beard. I don't know if he has dimples, but if he did my panties would melt right off me with that ridiculously sexy smirk.

I look to the ceiling and exhale. "Is that seriously all you took from what I just said?" This conversation has to end. We're going off the rails.

"I heard everything, but you said our kiss was incredible. I'm inclined to agree. Je veux encore t'embrasser." His eyes are twinkling. TWINKLING, dammit!

I rub my forehead, trying to smooth out the stress wrinkles embedding themselves into my skin. "I have to go."

I stand and am about to turn when he stops me. "Alis, wait, please. I won't apologize because I do want to kiss you again, but if you don't want this, I will let it be."

"Thank you."

"I'm not budging on the weekly meetings, but those meetings will be strictly professor/grader. Thirty minutes, tops. I won't pursue you romantically unless you ask me to."

Do I believe him? I don't know. I'd like to think he'll respect my boundaries, but his flirtatious demeanor during this meeting suggests otherwise.

"I think I can work that into my schedule. I'll talk with your secretary and find a good day and time each week."

He nods. "Sounds perfect. I'll email you the syllabi and some notes about each class. May I walk you out?"

"Thanks, but I can find my way back to Dr. Matthews. I'll keep an eye out for your email."

I walk to his office door and he follows, but he stops at the threshold. *One point to Dexter for respecting boundaries.*

I stop at his secretary's desk to grab her card and let her know I'll be emailing her to set up weekly meetings with Dr. Belanger. She smiles and bids me farewell.

I don't look back at Dexter. Looking back will only make him think I'm lying about the boundaries I've set.

He can't think that I want him. Forget *thinking* I want him — I straight up CANNOT want him. A professor/student romantic relationship is a line I won't cross, even if he doesn't see the problem. I know what happens when people blur the lines, and it's not worth the fallout.

Once I've retrieved my items from Dr. Matthews and bid her farewell, I head back to my car and sit in the parking lot. My thoughts are spinning, taking me back to the darkest time of my life, and I can't dig my way out of this mental sinkhole.

The drama surrounding my snap decision to drop out of grad school still haunts me to this day. I don't dwell on what happened, but those wounds are deep and I still feel the scars of betrayal and loss. You'd think after nine years I'd be over it.

I didn't expect the memories to resurface so forcefully with this fresh start, but life has a way of dishing out a gut punch when everything seems fine and dandy. Why can't anything be simple? All I want is to finish my degree, maybe continue on with my PhD, and teach. Is that too much to ask?

After what happened with Dr. Ryan I wasn't on campus to fight my way through the gossip, but social media painted a pretty clear picture of my tarnished reputation among the student body. The messages I received are still burned into my memory.

"Oh my gosh you whore how could you sleep with a married man?!"

"OMG OMG OMG you and Dr. Ryan?! You lucky bitch!"

"So you won't give me a second date but you'll suck off a professor? That's fucking sick."

"Please tell me you have dick pics."

"Where the hell are you? You get caught fucking a prof and then you disappear? Coward."

"Now we know how you landed the TA spot. You must deepthroat like a porn star to beat out students who actually deserved the job."

God bless the creator of social media. Who knew the Internet would give people the courage to say what they really feel? Never mind that their words destroy others.

Part of me wishes I had been on campus to defend myself and my character, but everything in my life fell apart in a matter of days and I didn't have the energy to fight off an insecure woman, a spineless man, and a student body full of idiots who believe everything they hear, no matter how absurd. Regardless of how hard I worked and how quickly it was destroyed, none of it mattered after that day.

For all I know I became a legend at Grant University. Dr. Ryan is charismatic and inspires devotion from his students. I have no idea what the man looks like now — *please, please be balding* — but a decade ago in his early forties he oozed geek chic. Who knew anyone could consider argyle attractive? I think the coeds were more attracted to his charisma than his looks — not that he was ugly or anything, but he wasn't Adonis by a long shot.

"Dr. Ryan — more like Dr. Ride Him!" I wish I was joking. No creativity points awarded to the sorority bimbos. This one girl, Michelle, used to stare at his butt and make comments under her breath about biting it. I don't think she realized I could hear her talking to herself about seducing our professor, and I never let on that her "secret" crush was actually public knowledge.

Skye always got a kick out of my weekly Michelle reports. "What part of Dr. Ryan did Michelle have for lunch today?" she'd ask. Now that I think about it, Michelle must have had one hell of an oral fixation. She always fantasized about biting, licking, sucking, nibbling — *Gross.*

Did I think Dr. Ryan was attractive? Sure. However, I was not a twenty-one-year-old girl with daddy issues, nor did I have an older man fetish. I was so consumed with my studies and goals that I didn't have time to date, much less lust after my faculty supervisor.

I tried dating in undergrad, but most of the guys I knew didn't hold my interest. Skye introduced me to my first — and only — long-term boyfriend, Ben, our junior year. We dated for ten months and then he dumped me because I didn't give him enough attention (see studies and goals above).

Annabelle Windsor surely gave him enough attention, though. Right after we broke up, I found out he'd been hooking up the girl for the last month or so of our relationship. I knew he definitely was not "the one" when I found myself less upset about the emotional betrayal than I was about his double dipping. Thinking about it still gives me the heeby jeebies. We always used condoms, but I still got tested after learning of his wandering dick.

Side note: Why don't we refer to cheating as wanderlust? That seems more accurate, and makes a hell of a lot more sense than an overwhelming desire to travel.

Ben was the beginning and the end of my boyfriend roster. I went on random dates over the next few years, but only because Skye couldn't help but try and set me up with whatever guys she met in class. None of them ever got a second date. The only reason any of them got a first date was to keep Skye off my back about my lack of romantic life. If I "gave him a chance" and went to dinner then I could go back to my books for a few months until Skye decided it was time for her to once again intervene. Wannabe cupid, that one.

After Hurricane Margaret (as I've dubbed the Dr. Ryan debacle) I wanted nothing to do with dating, relationships, romance — none of it. Add in my sudden and terrifying new role as guardian to a nine-month-old baby girl, mourning the loss of my sister and brother-in-law, and grieving my demolished life plan, and I was one hell of a depressing cocktail. Not even tequila could numb the pain that was my life back then.

I'll never knowingly set myself up for that level of betrayal and pain again — which is exactly what will happen if I don't douse all lustful thoughts of Dexter Belanger.

SEVEN

9 years ago

"I DON'T KNOW how to do this life without you." My parents have already spent their time alone with Belle and left me here to say goodbye while they retrieve Sunny from my aunt and bring her to visit her mama one last time.

"You've always been my sunshine. My happy place. My best friend. My home." I choke on my words, silent tears suddenly strengthening into gut wrenching sobs. My cheek rests on her bed, looking up toward her face with my hand gently stroking hers.

I know the machine is the only thing keeping Belle alive right now, that she's not really here, but I don't know how to accept that reality.

"You'll be with grandma soon." A small smile tugs at my lips, tears still pouring from my eyes. "Remember the summer we visited her and she gave us our nicknames? We were her Sunshine and Aurora Borealis. Sunny and Alis. The lights of grandma's life. I remember listening to her talk about how much warmth you brought to everyone around you. How a hug from you was better than a mug of hot chocolate during winter. It's like she saw into the deepest parts of us and knew us better than anyone else.

"Turns out the nicknames grandma gave us went deeper than us just providing light and beauty to her life. Sometime in high school I learned that the northern lights are actually dependent on the sun. Something about plasma shooting out from the sun, and then that stuff makes its way to earth and causes the aurora borealis.

"The northern lights don't exist without the sun. How am I supposed to exist without you?"

I bury my head into Belle's side and let out another strangled sob, clinging as tightly as I can to her and refusing to let go. "I — I can't. I know I'm being selfish but I can't lose you. You're my leader. My strength. My better half. Don't leave me. Please, don't leave me!"

Sobs shake my entire body and I can't say another word. I don't have anything more to say that isn't redundant. I know I should be assuring my sister that we will be okay, that Sunny will grow up in a loving home and she doesn't have to worry. That she can let go and know we will all be alright. But I'm too selfish to say any of that.

I've never had to go a day without at least talking to my big sister. She's the leader; I'm the follower. She's the strong one; I lean on her. She's great with people; I'd only have book characters for friends if she didn't teach me how to be sociable. She's charismatic and beautiful; I'm pretty but socially awkward.

God, Alis, snap out of it. This isn't about you.

I try to take a deep breath, but it's shaky at best. The tears are starting to slow a bit and my entire body is no longer shaking. Progress.

A soft knock comes from the door. "Alis? You ok, honey? We've brought Sunny." Mom is whispering, as if speaking at a normal volume will wake someone.

I look up and into the most beautiful, smiling cherub face. Gosh, Sunny looks just like her mom. All bouncing chestnut curls and round hazel eyes. She's got those two fingers in her mouth, as always. This girl is a mess.

"Come here, baby girl." I reach out to my mom to pass Sunny to me. She almost falls out of mom's arms trying to jump from one person to the other.

"Whoa now." I chuckle. She's now sitting on my lap, looking at my splotched face. Her fingers are still covered in slobber, and she presses her wet hand to my cheeks, trying to rub away whatever tear tracks are left. Good thing I didn't put any makeup on my face after showering — between tears and baby slobber I'm sure my face would look more like an abstract painting if I had.

I stand, pushing the chair back and setting Sunny on my hip. "Baby girl, we need to give your mama our best hug and kiss good-bye." I choke on the last word, hiding my face in her wild hair, and stifle a sob.

Sunny doesn't speak yet, but her babbles include a few "ba ba" and "ma ma ma"s, so I'm going to count that as her understanding we're with Belle right now. My sister definitely doesn't look like herself, covered in bruises and cuts with a tube attached to her neck and a bandage wrapped around her head. Her eyes are swollen and bruised, making her face nearly unrecognizable.

I prop my butt on the side of the bed, keeping Sunny closest to Belle, and lift my sister's hand so Sunny can touch her. "Ba ba ma ma," Sunny babbles as she pats her mother's hand.

"Do you want to give her a hug, baby?" I ask, pushing her curls behind her ear and kissing her on the cheek. Sunny looks at me and opens her mouth wide, leaning in to give me a 'kiss'. "Thank you, baby. But let's try and give your mama a kiss on her hand, yeah?"

I lift Belle's hand a bit higher and give it a soft kiss before offering it to Sunny. "Give mama a kiss, baby." She looks at me like I'm crazy. I kiss Belle's hand again. "Kiss kiss for mama."

Sunny finally leans over and gives a big open-mouthed kiss to Belle's hand, leaving a trail of spit behind. I know my sister wouldn't have it any other way.

"That's it baby girl. Good job." I try to smile but the tears are coming back. These things are relentless, I swear. "We gotta say goodbye to mama, because she's gotta go see Grandma Gilmore in heaven, ok?" Sunny just looks at me, not understanding a word.

"It's going to be ok, baby. Mama's going to be ok and so are we."

Maybe if I keep telling Sunny we'll be alright I'll start to believe it as well. Fat chance, but it's worth a shot.

I press Sunny closer to me, crying into her hair and trying to get a grip on myself. Suddenly, I feel a soft squeeze on my shoulder and look up to see my dad, eyes glistening with silent tears. "Everything is going to be alright, Alis. We'll get through this, together."

I don't say anything. I can't say anything right now. I just nod my head and look back to my sister, still holding her hand. I refuse to let go until I absolutely have to.

I hadn't even noticed my mom had left until she returns, accompanied by the doctor. A hush descends upon the room as the doctor approaches the opposite side of Belle's bed, close to the ventilator.

His gaze is heavy, burdened with the weight of the moment. He offers a faint, reassuring smile, the unspoken question evident in his eyes: are we prepared?

Dad envelops mom with one arm, the other firm on my shoulder, anchoring us all. He plants a tender kiss on mom's temple, then meets the doctor's gaze, giving a slight nod.

With a soft click, the ventilator falls silent. We remain by Belle's side, holding onto her and each other. Time blurs, and after what feels like both an eternity and an instant, she's gone.

She's really gone.

I feel like somebody just stuck their hand in my chest and ripped out my heart. This is a fucking nightmare.

EIGHT

Dexter

I STAND at my office door and watch Alis leave, rubbing my chin in confusion at her reaction to me today. It's not like I wasn't caught off guard when she was introduced as my new grader, but I was at least happy to see her again. Alis is beautiful and intelligent, and now I learn she speaks my mother tongue — I can just imagine the sounds she'd make as I whisper how much I want her.

I can almost feel the goosebumps spreading across her skin as I nibble on her earlobe — *Je veux lécher chaque centimètre de ton corps nu —* trail my tongue down her neck — *T'es la plus belle femme que j'aie jamais vue* — brush her hair off her shoulders and nip at her collarbone as I push her sweater off the side of her shoulder — *Je rêve de te toucher depuis notre première rencontre...*

"Dr. Belanger?" Deborah's voice shakes me out of my fantasy. Fuck. Please God don't let her see how tight my trousers are right now.

I cough. "Yes, Deborah. Do you need something?" She cocks her head to the side as if I should know what she wants from me.

"No, sir, I just wanted to make sure you're alright. You've been standing in your doorway staring at nothing for nearly five minutes."

"I'm fine, thanks. I have a few things to finish up. When Dr. Euler arrives, can you send him in?"

She nods, and I turn and shut my office door, letting out a deep breath and shaking my head to clear out thoughts of Alis. What is it about this woman? She says she doesn't want me — wait, did she actually say that? I get the feeling she wants me just as badly as I want her, but she doesn't WANT to want me.

But, why? Aside from her professor/student argument, which frankly is not a big deal given we are both in our thirties and I am not her professor, why is she so adamant about pushing me away?

I get that she just moved here, but I'm not asking her to marry me. I just want to get to know the woman. She's stunning and we have great rapport, our banter is sexy as hell, and if I'm guessing correctly, her professional aspirations closely line up with mine. If nothing else, we could casually get to know each other over the next few months and see where it goes from there.

I run my hands through my hair, push my back off from the door, and head back to my desk. I have a shit ton of work to finish before Leo — yes, his parents named him after that Euhler and yes, he's a math professor — meets me for lunch, and there's no way I'll get it all done with Alis invading my every thought.

Pushing thoughts of Alis aside, I sit and get to work rifling through the stacks of summer essays that litter my desk. I know my office is a cluttered mess, but I truly do have my own system. Just because others don't understand it doesn't mean that I'm a slob.

I'm halfway through grading the fourth essay when Leo knocks twice and walks into my office.

"Bro, you ready?" Despite his genius namesake and predictable career in mathematics, Leo is the most laid back of the friends I've made since moving back to the States. I'm surprised he hasn't been reprimanded for skirting the faculty dress code, but he looks professional enough when he adds a sport coat over his V-neck shirts.

"Yeah, just a sec. I'm finishing up this paper."

Leo nods and walks in, settling into one of the visitor chairs in front of my desk and setting his ankle across his knee. "Thank God I don't read essays for a living. My head would explode."

I laugh. "Yeah, well, I thank God that I don't teach polynomials to freshmen. That would drive me fucking insane."

"You're just pissed that you'd fail my class and get your ass kicked by my freshmen."

"Sorry, Mathlete. But I did, in fact, pass algebra with flying colors."

I flip to the last page of the essay, scribble some concluding notes and give the student a B-minus.

"That's that. Let's go." I stand and grab the blazer off my chair, and Leo and I head out.

"YOU OKAY, MAN?" Leo stops inhaling his lunch to inquire about my less-than-chatty demeanor.

"Yeah, why? Is there something on my face?" I grab my napkin, wiping around my mouth to find the rogue sauce. He shakes his head.

"No, but you look confused. Or maybe, constipated?"

"Shut up, idiot. I'm fine. I'm just thinking." I dip a fry in barbecue sauce and take a bite.

It's an unspoken rule among men that we don't pry, but Leo has never been able to read a room so, of course, he pushes.

"About?" he waves the back of his hand in my general direction, signaling me to go on.

If I say "it's nothing" he will continue to pry, and I'm a shit liar. So, I decide to let Leo help me sort through my attraction to my grader. "Remember last weekend when you and John dragged me to that club so you could meet up with those Tinder chicks you wanted to hook up with?"

Leo looks at the ceiling. "Fuck, Shelly... Sherry? Shelly. Yeah. She was so fucking hot. Didn't you bow out early that night?"

"Yeah, that was the plan." I start to rub my forehead. "But as I was heading out I met someone."

"Yeah?" A grin takes over his face. "About damn time, man."

I shake my head, laughing. "She gave me her number and then gave me the brush off when I sent her a text a few days later."

Leo's lifting a fry to his mouth as I tell him about Alis's brushoff, and he freezes, fry in hand, dumbstruck by this revelation. He shoves his fry into his mouth, cocks his head to the side, and scrunches his eyebrows together in confusion. After swallowing his fry Leo asks, "Aren't women usually waiting by their phones for the dude to text them for another date?"

"I guess. But not this one. She wasted no time responding and shutting things down before I could really entertain seeing her again."

"That's just brutal," Leo snorts. "Looks like your man bun lost its luster. Needs more fairy dust or whatever magic it gives off to make women drop their panties for you."

"Seriously, man. You're a child, I swear."

He laughs. "You know it's true, though! Every time we go out half the women in the bar spend the night eye fucking you from their stools. They dig your lumbersexual look."

"Lumbersexual? What the hell is that?"

"You know, like a sexy lumberjack. But you're too pretty to be a lumberjack so nevermind."

"Too pretty? Are you high? What is wrong with you? I'm Canadian! I'm rugged!" I'm not even convincing myself at this point.

Leo's cackling is getting louder, drawing attention from the people around us. "No, bro. I just meant that you don't have that rugged, outdoorsy look going for you. But still, women are always coming onto you and petting your hair, rubbing their tits all over your arm trying to get your attention."

He's right. Women do tend to flock toward me at bars and most of them try to touch my hair. It's kinda weird. Do they think it's hot to pet a man in public? I'm not a dog.

I brush off his words. "Whatever. She was different. We talked." I keep eating, thinking back to the smile etched on her face as we talked at the bar.

"Please, hold back," Leo goads. "Your overflowing details are too much."

I roll my eyes. "We talked. She's witty, and gorgeous. She knows Tolstoy and Dumas."

"Whoa now. Slow down." Leo holds up his hands in mock surprise. "She's read classic authors? How rare!"

"Shut up, dumbass. I mean she KNOWS them, knows them. She can quote their works. It was hot as hell."

"Damn. No wonder you actually contacted this one. She's into your nerdy literature shit."

"Don't be daft; you have a doctorate. You may act like an unintelligent manchild, but you know if some gorgeous woman at a bar started talking your ear off about tangents and cotangents you'd drool all over yourself."

He considers this for a moment. "Yeah. That'd be fucking hot. I bet that chick would actually understand my pickup lines."

"Like I said."

"So, why don't you just reach out to her again?" Leo asks. "Maybe she's changed her mind?"

I scoff and shake my head. "She certainly hadn't changed her mind when I saw her earlier today."

Leo starts coughing and choking on his soda. "Back the fuck up. What? You saw her today? Why didn't you say that already?"

"I hadn't gotten to that part of my story yet."

He waves his hand at me again. "Go on."

"I saw her today. In my office. Dr. Matthews introduced her as my new grader."

Leo stops mid-chew, eyes practically bulging out of his head.

"Yeah. At first I didn't know what to think. She was introduced by a different name, making me think she lied the other night. Then I mentally chastised myself for hitting on some young twenty-something. Turns out she didn't lie about her name, she usually goes by a nickname, and she's thirty."

"Thirty? And she's your grader?"

"Yeah. Apparently she started grad school, quit, and now she's moved here to finish."

"At thirty." Leo looks skeptical. "Don't thirty-somethings typically do online school or some shit? She picked up and moved to a different location for school? That's odd."

"I had the same reaction. She looked at me like I was being a dick, but I was just caught off guard. Anyway, I brought up taking her out and she shut me down, fast." I shrug. "Something about crossing the professor/student boundary. I mean, I know typically that stuff is frowned upon by the administration, but isn't that just for profs trying to hook up with the undergrads? Like the young twenty-somethings looking for extra credit or something?"

Leo shakes his head and laughs. "Or something. I don't think there's any official policy about it, but you should check. And I'm with you — the rules are different when you're the same age. It's not like this is some powerplay or whatever. You're thirty-six, not fifty. And she's thirty, not twenty-one."

"Yeah. She also gave me the generic 'now isn't a good time for me' speech. Since she just moved to the area says she doesn't want to get involved with anyone."

"Involved? That's presumptuous."

I chuckle. "Well, it's not like I was asking her out just for a hookup. I mean, I'm not saying I want to marry the woman but I would actually like to get to know her. Spend time with her. Talk with her some more."

"Shit, man. I've never seen you actually interested in anyone. I know you've hooked up with chicks every once in a while, but you've never gone past casual. Not in the three years I've known you."

Leo and I are friends, but he doesn't know my history. We've never delved into the past — there's really no need.

"Yeah. I haven't been really interested in anyone since my ex, and we split … six years ago? Seven? I don't know, it's been a long time though." If I brush off Laura like she wasn't a big deal, maybe Leo will leave this topic alone.

"You're divorced? How did I not know this? Why didn't you say anything when I walked through that shit? Misery loves company and all."

Leo and his ex-wife, Stephanie, split two years ago after she reconnected with her high school boyfriend through social media and decided he was the love of her life. She acted like it was some romance novel kismet shit, when really she just drove a knife through Leo's heart and abandoned her marriage.

"I'm not divorced," I explain. "I met Laura in grad school and a few years later we got engaged, lived together for a few years, then split. There's no big story to tell — we just wanted different things and went our separate ways."

"How many years are we talking?"

"Shit. I don't know. I haven't thought about her in a long time. I guess I was, what, twenty-three when we got together? So, seven years?"

Leo looks shocked by my revelation. "That's a long fucking time to be with someone and not marry them. And to just all of a sudden 'go your separate ways'."

I shrug my shoulders. "I dunno. We were in school, then I was working on my PhD and she was building her career. It's a good thing we didn't get married otherwise the split would have been messy. We didn't have to go through lawyers and split assets or anything. She just packed her stuff and moved out, started her new life somewhere else, and I kept the apartment and continued working on my doctorate. She wasn't crazy or anything. Like I said, we just wanted different things."

Nevermind the fact that I didn't have a say in whether or not our relationship ended. She informed me of her decision before work one morning, and when I got home that evening she was gone — left her keys on the entryway table. No note. No phone call. No text. Nada.

It's not like the end of that relationship ruined my life, but I'd be lying if I said it didn't affect me. She never explained exactly what she wanted that was different from the life we had. I would have been willing to compromise and adjust our lives to accommodate her wants and needs, but up until that very morning I honestly believed that she was happy — that we were happy. Obviously, I was wrong.

Leo sees straight through my feigned nonchalance. "Just wanted different things. No biggie. And the end of that relationship has nothing to do with your decision to not get serious about another woman for the last six years."

"Look, man, it's not that the breakup didn't hurt, but I also haven't spent the last six years avoiding relationships because of some tragic heartbreak. When Laura left I focused all my energy on finishing my PhD, then on finding a faculty position while doing adjunct work, and then moving here and starting a new life in Grand River. I didn't know anyone here and it's not like I'd have ever gone to a bar without you dragging me there. I'm surrounded by faculty members and young college coeds. When was I supposed to meet someone?"

Leo gives me a WTF look. "You have heard of this new invention called the Internet, yes? Dating apps?"

"I know those apps and whatever else are appealing to you and the other guys, but I dunno. I'm just not into it." I leave out my surprise that after the plethora of hookups Leo's had in the last two years, I'm surprised he hasn't caught an STI from his app women.

"And then there's Savannah …" Leo wiggles his eyebrows and smiles devilishly as he brings up Savannah Martin, the thirty-five-year-old psychology professor who has wanted to ride my dick since she met me three years ago.

I give Leo an annoyed glare. "You're fucking kidding me, right?"

"She's hot, man. She's single. And she wants you." Leo's smirking like I should get on that, stat.

Hell to the no. "And she's a walking red flag. I'm not touching that with a ten-foot pole."

"Red flag? What the hell is wrong with you? She's a dime." Leo has apparently spent too much time in the Tinderverse. His judgment is skewed and he no longer recognizes the metaphorical red, flashing WARNING sign that hovers above Savannah's head every time she enters a room.

"You're joking, right?" I start to count off on my fingers. "She has no concept of personal space — proven by the who-knows-how-many times she's grazed my dick with her hand or her hip; she has crazy eyes; she's about as subtle as a pit bull; she thrives off the attention she gets from her tight-ass clothing; we have absolutely nothing in common; and we work together — I don't shit where I eat."

"Yet, you want to fuck your grader." Just when I think he's lost his marbles, he calls me out on my own blind spots.

"Dammit, Leo. You know what I mean. I knew five minutes after meeting Savannah that she'd be a good time for a few nights but that's it. I'd tell her from the beginning I didn't want anything serious and she'd say she wanted the same thing, but whenever I ended our hookups she'd freak the fuck out as if we were in some sort of exclusive relationship. Stage five clinger, that one. No thanks. I wasn't about to deal with the aftermath of sleeping with a coworker who might be a good lay, but would cause a shit ton of drama when it was over. Not worth it."

Leo rubs his chin. "Yeah, I guess I see what you mean. But what if you hooked up with your grader, it didn't go anywhere, and then you had to see her all the time? That doesn't seem worth the risk either."

I blow out a breath, shaking my head. "It doesn't matter if it's worth the risk or not, because she shut me down, twice."

"Third time's a charm?" Leo's eyes are full of mischief as he smirks at me.

Why again did I choose to confide in him about this? "You do know that you're giving mixed signals, right?"

"Definitely. That's what friends are for."

I shake my head again and stand, gathering up my trash so we can head out. "Right. Friends aren't meant to help clarify jumbled thoughts, but to stir the pot of confusion even more."

Leo may not give the best advice, but telling him about Alis at least helped to get some of the thoughts out of my head so I could better sort through them.

I know I haven't been seriously interested in a woman since

Laura, until I met Alis. She's gorgeous, witty, intelligent — but aside from her attributes we just, clicked. I can't remember the last time I wanted to continue a conversation with a woman or the last time I spent the week after meeting someone thinking about them constantly. Not even half an hour with Alis that night and I wanted more. More of her attention. More of her words. More of her thoughts. More of her lips. More of *her*.

However, it seems the connection was one-sided, if her double rejection is anything to go by.

No. I know for a fact she wanted me the night we met. You can't fake chemistry like ours.

Either way, she said no. I've gone six years without pining for a woman, and that's just what Alis is — a woman.

Surely this sudden infatuation will fade. No need to be concerned. I've got this.

NINE

9 years ago

"WATERLOO, *Couldn't escape if I wanted to. Waterloo, Knowing my fate is to be with you. Wa-Wa-Wa-Wa-Waterloo, Finally facing my Waterloo ..."*

"Shut up!" I slap blindly at my nightstand, trying to find my ringing phone that I obviously forgot to put on vibrate only before crashing last night.

"Waterloo ..." Seriously though, it's so freaking loud.

My fingers find the phone and I grab it, bringing it close to my face to read the call screen as I push up my sleep mask onto my forehead. It's Dr. Ryan. Shit.

I swipe to answer before the call goes to voicemail, hoping my voice doesn't sound too much like a frog. "Dr. Ryan, good morning, sir."

"Alis, I apologize if I've woken you. I assumed you'd be awake at this hour." *This hour? What even is this hour?*

"Um, yes sir. I'm awake." I look over at my alarm clock. *Dammit.* It's 11:30 a.m.

"Right. Well, I didn't hear back from you after our email exchange and wanted to touch base. Is everything alright, Alis? Your email indicated a family emergency."

How in the hell do I answer that question? "The past two days have been very difficult for my family, sir. My sister and her family were in a car accident, and we spent that night and all day yesterday in the hospital."

"Oh my. I am so sorry to hear that. Is everyone alright?" No. Absolutely not alright.

"Um …" *deep breath* "no, actually. Both my sister and her husband passed away at the hospital, and the driver of the other car died on impact."

Silence. "Dr. Ryan?"

I hear him clear his throat through the phone. "I am so sorry for your loss, Alis. Is there anything Margaret and I can do for you and your family?"

"I appreciate the offer, sir, but I can't think of anything right now. We'll have the funeral for both of them this weekend, and after that I'll be commuting back and forth from campus for a few weeks to help my parents adjust."

"I see. Your parents aren't far from here, are they?"

"No, sir. They're about forty-five minutes away, in Moraine."

"Good, good. I read in your email that you'll need some time and won't be available to teach next week. I completely understand. I've already spoken to Brad about covering the classes for next week, but I'd still like to meet to discuss the next few weeks with you commuting and what responsibilities we'll need to redistribute to give you the time you need with your family." *Ok, so I'm not losing my job. Phew.*

"Thank you, sir. And yes, I can come Monday if that's alright?"

"Sounds great. I'll have Linda email you the time and I'll see you then. Again, Alis, I'm so sorry for your loss. Please give my condolences to your parents."

"I will, thank you." *Click.*

I sit up and stretch, trying to wake up my body after sleeping like the dead. Emotional trauma will do that to you — knock you out cold. I'm glad I packed an overnight bag when I went to my apartment yesterday so I didn't have to drive all the way back to Fort Ulysses and could crash at my parents' house.

Swinging my legs over the side of the bed, I stand and stretch some more, then head to the Jack and Jill bathroom my sister and I shared while growing up. The walls are still covered in the yellow and white striped daisy wallpaper Belle and I picked out when we were little. I can't believe mom still hasn't done anything to update this room since we moved out. She's sentimental like that.

I planned to brush my teeth and head downstairs, but the door that leads to Belle's room is ajar and I hear soft music playing from inside the room. I slowly open the door and walk into the bedroom to find Sunny's noise machine playing soothing music to help her sleep. She's not in her portable crib, but mom must have forgotten to turn off the machine when they went downstairs for breakfast.

As I look around the room, I'm surrounded by memories. So many memories.

Nights lying in Belle's bed, talking about the first boy I liked. He also happened to be the first boy to break my heart. Well, only if you count one week of having a fifth grade boyfriend worthy of love and heartbreak. I laughed about it later when I experienced my first real breakup, but my little fifth grade self was devastated and Belle took my feelings seriously. She was always great like that.

The green nail polish stain from halloween my eighth grade year when Belle helped me dress as a ninja turtle. I kicked over the bottle, not realizing I forgot to screw the lid back on, while showing off my "mad nunchuck skills." No, obviously I had no real skills in martial arts, but I was dressed as Michaelangelo so I had to pretend I was awesome like him. We tried and failed to scrub the nail polish out of her carpet, and eventually moved a standing lamp over the spot to hide it from Mom.

Seated at Belle's vanity, I prepped for my senior prom. Belle had generously skipped her Friday university classes, driving three hours back home to assist me. Instead of traditional dates, I was going with my two best friends, Skye and Tori. While we had male friends to dance with, we didn't want dates detracting from our girls' night out.

As for Tori, she and her boyfriend Chase were "on a break" (à la Ross Geller). That very night, after witnessing Tori dancing with another football player, Chase decided to end their break and whatever reason he'd had for instigating it. Before they got engaged, I doubted he would ever fully commit to her. But they're happily married now, and Chase hasn't had another bout of cold feet since before their engagement. It seems he's grown past his immature high school phase.

Distracted again — back to the topic of prom. My thoughts seldom travel in straight lines, even with the clearest directions.

With Belle's hair and makeup expertise, I felt and looked like a deity. As a sentimental touch, she secured the same gemstone hair clip she'd donned for her senior prom into the side of my styled tresses. Glancing at me through the mirror with mischief in her eyes, she casually inquired if I needed condoms for my clutch. The unexpected question caught me off guard, causing a spurt of sparkling grape juice to splatter across the vanity table. Her laughter was so raucous I half-expected her to lose her composure entirely. Meanwhile, I was left wondering who on earth she imagined I'd be spending the night with. I wasn't seeing anyone and had only recently had my first intimate experience with a guy from the previous month's spring break cruise. That memory was still vivid, and I had no intentions of diving into another one anytime soon.

Sitting down at the vanity, I find a picture from that same cruise on Belle's mirror. In the picture we're crazy tanned and I'm wearing the most ridiculous sombrero. I have my arms wrapped around Belle's neck and her cheek is smashed into my chest as we smile at the camera. *God, I miss her.*

Gently, I remove the photo and trace Belle's face with my fingertip. The memories from that incredible week remain vivid, as though it all happened just yesterday.

I let my mind travel to a happier time — a week full of laughter, love, and sun.

When Belle expressed her desire to spend spring break in Mexico with her friends, our parents were far from thrilled. In a compromise, Belle brought her girlfriends on a family cruise. I invited Skye and Tori along, and on our first night, Belle and her crew ushered us into the onboard college club.

With the help of their fake IDs, the college girls discreetly provided us drinks. As we chatted, laughed, and danced, we caught the attention of a striking group of east coast college guys, all conveniently single. Naturally, Belle, with her undeniable allure, caught the eye of their group's leader. I swear, Belle radiated sex appeal without trying. Soon enough, each of Belle's friends found a match from the group. Skye quickly got engrossed with a newfound companion in a secluded booth. Meanwhile, Tori, thinking of her boyfriend Chase back home, stood awkwardly at the table, shifting her weight from one foot to the other. I tried to keep my composure amidst the overwhelming surroundings, afraid that any attempt at flirtation would betray my age.

Just as we were about to leave and head to our stateroom, the tall guy with his arm around my sister shoved his friend toward our table and told him to, and I quote, "Stop being a pussy and talk to the girl." It appeared I was the girl in question. Moments later, I was introduced to DJ, a college senior whose appearance made my heart skip a beat — at least from what I could discern in the club's muted lighting. He nearly lost his balance from the nudge but steadied himself using our table. For a split second, a look of surprise flashed across his face, replaced by an unwavering gaze as our eyes met. His gentle half-smile and the dimple on his flawless right cheek left a lasting impression. With deep brown eyes that exuded warmth, he didn't come off as the typical college party-goer with questionable intentions. I sensed an immediate rapport with DJ. Our silent, prolonged eye contact stretched beyond the usual boundaries of social decorum. Eventually, breaking our mutual gaze, he brushed his hand through his medium-length, bleach-tipped hair.

Before I had a chance to introduce myself, Belle's voice cut through the music, "Meet Rory!" Puzzled, I turned to her. No one had ever called me Rory, and certainly not Aurora. Noticing my confusion, Belle whispered in my ear, "Play along. As Rory, you can be anyone. Let go for once. Remember, what happens in the Caribbean..." She trailed off, giving me a knowing wink, and then gracefully glided to the dance floor with her partner. Seizing the moment, Tori excused herself, promising to catch up later, leaving me alone with my unexpected companion for the night. Conversing was challenging over the music's blare. However, after a while, he laced his fingers with mine and nodded toward the dance floor. I accepted the wordless invitation, allowing him to guide my steps toward the crowd. Soon we, too, were immersed in the rhythm. Our movements synchronized effortlessly, and as I stopped over-analyzing and allowed the music to guide me, I felt a profound connection with Mr. Cheek Dimple.

I couldn't let him know I was still in high school. So, throughout our time with the guys and their circle, I remained intentionally ambiguous, letting down my guard only when discussing our favorite books and mutual love for literature. Although our group's whirl-wind of activities — from swimming and partying to mini-golf — limited our private moments, the brief conversations we shared created a bond I'd never felt with anyone else. While we shared heated glances throughout the day and stole secret kisses on the dance floor, our intimacy hadn't moved beyond that, given our ever-present friends. DJ and I didn't exchange personal details like last names, phone numbers, or social media accounts. On paper, I barely knew him. However, we had undeniable chemistry.

On our final night aboard the cruise ship, DJ and I found ourselves perched on a secluded staircase at the back of the vessel, the night sky strewn with stars above us. It was as if we had discovered our own secret haven, a place where time seemed to hold its breath, far removed from the bustling crowds and distractions of the ship.

DJ's kisses were nothing short of electrifying, igniting a fire within me that had been smoldering since the moment we met. We lost ourselves in each other, our lips locked in a passionate dance that stretched on for what could have been hours, although in that suspended moment, time was irrelevant. The hushed whispers of the ocean below were the only witnesses to the palpable sexual tension that crackled between us.

Immersed in the moment, I did not hesitate to acquiesce when he suggested finding somewhere more secluded. Eagerly, I nodded and whispered, "Yes, please."

He led me away from the stairs, searching for a discreet spot to continue our dalliance. I had no intention of revealing my inexperience to him. While I never overtly lied, I allowed him to believe I was a college student with a history of casual relationships. The truth about my age and high school status might have sent him running, and we'd come too far for him to run away now.

Finally, we found an unlocked door that led into a quaint and dimly lit library. The late hour gave us privacy, as the other guests had returned to their rooms or to more exciting evening activities, leaving the library to us. DJ directed his sexy half smile my way as he quietly shut the door and turned the lock. He wrapped his arms around me, kissing me while slowly walking us back toward a couch on the side wall in between floor-to-ceiling bookshelves. I was too lost in him to recall any previous fantasies of my first time with a man, but this no doubt surpassed them all.

DJ laid me back on the couch and nestled his body between my thighs, kissing down my neck toward my chest. He lifted his head and smiled, staring down at the birthmark just under my collar bone. Tracing the dots with his finger, he looked up at my face, curious. "Strange place for freckles, eh?"

"Birthmark," I breathed. He looked down at it again, still tracing the dots.

"Andromeda," he whispered. I stilled. No one aside from my grandmother had ever noticed the distinct pattern of my birthmark.

"Yes," I whispered. DJ looked up at me and gently brushed the long bangs off my face. His soft smile reached his eyes and he looked at me like I was someone beautiful, someone special. Before either one of us could breathe another word, I leaned up and captured his lips with mine, fingers gripping his upper arms.

We kissed, tongues dancing, bodies pressed together, and hands wandering greedily. Running his hand up my thigh, DJ slid under my skirt, squeezing lightly and pressing his thumb into my hip joint. Fingertips reaching the edge of my bathing suit bottom, he lifted his face to meet my eyes. "Is this okay?" My body was on fire, my desire in full control, and without hesitation I answered, "Yes." I then slid my hands up his chest and around his neck, pulling him in for another kiss.

Venturing into territory unknown, I didn't want to stop. After tonight I'd never see DJ again, and having the memory of my first *anything* with a man who made me feel so much all at once would be a dream come true. Not to mention, the thought of not having to fumble through talks of a future or dating after the cruise sounded like perfection. We both appreciated tonight for what it was — goodbye.

DJ slowly pulled loose the strings of my bikini bottoms, one and then the other, pushing aside the fabric so he could slide his fingers along my bare, wet flesh.

Holy mother of all things holy. I'd touched myself intimately before but it was NOTHING like having someone else touch me. As if electrocuted, my hooded eyes flew open as DJ found my clit and rubbed it in circles, finding a steady rhythm as I moaned and closed my eyes once again. I was almost there — ALMOST THERE — when he slid his fingers from my clit to my opening and pushed one finger inside. The penetration was new, and while I enjoyed it, the pressure of his fingers on my clit was OMFG-please-don't-stop good. I whimpered and he pulled his lips from mine, concern evident as he asked, "I'm not hurting you, am I?"

"No, not at all," I half moaned as I lifted my pelvis, trying to find friction for my clit with the palm of his hand. "Ah," he chuckled, "I see." Then DJ pressed his palm against my hood, rubbing it in time with the thrusts of his finger. Just as I was building back up, he curled his finger and rubbed some sort of magic button inside my sex. Euphoria exploded through my entire body, the throbbing in my core pausing momentarily as my inner walls clenched around him. (I later learned that magic button is known as a G-spot, which makes perfect sense being that it felt capital 'G' great.)

"That's it, baby. Come for me." He whispered as I rode out my orgasm, pulsing around his finger and digging my nails into his biceps. DJ resumed kissing down my neck as I slowly came down from my climax. "I want to be inside you," he whispered into my ear, kissing along my jaw before lifting his head to see my response.

"Y-y-yeah. Yes. Ok. Yes." I fumbled my words, suddenly confronted with the reality of having sex for the first time in my life. My thoughts scattered, as if understanding any focused thought would make this all too real, all too fast. I kept my eyes locked on his, my heart pounding in my chest. Surely my rapidly beating heart would give away my nervousness, my inexperience.

DJ furrowed his brow. "Are you sure? We don't have to." His concern for me helped to ease my fears.

"I'm sure. Yes." I nodded, wrapping my hands around his neck again and pulling him back down for a kiss. The last thing I needed was to welcome more conversation that would no doubt help him deduce I was, in fact, a virgin.

He reached into his pocket and pulled out a condom — I couldn't decide if this was great forethought or presumption on his part — and then untied the front of his board shorts and pushed them down his hips. I was too terrified to look; I had never seen a penis outside my biology textbook and knew if I looked now my face would surely give away my virgin status as my cheeks turned bright red and my eyes tried to bulge out of their sockets. So I looked up. At the ceiling. At the shelves lined with books. Not wanting him to mistake my wandering eyes for indifference toward what we were about to do, I returned my gaze to his and smiled, praying my expression was demure, yet sexy. I probably looked ridiculous, but I banished the thought as he slid the condom over himself and repositioned his lower half to press against me.

I was swimming in a sea of nerves and excitement, my stomach a whirlpool of butterflies. As I lay there, the weight of what was happening slowly sank in, the gravity of the situation becoming more and more evident with each passing second. He saw the apprehension in my eyes, the tension stiffening my body, and he paused, his hand lingering near my thigh.

He leaned down, his forehead touching mine, the intensity in his eyes piercing through me yet kind and reassuring, reminding me of our connection — the sparks we had felt throughout the week, the tender gazes we shared while surrounded by our friends, sitting by the pool getting lost in conversation about our favorite books, the way our bodies moved together each night at the club.

"Hey," he said softly, his thumb tracing lazy circles on my hip, his voice soothing, grounding, bringing me back to this moment with him. "We can stop, really. No pressure."

But despite the nerves, the fear of the unknown, I still wanted this, still craved this intimate connection with DJ, the mysterious, kind guy who'd captured my attention, who'd made me feel seen, cherished, and special. I took a deep breath, trying to find courage, to find the Rory that had blossomed this week, the Rory who had dared to embrace freedom, joy, and the thrilling tumble of new experiences.

I reached down, my hand finding his, intertwining our fingers, squeezing gently, a silent reassurance, a silent plea to continue. It was a strange paradox, the whirlpool of feelings inside me, fear and desire dancing in a precarious balance as he led me into unknown territory.

He kissed me then, a kiss that was a symphony of softness and urgency, a kiss that tried to convey understanding, patience, and sweet affection. And as he kissed me, he guided himself to my entrance, the touch of him there startling, hot, and hard yet achingly right.

My breath hitched, and I felt a rush of vulnerability like I'd never known. My whole being seemed to be on the edge of a cliff, teetering, ready to fall into an abyss of the unknown, into an ocean of sensation that promised pleasure but also carried the undercurrents of pain and fear.

DJ moved slowly, tenderly, giving me time to adjust, his eyes constantly seeking mine, asking silent questions, giving silent assurances, creating a rhythm that was tentative yet determined, gentle yet persistent.

And as we moved together in that quiet library, surrounded by tomes both old and new and under the silent witness of a million stars outside the window, I found myself crossing a threshold into womanhood, into a new understanding of my body, of connection, of pleasure and pain intricately woven together in a tapestry of human experience.

With each thrust, I felt the pain yielding, giving way to a burgeoning pleasure that started as a flicker and grew, steadily, surging, building, a crescendo of sensation that felt expansive and deep, as radiant as Andromeda herself.

We moved together, breaths mingling, bodies entwined in a dance as old as time yet utterly new and breathtaking in its intimacy and discovery. And when I felt the tide rising, felt the rush of warmth, the spiral of intensity winding tighter and tighter, DJ whispered encouraging words in my ear, his breath hot and erratic against my skin as he too approached his peak.

His lips dropped to my birthmark and gently sucked. My eyes rolled back and a moan broke free from my lips as I once again reached my climax. DJ buried his face into the side of my neck as he came, breathing heavily as we trembled together in the aftershocks. Lying in a tangle of limbs and satisfaction, the silent library around us felt transformed, a sanctuary of secrets, of shared experiences, of a connection that transcended words.

We lay there for what felt like an eternity, a bubble of stolen time where Rory and DJ existed in a space untethered from reality, from judgments, from expectations. We kissed and held each other in silent understanding that this was an ending. I expected guilt to overtake my heart when his eyes met mine, but all I felt was an overwhelming sense of calm. This night would forever remain etched in my memories, a night of passion forged in starlight and tender touches.

Eventually, we dressed, smiles shy and tender. And as we

unlocked the library door, stepping back into the world, we carried with us the secret knowledge of each other, a moment in time where I imagined Rory became a constellation in DJ's sky, and he became a treasured chapter in my unfolding story.

DJ held my hand and walked me back to the stateroom I shared with Skye and Tori. Once at the door he slid his fingers along my jaw until his hand gripped the side of my neck, thumb stroking my jawline as he looked into my eyes. "I had a really great time with you this week, Rory," he said.

"Me, too," I replied, my smile stretching clear across my face as I pushed up onto my tip toes and kissed him one last time. "Goodnight, DJ." I lowered my feet back down, opened the door, and glanced back at his unforgettable half smile as I slowly closed it behind me.

"ALIS, ARE YOU UP?" The knocks on my bedroom door pull me from my reverie.

"I'm in here, mom," I reply, indicating that I'm in Belle's room rather than mine.

"Good morning, sweetheart." Mom enters with Sunny perched on her hip and plants a kiss atop my head. "Morning," I respond, attempting a reassuring smile.

"Did you sleep alright?" I might have, but Mom bears the unmistakable pallor of restless nights.

"Yeah, you?" I ask, even though I suspect the answer.

"Briefly," she admits. "Listen, honey, your father and I need to pick up Alex's parents from the airport, then head to the funeral home to make arrangements. Would you watch Sunny while we're out?"

"Of course," I reply, standing up and reaching for Sunny. "We'll have a day filled with stories about mama, won't we, little one?"

Sunny beams, a thread of drool connecting her fingers to her lips, her eyes bright with anticipation. As morning light pours through the curtains, illuminating Sunny's radiant face, she seems untouched by the shadow of grief blanketing the adults. For a brief moment, I envy her blissful ignorance. I then gently take her from Mom.

Cradling Sunny, I'm reminded of both solace and the devastating loss of her mother. Memories of Belle — her infectious laughter, the countless hours we shared deep conversations and light-hearted banter — form a void in my heart, threatening to consume me. But today, for Sunny's sake, I must emulate the strength and warmth that Belle always provided.

Mom nods at me, her face a canvas of fatigue and sadness, yet adorned with a brave smile, one that tries to mask the pain but can't quite manage it. She kisses Sunny's forehead, lingering a bit, as if trying to absorb the innocence and the blissful ignorance bestowed upon the tiny life in my arms.

She turns and walks toward the stairs, her figure diminishing with each step, leaving a hollow echo in her wake. As the door clicks shut, I pull Sunny close to my chest, feeling her tiny heartbeat, so strong, so vibrant. It's a grounding pulse in a reality that seems so distorted, so unreal. I hug her a bit tighter, reassuring myself that life, in its purest, most innocent form, was right here in my arms, a fragment of Belle, untouched and untamed by the cruel circumstances.

"I love you, Sunny," I whisper to her, the words catching in my throat as I fight back tears. In this room filled with remnants of joyful memories and echoes of laughter, I make a silent promise to myself and to Belle — that Sunny will grow up knowing the depth of her mother's love, her spirit, and the beautiful soul that she was.

We sit there, the morning light wrapping around us like a warm hug, as I begin to tell Sunny stories. Stories of her mother's bravery, of her warmth, of the adventures we had, and the love she poured out to everyone around her.

TEN

Alis

THE FOLLOWING TWO WEEKS ARE, thankfully, uneventful. Sunny made a few friends in her class and she's starting to feel more comfortable in her new school. Skye got a job at a locally-owned coffee house downtown, and I am officially ready for the semester to begin on Monday.

"Navigating your filing system is like going digital spelunking. I have no idea how you find anything in all those subfolders." Skye is sitting next to me on the couch while I finish setting up grading folders in my drive.

"At least I have a system. You just dump everything onto your desktop. I have no idea how you find anything." Skye scoffs and presses her pointer finger to my right glasses lens. I immediately react by slapping her arm, using my other hand to slide my laptop to the coffee table as she tries to scurry away. I grab her ankle before she succeeds, only to be met with a pillow to the face courtesy of Sunny.

"Ugh, Skye! Why do you always do that?!" Skye and Sunny are laughing hysterically while I dig around in the side table drawer for a lens wipe, to no avail. *Dammit, I forgot to add a new pack of them to my grocery order.*

I have issues with dirty lenses. The easiest way to avoid this pet peeve is to wear contacts, but no thanks. However, my glasses have to be spotless or I can't focus on anything else until they're cleaned. Smudged lenses are like gnats — all up in my face and annoying as hell.

After finally finding a microfiber cloth in the kitchen, I clean my glasses and go to retrieve my computer. Skye and Sunny are once again curled up on the couch, entranced in some reality show as if they didn't just team up and attack me.

"I'm going to bed. Sunny, you have school tomorrow so make sure you're in bed by nine."

She looks up at me and pouts, "But the show goes until 9:30!"

"Sorry, kid. Nine. No later. You can catch up on whatever you miss tomorrow on Hulu. Spoiler alert — she says 'yes' to the dress." In true nine-going-on-nineteen fashion, she rolls her eyes and huffs, "Fine."

I grab my mug of ginger tea off the side table, tuck my laptop under my arm, and turn toward the hallway to head to my room.

"Night!" They don't respond; the show has sucked them in. I'd understand the draw if they were hooked on true crime documentaries or even period dramas, but their love for reality TV makes no sense to me. I used to arguing with them about how reality TV is basically garbage and a waste of time, until one day Skye snatched the remote from my hand, gave me a death glare, and said, "Just because you watch TV to *think* doesn't mean everyone else has to. We watch TV to veg out, not for a mental workout. Some people just like to be entertained."

I'd never thought of it that way until she said it, but she was right. After that, I never again fought Skye or Sunny on their shows of choice. My idea of vegging out is reading a book or working on a puzzle; they prefer to burrito themselves in throw blankets on the couch and watch crazy people try on wedding dresses or attempt to buy million-dollar houses on shoe-string budgets. *Whatever floats your boat.*

I enter my room and close the door, leaning my back against it. Now that I'm alone without any distractions, the dam breaks on my anxiety about being back on campus tomorrow. I've done so well at compartmentalizing anxious thoughts this week, but now that I'm one sleep away from potentially seeing Dexter again, my mind is racing and my heart is pounding.

I remember the words he spoke to me in his office, and I close my eyes at the memory of how he looked at me, eyes full of confidence and desire, unapologetically telling me how he wanted to recreate our incredible kiss.

"Je veux encore t'embrasser." Gah, that man and his French. I'd be lying if I said I haven't fantasized about him a time or six this past week. Remembering that night at the club, his fingers tracing my jawline — only in my fantasies he whispers enticing promises into my ear while his fingers trace down my arms and then up the sides of my body.

"J'ai tellement hâte de te goûter," he whispers, nibbling my ear lobe before kissing down my neck. "Je veux lécher chaque centimètre de ton corps. Je veux te mettre sur mon lit, les jambes écartées, et te baiser jusqu'à ce que tu perdes ta voix en criant mon nom. T'es une déesse, t'es parfaite, t'es à moi."

Is it getting hot in here? Somebody turn the fan on before I combust. Ok, Alis, get a grip, calm down. Touching yourself to thoughts of Dexter Belanger is not helping the situation.

"T'es à moi." If only.

I've spent the last nine years of my life working my butt off, raising my daughter, living with my parents, and I haven't once — *not once* — had any desire to start any sort of romantic relationship with a man. No boyfriends, no app hookups (because, ew), no casual flings with guys from around town — nada. And now that I'm "getting out there," chasing my dreams with a basically revirginated vagina, the one guy in a decade who has caught my interest is off limits.

Who the hell is writing this story? What kind of sick joke is it to dangle Mr. Sexy Man Bun in front of me, light my panties on fire, and then snatch him back, saying, "psych!"

Author of my life, I think I hate you. Can't a woman catch a break?!

You're the one who turned him down. Screw you, self.

Twice. Ugh!

I flop over onto my stomach and bury my face into my pillow. I have to be making a bigger deal out of this than is necessary. Sure, Dexter is the first guy in a decade I've wanted, but that's probably just because I'm in a new place with new people and thinking about my wants and needs for the first time in forever. It's not because he's special or one of a kind; not because his fingers on my skin made my heart race and his kiss felt like coming home. Nope. Nope. Nope.

Tomorrow I'll go to class, meet new people, spend time in the library prepping for my first Comp lecture, and not think about Dexter Belanger. If I run into him, no biggie. He's one of many hot guys I've seen in my life. He's a professor. He's my boss (kind of).

I didn't uproot my life and move four hours away from home only to detour from my goals once again. I have a degree to finish, a career to pursue, a daughter to raise. My life has enough responsibilities as it is.

Just as I'm diving headfirst into "woe is me" territory, Stewie's incessant nagging from my bedside table snaps me out of this pity party.

"Hi, Mom."

"Hi, honey. How are things? Have you girls had a good first week?"

"Yeah. It's been good."

"How did your meeting go with Dr. Matthews? Are you two a good fit? I know you were nervous about that."

"She's great. Very nice."

Mom is silent for a beat, obviously waiting for me to expound. "And? Tell me about your meeting! I want to hear all about it.

I exhale. "The meeting was fine. We just went over the upcoming semester, her class list, my teaching responsibilities — the same stuff I used to do.”

“Well, that sounds nice. Are you teaching at all this semester?”

“Yeah, I’m teaching one of her classes. I was originally supposed to teach more, I think, but something happened with the budget and they weren’t able to bring on new people they’d planned on having, so I’m taking on more grading and less teaching.”

“More grading?”

“Yeah. Two other profs needed help so I’m grading for them as well. Nothing too difficult, just Comp and French.”

“Three professors? That sounds like a lot to take on in your first semester, Alis.” She sounds worried, but she shouldn’t.

“Just grading. No teaching. Besides, Martin is an online-only prof so my grading is more basic moderating. Belanger is on campus, but he only teaches three classes so it’s not anything I can’t handle.”

“He?” I close my eyes and clench my teeth. *Why did I say that?!*

I swallow. “Yeah. He. I’m just grading for him; it’s not like he’s my advisor or anything.” Crap. Now I sound defensive.

“I know, honey, but the main reason you chose Middle Peak was so that you’d work for a female professor. I just want to make sure you’re going to be okay with this new arrangement.”

I’m not a child, mother. I’ll be fine. Can’t say that to her, though.

“I’m fine, mom. Really. Dr. Belanger is a nice guy. He’s young, too. That caught me off guard. I was expecting some old, graying pretentious guy, but, nope.”

I hear clicking in the background before mom says, “Oh my. He’s beautiful.”

I huff, “I know, right?” Oh, shit. Now I’ve done it.

I can hear the smile in her response. “You think so, too. How old is he? Is he single?”

I let out an exasperated sigh. “Mom. Stop.”

“What? He is handsome. And you’re right, he’s young. You two would make the prettiest babies!”

“MOM! STOP IT.”

“You can’t really blame me for wanting more grandbabies. I won’t be around forever, and I have so much more love to go around. Enough for a whole brood of grandbabies. Four? Five?"

Someone — anyone — save me from this conversation.

My silence lets her know I'm done talking about this. Thankfully, she takes the hint.

"Speaking of grandbabies, how is my darling Sunny? I miss her sweet face in our home every day."

"She's good, I think. Seems to be adjusting well at school and making some new friends. Everything is so different here, though. Not like home."

"That's definitely true, but what exactly do you mean by 'different'?" Thankfully, she doesn't sound worried, just inquisitive.

"Everything, really. We moved from a small town where the only strangers were tourists to a city with more people than we could ever meet. We live in an apartment instead of a house with a yard and nearly all her friends within walking distance. She spends so much more time inside than she used to, and I can't really encourage her to go out and explore because I don't know anyone in this complex. I can't send my daughter to venture into the unknown without supervision. What if some creep snatches her? What if she gets into some other sort of trouble? What if she gets hurt and can't find her way back to our apartment?"

"Alis, honey. You can 'what if' yourself into an early grave if you're not careful. Take a deep breath."

I close my eyes and do as she says. In, two, three, four. Out, two, three, four.

"I know, mom. It's just, all so new. I feel like for the first time since Sunny became mine, I'm having to actually *parent* her by myself. You and dad have always been there to fall back on, and now you aren't here."

I can hear her smile beneath her next words. "We're still here, honey. You can always call if you need us."

Mom's ability to talk me down from an anxiety attack is one of the many reasons I love her. Growing up, Mom and I weren't very close.

We didn't argue or butt heads, we just didn't have much in common. Still don't, if I'm honest. Dad and I are very similar, whereas Belle was always more like our mom. They both have always been more social, outgoing, laissez faire. Dad and I are easily overwhelmed, overthink everything, and prefer the company of books rather than people.

Mom was always Dad's safety blanket; Belle, mine. But then it all changed. Belle was gone, and I felt truly lost for the first time in my life. Sure, Tori and Skye helped keep me afloat in the wake of our loss, but Mom was my true life raft. My friends couldn't pause their own lives to guide me through grief. Both of my friends returned to Ft. Ulysses to finish the semester the next week.

For the next few months Tori and Skye came home every weekend to spend with me. As the semester drew to a close, Chase's patience wore thin, keeping Tori in Ft. Ulysses most weekends. The previous October Skye had committed to a year-long study abroad program that began in June, and before I knew it, I found myself waking on a Saturday morning without my friends to dictate the weekend's activities.

Enter, Mom. The woman who was simultaneously grieving the loss of her firstborn child, guiding her husband out of his darkness, caring for her infant granddaughter, and keeping the Gilmore household running like a well-oiled machine. She had too much on her plate, but still found room for the emotionally-shattered twenty-two-year-old to find sanctuary with her.

"I know, but you're not *here*, here. If I hadn't brought Skye with me, I would've already thrown in the towel and moved back home. If not for her, I would've already had a panic attack."

"Have you talked to Dr. Wilkes since the big move?" Of course, she would bring up my therapist.

"No, Mom, I've been a little busy adjusting to everything." Great, now I sound like a temperamental teenager.

"Isn't that what Dr. Wilkes is there for? I mean, I'm always happy to talk to you, but I can't really relate. I grew up and married in Moraine; I've never had a big move. I was born here and I'll probably die here. All this to say, I think it would be a good idea for you to make an appointment with her."

If I don't acquiesce, she'll keep prodding. "I will after this week."

"I think you should do it sooner."

Give me an ever-loving break. "Mom, I am thirty years old, and I think I'm fairly self-aware. I know when I need extra help."

"I know you are, sweetie. I just want to make sure you're taking care of yourself." I know she means well.

"Can we change the subject?" *Please?!*

"Of course. How's Skye?" She knows what she's doing. This woman helps combat my anxiety by reminding me that I'm not alone here in Grand River.

"She's good, she got a job at a coffee shop nearby."

"Oh good! Have you two made any friends?"

"Haven't really had the time. Last weekend Skye went home to see Tori and I'm pretty sure she's going back again tomorrow after work."

"Really, what for?" Good question. I've been so caught up in my own head I didn't think to ask.

"No clue. It's Skye and Tori — who knows what those two are up to. I think Skye mentioned a project or something a few days ago?"

"I haven't seen Tori since you left." Tori's always had her own life separate from Skye and me. That tends to happen when you meet the love of your life at sixteen and get married at twenty.

I chuckle and say, "Why would you if I'm not there?"

"I would've seen her at church the last two Sundays, but now that I think about it, I haven't seen her at church in a month. She and Chase are always there!"

Not sure how to respond to her frustration, I don't. If Tori is anything, she's a creature of habit. Missing a month's worth of Sundays at church *is* out of character. Mom doesn't seem to pause for my response before she barrels on.

"You don't know what this mystery project is?"

"Nope. Not a clue. Honestly, Mom, I only half remember the conversation. I'm pretty sure Skye was talking about ten things at once so she could have been referring to a project at the coffee shop for all I know."

Suddenly, as if she's come to a revelation, mom gasps. "Maybe Tori wants to open her own accounting firm! God knows she's been working for Roger for way too long, getting paid pennies no doubt."

I don't make a habit of prying into other people's business, but Mom is a meddler, albeit with good intentions.

Sunny knocks on the door and peaks in. "Monty?"

I smile at my sweet girl and pat the bed next to me. She climbs up and snuggles into me. "I'm on the phone with Grandma, want to talk to her?"

Sunny jumps up excitedly. "Ooooooh, Grandma!" So much for snuggling.

I say my goodbyes to Mom and hand over the phone to Sunny. Those two will gab at each other for God only knows how long, so I leave her on my bed and decide to take a shower before going to sleep.

The hot water beating down on my head, neck, and shoulders helps to relieve the headache I've been battling most of today. After washing I close my eyes and rest my forehead against the shower wall, relishing the feel of the water on my back.

Belle, what was I thinking moving so far away from home?! I've never had to worry if Sunny was happy, who her friends were, where she disappeared to outside, how she was faring in school. Sure, she seems fine, but what if she's not telling me everything? What if she hates it here but is afraid to tell me the truth? What if she's bullied at school and the teacher doesn't tell me? It's not like back home where most of the teachers and administrators knew our family. I feel like I'm wandering around, blind, with no one to guide me in the right direction.

What am I supposed to do about Dexter? Why can't I stop thinking about his smile, his kiss, his ... everything. I AM NOT THIS PERSON. I don't swoon or pine after men. Especially not when I'm overwhelmed by everything happening around me.

"Hey, here's an idea. How about we move Alis across the state to a new city, new school, new everything, and then, right when she's most excited and

confident about her choices, we'll kick her feet out from under her with … wait for it … A MAN!"

I can see the you up there, sitting on a cloud couch, having a good laugh at my expense.

Belle: "Oh, what's that? He's her BOSS?! This is too good."

God: "Quick, grab the popcorn! We're about to get to the really good part where her past hurts bubble up to the surface and she's forced to deal with them."

Belle: "Wait. I thought she spent the last nine years healing from all the trauma?"

God: "Concerning losing you, yes. She may have fooled herself into thinking she dealt with all the other drama, but she hasn't even scratched the surface of that shit storm." (I don't know if God would say 'shit storm', but in this instance it seems appropriate.)

*Belle: *rubs hands together* "Oh, goody. I'm sooo here for this. I can't wait to see what happens!"*

I bang my forehead against the tile wall, annoyed at Belle, the imaginary sadist sister. I know she'd never revel in my misery, but she would find some way to impart wisdom while simultaneously bringing levity to the situation. She'd coax me out of my analysis paralysis, give me the necessary tools to slay my past demons, and then swat me on the butt and say, "Good game, sis!"

I miss you. I need you. Help me through this, please. I can't do any of it alone.

After I dry off from the shower and slide into my most comfortable sleep shorts and camisole, I crawl into bed and dream of a life without so many complications and uncertainties.

ELEVEN

"PLEASE, please, please don't spit up on your outfit again. If you promise not to, I'll ensure you get sweet potatoes tonight instead of peas, okay?" I find myself negotiating with a baby, quite certain she doesn't grasp most of my words. On second thought, perhaps she does recognize "sweet potatoes" and "peas," given the former brings a gleam to her eyes and the latter, a defiant spit.

This morning's wardrobe wars with Sunny mark the second round, and with the funeral imminent, my search for another formal attire seems futile. While her attire might not be of utmost importance, I sense Mom would appreciate her dressed in tandem with the family's somber mood. Rather than hunting for a black dress, I settled for her gray sweater dress, dark blue cotton ones, and a maroon festive dress. As luck would have it, she drenched the most elegant one in regurgitated milk, and the next fell victim to a diaper mishap. The sweater dress is now the last resort unless she's game for footie pajamas at the service — a choice I'd personally favor over a dress any day.

"Alis, it's time to go!" Mom's voice echoes for the third time.

Evidently, the universe runs on a nine-month-old's timeline today, and she's not in the mood to align with ours.

"Hold on! I'm just putting Sunny's shoes on. We'll be right down!" I ponder, why bother with shoes for a baby who doesn't even walk?

Outfit complete, I snatch her diaper bag, sling my purse across my shoulder, and descend the stairs.

"Apologies, Mom. Another dress mishap meant a fresh start. Where are Alex's folks?"

"They left with your dad about thirty minutes ago. We agreed to meet at the church."

I exhale, relieved we didn't aim for a singular carpool. No limo will shepherd us today since the burial ground adjoins the church. I'm grateful we don't need to embark on an extended ride, followed by an endless procession to a distant cemetery. With nearly the whole community in attendance, that would've felt eternal. And today, of all days, I lack the fortitude to draw things out any more than needed.

Once Sunny is safely buckled into her car seat, we head to the church, the very place where I'm slated to eulogize my sister in front of the entire town. What was I thinking when I agreed to this?

Avoiding eye contact, I unbuckle Sunny and carry her into the sanctuary. While I realize it might come off as rude to ignore others, I bank on my preoccupation with Sunny to be a good enough reason. A moment alone before the service would have been ideal, but Sunny's wardrobe malfunctions set us back.

Belle's casket is closed. So is Alex's. I yearn for one last glimpse of them, even though I understand why open caskets were out of the question. A cold shiver travels up my spine at the thought of my sister enclosed in a box. She's not there, Alis. She's free. Now isn't the time to indulge your claustrophobia.

As we settle into our seats, the soft hum of background music fades, and Reverend Thomas steps up to the podium.

"Good morning, friends. On behalf of the families of Alex and Isabelle Donnelly, I welcome you to this celebration of life. Both Alex and Isabelle were cherished members of our congregation, and I was blessed to have known them."

The reverend continues sharing personal memories of his interactions with both Alex and Belle, including the day Belle was baptized, and when she brought Alex back from Ireland.

Before I know it, he signals me forward. The weight of the moment hits, and panic courses through my veins. *I'm not ready for this. I'm going to break down on that stage.* My palms are sweating as I adjust the microphone to my much-shorter stature.

"Hello, everyone. I deeply appreciate you all joining us today to remember Belle and Alex. The outpouring of messages, flowers, prayers, and comforting embraces over the past few days has been overwhelming. Loss like this is not something we could have ever prepared for, and I know it's because of the strength you've lent us that we've made it this far.

"I'd like to start by sharing my favorite memories of Alex. Despite being a newcomer, he quickly found his place in our tight-knit community. I still chuckle remembering his first solo grocery run after moving in with Belle. He returned, utterly bewildered, sharing how Julie at the checkout had never heard of 'black pudding.' I played along, feigning similar surprise, all the while clueless about what black pudding was myself.

"Alex was one of the smartest men I've ever met, and no matter what new hobby or sport he tried, he always seemed to be the best. He was never arrogant or pretentious, but had a humble heart and attitude in all things. He truly was the best brother I could have hoped for.

"More than anything, Alex loved my sister and their daughter, Sunny. Belle nagged me about my lack of dating life these past few years, but what she didn't realize was that between watching our dad love our mom all these years and then watching Alex love her and Sunny, I had two nearly perfect examples of how a man should love a woman, a father should love his daughter, and there's no way I'd settle for anything less.

"I miss my brother every day, and I'll miss him every day for the rest of my life. He was truly an incredible man, and our community will forever feel his loss."

I close my eyes and take a deep breath, fighting back the rush of tears threatening to spill out of my eyes as I transition to talking about my sister. Clearing my throat, I look back up at the crowd before me and use every ounce of self control to keep myself from falling apart.

"Belle was my first friend. My best friend. My big sister and my role model. Our grandmother called her Sunshine, or Sunny, because she always provided warmth, happiness, and light wherever she went."

Deep breath, Alis. Deep breath.

"To know Belle was to love her. She was everyone's cheerleader, and when she spoke to you she made you feel like the most important person in the world. Her ability to make even strangers feel at home in her presence was truly remarkable.

"We used to joke that once we were gone nobody could honestly say 'she never had a bad thing to say about anyone'. But the truth is, the only times Belle ever had something negative to say was when a person bullied or belittled someone else. And even then, her negative words didn't stand alone — she always had something positive to say or some constructive criticism to help that person grow. Her words were never wasted on gossip; she was a counselor and friend.

"Belle loved her family more than anything. She was dad's first princess, mom's right-hand woman, Alex's love and partner, Sunny's incredible mom, and my other half. She made sure to FaceTime her in-laws every week so Sunny could know them, even though they live across the pond. She loved this town and everyone in it, and I know she's smiling down on all of us right now. She wouldn't want us to be sad for long, but to remember the countless good times we spent with her.

"Alex, I love you, brother. And Belle, I love you and I miss you so much that sometimes I can't breathe. You both were taken from us too soon, but everyone in this room can say their lives are better for knowing you. We'll all love and take care of Sunny and we'll make sure she feels your love even though you can't be here with her."

Wrapping up emotional speeches has never been my forte. I offer a final word of gratitude to everyone in attendance and make my way back to my seat, flanking Mom and Sunny. To my relief, Sunny sleeps soundly. Her nestled presence in Mom's arms, I believe, offers Mom a semblance of comfort during this trying time.

The exhaustion in Mom's eyes speaks volumes. Days of ceaseless tears have left their mark, and her lack of sleep is evident. Dad, in his effort to remain our pillar of strength, keeps his grief under wraps. Yet, last night, I chanced upon him in his study, silently shedding tears as he lost himself in the warm glow of the fireplace. He seemed unaware of my presence at the door. Respecting his moment of solitude, I withdrew, seeking refuge in Belle's bed, hoping for a few hours of rest before the draining day ahead.

The service draws to an end with a reading of Scriptures, followed by a heartfelt prayer. The somber procession of pallbearers then escorts both Belle and her husband to their final resting place, nestled side by side behind the church. As Sunny stirs, I brace myself, sensing she's about to rouse from her nap.

"Mom, I'll take her. Walk with Dad and the Donnellys. We'll follow right behind."

Handing me the drowsy Sunny, Mom offers a gentle smile, though it fails to touch the depth of her eyes. I seize these brief moments away from the crowd to center myself, drawing strength from Sunny, hoping that will suffice for the burial.

A sudden squeeze on my shoulder jolts me. "Hey, babe, need help?" It's Tori, with Skye just steps behind. I'm grateful it's them – their mere presence provides a buffer against the looming swell of emotions.

"Hey. Could you prepare her bottle? I need to check her diaper."

Tori promptly retrieves the essentials from the diaper bag, while I lay Sunny on a pew. Sunny's eyes, now open, sparkle as they fixate on the stained-glass windows.

"Thank you for staying calm through the service and not causing another wardrobe mishap," I murmur, tickling her. As I lift her, Skye playfully warns, "You might've just jinxed yourself there."

Grinning, I retort, "Then I'll be sure she's aimed in your direction when disaster strikes." Skye's mock-horrified expression soothes my aching heart, providing a moment of solace.

Tori, ever the group's anchor, rounds us up. "They're waiting. Let's go." The role she assumes today, alongside Skye, becomes my lifeline.

The burial concludes swiftly. I hoped it would grant closure, but my heart still feels torn between numbness and engulfing sorrow. An emotional middle ground seems unreachable.

Back home, the house remains a sanctuary, devoid of visitors, save for Tori and Skye. They insist on staying, and I'm grateful, even though I put on a front of self-sufficiency.

"You've been on duty non-stop. Rest," Tori firmly advises.

Before I can protest, Skye chimes in, whisking Sunny from her car seat. The ease with which Sunny nestles into Tori's embrace attests to the bond she shares with my friends.

Tori reassures, "Chase knows I'm here for the night. I've got your parents. Skye, make sure Alis sleeps."

Obliging, Skye ushers me upstairs. "First, pee. Then, let's get you out of that dress."

Exiting the bathroom, my amusement peaks at the sight of Skye's audacious pajamas. "Is that... a unicorn?"

"The epitome of comfort," she declares with a mischievous grin.

"It looks like a mythical creature threw up a rainbow hairball all over you," I jest.

Skye feigns indignation, "Wait till we're snuggling. You'll be begging for one."

"How are we friends?" I mumble as I pull my dress over my head, unclasp this ridiculous stupid bra that's been stabbing me all day, and change into my comfy clothes. She just chuckles, handing me a sock to help wipe away the residual tears streaking down my face.

I feel like I'm moving through molasses as I shuffle into Belle's room. Skye pulls back the bedcovers, inviting me to sink into the familiar warmth. I comply, curling up in a ball, the weight of the day, the weight of loss pulling me down into the depths of the mattress. Skye slips in next to me, wrapping me in a warm embrace, her unicorn onesie surprisingly soft, albeit suffocating, against my skin.

"You're smothering me," I say into her onesie.

"Shut up; no I'm not."

"I'm inhaling rainbow fur."

"Ugh." She loosens her grip on me, and I readjust to lay my head on her shoulder.

"Thank you."

"No need to thank me. You're my person. I'm here for you, always."

"I know. And I'm grateful. Everything just feels so empty without Belle. I know I'm not alone, but I *feel* completely alone." I exhale, puffing out my cheeks while staring at the rainbow zipper on Skye's unicorn onesie. I can't bring myself to meet her eyes, feeling slightly guilty for feeling so alone when I'm so clearly not.

"I kind of remember feeling that way when mom died, but I was eight and I'm an only child so I have no idea what it feels like to lose a sister," Skye whispers, running her fingers through my loose hair. "I remember feeling safe when you and Tori climbed into my bed after the funeral and stayed for the next three nights. I felt alone, but I didn't completely lose it because you guys held me together."

I squeeze her tightly, and she echoes the gesture, holding me together when all I want to do is fall apart. "I'm glad we're still together."

"Me, too, babe. Me, too." Skye's fingers against my scalp are slowly but surely lulling me toward unconsciousness, and I welcome the becoming oblivion of sleep. "I don't think Tori's big butt would fit in this bed with us so it's a good thing she's in boss mode downstairs."

I chuckle, grateful for the reprieve of laughter, though still longing to not feel anything for the night. "You're probably right. If she tried to climb in here with us I'd suffocate in your rainbow fluff."

"Whatever. You're about to have the best sleep of your life cuddled up to this heavenly unicorn."

"Or the sweatiest."

We both chuckle. "Or that. Yeah."

We're quiet after that. Skye continues running her fingers through my hair and I stare blankly at the bathroom door across the room. We lay there in the quiet room, her steady breathing a calming backdrop to the whirlpool of emotions spiraling in my chest. The tight knot of grief, of loss, of heart-shattering sadness twists tighter with each passing moment. I feel tears well up again, spilling down my cheeks, soaking into the pillow beneath my head.

Skye holds me tighter, her arms a firm, comforting presence around me. She doesn't say anything, doesn't distract from my pain. She just holds me, allowing me space to grieve, to feel the sharp sting of loss.

At some point, exhaustion takes over, and my tears dry up, replaced by a heavy, oppressive numbness. My body feels heavy, my limbs like lead, a strange detachment setting in as I drift on the edge of consciousness. Skye's warmth, her presence, slowly soothes the chaotic storm in my heart as I fall into dreamless sleep.

***

AFTER A NIGHT OF SOLID, albeit overheated, sleep, I head downstairs for coffee. I can already hear Skye talking to Sunny, and I assume she's bribing the baby to get her to eat. I don't hear anyone else in the kitchen, so now I'm confused about where my parents could be at 7 a.m. on a Sunday. It's not like they're going to church the day after their daughter and son-in-law's funeral.

"Open up big, Sunny-bunny." Skye is airplaning eggs near Sunny's face, and that sweet baby smile convinces Skye that she'll actually open for the food. Just as she goes in for the feed, Sunny slaps the fork and giggles as scrambled eggs fall to the floor.

"Having fun?" I ask, standing with my hip propped against the entryway to the kitchen. Skye looks at me, deadpan. "So much. You have no idea." She stabs another piece of egg and once again attempts to entice Sunny to eat it. "Your parents refilled the Keurig basket with that dark roast you like. Beware of the hazelnut — it's gross."

"Noted." I walk to the counter and reach up into the mug cupboard, trying and failing to find the mug I always use when I stay with my parents. I look around and spot it, currently in use, sitting on the table next to Skye.

Great, just my luck. Now I'm relegated to using one of those oversized mugs from my parents' collection — the kind that's so roomy the coffee turns lukewarm before I can even take a second sip. Aren't these designed for soup? If I ever felt like chugging a bowl of coffee, I'd at least be practical and use a thermos to keep it hot.

With my coffee made, I snatch an apple from the fruit basket and settle at the table. "Where's Mom?" I ask, attempting — and miserably failing — to prevent apple juice from trickling down my chin.

"I think she and your dad are in the study. When I brought Sunny downstairs they were in the kitchen drinking coffee, and after saying good morning and assuring them I've got the kid they stood and walked off down the hall. I think I walked in on a private conversation. They looked super serious."

Super serious? Can't we get a break from serious, heavy, depressing, etc. for just one day? "Hm. Okay. Mind if I go find them?"

"No prob. I'll just sit here and pretend to feed this kid her breakfast." Sunny is using her highchair tray as a drum, knocking fruit and eggs to the floor and smashing bananas in the process.

"You have fun with that. I'll be right back." I stand, coffee bowl in hand, and head toward my dad's study, hoping to figure out what my parents are working through. I thought they had everything sorted now that the funeral was over, but I stand corrected.

The door isn't closed all the way, so I don't feel bad about intruding. "Dad? Mom? You guys in here?" I ask, pushing the door the rest of the way open. They're sitting on either side of the desk, which is strangely formal for an early-morning conversation.

"Hey, honey, come on in." Dad gestures for me to sit next to Mom, and the ambiance suddenly feels as though I've walked into an attorney's office.

"You guys okay?" I venture, sipping my coffee as a shield against the mounting wave of anxiety.

"Fine, fine. We're just going through some legal matters concerning Alex and Belle. It's good you're here, because this conversation involves you."

"Me? What does this have to do with me?"

Dad aligns the papers on the table before meeting my eyes. "Alis, Alex and Belle designated you as Sunny's guardian if something ever happened to both of them."

I choke on my coffee, attempting to swallow and gasp simultaneously.

"Guardian? I'm only twenty-one. How can I be responsible for someone else?" Their faces remain inscrutable, revealing no insights into their thoughts.

Mom gently pats my knee. "We've deliberated since last night. If you don't feel ready, we're here to step in and legally care for Sunny."

"Handle?" I snap. "Why would they even choose me? That's... it's unexpected."

Mom's smile is soft, meant to comfort, but it fails. "Belle left a letter for you in her legal documents. Maybe it'll provide clarity. You shouldn't rush any decisions."

Dad's gaze is steady on Mom, a silent message passing between them. "It's a lot to process, Alis. Reading the letter might help. While we'd gladly raise Sunny, remember that you were their chosen one. I believe they made that decision with care. It might seem dismissive to their memory not to at least ponder their wish."

His words strike a chord. "You think I'm up to the task?"

Dad nods. "You're capable of anything. And you won't be alone; we're here to help. Give it some thought; no need for immediate decisions."

"Alright." My voice is soft, eyes fixated on the mug cradled in my hands. Dad slides an envelope labeled "Aurora Borealis" across the desk. My fingers tremble as they touch it, recognizing Belle's familiar script.

"I, uh, I'm going to read this upstairs." I stand, gripping the envelope tighter than necessary in my free hand. I don't wait for a response. I simply turn and walk toward the study door, still in shock at the thought of becoming Sunny's guardian.

Why the hell would you leave an infant to a twenty-one year old?! Leave it to Belle, the fun one, to take an already unstable situation and add another plot twist. I rub my forehead as I ascend the stairs and head back to Belle's bed. I need to be surrounded by her if I'm going to digest her final words to me.

I place my coffee on the vanity and settle on the floor, my back against the bed. "Here goes," I mutter, carefully breaking the seal of the envelope.

Unfolding the handwritten letter, I spot Belle's signature purple ink — a small detail that brings an unexpected smile.

Aurora,

I hope you'll never have to read this letter, and if you are reading it I hope you're in a good place in life. Who am I kidding? You're always in a good place because you're Alis — kind, mature, and responsible. Even though you're my little sister, I've always looked up to you. Your passion and commitment to your dreams is inspiring, and I'd like to think Sunny will inherit that same drive from you.

Thinking about dying and assets and guardianship is all incredibly depressing, but I'm glad Alex and I are handling the legal stuff in case something ridiculous happens. We've talked through all the different options for who would take care of Sunny in the event she's left without either of us, and we both agree that you are the best person for the job.

I know I should have talked to you about this

first, but like I said, I'm hoping this letter never leaves the envelope. I know you hate to be caught off guard, that you thrive on schedules and carefully thought out plans, but I know you can do this because even when everything goes awry you find a way to shine light and beauty into the darkness. You truly are Aurora Borealis — my northern lights. And now I need you to be that for Sunny.

I know she could live with Mom and Dad or even Alex's parents, but she will find the most joy and adventure with you. You have a special way of loving people, a way that cares for both the person and the soul. I want my daughter to be surrounded by your love every day of her life if she can't have us.

I know you're young, but we both know you're the adult in our relationship. You're my best friend, my confidant, my encourager, and now I need you to be all those things for my little girl.

I love you, Alis. And I know you're going to be an incredible Monty for Sunny. (What is a monty? It's a word I just made up in an attempt to Brangelina the words mom and aunt. Just go with it, k?)

Still hoping you never read this letter, and also hoping I get to rewrite it when you're thirty and married and probably already have kids of your own. If not, you got this, sis. Trust me.

Your Sunshine, Isabelle

The tears spill over, a steady stream falling onto the paper, blurring Belle's words, smudging the ink. *God, I can't even cry without messing things up.* I use the back of my hand to wipe away the tears; try to salvage the precious words on the paper.

Belle believed in me so much, saw in me a maturity, a capacity to love and nurture and *fortheloveofallthatisholy* to *parent*, that feels almost foreign. And yet, here I am, twenty-one with ambitions stretching far and wide, but with resources so limited, it's laughable. I'd have to put those dreams on hold, reroute the carefully laid plans I had for myself. Could I do that? Could I be that for Sunny?

A rush of thoughts inundate me, painting pictures of different futures, varying paths — some converging, some diverging drastically. I envision waking up in the early hours to feed Sunny, bidding farewell to her and Mom before embarking on the long drive to campus, coming home after a full day of school to hold her in my arms before she falls asleep.

I could balance school and raising her, couldn't I? Commuting, coordinating with family, living a life interspersed with baby laughter and serious study sessions. I could morph into this person that Belle envisioned, someone steady and nurturing, even in the whirlpool of academics and research projects.

But then another reality dawns on me — the post-master's phase, the relentless pursuit of a Ph.D., late nights turned into early mornings in the library, a life dictated by an ever-evolving thesis. Could I ask Sunny to adapt to a life like that? Could I give her the time she deserves amid the demanding hours of academia? I wouldn't be the only guiding figure in her life — we'd have both Mom and Dad — but I'd be her guardian. Her mother figure. Her Monty.

I'm trying to breathe, to maintain a semblance of control as the burden of choice weighs heavily on my shoulders. I can feel the enormity of it, a pressure building in my chest, a tightness that is both terrifying and sacred. I'm torn between being *Alis*, the sister engrossed in books and dreams, and becoming this person, *Aurora*, this guardian, this light in the darkness, who could offer Sunny a life filled with love and unwavering support.

And yet, despite the whirlwind of doubts and fears spinning in my mind, Belle's words resound with a clarity that pierces through the chaos. A plea from someone who knew me more than anyone else, who saw in me a potential that even I find hard to see sometimes.

I glance down at the paper again, tracing the words with my fingers, feeling the ridges of the ink as if trying to grasp onto Belle, to bring her here, to ask her a thousand questions, to tell her that she's asking too much and not enough all at once.

Belle called me her northern light, her beacon in the darkness, the constant glow that could bring warmth and light to Sunny's world. Was that really who I was to her? Could I be that for someone else as well?

And I feel it then, the gentle flicker of a flame deep within me, a blend of resolve and love, slowly growing, warming the cold corners of doubt and fear in my mind. It's a fragile light, one that flickers uncertainly but holds promise, a potential to grow into a guiding force, a steady glow.

Because while Belle didn't waste her words on negativity, she also wasn't one to hand out direct praise lightly. She saw something in me, believed in it with her whole heart. And how could I turn my back on that belief, that unyielding faith she had in me?

Grandma named us Sunny and Alis, names woven with threads of light and warmth. Perhaps it's time to embody the spirit of my name, to rise to the occasion, to be the light that guides Sunny, nourishing her with love, teaching her to chase her dreams just like Belle taught me.

Yeah, it's terrifying, and there are a million ways this could go wrong, but there's also a chance, a possibility of creating something beautiful, something radiant. And maybe, just maybe, with Belle's blessing wrapping around us like a warm embrace, Sunny and I can find our way, lighting up each other's paths as we venture into this new beginning, hand in tiny hand.

TWELVE

Alis

"SHOOT, shoot, shoot, shoot, shoot, shoot — SUNNY!" I bolt up out of bed, grabbing my glasses and phone to see that it's already 7:15 a.m. and we were supposed to be out the door ten minutes ago.

"SUNNY! ARE YOU AWAKE?!" I yell out into the hallway as I rip off my t-shirt and sweats, looking frantically around the room for a pair of pants, a skirt — anything clean, really.

Sunny's bedroom door opens and she stands there, rubbing her eyes, bed head to the max and yawning. "I'm awake. Why are you yelling?"

As she's talking, I find a pair of jeans balled up near my closet and start to wiggle them up my legs. "Because it's 7:15 and we were supposed to leave by 7:10. We have to go. Throw something on and grab your bookbag. I'll give you some mint gum in the ca— ah!"

I trip while trying to get my pants on and slam my hip into the dresser. Grunting and uttering useless expletives under my breath, I right myself and finish buttoning my jeans. When I look up Sunny is still standing in her doorway, in her pajamas, laughing at me.

"Seriously? Did you not hear a word I just said?! GET. DRESSED.

NOW!" She turns and bolts into her room, hopefully dressing herself so we can get out of here.

Thank goodness I at least had the forethought to pick out a top for my first day of class, so I snatch it off the hanger in my closet and pull it over my head. Now for shoes. Shoes, shoes, shoes — where the hell are my yellow flats?! I could have sworn I put them in my closet. Maybe they're by the front door. I decide they must be, and instead of checking to make sure I run into my bathroom to brush my teeth and throw on some deodorant. I look at my face in the mirror as I brush my teeth and see that, of course, I woke up with a serious case of chin acne. I guess I am due for my period any day now, but I don't have time to put on makeup and I really don't want to stroll into class sporting an uncovered puss volcano on my face. I rinse my toothbrush and mouth, set the toothbrush back in its holder, grab my makeup bag, and sprint back into the bedroom to find my messenger bag.

"Sunny?! Are you ready?!" I yell out into the apartment, hoping that my child is dressed and at least has her shoes on and backpack located.

"Yes, Monty. You're the one taking forever. I thought we were late?" I can hear the eyeroll in her tone and today is not the day for sass. I also don't have the time or energy to reprimand her, so I decide to leave it for now.

I grab my laptop and shove it into my bag, zipping it shut before slinging it over my shoulder and running out into the living room.

"Did you eat?" I ask, not looking at her because I'm now scouring the shoe pile by the door.

Sunny responds with a mouthful of food. "Yes, I'm eating a granola bar." Though it sounds like, "yesh, I'm eeing a gwanohoh bah."

"Have you seen my shoes? Where the hell are my flats?!" I'm now tossing shoes out of the basket near the door looking for a pair I've deemed professional but jeans appropriate.

"Which ones?" Sunny looks at me, confused.

"Seriously? The yellow slip-ons I just bought. The ones I bought for work."

"Oohhhhh. Yeah. I have no idea where they are." Thanks. Super helpful, kid.

I look at the clock on the microwave and see it's now 7:27. Shit, we have to leave. I see my bright red Mary Janes, shove my feet into them, and turn back to Sunny. "Come on. We gotta go. Now."

She tosses a granola bar my way. Mercifully, I catch it, shoving it into my purse on the entry table before I sling the crossbody bag over my head, grab my keys, and open the door. Sunny is thankfully right behind me and she locks the door as we run toward the parking lot. I've at least got one thing going for me this morning — yesterday I lucked out and landed the parking spot closest to our apartment. The only downside to this spot is that it's not shaded, and my black leather seats are hot plates in the August heat. Beggars can't be choosers when you're running late.

I toss my bag and purse into the back, climb into the driver's seat, and crank the vehicle. I back out of the spot and then we're on our way — thirty minutes later than intended, but whatever.

"I didn't have time to pack anything for lunch. I'll need cash for food," Sunny says as she buckles her seatbelt. I have no idea if my wallet holds any cash, but I tell Sunny to grab my purse off the back seat and check anyway. Glory hallelujah, she finds a twenty.

"Did you forget something?" Sunny asks as I stop at a red light.

"No? Maybe? What did I forget?" I frantically look around and then pat down my body looking for a missed necessity. Just as I'm about to ask again what the hell she thinks I forgot, Sunny pulls a hairbrush out of her backpack and offers it to me. "Please don't go out in public with your hair like that."

"Like what?!" I scoff, but quickly clamp my mouth shut when I see the half-fallen messy bun in the rearview mirror. How did I miss that?

Traffic is thankfully not backed up yet, so I get Sunny to school right before the tardy bell rings.

"Keep the brush," she says, opening the door to hop out before I've fully stopped.

"Love you! See you tonight! Skye is picking you up today." I yell out the window as she jogs toward the school. She doesn't look back or say anything, just sticks her arm in the air and gives me a thumbs up before slipping inside the front door.

My class begins in ten minutes and I'm twenty minutes away, more if traffic sucks. I cannot believe this. I'm thirty years old. I thought I had my crap together and now I can't even make it to class on time on THE FIRST DAY OF THE SEMESTER.

I try to maintain the speed limit on my way to campus, changing lanes more than usual to weave through traffic. I saw a study once that said weaving actually makes traffic move slower, but my brain isn't functioning well enough to remember that right now.

"Come on, come on, come on." I'm literally two blocks away from my destination and this red light is taking forever to change. Class began ten minutes ago, and I still have to park and walk to class — oh, and fix my hair. So much for makeup. Don't have time for that now. I really hope I can sneak in quietly and find a seat in the back.

The light turns green — finally — and a few minutes later I'm parked and jogging across the parking lot toward class. It has to be ninety degrees outside already and my hair tie broke when I wrestled it out of my nest, so my now-frizzy, but brushed, mop of blonde hair hangs loose down my back as sweat builds on my skin.

This blouse is thin and will most likely stick to my skin when I slow down. At least I wore deodorant — wait, I did put on deodorant, right? Yes. Yes, I did. Ok, so I shouldn't have pit sweat but who knows what my back and underboob will look like. I can't think about this right now. Where is my class again? I stop and look around, realizing I passed the English building while lost in my thoughts of sweat-soaked clothing. I spin on my heel and jog up the stairs, looking at my feet to ensure I don't trip on my way to the front door.

Smack. I crash into someone and start to fall back down the stairs when a strong arm wraps around me, pulling me back up and steadying me on my feet. Thank God I'm not running with a drink in hand.

"Whoa now, you ok?" His words don't register because all I can smell is sandalwood and spruce. *Heaven.* "Alis?" Wait. I know that voice. I know this smell. Dexter. Oh, fuck me. *Yes, please do.* No!

I take a step back and brush my hair from my face. "Hi, Dr. Belanger. Sorry I ran into you. Literally." I look up at him from beneath my lashes, suddenly thankful for the heat because my sweat-flushed skin hides my embarrassment.

"No worries. You ok?" He asks, his eyes are concerned, but he still manages to aim that sexy half-smile right at me.

Am I ok? No, I am not ok. I'm late for class, my hair looks like I've been electrocuted, it's so freaking hot outside that I'm sure I have underboob sweat staining my shirt, and the one man I want and can't have is now all up in my space.

"Yeah, sorry again. I have to get to class." I smile, awkwardly, and scoot around him to pull open the door and head into the building. I find the directory on the wall near the elevator and see that my class is on the first floor, but I swear the hallways on this map look more like a maze than a grid. I find the room number and trace the hallway route with my eyes before walking deeper into the labyrinth, hoping and praying I don't get lost and make myself even more late than I already am.

Five minutes and two wrong turns later, I peer through the glass window on the classroom door and see my professor is turned around writing something on the whiteboard. I open the door as slowly and quietly as possible and slip in, looking to my left and then right to hopefully find an open seat near the door. Ah-hah! I find one in the second row from the back and slide into the aisle, whispering "sorry" and "excuse me" before plopping down into the open seat and lifting up the desk attachment. The professor is still writing on the board and I don't think he heard me, so I should be in the clear.

Everyone around me seems to be copying whatever the professor writes, so I reach into my bag, grab a notebook, and search for a pen to follow suit. When my fingers fail to find one, I hear a tap on the side of my desk and look up to see the guy next to me offering one of his extras.

"Thank you," I mouth with a friendly smile before looking back to the front of the class. The professor turns and continues his lecture, none the wiser about my late arrival. *At least something went right this morning.*

Thirty minutes later class ends and I'm scribbling down the last bullet point from the board when I hear, "Miss Gilmore, a word." I close my eyes. *Of course. Nothing can go right today.*

I look up toward my professor and smile stiffly. "Of course, sir."

I pack up my belongings and slide my bag over my shoulder before walking down the auditorium-style classroom to apologize for my tardiness. "Dr. —" I don't even finish saying his name when he cuts me off.

"I don't tolerate tardiness in my classroom. This is a graduate-level course and you've been in school long enough to manage time appropriately and arrive on time. See that it doesn't happen again." He stops talking and looks back down at the papers in front of him, and I'm not sure if I should respond or wait for him to say more? After ten seconds of silence I'm about to speak up when he looks back up at me and says, "Is there something you wish to say?"

I stand there with wide eyes, my mouth opening and closing like a fish. "I, uh, I'm sorry, sir. It won't happen again."

He nods once and looks back down at his papers. I guess I'm dismissed? I turn and make my exit, feeling like a scolded child. I don't know whether I'm more embarrassed or annoyed, but my stomach flips and I kind of want to throw up after that interaction. Awesome. I was just reprimanded by a professor on my first day back to college.

What am I even doing here? Am I too old for this? I had a good life back in Moraine. I liked my job, I knew everyone around me, Sunny was happy and content, and I didn't even have to pay rent because we lived with my parents. I shake my head and let out a breath as I push open the door and step into the hallway.

Before I can sink deeper into my internal tale of woe, someone touches my arm and says, "Hey." I look up and see pen guy from class smiling at me. Was he waiting for me? Surely not. This guy is like twenty-two, tops.

"Uh, hi," I say, reaching for the pen in the side pocket of my bag. I offer it back to him. "Thanks for the pen save. All mine decided to become hide and seek champions today."

He smiles and nods. "Keep it." Um, okay. I'm not one to turn down a perfectly good pen, *thankyouverymuch*. I slide it back into my bag and thank him as I turn to walk back through the maze of hallways to the exit.

"I'm Brody," he says as he slides into step next to me. "Hi, Brody, I'm Alis." I give him a small smile and leave it at that. I really don't have anything more to say now that I've thanked him for the pen, so I'm not sure why he's walking next to me.

"New here?" he asks, apparently wanting to continue this non-conversation.

"Yep." I am incapable of talking and walking when I'm unfamiliar with my surroundings. I need to find my way out of this building so I can meet with Dr. Matthews, and I'm not a cougar so I don't really want to flirt with Mr. Young Buck here.

He chuckles. "My, my, you're quite the chatty Kathy. Wanna tell me anything more about yourself?" *Nope. Not really.*

I stop and turn to look at him. "I'm sorry; I'm not trying to be rude. This building is confusing as hell to navigate and I'm just trying to concentrate so I can make it back to the exit without walking in circles … or into a wall." *Also, I was just called out by my professor so I feel super awkward, and I avoid meeting new people when at all possible, especially men.* I leave out that last part.

"No worries. I got you. I'm heading out also." I nod and we resume walking. Brody takes my nod as an invitation to continue conversing, so I just go with it. *Not every guy that talks to you is interested in you, Alis. He's probably just a nice guy wanting to get to know a new student.*

"So, this is your first semester at Middle Peak. Are you new to the area or just to the school?"

"New to the area. I moved here a little more than a week ago for school."

"English, right?" I want to make a snarky comment about him being a stalker, but considering our class is only offered to grad students in this specific program, I try to remember his question is more *duh* than intrusive.

I nod. "Yeah. You?" Looky looky; we can both ask stupid questions.

"Same. This is my second year. After this semester I'll finish my thesis and will hopefully graduate in the spring." We reach the front door and he opens it, gesturing for me to walk ahead. I nod my thanks.

"Nice. I should be graduating next December, but that's only if Dr. Matthews will let me write my thesis and take my last seminar courses at the same time. She seemed fine with it when we worked through my transfer credits, but I know profs usually prefer students to focus solely on their thesis in their last semester, so who knows. I may end up graduating later instead." That's a heck of a lot more words that I thought he'd pull from me.

"Where'd you transfer from?" he asks.

"I'm not exactly a transfer student, but kind of? I took some time off and am just now able to get back into the swing of things and finish. Dr. Matthews pulled some strings to transfer in old credits so I wouldn't have to start from scratch." *Atta girl. Way to sidestep that question.* With him studying English I knew as soon as I said Grant University he would have gone all fanboy about Dr. Ryan.

He looks at me, obviously confused. "Old credits? I thought all credits transfer as long as you took the courses within the last five or six years. You shouldn't have had any issues transferring in unless your school had accreditation issues or something."

I laugh. "No accreditation issues. And you are correct. My transfer credits are from nine years ago."

Brody's eyes go wide. "Wait, what? Were you a child prodigy or something?"

"Now Brody, didn't your mom teach you it's never okay to ask a woman her age?" I smirk up at him and cut him off as he's about to apologize. "I'm just kidding. Not a prodigy. I'm thirty."

He's shocked. "Thirty? You don't look thirty."

"Thanks? I guess?"

He smiles and looks me up and down. "Definitely not thirty. I would have guessed twenty-four, twenty-five tops."

I chuckle and fold my hands under my chin, fluttering my eyes like a smitten cartoon character. "Why Brody, that's the sweetest thing anyone has ever said to little 'ol me." *Where the hell did that come from? Gosh, I'm so awkward.*

He nudges my arm. "I doubt that. Surely all the guys tell you you're beautiful."

Oh no. He's flirting. Abort! Abort! "Uh, maybe? I don't know." How am I supposed to respond to that? I don't want to compliment him back because that will send the wrong message. *No, sir, I am not interested in dating you.*

"I'm twenty-five, in case you were wondering." I wasn't, but knowing he's older than twenty-two makes this conversation a bit less unnerving.

I offer a stiff smile, but don't say anything. We spend the next few minutes walking in silence. I wish I could say it's comfortable, but the awkward cloud surrounding us is so thick I might choke on it. I stop as we approach the building that houses Dr. Matthews' office and look up at Brody, trying and failing to look calm and cool.

"Well, I have to get going. It was nice meeting you, Brody. I'll see you in class, yeah?"

He runs his hand through his tousled dirty blonde hair and nods, smiling. "Yeah, definitely. See you in class."

I turn and latch onto the door pull, but Brody stops me as I pull it open. "Hey, Alis?"

I look over my shoulder at him. "What's up?" Please don't ask me out. Please oh please oh please do not ask me out.

"Wanna meet for lunch sometime this week? I could show you around campus and we could grab a bite at Nico's?"

"Nico's?" That was the wrong answer. I didn't say no and now he thinks I want to have lunch with him.

He nods. "Yeah, Nico's pizza. It's the closest thing to legit New York pizza you'll find on this side of the country." Well now, there's the one word that could change my mind: pizza. Pizza is to Alis as ice cream is to a teenage girl with a broken heart. You simply cannot have one without the other.

Brody seems nice, not creepy. Maybe he'd be down for living in my friend zone? I mean, he didn't ask me to dinner — he asked to show me around campus and meet for pizza. Friends do that kind of stuff. So do nerdy student government kids in high school when the new kid shows up. I'm the new kid. He's the not nerdy but definitely enthusiastic class president.

"Yeah, that sounds good." I mentally scroll through my schedule this week and find a few hours free on Wednesday. "I could do Wednesday at 10? Show me around a bit and we can grab lunch after?"

His face lights up. I hope that smile means "yay, new friend!" and not "pretty girl like boy!"

"That works for me. Give me your number and I'll text you to meet up." How do I say no without sounding like a total bitch? Wait, I'll see him that morning in class.

"I gotta run, but we can make a plan Wednesday morning in class? See ya then!" I turn back toward the building and walk through the door before I can hear his response.

I've been here less than two weeks and have had two different guys ask me out. Aside from tourists, I haven't had one flirty comment tossed my way from a man my age in nearly a decade. That's what happens when you live in a small town where everyone knows each other and the only single men are tourists or like brothers. The few times a year I headed into the city I always had mom and Sunny in tow. Very few men try to pick up women with their mother and child in tow at Old Navy and Pottery Barn.

Does having lunch with a man communicate that I'm interested? Or is it normal for single men and women to have lunch together, strictly platonic?

Brody didn't try to touch me, so that's good. Maybe he's not interested in more than friendship. Wait, I think he nudged my arm at one point. Maybe he's just being nice to the new girl. Maybe he's gay? Or, better yet, maybe he's in a committed relationship and his girlfriend will join us on Wednesday so I won't have to question whether or not anything I say or do can be misconstrued as flirting!

Or, maybe you should stop overthinking everything and get excited about pizza. Noted.

THIRTEEN

I'M HOPING today's meeting proves beneficial and that Dr. Ryan can accommodate my new commuter status. I still need to find someone to sublet my apartment through the end of my lease, pack up my belongings, and officially move back in with my parents.

I can't store my apartment furniture, so I'm hoping I can either sell it online or the subletter can offer a decent price for everything. Overthinking has resulted in an epic tension headache, and the end is nowhere in sight.

As I pull into the parking lot near the faculty offices, I see students and professors alike walking to and from spring break intensive classes. Some sit on benches, deep in conversation. Others seem in more of a hurry and struggle to keep their books in hand.

The weather is kind today, for March. Had last week gone differently, I'd be spending my morning preparing to give the afternoon lecture to Dr. Ryan's undergrad English Lit class. I've taken advantage of how carefree my life has been up to this point. Sure, my life was busy, but I lived on my own terms. I didn't have to think through how my daily schedule affected my family, how I would budget for both school and raising a child. I wish I could switch off reality for a few hours and bask in the simplicity of last Tuesday.

No such luck.

My dashboard clock says I have fifteen minutes until I'm expected in Dr. Ryan's office, so I gather my purse, secure my favorite wool infinity scarf, and step out into the sunny thirty-four degree day. I love the weather here. The crisp, clean air on days like today breathes life into me. I'll miss living near campus, but at least I'm only moving an hour back home.

I step onto the sidewalk and head toward the faculty offices, staring up at the three-story historical brick building with a soft smile on my face. Although the rest of my life is currently in disarray, the comfort and stability I find on this campus calms me and helps redirect my focus to the task at hand — convincing Dr. Ryan that I can perform my TA responsibilities perfectly fine as a full-time commuter student.

Once inside, I remove my jacket and scarf and fold them over my arm as I walk toward the English pod — a cluster of offices on the first floor that house all five English department faculty members, and their shared faculty secretary.

"Lisa, hi. I have a 9:30 with Dr. Ryan. Is he ready for me?" Lisa looks up from her computer, her smiling face not revealing if she knows about my sister's accident.

"Alis, so nice to see you. Dr. Ryan is in his office and he hasn't had any other visitors this morning so I'm sure you can head right in."

I thank her, hang my jacket and scarf on the coat rack near her waiting area, and head into what I hope is a productive and helpful meeting.

I knock lightly as I enter. "Dr. Ryan? It's Alis."

"Come on in, Alis. I just need to finish typing this email and I'll be right with you. Please, take a seat."

As the department head, Dr. Ryan has the largest office in the pod, complete with a separate sitting area. I'm not sure if I should sit at a chair near his desk or on the couch, but I choose the couch so I don't crowd his space.

Why am I acting so nervous? I've worked with Dr. Ryan for more than a year now, and before that we had a great relationship in undergrad. I've earned my position as his TA and we work very well together. I should not be afraid that he'll cast me off as if I don't matter just because I need to adjust my schedule.

"Right then." Dr. Ryan stands from his computer chair and walks toward the couch, greeting me with a warm smile. "How are you, Alis? I'm sure these last few days have been extremely difficult."

I stand to shake his hand in greeting, and he places his left hand on top of our clasped hands in a comforting gesture. "I'm alright, considering the circumstances. Thank you for asking, sir."

He releases my hand and we both sit, he in the leather chair across the coffee table, and I back onto the couch. I don't know if I'm supposed to lead this conversation or if he will.

"So, I've taken care of the guest lecture rescheduling for this week." Alright, we're going to dive right in, I guess.

"Thank you, sir. I appreciate you finding fill-ins for me this week. I know, in my current mental/emotional state I wouldn't be able to teach to the best of my ability right now."

"No worries. You know how the other grad students can be — they're like piranhas chomping at the bit for any opportunity."

"Right," I chuckle, suddenly more nervous about asking for more scheduling accommodations since he's just reminded me of the competition.

"You plan to commute for the next two weeks? Three?" Dr. Ryan asks, removing his glasses and using his sweater to clean them. Gosh, I hate when people do that. That's the easiest way to ruin perfectly good lenses. They make alcohol wipes for a reason, people.

I clasp my hands tightly on my lap, trying but failing to quell my nerves. "Actually, sir, I'm here to talk about extending my commuter status." He pauses mid-cleaning, looking up at me with a blank expression. I have no idea what this man is thinking right now.

"Extending? As in, a month? Or longer?" He replaces his glasses and maintains his poker face.

"Longer. I actually need to become a permanent commuter student." I pause, waiting for his reaction. Nothing. Great. I continue, "I learned this weekend that my sister and brother-in-law named me legal guardian of their daughter, so I'll be moving back home this week and commuting to and from campus each day for the rest of the semester."

"Guardian? Aren't you only twenty-two?"

"Twenty-one, sir. But this is what my sister wanted, and I have my parents to help out and we'll be living with them, so I won't be alone. My parents support my continuing with my master's degree, and with my mom at home I won't need to sort out childcare while I'm on campus."

Dr. Ryan steeples his hands, tapping his closed mouth with his joined fingertips. "I see. And what about evening classes? You're scheduled to teach two undergraduate evening classes next semester."

Shit. I forgot about those. "Do you know if those are block classes or are they multi-day?"

He stands, walks to the office door, and calls out. "Lisa, can you bring me a print-out of my next-semester schedule?"

I can't make out her response, but Dr. Ryan returns to his armchair so I assume she'll bring it in shortly.

"What do you plan to do for your own class schedule? You typically take nine hours. That, on top of your TA responsibilities, and commuting, and serving as a guardian — that all seems like a lot, don't you think?"

"Yes, sir. I plan to lighten my class load, and hopefully with fewer classes and just the two classes to help teach, I won't have to commute all five days of the week."

Lisa walks in and hands Dr. Ryan a print-out, then pulls the door closed behind her as she returns to her desk.

"That's a tall order, but let's see if we can figure something out." *Oh thank God. He isn't kicking me to the curb just yet.*

Dr. Ryan stands, retrieves a pen and notepad from his desk, then sits next to me on the couch to brainstorm possible schedules that better accommodate my new life as a parent.

After an hour of mapping both teaching and class schedules, I think we have next semester figured out. I'll have to give up one of my teaching slots, but Dr. Ryan doesn't seem perturbed by it and I'll still grade for every one of his classes.

"That should do it, yes?" Dr. Ryan adjusts his glasses as he looks over to me and smiles.

"Yes. Yes, thank you so much!" My eyes are watering. Shit, not now. Don't cry in front of your professor, idiot!

I wipe my eyes but the tears keep falling. "I'm so sorry, sir. I'm just overwhelmed by the last week and I was worried coming into this meeting that I'd have to give up my position as your TA. I didn't know if my need to commute and lighten my workload would result in you needing to find someone else, and I've worked so hard to earn this position I couldn't imagine giving it up. Everything is up in the air right now and I don't know left from right. I'm a complete mess." *Cheese and Rice, Alis. Word vomit much?* I'm still crying, now wiping snot from my nose with my shirt sleeve. Lovely.

"Shhh, Alis. Everything is going to be alright." Dr. Ryan places his hand on my shoulder and squeezes lightly to offer some comfort.

That one touch breaks the emotional dam inside me and suddenly I'm sobbing into my hands, unable to calm the hell down.

"I'm so sorry. I just..." My voice breaks, overwhelmed with emotion and the words sticking in my throat.

Before I know it, Dr. Ryan's comforting arms are around me. "Alis, it's going to be okay. You'll navigate this. And if extending your degree means you stay on as my TA a bit longer, then that's just a bonus."

I manage a weak laugh, pulling back slightly to meet his understanding gaze. "Thank you, Dr. Ryan. This means a lot."

As our conversation concludes, the door swings open, revealing Margaret Ryan. Her gaze scans the room — first, landing on me, visibly shaken, then to her husband, comforting me. I see the moment the sight is misinterpreted in her eyes.

"Margaret, this is a surprise," Dr. Ryan begins, removing his arm from my shoulder and rising to meet her. *Of all the responses, he went with 'this is a surprise'?!*

"What is going on here?" Her voice is filled with suspicion.

"Going on?" Dr. Ryan is obviously confused at her accusatory tone. "Margaret, Alis had a rough week, and we were discussing some adjustments for the next semester."

Her eyebrow arches, unimpressed. "So, you make a habit of cuddling with students when 'discussing' things in a closed office?"

Trying to defuse the situation, I interject, "Mrs. Ryan, we were—"

But she cuts me off, her eyes flashing with anger. "I don't believe I was speaking to you."

"Margaret, stop. This is ridiculous. Alis is my student and my teaching assistant, nothing more."

"Your teaching assistant who stays late to teach night classes with you. Who you talk about more than any other student in your program. Who you are up emailing at all hours of the night. 'Can't sleep and need to get some work done,' my ass. She worships the ground you walk on. And you talk about her like she's your favorite fucking pet." *What?!*

Dr. Ryan's voice is remarkably calm, considering the tantrum his wife is throwing. "Margaret, I've told you before. She is my student and my employee and that is all. I have no romantic feelings toward her whatsoever."

Before?! What the hell is he talking about? This isn't the first time they've had this conversation?!

"You can tell me that until you're blue in the face, John, but that doesn't change the fact that I just walked in on you about to kiss her." *Nope, I've had enough of this.*

"Mrs. Ryan," I interject, standing and walking toward her.

"I told you to stay out of this, tramp." I've had the worst week of my life, I'm mentally and emotionally spent, and I have no room left for niceties, nor do I have the ability to think before I speak.

"No, I won't. Dr. Ryan is my professor and my boss. He's my educational mentor and nothing more."

"I know what you college girls think of men like John. He's older and wiser and you get off on the fantasy of being with him." *The fuck did she just say?!*

"You're wrong, and you're not only implying that your husband is unfaithful, but that I'm some scheming homewrecker out to ruin your marriage. That's the farthest thing from my mind, especially given the fact that my head is currently filled with my dead sister and brother-in-law and my newly-acquired role as a parent."

She pauses, looks from Dr. Ryan to me, and spews the most venomous thing anyone has ever said to my face.

"You seriously expect me to believe that you aren't using your grief to manipulate my husband into your bed? I see how you look at him with your bedroom eyes. It's hero worship. Lustful, manipulative, hero worship. You may have him fooled into believing your innocent act but I see straight through you. Get out!"

I'm flabbergasted. To suggest that I would ever insert myself into someone else's marriage or use my personal pain and grief to manipulate another person is inconceivable.

I look to Dr. Ryan and his shocked face is frozen on his wife. He's silent. No words.

Is he going to come to my defense? Put this psycho bitch in her place? Call for Ashton to come out from behind a bookshelf and tell me I've just been Punk'd?

Seconds pass. Still, silence. Say something. Anything. Please!

"I'll just go." I grab my purse off the couch and push past this incredibly dysfunctional couple, practically sprinting to Lisa's coat rack to grab my jacket and scarf.

The office door slams behind me, and unintelligible yelling carries out into the waiting area. Lisa looks at me, eyes wide, seemingly unable to speak. *You and me both, sister.*

What just happened? And what am I supposed to do now? I try to calm myself down and walk away instead of sprinting, and somehow I manage to say, "Have a good day, Lisa. It was great seeing you."

I'm in shock when I start my car and wait for it to warm up. I don't understand how one of the most encouraging meetings I've ever had turned into a circus with Margaret Ryan as the deranged ring master.

I try to sort through the jumble of accusations thrown at me in the last ten minutes:

1. Hero worshipper
2. Night stalker
3. Emotional Manipulator
4. Seductress
5. Tramp

I don't think any of those will look good on my résumé. I also never thought any of those titles would be attached to my name.

And Dr. Ryan's silence? What even *was* that? He stood there while his wife verbally attacked me and said nothing to defend my character. Defended himself, for sure, but left me hanging out to dry. I mean, I can see now that Margaret Ryan is terrifying, but is he so weak that he can't stand up for an innocent person when they're being wrongfully accused of coming onto a married man?! And she — she's met me maybe three times? Four? That woman doesn't know me at all, so to accuse me of seducing her husband as if she monitors my every interaction with him is absurd.

I have enough shit blowing up in my life right now, and I can't handle one more thing.

Once my car is warmed, I shake my head to clear the internal fiasco and pull out of the parking lot.

When I arrived here today this place was my sanctuary. Little did I know when I left it'd be the last time I ever step foot on this campus.

FOURTEEN

Dexter

I'M SITTING in the lounge chair closest to my office window reading fiction entries in the newest publication of the *Colorado Literary Journal*. But no matter how hard I try to focus I keep rereading the same sentence. I honestly believed I had my thoughts under control concerning Alis, but then we walked into each other and the smell of her perfume overtook me.

A combination of cedarwood, vanilla, and maybe something floral? I have no idea what perfume she uses, but it's intoxicating. Distinctly, Alis. I've never met another woman who wore that same perfume, yet somehow her scent reminds me of an old friend. No one in particular, but the scent calms me and excites me at the same time, making me feel like everything is right in the world. Her lingering scent on my shirt triggers thoughts of the two of us standing close, my hand on her jaw as I was about to kiss her the night we met. I wish I could go back to that moment and freeze time while I bury my nose in her hair and then trail kisses from her earlobe, down her neck, and to her collarbone. I bet her skin tastes as delicious as her scent. Her kiss tasted of vodka and pomegranate lip balm; her lips, full and soft, felt like coming home.

I shake my head and rub my eyes, trying to push thoughts of Alis from my mind. I'm a words man, but I've never mentally articulated personal feelings like this before. My work has never competed for my attention, not even with Laura. When I'm working, I'm working. When I was with Laura, I was with Laura. She had her own compartment in my brain, and she stayed there. I loved her, she was always a priority in my life, but my work was always my favorite pursuit. It's still my favorite pursuit, right?

Focus, man. She's your grader. She won't always be my grader. She won't always be off limits. And I know she wants me just as badly as I want her. Every time she turns me down I can't help but think *her lips say one thing, while her heart says another.* Dumas always did have a way with words. Perfectly poetic truths that cut to the core.

Just as I'm about to give up on reading and work on emails instead, a line in the student author's bio catches my eye: "in collaboration with Dr. Jonathan Ryan, PhD, Grant University." I smile. I haven't seen that man in years. I wonder how he's doing? He and I both presented at the Surrey International Writers' Conference five or six years ago while I was drafting my dissertation. I was stuck in a rut and couldn't dig my way out of writer's block no matter how hard I tried, and one conversation with him cleared away the fog and put me back on track. I would have finished my PhD with or without his advice, but there's no doubt in my mind that our conversation over lunch that day was the catalyst that transformed my research from good to incredible. I've met a few of his pupils at various conferences, and simply having his name attached to their studies has secured them tenured positions at universities across the country.

Oh, to be a disciple of Jonathan Ryan. I laugh to myself. I didn't have the advantage of "who you know" when I began my hunt for a faculty position. The closer I got to finishing and defending, the more anxious I felt about the lack of job prospects coming my way. Finally, I lucked out meeting Abigail Matthews while finishing my PhD in French Literature at the University of Montreal. She served as a guest lecturer in an intensive seminar co-taught by my major professor and ended up serving as an external reader for my dissertation.

I had just finished my first year post-PhD adjunct teaching online for a few universities across Canada when I received a call from Dr. Matthews asking if I'd be interested in teaching at Middle Peak. Their French language professor was set to retire before the beginning of the next academic year and, being the head of the Literature and Languages department, she was tasked with finding his replacement. Originally I had hoped to stay closer to home in Montreal, but teaching here has been a dream come true. I attended undergrad in New England before returning to Canada for graduate school and PhD work, so I was no stranger to America. I can say, however, that eastern culture is vastly different from western. Aside from being in the same country, Rhode Island and Colorado are two different worlds.

My mobile alarm sounds and promptly ends the mental stroll down memory lane. As I stand to gather my things and head to a faculty meeting, I see Alis out my office window. She's walking across campus with Brody Davenport, and she's smiling up at him. I clench my fist at the thought of her cozying up to him, giving him her undivided attention and affection.

Calm down, Dex. They're just walking and talking. People do that. I close my eyes and take a deep breath, releasing the tension that took hold of me at the sight of them together. One, I have no right to feel possessive of her. Two, Brody's a good kid, but he's too young for Alis. He's what, twenty-three? I have no clue. Either way, I don't see Alis being interested in younger men.

It doesn't matter if she is or not, because she's your grader and she turned you down — TWICE. I can't think about this right now. I have five minutes to get across campus for the faculty-wide beginning of the semester meeting and walking in frustrated can only result in a hundred probing questions from Leo about my sour mood.

Just as I arrive at the auditorium door a small hand slides down my arm, caressing my bicep. "Hey, Dex. I haven't seen you in, what, two months?" I cringe at the sound of Savannah's voice but plaster on a smile as I turn to greet her while walking to find a seat.

"Hi, Savannah. Yeah, it's been a while. How have you been?" *Be pleasant. Be kind. Don't be an asshole.*

Her eyes light up at my inquiry. "I've been great! I spent most of the summer traveling …" she shakes her head and laughs, "but you already knew that. I still wish you and Leo had decided to join the group of us in Florida. The beaches were to die for and the little bungalow we stayed in had a private beach just for us. I can't begin to express how incredible it was to lay out in the sun without worrying about tan lines."

Of course, she went there. I don't even know how to respond to that. "Uh, yeah. Sounds like you had a great time. You know why we couldn't tag along, though. Leo and I both had a shit ton of work to do this summer and besides, you went with your sisters. Don't you think it would have been a bit awkward taking a trip, just the five of us?"

I see Leo about halfway down on the left. I lift my chin in acknowledgment and head in his direction. I failed at ending this conversation before it even began, so Savannah follows close behind, speaking quietly so only I can hear.

"I think we could have had a great time," she croons. "And it wasn't just my sisters — a few friends from college came, too. You guys missed out on a week of relaxation, surrounded by topless women. We could have enjoyed the hot tub together, or the outdoor shower."

I swear, this woman is disgustingly forward. I don't want to hear another word about her trip but I also don't want to cause a scene by telling her to fuck off. I stop at the end of Leo's row and, before making my way toward my seat, turn and look down at Savannah.

"Look, Savannah, I'm glad you had a good summer and had fun with your friends in Florida. However, I've told you more than once that I'm not interested and I'd appreciate it if you respect that." Direct, but considerate. I try my best not to beat around the bush when it comes to women, but no matter how many times I say no to her, she still thinks we are going to happen.

She laughs and slaps my arm, no doubt an attempt to make everyone around us think I'm telling her some hilarious anecdote. Her mouth may be laughing but her eyes are … sad? Angry? Resentful? I'm not sure but I think it's some combination of the three.

Gripping my bicep once again — much harder this time; fuck her nails are sharp — she finishes her laughing charade. "Oh, Dexter. You are too much. I'd love to chat some more but I need to go find Jessica. Talk later! Hey, Leo!" Savannah twiddles her fingers his way and then walks off to find her friend and colleague.

Leo looks at me as I sit down next to him, a questioning look on his face. "What was that about?"

"Not worth rehashing. Where's the dean? I have so much to catch up on today; I hope this meeting doesn't drag on."

Leo drops his voice, impersonating our ancient dean of faculty who speaks slower than a turtle crawls. "Ladies and gentlemen, thank you all for coming today. It's always a pleasure to begin a new semester surrounded by such competent faculty and staff."

I shake my head, rubbing my forehead. "One day he's going to hear you and then you'll be fucked. You know that, right?"

Before Leo can respond, Dr. Daniels clears his throat in the podium microphone, calling all to attention. "Ladies and gentlemen, thank you all for coming today …"

As I walk back into my office suite nearly an hour later, I see Deborah typing away at her desktop. I swear that woman is like the Energizer Bunny. I've never seen fingers fly across a keyboard as quickly as hers.

"Deborah, have you already set up my weekly meetings with Alis Gilmore?" She looks up at me, pushing her sliding glasses up her nose.

"Not yet. She took my card and said she'd reach out, but I'm happy to email her and get them on your calendar if you'd like." Yes, I would like. I would like very, very much. The sooner the better.

"Perfect. I know Wednesdays I have an hour open for lunch. Can you put her down for 11:30 and tell her to meet me at Nico's?"

Deborah eyes me suspiciously. "Nico's? Isn't that place packed during the lunch rush? How are you supposed to have a productive meeting surrounded by frat kids with no concept of volume control?"

I rub my chin. "Good point." But I want to share a meal with her. A non-date meal, of course. Strictly professional.

"They deliver around campus, right?" Deborah opens a drawer to her right and shuffles through a stack of menus. This glorious woman is always prepared for anything. She finds the Nico's trifold and scans the front page from top to bottom.

"Yep. Thin crust, pepperoni and bacon?"

I smile at her. "You know me so well. What would I do without you?"

She smirks. "Forget every meeting, be late for class, walk around with coffee stains on your shirt. My ability to remember superfluous details like your topping preferences should garner me a raise, yeah?"

"You know I would if I could. Next time we do employee evals I'll drop a hint to Matthews, sound good?"

"Most definitely. And until then, Dr. Belanger, don't forget I accept gifts of appreciation in the form of coffee and breakfast pastries."

I wink at her before heading to my office. "Only for you, Deb. You're a gem."

"A diamond!" she hollers at my back as I enter my office and close the door behind me.

FIFTEEN

Alis

"THAT'S ALL FOR TODAY. Make sure to grab a hard copy of the syllabus on your way out if you don't already have one, and don't forget to complete this week's reading before our next class." I disconnect my laptop from the lecture hall media before shutting it down and gathering my things into my messenger bag. *Not bad for my first time teaching in a decade.*

Teaching is home for me. Until this morning I didn't realize just how displaced I've felt since I left school. Maybe displaced isn't the right word. I've just focused so much of my energy on other people for so long. Now that I'm doing something for myself, it feels like I'm breathing new air, seeing brighter colors.

I don't regret leaving school to raise Sunny. I don't regret moving home, working at the bookstore, or living with my parents. I needed time after Belle died — not just to adjust to motherhood, but also to grieve my best friend.

Sliding my messenger bag over my shoulder, I turn to walk toward the door when I see Brody sitting in the front row near the podium. He has an athletic build, which I find strange for an English major. Today he's wearing a light blue button down with the sleeves rolled up his forearms and khaki pants that hug his muscular thighs. Brody really is a good looking guy. He's also twenty-five, so just … no. If ever the day comes that I meet a man I want to spend the rest of my life with, I highly doubt he will be younger than I am. I had to grow up at warp speed when I became a mother overnight, and considering men tend to mature much slower than women, I doubt I'll meet a younger man I'd want as my life partner.

Brody's sporting a half smile and he quickly scans my body before he meets my eyes. "Hey." *Does he really think I didn't notice him checking me out?*

"Hey. I didn't hear you come in." I hope I sound friendly and not flirty. I really don't want to give this guy the wrong idea.

"Yeah, your students were filing out when I slipped in so you probably couldn't hear me over the commotion. Ready for your tour?" He stands from the seat and gestures for me to walk ahead of him.

"Sure. Sounds good. I thought this morning we planned to meet by the gazebo?" I ask innocently as I pass by him on the way to the door.

"I know we did, but I remembered you mentioned teaching this class before our tour and I decided to fetch you here instead." I can't see his face, but I'm positive his tone is flirtatious. Also, did he just say 'fetch'? Am I a pail of water? Who uses the word 'fetch' outside of talking to a dog? Bro, you are definitely not going to make 'fetch' happen. *Regina, you'd be so proud of me right now.*

We exit the room and turn down the hallway toward the exit. I am stuck in my head right now, assessing his flirtatious tone and strange word choice, so we walk in uncomfortable silence. I think he's waiting for me to say something. I turn and look up at him and he's already looking at me.

"So, uh, where do we begin?" I ask, adjusting my bag strap and plastering on a fake smile like I'm not an awkward turtle.

For the next hour Brody guides me around campus, pointing out the different department and classroom buildings, the library, the small plaza that includes a Barnes & Noble, the campus coffee shop, and a few eateries. The campus truly is beautiful. It's not as old as Grant, so it lacks the detailed late-nineteenth century architecture I love so much. Middle Peak is full of sharp angles and glass — super sleek, super modern. Even if I was unfamiliar with MPU's emphasis on the arts, I'd no doubt feel their importance from the twenty or so sculptures erected in various places around campus. I love that no two sculptures are alike — of the few I've seen so far, the one that most takes my breath away is a tribute to the Ludlow Massacre of 1914. The sculpture depicts a coal miner, hunched over with exhaustion, being held by a young child dressed in contemporary clothing.

"Wow," I breathe, staring in awe at the sculpture. "I've never seen so much pain and gratitude captured in one piece of art."

"It really is spectacular," Brody comments. "Did you know the Ludlow Massacre was the catalyst for child labor laws and the eight-hour workday limitation?"

I look up at Brody, perplexed. "No, I didn't. That's really interesting, though. I haven't given it much thought, but I probably would have guessed factory workers on the east coast would have fought to implement them."

"Nope. It was coal miners in Ludlow." Brody looks over at me with a pensive expression on his face. "I wonder if anyone outside Colorado ever learns about that in American history?"

"No idea," I shrug. "I've only ever lived here and I think we learned about Ludlow in middle school."

"Here?" he asks, "I thought you said you were new to the area?"

"Here, as in, Colorado. I grew up about four hours from here. Small town."

"Gotcha," he nods. "I'm from Colorado Springs. Spent my whole life there until I moved here for college; then decided to stay for grad school."

"Cool." I have no idea what to say from here. Why can't I be better at carrying a conversation? *It's not difficult with Dexter.* Shut up, brain!

Awkward silence settles between us as we continue walking

around campus until I pull my phone from my pocket to check the time.

"Shoot. I'm sorry to cut this short, but I gotta run." I look up at Brody apologetically. "I have to meet someone in ten minutes across campus and I don't want to be late."

Brody looks confused. "Meet someone? I thought we were supposed to have lunch at Nico's after the tour?" Ah, shit. I knew I forgot something. I saw the email from Deborah about meeting with Dexter — no, Dr. Belanger — yesterday and said yes without even thinking about lunch with Brody. Then, once I realized I was double booked, I made a mental note to tell Brody this morning in class. That mental note apparently flew right out of my brain as soon as it entered.

"I'm so sorry, I forgot to tell you earlier." I hope he can see the sincerity in my eyes. "I'm grading for a few different professors this semester and one of them needs to meet with me at 11:30 today."

Brody relaxes and looks relieved that I'm not ditching him just to get out of spending time with him. Then, he gives me a soft smile and pivots toward east campus where the Languages and Literature offices are located. "No problem. I'll walk you. We can grab lunch another day. Which profs are you grading for?"

"Matthews, Miller, and Belanger." Brody's eyebrows raise. "Damn, woman. That's a load, yeah?"

I laugh. "It is, but it's not too bad so far. I only have to teach for Matthews — the other two just needed a grader."

Brody still looks concerned at my workload rather than appeased. "Seems like working for Matthews would be a fulltime job in itself. I can't imagine adding two more profs on top of that. And Belanger — doesn't he teach French? That can't be easy. Don't let them take advantage of you, okay? You don't want to burn out in your first semester."

His concern is sweet, but also unnecessary. "I appreciate you looking out for me, but I promise I have everything under control. I'm only taking one class this semester so I could pace myself while readjusting to grad school. I don't have much of a social life, so it's not like I'll be neglecting any friends with the extra work. Besides, Miller only teaches online courses and most of her stuff is automated. And Belanger only teaches a few classes so it's not really a burden."

Brody laughs and kicks a pinecone off the walking path and into the grass. "Ok, Miss Badass. I think you underestimate how difficult grading for a foreign language prof can be. I graded for Dr. Morales before he retired and working through student translations was exhausting. Don't come to me for help mid-French translation because I can't even count to ten."

"You speak Spanish?" I ask, readjusting my messenger bag strap so it doesn't cut into the side of my neck.

Brody shrugs his shoulders. "Kind of, yeah. I'm not fluent or anything but I can read it well. I've never been able to hear it, you know? So conversational Spanish is a no-go. As long as you can read French, I'm sure you can pull off grading for Belanger."

I don't want to lie and pretend like French is a challenge for me, but I also don't want to embarrass Brody by brushing off his encouragement as if I'm somehow better than he was as a foreign languages grader. I settle for a middle ground.

"I should be good then," I say and smile up at him. I elbow his arm playfully. "I'll definitely vent to you if it turns out to be *une prise de tête*. Misery loves company and all."

Brody chuckles as he shakes his head. "I have no idea what you just said, but I'm assuming it's French."

"I'd hope so, otherwise I'm grading for the wrong professor!"

We laugh and talk some more, eventually making it to the Languages and Literature building. Just as I'm about to pull open the door and bid farewell to Brody, he reaches around and opens it for me, ushering me in before closing it behind himself. *Oh, so when he said he'd walk me he meant all the way to Dr. Belanger's office. Just what I need — to show up with another man.*

As we enter Pod A, I find Deborah kneeling in a supply closet behind her desk. I don't want to startle her, but by the way she's huffing and talking to herself I deduce she needs help finding something. I set my bag down with a thump to signal my presence before speaking.

"Do you need help finding something, Deborah?" I ask. She sits up suddenly, smacking the top of her head on the shelf above her. So much for not startling her.

I rush around her desk and squat next to her inside the closet, placing my hand on her arm while she rubs her head with the other. "Are you okay? I'm so sorry I caught you off guard. I didn't mean to scare you."

"Oh, Aurora. It's so nice to see you again. I know I have a package of paper plates somewhere in this closet, but they seem to have sprouted feet and walked away."

"Paper plates? Do you need them for a meeting or something? I can grab some from the store after my meeting if you need them today," I offer. "And please, call me Alis."

"Alis, yes. We should contact IT and have them change the name on your student email account so it's easier to remember. And you are so sweet for offering, but I actually need them for your lunch meeting that starts in," she looks down at the watch on her wrist, "four minutes."

As I help Deborah back to her feet, I hear Brody's voice just as he presses up against my back and reaches over my head to a higher shelf. "Found 'em."

He grabs the unopened package of paper plates and hands them to Deborah before the three of us exit the walk-in supply closet.

"Oh! Brody! So nice to see you." Deborah beams at him affection-ately. "How are you, dear? How's Rebecca? I haven't seen that girl since before summer break. She didn't graduate, did she?"

Brody rubs the back of his neck, suddenly looking very uncom-fortable. "It's nice to see you, too. I've been good. And no, Rebecca won't graduate for another year and a half. I actually haven't spoken to her in a few months, but I assume she's well."

Deborah gives Brody a sympathetic smile and pats his arm. "I'm sorry to hear things didn't work out."

Before Brody can respond, Dexter walks out of his office and sees our trio talking in the waiting area. More specifically, he zeroes in on Brody standing to my right. He tightens his jaw before forcing a smile that doesn't reach his eyes.

Walking toward us, Dexter extends his hand in greeting. "Brody, I didn't expect to see you today."

Brody accepts his hand and offers a warm smile. "Dr. Belanger, it's great to see you, sir. I was just showing Alis around campus when I found out you commandeered my lunch date for a work meeting." *Seriously, Brody? Date? Why the heck would you say that?*

I laugh, awkwardly, not sure what to say in response to Dexter's penetrating gaze and quirked eyebrow. *Even his frustrated face is hot.*

Brody releases Dexter's hand and turns to place a hand on the small of my back. *We're touching now. Why are we touching?* Quirked eyebrow gone; I feel the full force of his glare. *Still hot, though much more intimidating.*

"I'll see you later, yeah?" Brody slowly moves his hand, grazing his fingers a bit before completely backing away. He no doubt felt how my body tensed as soon as he made contact. I try to smile at him and nod, but I'm pretty sure I just look constipated.

"Um, yeah. See you later." I grasp my messenger bag strap tightly, rotating my grip back and forth to channel the nervous energy into my hands instead of my words. Brody winks at me before saying goodbye to Deborah and heading out of the pod and back into the hallway.

I look up at Dexter, and he looks pissed. He has no reason to be. We aren't dating — he's one of my bosses for crying out loud. He's a professor, and I'm a student. And if I decide to date anyone else it's really none of his business. I thought I drew the line in the sand and he had decided to respect my boundaries. Based on the possessive, jealous look in his eyes, I was mistaken.

Awesome. This meeting should be *loads* of fun.

SIXTEEN

Dexter

I DIDN'T EXPECT to find Brody with Alis when I stepped out to ask Deborah if she found the plates I requested a few minutes ago. Why is he here? Why is he standing so close to her? *Pull your shit together, Dexter. Now is not the time to act like a jealous boyfriend.* I'm not her boyfriend. I'm her boss. Kind of; not really. She's my grader. That's all. For now.

I walk toward them and extend my hand in greeting. "Brody, I didn't expect to see you today."

Brody shakes my hand, smiling in a way that conveys he does not register the frustration emanating from my eyes. "Dr. Belanger, it's great to see you, sir. I was just showing Alis around campus when I found out you commandeered my lunch date for a work meeting."

I look at Alis with a quirked eyebrow that says, *Date?*

She laughs, clearly uncomfortable, and Brody releases his grip and moves his hand to the small of her back. *The fuck?!*

She looks stunning today in a navy blue sundress and yellow flats. I've noticed since her first day on campus that she has an eccentric sense of style — especially pertaining to those yellow shoes. Other than the night I met her in those sexy as fuck strappy heels, every time I've seen her she's wearing brightly colored footwear.

Her long blonde hair is in a low ponytail, its waves trailing halfway down her back. *The back another man is currently touching.*

I don't hear their goodbyes; I'm too busy trying to control the rage welling up inside me at the sight of another man touching Alis. My only consolation right now is that she is clearly startled by his misplaced hand. Her body tenses and she pushes her glasses up her nose, averting her eyes as best she can. *Ok, so either she doesn't welcome his touch or she doesn't want him touching her in front of me.*

Next thing I know, Deborah pushes a few paper plates into my hand. From the nudge she gives me, I deduce she tried to get my attention and I didn't hear her first attempt. I remove my gaze from where Brody's hand was moments before and look at Deborah with an appreciative smile.

"Thanks, Deborah. Alis?" I nod my head toward my door and turn to walk into my office. I need to gather myself before I look at Alis again. I told her these meetings would be strictly professor/grader, and I can't renege on that five seconds into our first meeting by asking about her relationship with Brody.

She's my grader. She's my grader. She's my grader. I scan the room as I reach one of the chairs in my office, setting the plates next to the pizza box on the coffee table before gesturing for Alis to take the chair next to me.

"Thanks," she says, setting her bag on the floor next to the chair before sitting down.

I still haven't looked at her, busying myself with opening the pizza box and making sure I didn't forget to grab the napkins off my desk. When I have no reason to keep looking down at the table, I look up at Alis and offer her a plate. "I assumed you'd be fine with pizza for lunch. Nico's has the best pizza in town and it's conveniently right across campus."

She takes the plate and then reaches to pull a slice from the box. "Pizza is great, thanks." Once she has her pizza, I motion toward the water bottles on the other side of the table and she takes one, wedging it between her thigh and the chair.

We eat without talking for a few minutes, and she's the one to break the silence. "This is delicious. I was originally supposed to eat at Nico's for lunch today so this was a pleasant surprise. I didn't have to miss out."

Well, if she is going to bring Brody into this conversation then it'd be rude not to acknowledge his unwelcome presence in my office. Happy to oblige.

"Brody was going to take you to Nico's?" I ask, careful to keep any trace of accusation or jealousy out of my tone.

She nods, blotting her mouth with her napkin before responding. "Yeah, he offered to show me around campus today."

"And then out to lunch." It's a statement, not a question. She narrows her eyes the slightest bit. Dammit, I guess my tone isn't as impassive as I thought.

"Yep." She pops the 'p' and takes another bite of her pizza, not offering any other explanation. Why does she do that? She did the same thing the first time we talked in my office — shut down a line of questioning with a single word, leaving me without anything more.

Do I push for details or let it go? The man in me wants to know why the hell she'd be having lunch with Brody when she shut me down with the excuse that now is not a good time for her to get involved with anyone. The professor in me reminds the man that this is a work meeting and it's none of my business who she dates.

After being blindsided seeing Brody's hand touching Alis, I garner what's left of my self control and shove the jealous man aside. *She's my grader. She's my grader. This is a grader meeting.*

I stand and walk toward my desk, disposing of my plate and napkin in the bin. I decide to sit in my desk chair, creating more space between us and thus enforcing the professional nature of this meeting.

"Oh, I'm sorry. I thought we were meeting here." She gestures around the seating area.

"Take your time. I'm just pulling up some notes about this week's assignments. You can move over here when you're finished eating." I don't want her to feel rushed; I just needed the barrier between us to keep myself from venturing into personal conversation. She asked for professional; I can be professional.

She finishes her lunch and disposes of her plate and napkin, opening her water bottle and taking a sip before she reaches into her bag and pulls out a notebook and pen.

"I see you brought your own writing materials this time." I grin at her and she rolls her eyes before sitting in the chair across from me.

"Figured asking you for a notepad would be a lost cause." Cheeky. Alis's eyes twinkle playfully, something I wasn't expecting from her.

"*N'importe quoi. Ta gueule, casse-couilles,*" I snap back. Alis snort-laughs just as she takes a sip of her water. That laugh is so unbearably cute.

"Ah!" She covers her mouth and nose with her hand, still laughing. "Now I've got water in my nose!"

"That tends to happen when one acts like a smartass." She just shakes her head, still laughing, clearly sensing my teasing tone. Adopting my professorial demeanor, I say, "Alright, Miss Gilmore, we have work to discuss."

"*Je suis prête.*" She crosses her legs and opens her notebook, pen poised and ready.

Thirty minutes later, Alis stands to pack her things. Our meeting has finished, but I'm not ready for her to leave. She bids me adieu and heads out, gently closing the office door behind her.

While going over upcoming assignments and grading deadlines we fell into an easy rapport, bantering back and forth like old friends. I get along with others pretty easily, but with her it feels so much deeper than cordiality. Her smile is warm, her eyes alluring, and that tongue of hers — sharp as a tack. I haven't had the opportunity to banter back and forth in my mother tongue for the past three years. Sure, I have students who speak French incredibly well, but Alis's fluency in French colloquialisms is incredible. I wonder how she learned those? Maybe she spent some time in France or Quebec?

When we spoke last week she alluded to a life circumstance that took her away from graduate work. I can only guess at what happened. Maybe she had to care for a sick parent? Financial responsibilities? Has she spent the past few years traveling? That would explain her pristine French. Perhaps she endured a painful breakup? No. Alis doesn't seem like the type of woman to walk away from academic aspirations due to a broken heart.

I continue to ponder what could have changed the course of her life so drastically until a knock sounds at my office door and I'm startled out of my wandering thoughts.

Just as I stand to walk toward the door and open it, my visitor lets himself in, plops into an armchair, and greets me with, "Bro, you are not going to believe the day I've had."

I take the seat next to him, wave my hand in his direction and say sarcastically, "Please, come in. I'm not in the middle of working or anything."

He scoffs. "Just give me ten minutes, okay? I've had the day from hell and it's not even 2 p.m." His hair is disheveled, a sure sign he's been pulling at it.

"Pizza?" I tilt my head toward the box in offering.

"Fuck yes. I'm starved." Leo grabs a slice from the box along with a napkin and begins shoveling it into his mouth.

I check my watch and see that it's 1:17. I teach a class at 2 so I guess I can give him a few minutes of undivided attention.

"I'm walking out of this office at 1:45, which gives you twenty-eight minutes to vent. Proceed."

Confirming my earlier suspicion, Leo runs his hands through his hair, clearly frustrated at whatever he's experienced the last few hours. Then, with his face in his hands, he mumbles, "She called."

"She?"

Leo looks up. And for the first time since he arrived I see, pain? His eyes begin to water before he sinks his face back into his hands and lets out an agonizing sob. *Whoa.*

Just as I reach to squeeze his shoulder he says, "Stephanie." My hand freezes.

I retract my hand and lean forward, elbows on my thighs. Stephanie hasn't come up in more than a year. "The fuck?! Why the hell is your ex-wife calling you? What did she want?" I stand to retrieve the tissue box off my desk and hand it to Leo.

As I sit back down, Leo pulls a tissue out of the box and blows his nose before grabbing another and wiping his eyes.

"She and her high school has-been are having problems, and she wanted me to help her sort it out. She was upset and crying and I didn't know what to say. I was in shock that she called in the first place, and when she asked for my advice I didn't know what to do. It's not that I want her back — hell will freeze over before that happens — but part of me will always love her, and I hate that she's hurting." Hurting? Her? What about Leo? Doesn't she realize that calling him will only hurt him? That bitch tore him apart and left him in pieces, and now she's running to him to help save her new marriage? The marriage that began as an affair and demolished her marriage to Leo?

I lean forward and clasp my hands, elbows back on my thighs. I need to choose my next words wisely, because I don't want to add insult to injury. However, the fact that he feels one iota of responsibility to help her sort through her shit makes me want to slap him upside the head.

"Leo, it is not your responsibility, nor your place, to offer marriage advice to your ex-wife. I know you care for her, but she doesn't deserve a second of your time or concern." I may give him a hard time for acting like a callous frat boy, working through his anger one Tinder hookup at a time, but I'll take that man-child over a sobbing, broken friend any day of the week.

Leo nods his head while staring down at the wet tissues in his hands. "I know. At first I was sympathetic but I think my response was triggered by shock. I haven't spoken to her since the divorce was finalized, and to hear from her a year and a half later caught me off guard. I've been stewing on this all morning, growing more pissed by the second. She has the nerve to call me? Does she think I'm a fucking idiot? That I don't see through her bullshit? This is exactly how she lit the fuse that blew up our marriage. She confided in her punk ass ex about our private issues. Who the fuck does that?"

He pauses and looks at me, rage added to the pain in his eyes. His chest rises and falls, he squeezes his eyes shut and begins spearing his fingers through his hair again. When he doesn't say anything after nearly thirty seconds, I assume he wants an answer to his rhetorical question. "Stephanie. Stephanie does that. And you're no fool, so you won't fall for her manipulation."

"Fuck no I won't!" Leo yells. I gesture for him to keep the volume down and he continues. "God, Dex, you should have heard her. She said they have the same fights we used to have; like it's déjà vu or something. I told her I'm sorry she's having a hard time but I'm not the person she should be talking to about it. It was like she didn't hear a word I said. She started yelling about Justin being selfish and lamenting about how she's underappreciated — you know how she is."

And I do. I know exactly how she is because being Leo's confidant meant I had a front row seat when all their shit hit the fan.

"Well, what did you say to her when she finished her rant?" I ask.

"Nothing. I hung up on her mid-sentence. I have no fucking clue what else she said."

Atta boy. "I think you made the right call. Has she reached out any more since this morning?"

Leo nods, looking exhausted. "Yeah. Like three more times. I sent her to voicemail each time."

"Have you considered blocking her number?"

"I hadn't before today. It never crossed my mind to block her. She just stayed away after signing the papers. I didn't think I'd ever hear from her again. When I saw her name on my caller ID, I answered without thinking. Then when I heard her sobbing I thought maybe something had happened to her dad. I'm still close with George and Linda, so if his cancer spread or something I'd expect a call."

I rub my chin, pondering whether or not he should block her

number. "Would Linda contact you if something were to happen to George?"

He shrugs. "I mean, Linda and I never had any issues. I assume she'd call me but I'm not certain. Why?"

"I'm trying to think through the best way to rid yourself of Stephanie without cutting out her father. If you block her number and something ever did happen to George, she wouldn't be able to reach you. I guess I'm wondering if Linda would think to call you in the same circumstance. If that's the case, then you don't have anything to worry about by blocking Stephanie. However, if she won't keep you in the loop and you found out George passed from an online obituary or something, I know that would crush you."

Leo's eyes fill with tears and I know he's thinking about losing the only true father figure he's ever known. "He's more of a dad to me than my own piece of shit father ever was. He stood by me when Stephanie's affair came out and all through our divorce. I don't visit him at their house anymore, but we talk at least once a month. He never talks about his cancer and whether or not the treatments are working. Every time I ask he brushes me off and says, 'Son, don't you worry about this old man' as if his illness is not something I should worry about. It fucking kills me not knowing how much longer he has left. If he's getting better or worse."

"Shit, man. I didn't realize you talked that often." I'm seriously dumbfounded by this revelation. "I knew you guys were close when you were married to Stephanie and that he's still important to you, but I didn't realize you talk to him regularly. Isn't that uncomfortable? I'm sure Stephanie's name comes up in your conversations."

Leo lets out a huff and shakes his head. "Never. We talk about literally everything but Stephanie. He hasn't mentioned her to me since everything was finalized."

"Damn. That man must really love you."

A sad smile stretches across Leo's face and he nods. "Yeah. He does. Like his own son."

The smile disappears and Leo rubs the heels of his hands into his eyes, trying but failing to rid himself of the clusterfuck of emotions running through his mind at this very moment. "I don't know, man. She just caught me off guard and I don't know how to process this curveball."

I nod to show I'm here for him, but keep my mouth shut. I don't know how I would react to a call from an adulterous ex. I haven't spoken to Laura in six years, but she never cheated on me — not that I'm aware of, at least. I'd like to think if she called or if we ever ran into each other we'd have a slightly awkward, yet cordial, conversation.

Suddenly I start to feel claustrophobic with Leo's varying emotions encircling my sitting area. "Let's table this discussion and grab a coffee. I now have nineteen minutes before class and the Java Hut is on the way."

Leo looks relieved that I'm forcing his attention away from his inner turmoil. "Sounds good. Talk to me about something good. Something light. Hockey. Talk to me about the Canadiens."

I laugh as we stand, grab my things, and we head out of my office. "You hate the Canadiens."

"I hate Stephanie more." Leo pushes open the door to exit the building and we walk down the steps and toward a much-needed caffeine fix.

"Touché. Considering it's the end of August I have just as little to report about my team as you do about the Canes." I shrug and pull my keys out of my front trouser pocket, hooking the ring around my finger before flipping them around in my palm. Leo hates when I do this, so hopefully channeling his annoyance into his biggest pet peeve will distract him from thoughts of Stephanie. "I don't have much going on right now that's worth talking about."

Leo gives me the side eye, then looks down at my hand and rolls his eyes. I'm surprised he doesn't slap my keys out of my hand to stop my fidgeting.

"What about the hot grader? Any movement on that front?" Nope. Not unless you count my ever growing jealousy toward a certain man-child who had his hands on her earlier today.

"Nothing to report," I shrug again, keeping my eyes fixed on the brick pathway before us. Leo's not buying it.

"You know you're full of shit, right? As soon as I mentioned her you stopped flipping your keys around and got all tense. What happened?" Damn. Someone's an observant mother fucker today.

I let out a sharp breath, trying to decide which details to share and which to hold back. Maybe if I give him an inch, he'll be satisfied.

"Considering I told you about her a little over a week ago and hadn't seen or spoken to her again until this week, I really don't have anything to report other than I think she's going to be an awesome grader. I'm thankful I won't have to do it myself this semester. When Matthews announced the budget cuts to our department and said she couldn't hire any more TAs, I thought I'd be grading everything myself. None of the TAs in our department speak French, and I didn't realize Matthews' new TA was fluent. She literally sent me an email about Alis an hour before she brought her to my office to introduce us."

"Oh, sweet. She speaks French?" Leo looks surprised by this revelation.

"I teach *French*, so it would obviously be necessary for my grader to know the language, don't you think?" Dumbass.

"Well, I mean, I guess. But I thought this semester you're teaching more English than French. I guess I assumed she'd cover your English stuff and leave the *bonjour, merci, si vu ple* to you."

We arrive at the coffee shop and, thankfully, the line is short. I check my watch again before saying, "Your French is shit, my friend."

Leo laughs and says, "It'd be better if someone would teach it to me."

"You only want to know curse words and come-ons. I'm not wasting my time teaching you French just so you can fulfill some stupid Don Juan fantasy."

Leo shrugs, unperturbed and all but confirming my accusation. "Don Juan is a legend. And he was Spanish, not French."

Before I can respond, the barista asks, "What can I get you today?"

Without even glancing at the menu, Leo orders for us. "One small black coffee with room for cream and a large white mocha with extra syrup." He slaps me on the back and says, "He's paying." *Of course, I am.*

After paying I venture to the other side of the bar to wait for our order. Before Leo can continue his questioning about Alis, I divert his attention with questions about how his classes are going. He's mid-complaint about some aloof freshman when the barista sets my coffee and his sugar-coma-in-a-cup on the pickup counter. I don't know how he drinks that shit. It's straight sugar *before* adding extra syrup. The day he is diagnosed diabetic, I'll remind him it was his own doing.

I'm glad he's talking about his new students so I can just listen and sip my coffee as we walk to the auditorium where I teach my one undergrad course. The class is a Wednesday block, so this is my first time meeting the students. Based on Leo's never-ending list of annoying behaviors from the freshmen in his college algebra class, I'm in for a treat.

We stop at the entrance to the building and I pat Leo's shoulder before walking inside. "Thanks for the heads up, man. I get to spend the next three hours with those same freshmen."

Leo calls from behind me, "At least you get it over and done with! I spend three days a week with them!"

I laugh to myself and walk into the auditorium, fortifying myself before facing the eighty students in this class.

SEVENTEEN

Alis

THE NEXT SIX weeks fly by without incident, thank God. Dexter keeps our weekly meetings professional, but friendly, which makes me more drawn to him as time passes. I'm honestly surprised that he hasn't asked me out or made any suggestive comments, nor has he shown any more jealousy toward Brody whenever he sees us together. Brody and I are just friends, but I neither confirm nor deny our lack of romantic connection to Dexter.

I'm careful not to let any conversations venture into my personal life because I know that will lead to knowing more personal information about him, which will in turn make me want him even more. I'm already using every ounce of self-control not to let my ever-growing feelings show.

That control tends to slip late at night when I'm alone in bed. Especially on weekly professor-grader meeting days. Spending time in his presence lights a fire in my core, and by the end of the day, I'm literally aching for relief between my legs. I swear, my vibrator has gotten more use in the last few months than it had the previous however many years.

I may not be an overtly sexual person by nature, but even I have to get myself off every once in a while. (Read: daily.) I don't know if some switch flips when a woman hits thirty or if it's Dexter's proximity, but my libido has become hyperactive since moving to Grand River.

I'm walking out of one of the campus coffee shops, heading to my Wednesday morning class, when my phone rings. I fish it out of my messenger bag and see a local number I don't recognize. I keep forgetting to program Sunny's school into my contacts, so I answer the call just in case it's about her.

"Hello? This is Alis."

"Hi, Miss Gilmore. This is Ms. Johnson from Peakside Elementary School."

Good thing I answered. "Hi, Ms. Johnson, is everything alright with Sunny?"

"We've had a stomach virus spreading among our students and Sunny is showing symptoms. We'll need you to come get her."

Of course. I have to teach after this class. I can't remember Skye's schedule today, but maybe she'll be okay to call out? It's easier for her to miss a day of work than it is for me to get my class covered on such short notice. Not that her job isn't important.

"Yes, I can do that. Will you please let her know that either myself or my roommate will be there to pick her up as soon as possible?"

"Yes, ma'am. I'll let her know. I'm assuming your roommate is on Sunny's approved check-out roster?"

"Yes. Her name is Skye Kennedy. She's listed as an emergency contact."

"Sounds good. We'll see you soon."

"Thank you, goodbye."

As soon as I disconnect the call, I scroll to my favorites and call Skye. *Please pick up. Please oh please oh please pick up.*

"Sup, honey pot?" Honey pot? That's a new one.

"Hey, are you busy right now?"

"If kicking ass and taking names barista-style is busy, then, yes. Why? What's up?"

Thank God she answered even though she's working. "Sunny's school just called and said she caught some stomach virus that's been going around. Someone needs to pick her up and take her home. I wouldn't typically ask you to ditch work to retrieve her, but I'm teaching in a little more than an hour and I don't even know where to begin to find a replacement. I haven't met any of the other TAs in my department, and Dr. Matthews teaches another class at this time, so I can't ask her."

Skye pops her gum in my ear. "No problem. I'll head out now. Is she puking? Do I need to bring a bag or something so she doesn't puke all over my car on the drive home?"

"I have no idea. The lady who called didn't give details, and I forgot to ask because my mind was all caught up in figuring out whether I should miss class or call you. I'm assuming stomach virus includes throwing up, so better to be safe than sorry?"

"Ten-four good buddy. Do I need to swing by the pharmacy or anything?" *What would I do without this woman?!* Easy. I'd die.

"I'll put in a drive-up order for Gatorade, soup, crackers, and Pepto. I'll let you know when it's ready."

"Cool beans. I'll call you when I have her with an update."

"You're the best." That's an understatement.

"Truth."

I laugh. She's a mess. "Thank you!"

"Ciao, mama."

Skye ends the call and I see that I have three minutes to get to class. *Shit, I can't be late again.*

I sprint toward my classroom, thankful that I've now mastered the maze from the front door to the auditorium. I swear, whoever designed this building was an idiot. I pull open the door just as the clock strikes 8 a.m. and take my seat next to Brody.

I breeze through class and then teaching, thankful to then head home to check on Sunny. I'm halfway home when I remember my weekly meeting with Dexter is today. *Dammit.* I totally forgot.

Not one to text and drive, I wait until I hit a red light before scrolling through my contacts to find Deborah's office number. I'd prefer not to call Dexter directly, especially since I don't have his office number, just his mobile. *At least he's no longer listed as Sexy Dexy.*

The phone starts to ring and my eyes are back on the road when the light turns green.

"Foreign Languages, this is Deborah." I hear the *click click click* of her keyboard in the background.

"Hey, Deborah. It's Alis. Something came up and I need to cancel my meeting with Dr. Belanger this week."

"Everything okay?" she inquires.

"Just dealing with some sickness so I'm heading home. Can you let him know I can't make it? He can email me whatever deadlines he wants to discuss."

"Sure thing, dear. Get some rest and feel better. Goodbye."

Deborah hangs up before I can say anything else, and I'm glad I didn't have to provide more explanation. I don't hide Sunny from anyone, but I prefer to keep the personal and professional separate when possible. Dr. Matthews knows about Sunny and I think I told her I'd bring her with me to campus one day, but considering I'm only on campus while Sunny is in school, that won't happen any time soon.

As I walk through the front door to our apartment I'm greeted with the cringeworthy sound of my daughter vomiting her stomach contents into the toilet. I drop my bag on the entry table and walk to the washroom, kneeling next to Sunny and rubbing her back.

"I'm so sorry, Sunshine. I'm home now and I'll stay with you."

I see tears streaming down Sunny's face as she coughs and spits to rid her mouth of lingering stomach acid. I hate seeing my sweet girl in this state. She becomes overly emotional when she isn't feeling well, and it breaks my heart to see her so emotionally and physically distraught at the same time.

Sunny squeezes her eyes shut, still crying, and croaks, "My throat hurts."

I start to push her hair back from her face and feel her scorching hot forehead in the process. "I know, baby. I'm so sorry. We'll get you a popsicle after you rinse out your mouth, okay?"

Sunny nods and lets out a few sobs into the toilet. "It was so embarrassing. I threw up all over my lap in front of the entire class. Hailey and her friends made fun of me and the boys started laughing and making fake gagging noises."

Kids are assholes, I swear. I resume rubbing her back, letting her have this moment to be upset. I know she doesn't want me to say it'll be okay or that I'm sorry. She's a lot like me in that she wants to get all her frustration and feelings out, but she wants to sort through them herself. Still, I wish I could slap the snot out of those kids in her class. Any one of them could have found themselves in the same situation, and I'm positive they'd hate to be bullied right after getting sick in front of everyone.

"I'm going to grab a wet washcloth for your face, alright?" Sunny nods in affirmation and I stand to grab a washcloth out of the linen closet. I soak it in cool water before wringing out the excess and then hand it to Sunny, who is now sitting back on her heels, head out of the toilet bowl. She looks absolutely miserable.

"Do you want to take a shower or a bath?" I ask. "It might help you to feel a bit better. It'll have to be lukewarm at best, though, because you're burning up and we can't risk your temperature getting any higher."

Sunny shakes her head, wiping the last bit of tears, sweat, and sickness off her skin. "Not right now. Can I just go to bed?"

"Of course. Let's get some medicine in you and then you can take a nap."

The poor girl's eyelids are heavy and swollen from crying. "Skye just gave me some pink chalky stuff and I think Tylenol or something."

"When?" I ask.

"I don't know. Ask her," Sunny moans, arms crossed over her bent knees, face buried.

I go to stand up to do just that when my foot catches on the edge of the bathroom rug and I trip and stumble face-first into the hallway.

"Ah!" I yell, throwing my arms out before me to catch myself.

Skye's door swings open and she sticks her head out, looks down at the back of my head that is currently face-first in the carpet in front of her feet, and busts out laughing.

"Gravity's a bitch, right?" she snickers. Sometimes I wish her default responses were helpful instead of antagonistic. However, then she wouldn't be Skye.

I roll over onto my back and stare up at her. *"Are you ok, Alis? Did you hit your face on anything? Can I help in any way?"* I deadpan. Just as she's about to spew out another snarky comment, Sunny gags and pushes back onto her knees, hugging the toilet as she vomits once again. *How does she even have anything left to throw up?*

"Fuck," I say, sitting up and crawling back to her. I call over my shoulder, "Hey, when did you give her meds?" Before she can answer, it occurs to me that Skye has been here the whole time, yet Sunny was throwing up, no Skye in sight, when I walked in. "And why was Sunny in here alone, throwing up, while you were tucked away in your room?" I'm stressed and concerned, but lashing out at Skye won't help anything.

Skye steps from her doorway across to the bathroom, her joking demeanor appropriately tucked away in lieu of sympathy and chagrin. "The last dose was about an hour ago? And I had my earbuds in. She took her medicine and went to take a nap, so I didn't expect her to need me."

"She's nine, Skye. You can't just tune her out when she's sick." Sunny has stopped gagging at this point, but she hasn't yet left her perch. Her face is once again buried in her folded arms, but she's resting on the toilet seat rather than her knees.

She mumbles into her arms, "Stooooooooooop. Please. I just want to go to bed." I continue rubbing her back, still frustrated but knowing she's right. Bickering with Skye isn't helping anything.

Sunny looks up and whines, "Do I have to drink chalk again?" Good question, kiddo.

"Erm, actually, hold that thought." Sliding my phone out of my back pocket, I hit Mom's contact and wait for her to pick up. Skye is still leaning against the bathroom door frame, eyebrows furrowed in concern and what I assume is remorse.

"Hi, honey. How is everything?" Mom asks, thankfully sounding like I'm not interrupting anything and she's free to talk.

"Hey, Mom. So, uh, Sunny caught a stomach virus at school and she's been throwing up off and on all day."

"Oh, dear. Is she alright? Have you or Skye caught it yet?" Shoot. Didn't think about that. Let's hope we don't.

"I think she's ok? She's running a bit of a temperature and like I said, throwing up, but she basically just told us to shut up so her personality is still intact." *Now who's the one trying to suffuse humor into things?* Sunny rolls her eyes at me before sitting back and pulling her knees close to her chest again, once more folding her arms over her knees and burying her face.

"I wouldn't expect anything less from my girl. Do you need me to come down? Is that why you're calling?" I know she'd hop into her car and be here tomorrow if I asked, but I really don't think that's necessary.

"I appreciate the offer, but we've got it. I called because Skye says she took some meds about an hour ago, but then she started throwing up again like..." I look at Sunny for a timeline, but she just shakes her head into her arms. "I don't know. Let's say twenty minutes ago, tops. I'm trying to figure out if I should give her more Tylenol or not."

"I wouldn't recommend it. Have her lie down with an ice pack on her forehead. Make sure she has a bowl nearby so she isn't constantly up and down to the bathroom every time she feels sick. You can give her more Tylenol at the recommended follow-up time, but not before." *What would I do without her?*

"That, I can do. Anything else I should know?" I ask, planning to get as much information as possible now so I don't have to call back. I've been Sunny's mom pretty much her entire life, so calling my own mother because I don't know how to treat a stomach virus in my own kid is pretty embarrassing.

"Keep her hydrated, and don't hover. You know how she hates that." Yes, I definitely know that.

"Got it. Thanks, Mom."

"Anytime, honey. Give Sunny and Skye my love. And let me know if you need anything else. Love you," she says in her comforting, sweet voice.

"Love you too." I hit the end button and slide the phone back into my pocket before reaching up to the vanity and pulling myself to stand.

"Good news, kiddo. You won't be taking any more medicine for a few hours yet." I try to infuse excitement into my tone, but it falls on uninterested ears.

"I just wanna go to bed," she groans, but doesn't make any move to get up from the floor.

I turn to Skye and say, "You want to tuck in the patient or find an ice pack and a bowl?"

"Supplies. On it," she responds and heads to the kitchen.

I squat and gently grip Sunny's arms under her biceps to help her up and to her bed. "C'mon Sunshine. You're just a few steps away from a dark room with a fluffy pillow."

"Sounds like heaven," she says as she trudges to her bedroom.

Have I mentioned how much I love being a parent?

And my mom thinks I need a man in my life. I've seen my dad in man-flu mode — the guy becomes useless for days and mom suddenly loses a partner and gains another child.

With Sunny down for what is hopefully a few-hour nap, I head to the kitchen and see Skye pouring a sports drink into popsicle molds. "Well now, that's pure genius."

She grins and nods her head. "I know, right? This is what my mom used to do when I was sick. Cools down the throat and replenishes electrolytes at the same time. Two birds, one stone."

"Are you here for the rest of the day?" I ask, leaning my hip against the cabinet.

"Yeah, I'm staying here. I've been in close proximity to the puke monster so I'll probably skip tomorrow as well just to make sure I didn't catch the same thing." Skye sets the filled popsicle molds in the freezer and says, "I'm going to take a nap."

I nod at her and then take advantage of the quiet and use the downtime to shower and change into pajamas before opening my laptop to work on a paper that's due next week. As soon as I open my inbox I see an unread email from Dexter.

> To: aurora.gilmore@middlepeak.edu
>> From: dbelanger@middlepeak.edu
>> Subject: Checking In
>> Alis,
>> Deborah let me know you won't make it to our meeting today. No worries. I've attached a list of upcoming assignments and grading deadlines for each.
>> I'm sorry you aren't feeling well. Please let me know if I can bring you anything to help. I'll see you next week for our Wednesday meeting.
>> *Cordialement,*
>> D. Belanger, PhD
>> Associate Professor of French Language and Literature
>> Middle Peak University

Please let me know if I can bring you anything to help. Two things cross my mind as I read this. 1) So much for being professional, and 2) Does he actually mean that, or is the offer akin to asking "How are you?" when you only expect the person to say, "Good! How are you?" I'm fairly certain having a professor offer to bring his grader soup or meds to her home is outside the strictly professional boundaries we've established, so it's safe to assume the offer is rhetorical.

Should I respond to him? Of course; I need to acknowledge receipt of the list. I'll just ignore the other part of his email. Better not to address it than to make things awkward.

> To: dbelanger@middlepeak.edu
>> From: aurora.gilmore@middlepeak.edu

Subject: Re: Checking In

Dr. Belanger,

Thank you for sending the list. I'll get to work on those assignments ASAP.

See you next week.

Alis

There we go. Short, to the point, but not necessarily rude. I have a hard enough time not wanting the man when he stays within the professional boundaries we've set. If he starts blurring those lines now I don't know how much longer I'll be able to resist him. We've been working together for just over a month and a half, and with every interaction the forbidden fruit that is Dexter Belanger becomes more appealing, damn the consequences.

Thankfully, Skye has stopped hounding me about him — whether that's because I stopped bringing him up or because she's preoccupied with something else, I don't know. She's driven home four out of the last six weekends to stay with Tori. Something is going on there, but Skye has been tight-lipped whenever I bring it up. Skye isn't usually so cryptic, but nothing else about her seems off so I haven't yet pressed for more information.

"Hey there, daydreamer. You okay?" Skye's question snaps me out of my wandering thoughts and I realize I've been staring blankly at the turned-off television for who knows how long.

"Yeah, I'm good. Just thinking." I give her a soft smile before returning my focus to the laptop. Skye walks around the coffee table and plops down on the couch next to me, bowl of cereal in hand.

"Thought I wanted a nap. Turns out I actually want Lucky Charms." I look over at her as she slurps her first bite and ask, "Brunch of champions?"

Mouth still full of half-chewed cereal, Skye says, "You know it." I'm thankful milk didn't spurt out of her mouth when she opened it to speak.

"You're gross," I tease. "Every time you talk with food in your mouth, you lure Sunny one more step toward your pubescent behavior patterns."

Skye swallows and smiles. "She's nearly a tween anyway; I'm just meeting her in the middle. You're too much of a grown-up to guide her into adolescence. Truly, I'm doing you a favor."

I shake my head. "You're ridiculous."

Skye lays her head on my shoulder and blinks up at me with puppy dog eyes. "But you love me." It's true. I do love her. I wouldn't have been able to move so far away from home and finish grad school without her.

She sits up and grabs the remote on the couch armrest. "You cool with me watching TV in here?"

"Yeah, no problem. I'm just going to work on some grading for Miller until Sunny wakes up. Thanks again for your help with her today."

"I told you, it was no trouble. That's why I'm here. I know she's *technically* your kid, but she's mine, too. She has two moms at home!"

Skye's eyebrows shoot up and she sits up straight, excited by whatever thought just popped into her head. "Ooooooooh you know what? That's how Sunny can rise in the ranks with her friends! She'll be the coolest girl in school if she's the girl with two moms. Her friends don't need to know we're friends without benefits — we'll be the cool, up-with-the-times, lesbian parents and all those kids will wish their parents were as cool as Sunny's."

I close my eyes and rub my forehead. "How in the world do you come up with these ridiculous ideas? And also, why would Sunny need to 'rise in the ranks'? She's made friends at school. She doesn't need a popularity boost, nor does she need to lie to get people to like her."

Skye laughs and elbows my ribs. "I was joking, dummy! See, this is what I mean. You are too grown up for your good. You can't even recognize a joke when it's right in front of you." I roll my eyes at her before turning my focus back to my computer.

Skye squeezes my thigh and wiggles my leg. "Oh, come on, party pooper. Are you upset that I don't really want to be your lesbian lover? Don't get me wrong — if I was into chicks I'd be all up in your business, but right now I've got my eye on someone else."

That gets my attention. "What? Who? Why is this the first I'm hearing about this?"

A smirk plays across her face. "He's nobody right now. Just an enigma who crosses my path each morning at the coffee shop."

"An enigma, you say?" Skye is typically great at reading people, especially men, so for her to consider him an enigma is a definite change of pace.

"Yeah. I don't know that I'm interested in him in the 'fuck me, please' sense, but I definitely want to figure him out. He's a suit — so not my type. And he shows up every morning between 7:27 and 7:30 a.m. Like a robot or something. Never fails."

"Never?" I look at her, questioningly.

"Not since I've started working there," she replies.

"I wish I had that much discipline with time management. Maybe then Sunny could show up to school with matching socks once in a while."

"Life's too short for matching socks."

"You're right," I concede. "But hey, be nice to Mr. Suit. He obviously likes his routine considering he sticks to it so diligently. Resist the temptation to trip him up. It never ends well."

"Yeah, yeah." Skye waves me off, then turns back to the TV so she can catch up on whichever reality show she and Sunny are currently following.

EIGHTEEN

Dexter

IT'S Sunday night and I'm sitting in my office preparing lectures for the week when I receive an email from Alis. I haven't seen her since Tuesday, and aside from our initial email exchange and grading notifications sent from the student portal, we haven't had any interaction. I'd like to say the distance has helped me to focus on work without getting carried away in daydreams about my grader, but the truth is the longer she works from home, the more concerned I become about her.

Her email does nothing to quell my concerns — she won't be on campus again on Monday or Tuesday. What the hell is going on with her? Does she have some sort of autoimmune disease that keeps her down longer than most people who catch a virus?

I've tried texting her but she never responds. I understand her desire to keep things professional between us, but surely we've developed some semblance of a friendship and familiarity during these past two months working together. I decide I should text her one more time in the hope that she'll at least let me know if she's improving.

> Dexter: Hey Alis, I saw your email about staying
> home for the next two days. I'm just checking in to
> make sure you're alright. Please let me know if I can
> help in any way.

Geez, I sound pathetic. I don't consider myself a selfish man, but truth be told I wouldn't give a second thought to another TA or student out for a week due to illness. I'd take their email updates at face value and go about my day.

WHAT THE HELL *am I doing?* It's Tuesday afternoon, and I'm driving slowly through her apartment complex, studying the numbers on each building to find Alis's apartment. When I sent her another email checking in and she didn't respond, again, I decided to drive to her apartment to make sure she's alright. I'm fully aware this is highly inappropriate for a professor, but hopefully not for a friend. The fact that I have to repeatedly convince myself that we are friends speaks to the weak foundation on which I stand, but I'm here now so there's no point turning back.

2300–2310… 2311–2320… *ah hah!* Deborah's text said she lives at apartment 2318, so now I just have to find an open parking spot. I swear this parking lot has so many twists and turns, I don't know if I'll be able to find my way out.

I park in an undesignated spot on the side of the building and shut off my car, hands at ten and two as I press my forehead into the steering wheel. I laugh to myself, imagining the scowl she'll give me when she answers the door.

I am just making sure she's okay. Any friend would be worried if someone they care about was homesick for a full week without explanation.

Grabbing the pharmacy bag filled with cold medicine, cough drops, and a sports drink, I exit the car and make my way toward the door. I really hope I don't need an access code to get into the building, otherwise I will have made this trip for nothing.

Just as I reach the top of the steps leading to the entryway, an elderly woman pushes it open. I grab onto the handle and hold open the door for her, deeming my act of chivalry to be payment for barging in on Alis so unexpectedly. Once the way is clear, I step inside and let the door close behind me, looking right and finding the directory on the foyer wall. Her apartment is on the first floor. Good. I don't have to climb any stairs on my quest.

I head down the hallway, noting the even-numbered apartments on the left side. I stop in front of 2318 and hesitate before knocking three times. I hear movement on the other side of the door. She's up and moving, not bedridden. That's a good sign.

"Coming!" I hear a high-pitched voice come near the door and turn the lock. I'm having trouble placing that voice with Alis, and as the door swings open I see why — the person projecting that voice is half the size of the woman I'm here to see.

I stand there, frozen, not sure what to say. I didn't expect to see a child. Is she Alis's? Her hair is darker, but then again her father could have dark hair. *Her. Father.* Oh God. Please don't tell me Alis is with someone. Surely she would have said something. Surely she wouldn't have kissed me that night at the club had she been involved with someone else.

The little girl cocks her head to the side and inspects me from head to toe. Shit, I still haven't said anything.

"Who are you?" she asks, her tone filled with curiosity.

I swallow nervously, still thrown off by the appearance of this young girl in the doorway. Do I have the wrong apartment? "Hi. I might have the wrong apartment. My name is Dexter. I'm here to see Alis?" The girl eyes me up and down once more; I can see the wheels turning in her head, trying to decide how to respond to me.

Suddenly she turns, door still ajar, and yells at the top of her lungs, "MONTY!" *Who the hell is Monty?* Oh God. He's probably some bouncer-sized man coming to tell me to get the fuck out of here.

Then I hear her — Alis. "Sunny, why are you answering the do—" Just as she pulls the door open wider, she stills as her eyes lock with mine. "Dexter. What are you doing here?"

The girl sidles up next to Alis, looking back and forth between us.

"Looks like you have the right house, dude. Here she is." Then she shrugs — shrugs, as if this is not unusual — and walks deeper into the apartment.

"Dexter?" Alis prompts, knocking me out of my momentary stupor. I shake my head to clear it and look Alis in the eyes.

"Hi," I say, my signature half-smile aimed directly at her. *God, she's beautiful.* She doesn't look happy to see me. She looks, annoyed?

"Hi, " she deadpans. "What are you doing here? And how do you know where I live?" She props her hip on the door frame, arms crossed over her chest.

"I, uh, wanted to make sure you were alright. You've been out sick for a week now and I was worried something was wrong."

Her face softens, just a tiny bit, and she looks at the floor as she tucks a loose strand of hair behind her ear. "Oh. Well, thank you, I guess. I'm fine." She offers no more words. No more explanation. No clue about the girl. What do I expect? She keeps treating me like just a professor and I keep wanting to read into our interactions as if she is somehow affected by me the same way I am by her. Sometimes I wonder if I imagined our chemistry and easy conversation the night we first met.

"Right. Well, I wasn't sure what type of illness you have — or had? I brought you a few things in case you have a cold or a stomach virus. Electrolytes and such." I present my offering and she looks down at it before her eyes return to my face. She doesn't make a move to take the bag, so I'm standing here holding it out, looking like an idiot.

The silence between us grows awkward and just as I'm about to apologize for intruding and then leave, the young girl returns to the door and says, "We're not contagious. You can come in!" Alis gives the girl a disapproving look before looking back to me. "You don't have t—"

"I'd love to. Thanks." I cut her off mid-sentence and take a step forward. Thankfully, Alis moves from the doorway and allows me to pass. *Thanks for the break, kid.*

Her apartment is cozy. Not very spacious, but it looks comfortable. I am a man and I do not decorate things — Laura decorated our apartment when we lived together — but even I can tell this living area doesn't have any specific theme or design. Her couch, up against the wall, is covered in different colored and shaped throw pillows and a superhero-printed throw blanket lies balled up on the floor to the side. Next to the couch, in the corner near the sliding glass door, sits a club chair piled high with more random pillows, books, and an open laptop. The chair is — purple? No, more maroon? The floral print on the upholstery looks straight out of my grandmother's sitting room back in Montreal.

As I continue looking around, Alis clears her throat and asks if I'd like to have a seat, gesturing toward the couch. I look at her and smile, happy to be in her space and see more of her life.

"Sorry about the mess. We, uh, weren't expecting company." She's looking at her feet while she talks, refusing to look me in the eyes. *We.* Who is we? She and the girl? She and the girl and the girl's father? Maybe she's just babysitting? If she's sick, babysitting wouldn't make sense.

I set the pharmacy bag on the round dining table to my right in the open kitchen/dining space and then take a seat on the couch. "Tea?" Alis asks, and I nod. "Thank you, that sounds great."

I can sense her discomfort, and it pains me to consider that I might be the cause. My intentions were genuine – to ensure she was okay. Admittedly, perhaps a part of me just missed her presence and sought to shorten the gap between us sooner rather than later.

My eyes linger on the eclectic decor of her living room, providing a momentary distraction until a young girl makes her entrance. With an unceremonious plop onto the floor in front of the club chair, she grabs a throw blanket, swaddling herself within its folds, and then lifts her gaze to me.

"So, who are you?" she asks. Direct. Authoritative. Dare I say, protective?

"I'm Dexter," I say, not sure how Alis will feel about me talking to the child.

"Well, duh," she gives me an exasperated look. "I already knew that. You told me your name at the door." The girl has a lot of attitude for her age.

"How do you know Monty? And why are you here? I've never met you before."

Ah, so Monty must be what she calls Alis. That's a strange nickname. Thank God it's not the Hulk I imagined.

I chuckle out my relief. "I work with … Monty? At Middle Peak. She's a friend and since she's been out for the last few days I wanted to check and make sure she was alright."

The girl nods and pulls her knees up to her chest. "She's never mentioned you." *Way to boost my ego there, kid.*

"Ah, well, I haven't heard about you either. What's your name?"

"Sunny. I'm nine years old but I'll be ten soon. Monty says when I turn ten I can finally get my own TV in my room so I don't have to fight with Skye about what to watch anymore. She likes the Kardashians, but I like Say Yes to the Dress better. The Kardashians are really annoying and their butts are too big. How do they even fit in chairs? It doesn't make sense."

This kid is not shy, that's for sure. She continues to ramble and I sit and listen, not quite understanding all her references to various reality TV programs. I'm lost in a flurry of Randy, slore, lace, Bible, and bridesmaids when Alis appears in the living area, two mugs of tea in hand.

"Sunny, you do know that Dexter has no idea what you're talking about, right?" Alis hands me a mug and I nod in thanks. She sits at the other end of the couch, nearest the hallway and kitchen, and Sunny rolls her eyes.

"I was just telling him about when Randy talked that crazy lady out of wearing a black wedding dress just because she wanted to be different. Seriously, who wears a black wedding dress?! That's just ridiculous." I laugh at her blatant disregard for Alis's attempt to change conversation topics.

"Who indeed," I reply, smiling at Sunny before taking a sip from the mug.

"Sorry," Alis says to me. "She watches way too much reality TV for her own good. I've tried to steer her more toward books, but she's one of those 'rather watch the movie' people. I don't even know how we're related."

Related. So, this is her daughter? Maybe? Sister? I have so many questions but I don't know where to begin. I also suspect Alis will close up as soon as I ask anything probing. I'm insanely curious, and also so completely confused right now.

I decide to avoid personal questions and direct my attention back to Sunny. "You'd rather watch the movie? But the book is always better!"

Sunny scoffs. "Gah, you sound just like Monty. 'You need to read a book. Movies are worse than cliff notes. They never get it right.' blah, blah, blah."

Gotta hand it to her, this kid's Alis impression is pretty spot on. She's hilarious. And she tells it like she sees it. I am smitten.

"She's right, you know." Just as Sunny goes to roll her eyes again, Alis touches my arm and exclaims, "Finally! Someone in this house sees things my way instead of constantly succumbing to Skye's influence!"

Alis touched me. The contact was brief, yet intentional — a gentle, voluntary squeeze on my arm. That's not something you do to a colleague, is it? Arm squeezes are for friends. She's never engaged in such casual contact with me — at least, not since our reintroduction in my office months ago.

"Skye?" I ask. Before Alis can answer, the front door opens, and in walks a short, curvy, pixie-looking woman with bright purple hair. She's wearing rolled-up overalls with a red and white striped t-shirt underneath and combat boots. She drops her keys into the bowl on the entryway table as she steps on the heel of her boot and wiggles a foot out before tossing it into the basket underneath the table.

"You're not going to believe what that asshat suit said to me this morning. I swear he's infuriating!" She huffs and turns to face us. Stopping in her tracks, a huge grin spreads across her face. "My, my, if it isn't Sexy Dexy!"

I nearly spit out my tea just as Alis buries her face into her hands.

"I'm sorry, what?" I'm trying not to laugh, to no avail, because just as Alis groans into her hand, Sunny jumps up and yells, "THIS is Sexy Dexy?! Ohmygosh. I didn't know you still talk to him?! Why am I just now meeting him?!"

Alis pulls her hand away from her face and gives Sunny a stunned expression through beet-red cheeks. "How do you know who Sexy Dexy is in the first place?"

She doesn't realize her slip-up — she referred to me as Sexy Dexy. That's all the confirmation I need. I am not just a colleague.

"I mean, Dexter. Dr. Belanger. Whatever." She corrects herself. She wouldn't have tried to save face by correcting herself if she wasn't talking about me, right?

Sunny looks at the purple-haired woman and says, "Skye was talking about him with Tori in the car one day! She said you needed to stop being such a prude and date the guy."

If Alis's eyes could pop out of her head, they'd be rolling on the floor right now. "WHAT?!" Alis looks at — Skye? I'm guessing — and her friend bats her hand like Alis is overreacting.

"Psh. Don't act surprised. It's not like I keep anything from Tori. You know this."

"That's not the point!" Alis's voice grows louder with frustration. "Why the hell were you talking about my sex life in front of a nine-year-old?!" *Sex life?* That escalated quickly.

Alis covers her mouth with her hand and squeezes her eyes closed. Her cheeks burn brighter. I don't think she meant to say that in front of Sunny. Or me. I try to stay quiet. *I'm so glad I came over.*

Skye laughs. "Be careful, Alis. Your word vomit is spewing."

Alis gives Skye a death glare and Sunny takes that as her queue to leave. "I'm going to my room. To read a book. Dexter has officially inspired me. You guys have fun! Bye-eeeee!" And then she bolts down the hallway and shuts what I assume is her bedroom door behind her.

Alis is still fuming, her eyes matching her red cheeks; Skye is still laughing. I have no idea what all just happened, but I know that I definitely don't want to leave.

I try to lighten the mood and nudge Alis with my elbow. "So,

Sexy Dexy, huh?" I wink at her and she rolls her eyes, blushing again, and lets out a huff. "This is not happening."

Skye walks across the room to Sunny's previous sitting location and reaches out her hand before sitting down. "Hi, Dexter. It's nice to see you again." Ah, she must be the friend from the club.

"Nice to see you again, too. I like the hair," I say, nodding toward her purple locks. "I don't remember the purple from the first time we met."

"Yeah, the purple is new. I think that night my hair was red? Or maybe black. I don't remember." She shrugs. "So, what brings you to our humble abode?" *Our.* Ok, so they all live together. Does Sunny belong to Skye, then?

"I just came to check on Alis. She's been out for a while and I wanted to make sure she was feeling alright."

"Aw, Alis! He came to check on you," Skye croons, hands folded over her chest. "You are so sweet to think of her, Dexy-Poo. And now that you're here, you should stay for dinner!" She claps excitedly. Alis isn't having it. *Dexy-Poo?*

"Sorry, Skye, but Dexter was just leaving." She stands and gestures toward the door. I don't want to leave, but I take the hint, set down my mug on the coffee table, and stand to follow.

"Aw, but I just got home! I didn't even get to talk to him!" Skye whines.

"You'll live," Alis replies and she opens the door and steps out into the hallway. I wave goodbye to Skye and follow Alis, pulling the door closed behind me on my way out.

Alis is leaning up against the hallway wall, watching as I exit her apartment. "I am so sorry about that. I swear those two have no filter. I hope they didn't make you uncomfortable."

I smirk at her. "I think *you* were the uncomfortable one. They're hilarious! I didn't realize you had a roommate, or a ..." I purposefully leave the sentence hanging, hoping she'll fill in the blank.

"Spitfire? Yeah. They're both crazy." Way to avoid the question, woman. Looks like I'm going to have to ask her straight up.

"Is she yours?" Alis looks at her feet. Her face doesn't look ashamed, but worried about answering my question. Why would she be worried about answering?

"Yes. And, no." I quirk an eyebrow at her. That makes no sense.

Returning her gaze to meet mine, a myriad of emotions fill her eyes. She seems to be wrestling internally about what to say next. Finally, she makes the decision to trust me and shares a bit of her story.

"I adopted her when she was a baby. Her mother was my sister. She and Sunny's father died in a car accident when she was nine months old." Nine months old, and she's about to be ten, which puts the car accident around … eight? Nine years ago? Right about the time Alis dropped out of grad school.

"You left school to take care of Sunny." It's a statement; not a question. Alis nods her head.

"Yeah. I had a lot happening around me and ultimately decided it would be best for Sunny, and for myself, if I left school and focused on raising her. We lived with my parents until we moved here in August."

This woman continues to intrigue me. Becoming an adoptive mother in her early twenties? Losing her sister and brother-in-law at the same time? I can't imagine how difficult that must have been for her, for her entire family. God, this woman is incredible.

This is the most information she's given me about herself since the night we met. It's nice to see Alis, the woman, and not just Alis, my grader.

"Wow." I don't know what else to say. I'm overwhelmed by Alis, and I'm sure there's so much more to learn about her. "Why didn't you tell me that day in my office when I asked about why you left school?"

"Because I didn't really know you, and I had no reason to divulge personal details about myself to you." She makes this statement so matter-of-factly, so directly, that I don't know how to respond. After a few seconds I recover from the jab her words aimed in my direction.

"You're right. I'm sorry. I didn't mean to pry." Not knowing how to steer the conversation from here without prying, I look toward the exit and then back at Alis. "I should be going. I'm glad you're feeling better, Alis."

She stops me with a hand on my arm before I can take a step away from her and looks into my eyes. That's twice now she's touched me, casually, dare I say, affectionately.

"Dexter, *I'm* sorry. I'm not trying to be rude or overly closed off; I just haven't opened up to anyone new in a very long time. Aside from college, I've lived my entire life in the same place, with the same people. I've always had the same friends, interacted with mostly the same crowd. Moraine isn't very large, so everyone already knew what happened with my sister. I've never had to explain things about my life to anyone because they all lived through it with me."

Her hand is still on my arm. I want to place my hand over hers, but I know if I move an inch she'll retreat. I want to tell her she doesn't have to rehash all of this right now, but I've felt drawn to Alis from the moment I met her and I won't waste any opportunity to get to know her better. After another deep breath, she continues.

"Moving to Grand River has been ... different. I had a plan in place to move here and finish school, to keep focusing on work and Sunny. I never considered how moving to a new city would impact me personally." She laughs. "For crying out loud, before the night we met, I hadn't kissed a man in nine years!"

That catches my attention. "Really?" I ask. She nods slowly, a small smile gracing her lips. "Really. My life has revolved around work and Sunny. And now, work, school, and Sunny. I didn't even consider meeting someone or changing up my routine."

Screw caution. I take a small step closer to her and sweep an errant hair behind her ear. Looking into her eyes, I ask, "Is changing up your routine so bad?"

Alis swallows. "I don't know if it's bad, but it's overwhelming. Not to mention terrifying." I want to kiss her again so badly, but the vulnerability in her eyes assures me that kissing her will only scare her away.

I smile at her and slowly take a step back. "I understand. And I'm sorry if I've contributed to you feeling overwhelmed."

"It's not just you. It's everything. I'm still trying to find my footing in a new place, with new people. I'm not only working through my own transition but also helping Sunny acclimate to a new school and new friends. I'm sure I'll get the hang of it eventually and be more open to people, but right now I need to navigate within my own boundaries. At least for a while."

I nod. "I respect your boundaries — well, today's behavior aside."

She laughs. "I definitely didn't expect you to show up on my doorstep."

I run my hand through my hair. "Yeah, well. I really was worried something serious was wrong with you. Your emails haven't been very forthcoming."

"I know. And I apologize for that. Last week when I left it was because Sunny was throwing up and had to leave school. I thought I'd be back in a day or two, but then I woke up Friday with the same virus. I finally started feeling better yesterday afternoon and took today as a final recovery day before Sunny and I get back into our normal routine."

"I'm glad you're both feeling better and that you took the time you needed," I assure her. "I'll see you tomorrow, then?"

She nods, her smile gentle and soft. "Yeah. I'll see you tomorrow."

As she opens her door, she offers a small, warm wave. I pivot, steering myself toward the exit. The sound of the door closing doesn't reach my ears, but I don't dare turn to check in case she's watching me. That's not true. I don't turn to check because I don't want to feel the disappointment of *not* seeing her watch me leave.

NINETEEN

Alis

TO SAY the last few days have been overwhelming and annoying is an understatement. Not two seconds after walking back into our apartment, Skye and Sunny were on me like white on rice.

"Oh. My. God. I CANNOT believe he actually came over!" Skye went full-on woo girl for the next few hours, turning every sentence into an exclamation followed by squeals released at unprecedented decibels. I'd never seen her that hyper and loud when sober, but apparently a hot guy showing up at our place is stronger than any liquor.

Sunny wasn't much better. She kept trying to weasel her way into the conversation, which was really one-sided — Skye blabbing all around me while I kept quiet and tried to ignore her. I still can't believe Skye talked about Dexter openly in front of her. Not once in her entire life has Sunny seen or heard of me with a man in a romantic sense. The men back home were either married, solid cases of failure-to-launch, friend-zoned, complete imbeciles, or tourists passing through. No thanks. And even if I had met a single, eligible bachelor in our hometown, I doubt I would have paid attention because I was laser-focused on work and Sunny.

I still can't believe how many conflicting emotions have run through me since we moved to Grand River. I mean, seriously, hasn't life messed with my carefully-laid plans enough for one lifetime? I know if we had stayed in Moraine I'd have had a happy, calm life. I also know I'd always wonder what I could have accomplished had I gone back to school.

I pride myself on thinking through every possible outcome before making a decision, but none of the scenarios I played out in my head come close to reality. I guess because I hadn't been attracted to anyone in so many years, I didn't factor in any sort of romantic entanglement in my mental list of potential complications resulting from moving and starting afresh.

It's not that I have never desired the love story; I just haven't ever met someone who piqued my interest enough to distract me from my educational and career aspirations, or from raising my daughter. Every time I refer to Dexter as a 'distraction' Skye reprimands me and says, "Having a partner is not a distraction. You can't cut a steak with only a fork." I have no idea where she comes up with her analogies, nor do I always understand them, but I've decided to keep quiet and nod in agreement whenever she dishes out her 'wisdom' to avoid poking the bear. *More like poking a pissed-off chihuahua.* Snippy, that one.

Finally, Friday has arrived, Skye is once again out of town for the weekend, and today is my last day on campus for a few days. Praise the Lord, I can finally take a deep breath and decompress after a week of conflicting emotions and constant badgering.

I'm strolling through campus, enjoying the crisp fall air and marveling at the many-colored leaves painting the trees, when Brody approaches and disrupts my moment of serenity. *Why can't I have one day when people just leave me alone? I just want to enjoy all the colors of fall in peace.*

"Hey, Alis, how's it going?" Brody readjusts his backpack straps that slipped down during his apparent jog to get to me. I try my best to wipe the look of annoyance off my face before turning toward him.

"Hey, Brody. I'm good, and you?" I manage to put a smile on my face, but I know it doesn't reach my eyes. He doesn't seem to notice and starts to prattle on about how he's doing well and how his week has gone. I'm only half listening to him, continuing to stare up at all the orange, red, and yellow leaves hovering overhead as we continue to walk across campus toward my meeting with Dr. Matthews. Out of nowhere I step on an untied shoelace and stumble forward, bending my knees to break the fall. Before I hit the ground Brody wraps an arm around my waist from behind and pulls me in close to him.

"Whoa now. You okay?" he asks. His mouth is too close to my ear and his arm is still locked around my midsection.

I try to wiggle out from his hold on me and say, "Yeah, thanks. Stupid shoelace." Once his arm slackens and I can take a step away from him, I kneel to re-tie my Converse, making sure to double knot them. I stand back up and brush off my hands on my skirt, checking to make sure I didn't rip a hole in my favorite tights while kneeling. Before I can say anything else Brody asks, "So about tomorrow night. You in?"

Um, what? Clearly, I missed something. "Tomorrow night?" I ask, trying to sound like I'm having a momentary lapse in remembrance rather than the truth — that I have no freaking clue what he's gone on about for the last few minutes.

"The hockey game. Do you want to go with me?" *When did he start talking about hockey?* Brody flashes a flirty smile and his eyes show just how much he wants me to say yes.

"I'm sorry," I say, "I can't this weekend." I resume my walk and Brody doesn't miss a beat, falling in step beside me.

"Why not? Got plans? We could go next weekend if you're free." His tone sounds hopeful, and I don't want to upset him. I also don't really want to hang out with him outside of seeing him on campus.

"Yeah, I'm slammed this weekend." Not really, but Skye isn't here to keep Sunny and I don't need to explain my reasoning to anyone. "Maybe another time, yeah?" That should do it. Not a yes, not a no. Don't smash his hopes, but also, hopefully, don't lead him on.

Why am I so spineless and awkward when confronted with

uncomfortable social situations?!

Brody seems placated for now. He smiles and runs his hand through his dark hair, then grips the back of his neck. "Yeah, another time. Maybe sometime in the next few weeks." It's not a question; it's a statement. I don't respond verbally; I just give him a small, friendly smile in acknowledgment of his words.

Once we arrive at the Languages and Literature building, I turn to say goodbye and Brody reaches out and grasps my wrist lightly. "I'm really glad I ran into you today. I've missed seeing you on campus this last week."

This isn't awkward at all. "Um, yeah. It was great seeing you, too. Hopefully, I won't get sick again anytime soon so I won't have to miss class and play catchup." Brody chuckles, hand still on my wrist, refusing to break eye contact. "Don't worry about the classes you missed. I'll email you the notes."

"Thanks, I really appreciate that." I offer him a genuine smile because I'm incredibly thankful that I don't have to track down the notes I missed taking. The PowerPoints in that class are useless, as our prof goes off on tangents frequently and the sidebars hold the truly important information.

"I'll see you next week, yeah?" I ask, taking a small step away from Brody in hopes he'll release his grasp on my wrist. "Yeah. Have a good weekend, Alis." Before I can step away any further, Brody pulls on my wrist slightly, leans down, and grazes my cheek with his lips.

I don't know how to react to his obviously more-than-friendly goodbye, so I just say, "Bye" and march up the building stairs as quickly as possible without looking back. *Am I thirty or am I thirteen?*

Shaking out of my stupor, I turn back to look at him before opening the door and say, "You're a great friend, Brody. Thanks for helping me adjust to life here these last few months. I really appreciate it." He smiles up at me and I see the disappointment in his eyes, which means I must have communicated my intentions clearly, and read his just as well.

"Anytime, Alis. See you next week." Then he turns and walks

away, and I head in to meet with Dr. Matthews.

I climb the stairs, evaluating the thoughts and feelings that coursed through me as Brody kissed my cheek. Not that I'd ever entertain a romantic relationship with him, but my internal reaction to his lips on my cheek was stronger than non-interest. I felt annoyed, frustrated, and most curiously, I felt as if his lips on my skin was a form of betrayal.

Betrayal? To whom?! Why am I even asking myself that question? I can push aside my attraction and pull toward Dexter Belanger every chance I get, but with each suppression the feelings strengthen and the internal pressure builds.

Maybe I can appease this felt need for him with a timeline. Alis, you will not succumb to your desire for Dexter Belanger until you are no longer his grader, nor a student at Middle Peak University. That's what, two years tops? Five if I stay here for my Ph.D.

I can't decide whether admitting my feelings for Dexter to myself is helping or hurting my cause. On one hand, I'm no longer lying to myself. On the other, being honest with myself about how much I want him makes the temptation to cave that much stronger.

Two years of pent-up sexual tension will only serve to make the release all the more blissful when it happens. That is, if it doesn't erupt like a volcano before then. What if he meets someone else before I'm ready? How will I handle seeing him with another woman, touching another woman, or, heaven forbid, kissing another woman? *Ugh!* This is why I refused to admit to myself that I want him. Now I've gone and made myself vulnerable to the possibility of a broken heart and unrealized dreams. I've had enough heartbreak in this life; I don't need any more.

Head on straight, Aurora Jane Gilmore. Focus on what's important, not on messy, overwhelming, unstable feelings toward a man. A gorgeous, six-foot-tall, swoon-worthy man. Nope. Don't go there. Focus. Sunny. School. Work. Priorities.

Lord, help my resolve.

Dexter

I've just stepped onto the sidewalk from the parking lot when I see Alis and Brody nearing the L&L building together. I don't have a meeting scheduled with her today, but maybe she plans to stop in and say a quick hello? Most likely not, but a man can wish.

I'm still a good twenty meters away when I see him reach for her wrist. She doesn't stop him; she doesn't pull away. Then he leans down and kisses her cheek before she ascends the stairs to my building. Just before entering she turns and says something else to him, a smile spread wide across her face. *Are you fucking kidding me? That boy is a child. Why the hell were his lips on her?!*

She enters the building without noticing my approach, but Brody sees me when he turns to leave. "Hey, Dr. Belanger! How are you?" His laid-back demeanor conveys no discomfort, like kissing Alis and then seeing me is a normal part of his every day.

"Brody. Hi," I say, giving him a stiff smile and a nod before walking up the stairs to head to my office. I don't want to be rude to the kid, but I also don't think I can keep my true feelings unreadable.

I'm still reeling from the thought of Brody's lips on Alis when I enter the lobby area of Pod A. Deborah looks up from her computer as I enter and stops mid-smile when she sees me. Before she can get a word in I ask, "Is Alis in my office?" Deborah looks confused, as she should. "No, sir. I haven't even seen her in the building today. Did I miss an appointment on your calendar?"

"No. You didn't forget anything. I have the days mixed up in my head," I say, easing her worried expression. "Any messages?"

"No, sir." Deborah looks back to her computer, clicking a few times in search of my calendar, adding, "And no meetings the rest of today."

"Perfect," I nod, my tone sharp. "Please set my line to 'do not disturb'. I'll be in my office the rest of the afternoon working on some things and would prefer not to be interrupted." Deborah nods in acknowledgment and I walk into my office, closing the door behind me.

I don't understand my visceral reaction to this woman. I spent years with Laura, and I genuinely loved her, but I don't remember ever feeling this crazed when another man paid her any attention. Perhaps I never felt threatened because I knew she was mine — Alis, however, is not mine. Is there something special about her or is the thrill and frustration of the chase messing with me?

I honestly have no idea. Alis and I certainly have more in common than Laura and I ever did. We like the same books, have similar personalities, and have nearly identical senses of humor. I hate it when people say "we're the same person!" but I'll be damned if I've ever met another woman who harmonizes with me so well. We're singing the same song, and if we could only sing it together the resulting duet would be symphonic.

Why can't I think in such romantic prose when I'm around Alis?! Now that I think about it, the night we met I remember our conversation flowing seamlessly, filled with wit and conversational caresses.

I'll never forget how beautiful she looked that night. Her shimmering black dress and soft, blond waves falling down her back caught my attention, but the moment I saw her reflection in between shelved bottles of Patrón and Casamigos I knew I had to talk to her. She sat alone, but not uncomfortably. Her smile was soft and supple, her eyes revealing an internal monologue she seldomly shares with others. She was stunning, warm, and I wanted to be nearer to her.

The spark of recognition that lit in her eyes when I subtly wove a line from *Marguerite de Valois* into our conversation was my breaking point. I've never written a list of qualities I desire in a life partner, but in that one, fifteen-minute interaction I knew I wanted more. More talking. More smiling. More laughing. More literary innuendo and witty banter.

And when I kissed her — God, when I kissed her — I never wanted to stop. Being the well-read man that I am, I can provide centuries of documented proof that an intangible, soul-deep connection is something all of humanity longs for. I don't believe in soul mates, nor that some supernatural power has designated one person to be your perfect complement, but I do believe a deep and unmistakable connection can exist with another person. Just as we meet certain people who trigger instant wariness, discomfort, or annoyance, sometimes life is kind enough to introduce us to people who inexplicably kindle feelings of serenity, of peace, of home.

Kissing Alis felt right, familiar. Touching Alis felt like coming home. I wanted to pull her closer to me, feel her arms around me, feel her warmth in every way possible.

That's it. That's why I can't keep my head on straight when it comes to Alis. It's not the chase; it's not her infuriating determination to keep me at arms' length — it's quite simply that being with Alis makes me feel centered in a way I never felt with Laura.

I still barely know the woman, but I want to. I want to know everything about her. Every thought. Every dream. Every desire.

This feeling of familiarity and rightness cannot be one-sided. Is she fighting against it intentionally, or does she not feel as drawn to me as I am to her? And how do I gently, subtly break down the walls she so forcefully erects around herself?

I wish my pépé was still alive. My mémé was very independent, strong-willed, and made pépé work to gain her trust and her heart. If I could call him and talk with him about Alis, I'm sure he'd draw from his never-ending fountain of wisdom and guide me in the right direction.

I laugh to myself, imagining the conversation, had it ever happened. First, he would throw his head back and laugh that I'm stuck on a woman who refuses to entertain my advances. Then, he'd call out to mémé to let her know his relentless pursuit of her stubborn heart has influenced generations of Bélangers and that his example is no longer seen as insanity, but wisdom. Mémé would shout back at him, *"T'es donc ben niaiseux!"*, refusing to leave her precious peonies mid-serenade. I never understood why she sang to her flowers each day, but she swore that singing helped them grow.

I know, without a doubt, that Thibaud Bélanger would describe the years he spent in pursuit of his beloved Ruby as absolutely, unreservedly worth every second. I hope at the end of this I can say the same.

TWENTY

Alis

AMELIA MUST BE out to lunch because when I arrive for my meeting with Dr. Matthews, she's nowhere to be found. The light is off in Dr. Matthews' office, so I take a seat and enjoy the quiet while I can.

Brody revealed his cards today, and so did I. The look on his face made me feel terrible for hurting his feelings. Did I lead him on? Wait. No. I did not lead him on. I have no reason to feel guilty or negative at all about establishing my boundaries. I'd like to maintain a friendship with Brody, but that's all. He can accept that or reject it; that's his prerogative.

Would I consider him more than a friend if I didn't know Dexter? No, I don't believe I would. I don't make my relationship decisions based on other people. However, I would be lying to myself if I said I didn't wish Dexter was the one with his lips on my cheek a few minutes ago.

Lifting my hand to my face, I close my eyes and think back to the other day in my apartment corridor when he tucked the loose hair behind my ear. In my daydream he doesn't pull back, but instead leans in close and is just about to brush his lips across my cheek …

"Alis, I'm so sorry to keep you waiting." I'm pulled from my daydream by a flustered Dr. Matthews. I stand and brush my hands down my blouse and skirt, smoothing out any wrinkles that popped up while I waited for her to arrive. The cat print on this skirt is just fun enough to convey "nerdy but flirty" instead of "I'm a crazy cat lady!"

"No worries. I haven't been here long." I give her a reassuring smile as she nods, pauses for a second to give my outfit a curious once-over, and then leads the way into her office.

"That view gets me every time," I breathe, stopping for a moment to stare through her glass panel wall that boasts a perfect view of the nearby mountains, before heading to a chair in her seating area. "How do you get any work done with a view like that in your periphery each day?"

Dr. Matthews chuckles. "It never gets any less beautiful, but in time it serves as a de-stressor rather than a distraction."

"I could see that," I nod. "Hopefully one day I'll have an office with a view like this."

"I'm sure you will," Dr. Matthews smiles at me. "With the academic prowess I've observed from you these past few months, I hold no doubt that with the right connections and direction schools across the country will fight to snatch you up when your dissertation is complete."

I blush. I don't take compliments well. "Thank you, Dr. Matthews. It means a lot to hear you say that." I toy with the hem of my skirt and offer a moment of vulnerability. "I had been away from academia for so long, I feared finding my footing would take longer than it has. Not only that, but I left so suddenly and I've often wondered how that could negatively affect my future career prospects."

"In a lot of ways, reentering the academy is like riding a bike," she says.

I nod, "Like riding a bike."

"And as for how leaving has affected your future, I wouldn't worry about it. The only way leaving could have negatively affected your future was if you didn't come back. Which you did."

Again, I nod, still staring down at my lap to hide the blush on my face.

"Ok, let's get to it," Dr. Matthews says, tapping a stack of papers on her lap. I pull a notebook and pen from my messenger bag and open it to the next blank page.

Now that we're past the compliments, I'm able to resume a professional demeanor and look at her. "The intensive I spoke with you about at the beginning of the semester is in two weeks. I assume you remember that I'll need you with me the entire week?"

"Yes, ma'am," I reply. "I've got my schedule situated and I'm yours all week."

She continues. "Excellent. I have an overlap with a few meetings I cannot reschedule, but I've talked with Belanger and he's going to teach those segments."

I pause in my note-taking when she says his name and look up at her. "Dr. Belanger? Are those segments not something I could teach?" *Way to be subtle, Alis.*

Dr. Matthews looks up from her planner, removing her glasses. I try to put on my best "nothing going on here" face, but she probably senses something's off with my tone.

Placing the foot of her glasses in her mouth, Dr. Matthews ponders for a few seconds before responding. "You know what, you make a great point. You could teach most of them yourself." *Oh, thank you, Jesus.* I let out the breath I was holding and hope she didn't hear my obvious sigh of relief. *Wait, did she say 'most'?*

"Not all of them, though," she continues. *Son of a bitch! Celebrated too soon.* "Two of the segments are in Belanger's wheelhouse and I believe the students would benefit from his teaching in those areas. Not to mention the students will want a reprieve from my blunt nature and could use some eye candy with a fun uncle demeanor." She laughs to herself and I try not to react to the fact that she just referred to Dexter Belanger as eye candy.

Apparently, I'm trying too hard not to react, thus painting an awkward expression on my face. "Do you not agree?" she inquires, teasingly.

I don't want to answer that. "Um, sure. Yeah." Smooth. Real smooth.

Dr. Matthews laughs, "You don't have to play coy. Any woman with eyes can see that man is gorgeous."

I blush and shrug. "Yeah, I guess you could say that."

"Anyway, moving on," she chuckles as she returns her glasses to her face. *Thank God.*

An hour later I leave her office armed with an updated schedule for the intensive, which includes two celebrity appearances by one Dexter Belanger. *At least I have a heads-up.*

As I walk back through campus after the meeting, I reflect on the last few weeks' grader meetings with Dexter. I've grown more comfortable in his presence, and I can confidently say Dexter Belanger has become more than just a professor I grade for — he's a friend. We don't talk about anything truly deep in our meetings, but the fact that we share lunch together at each meeting encourages conversation topics outside his upcoming assignments and my responsibilities toward his students.

I expected Dexter to ambush me with questions about Sunny after he met her, but thankfully he's kept questions light — focusing mainly on favorite authors and books, my career aspirations, and the like. I haven't had anyone to fawn over French literature with in nearly a decade, so it's nice to lose myself for half an hour in conversation about Duras's *The Lover*, Zola's *Thérèse Raquin*, and even modern French novelists such as Gilles Legardinier and Guillaume Musso.

My life the past nine years may have seemed boring to some, but I never stopped reading. Physically, I was in Moraine, but for at least an hour a day I lost myself in worlds created by some of the world's best authors — not just French.

I've loved learning about Dexter's varying tastes in books and I respect his opinions concerning French literature, both new and old. We don't like all the same books or writers, but we love literature as a whole.

I imagine what it will be like to sit in the lecture hall while he teaches. I hadn't expected this opportunity since I never plan to take any of his courses, and honestly, I'm looking forward to it.

I briefly close my eyes and revel in visions of him at the front of the room, hair knotted back away from his face, his button-down shirt neatly tucked into his trousers with the sleeves rolled up his forearms.

I'm just getting to the good part of my daydream — the part where he looks at me in the back row, smiles, and winks — when I trip for the second time today. *Dammit!* Brody is not here to catch me this time, so I hit the brick walkway, hard, and tear a hole in the knee of my favorite red tights.

To make matters worse, my glasses fall off my face when I trip and land face down on the brick. *Fuck. My. Life.* I retrieve my glasses and inspect them for scratches. A damp yellow leaf clings to one lens, but other than that I don't see any irreparable damage. I'll find out for sure once I'm home and have better lighting.

Did anyone see that? Of course, they did, Alis. You're walking across campus in the middle of a weekday afternoon.

Thankfully none of the passersby are close enough to lend aid and draw more attention to my blunder. I stand, brush the bit of dirt and leaves off my skirt, knees, and shins, readjust my messenger bag across my front, and carry on. *Nothing to see here, folks.*

Scuffed palms, ruined tights, a scraped and slightly bloody knee, shattered confidence in my ability to walk and do *anything* else simultaneously — the consequences of fantasizing about Dexter Belanger.

As if I need any more reasons to keep him at arms' length. *Sorry, Sexy Dexy, but you're a hazard to my person.*

Dexter

I'm walking toward my car at the end of the day when I hear my name being called by a familiar voice. I turn and see Dr. Matthews walking toward me, briefcase in hand and her long peacoat buttoned and knotted at her waist with a popped collar in an attempt to keep out more of the chilly autumn air. Add a deerstalker and she'd be a right Sherlock Holmes.

"Dr. Matthews," I give her a nod, acknowledging her as she approaches me.

"Dexter, I'm so glad I caught you. Do you have a minute?" She's winded from her power walk.

"Sure thing. Everything alright?" I ask while she calms her breaths, now only the cool temps are affecting her.

"Yes. It's about my intensive and the lectures you're presenting that week." Ah, she must be adding to my workload, yet again. Not that I mind. More time filling in for Abigail means more time with Alis.

"Need to add on another? No problem. It's fall break that week so I don't have any other classes to attend."

"Actually, quite the opposite. I met with Alis earlier today and she reminded me that she's already teaching a handful of these topics in my Wednesday class. I've been so scatterbrained lately with the overlaps and extra workload with fewer staff, it completely slipped my mind that my TA is just that — my teaching assistant." Dr. Matthews gives a self-deprecating laugh and shakes her head. "So, you're off the hook. Well, except for two. At the moment I can't remember which two, but I do remember that you only have to present two lectures and Alis will take the rest while I have overlap."

That's not what I wanted to hear. Less time with Alis? That's the opposite of what I want.

"Are you sure?" I press. "It's really no burden for me to cover the lectures we discussed. I'm sure Alis has a lot on her plate." Do I sound desperate? Not yet? No, not yet.

Dr. Matthews waves me off. "Nonsense. As I said, she brought it up. I'm sure she wouldn't have if she didn't want more teaching opportunities. When we talked at the beginning of the semester she marked off the dates for this class so she could dedicate her entire workweek to it. And you could use the time for planning, especially with Jonathan Ryan looking to teach a J-term intensive next year."

My eyes go wide. This is news to me. "What?! Since when?" Dr. Matthews smirks; she knew I wouldn't know and she no doubt anticipated my reaction.

"Keep it hush, but I caught wind of a lecture series he's presenting during his upcoming year-long sabbatical and figured I'd capitalize on the opportunity to boost the program with a class taught by him as a guest lecturer."

I can barely contain my excitement. "So it's for sure happening?" I ask, chomping at the bit for an opportunity to finagle my way into co-teaching with him.

"Nothing is set in stone, but I've opened dialogue with him about it." Her eagerness to solidify her plan is evident. "He'll be teaching in the US and Canada during the spring semester, then heading to Europe for the fall. The plan is to have him teach the entire lecture series as a two-week intensive as a sort of scrimmage presentation before he leaves Colorado for the start of the official series."

"That's genius. Think he'll go for it?"

"I hope so." She shrugs, "We'll have to wait and see. In the meantime, I want you to get your hands on his series outline and start building a syllabus for the class. If we have everything pre-organized, he's more likely to sign on."

I smile like a kid on Christmas morning. Me. Dexter Belanger. Build a class from Dr. Ryan's lecture series for him to teach at Middle Peak. I'm not thinking clearly when I nod my head enthusiastically and reply, "Yes. Yes of course I can do that. Anything I can do to help just let me know."

"I want the syllabus completed in three weeks." She cocks an eyebrow in question — or is that challenge? Does she think building a syllabus in three weeks when the content is provided *for* me will be an issue?

"Not a problem," I nod.

"Great. I'll see you tomorrow then."

I start to walk back toward my car when Dr. Matthews calls after me, saying, "And Dexter ..." I stop and look her way, letting her know I'm listening. "Keep this between us for now. I'd hate to get anyone's hopes up and have it fall through."

"Sure thing, boss," I say, saluting her with two fingers before unlocking my car with my fob.

Dr. Ryan teaching at Middle Peak. This is going to be incredible. And I get to build the syllabus for the class.

Me. Dexter Bellanger. Thirty-six-year-old, bottom-of-the-totem-pole French lit professor building a syllabus for the most celebrated scholar in our field. *This is amazing.*

Just as I close my driver-side door and slide my keys into the ignition I'm hit with a sudden rush of imposter syndrome.

Me. Dexter Bellanger. Thirty-six-year-old, bottom-of-the-totem-pole French lit professor building a syllabus for the most celebrated scholar in our field. *What the hell is Abigail Matthews thinking trusting me with this?!*

TWENTY-ONE

Alis

HE SHOULD WEAR *vests more often.* I'm sitting in the back row in the far right corner, supposedly grading quizzes while Dr. Belanger finishes up his lecture about research essays. I say *supposedly* because every few minutes I find myself staring at him as discreetly as possible, and before I know it I've wasted another ten minutes in a lustful trance. I can't help it — the man is next-level beautiful in a gray suit vest over a button-down with rolled-up sleeves and the top two buttons open. Seriously, delicious.

I'm still adjusting to this new facet of my personality — the formerly dormant wannabe sex kitten now fighting her way to the surface. I've stopped shoving her back into my mental vault. Turns out her claws are long enough to pick locks and free herself. Since she's not going anywhere, I may as well get to know her and grow comfortable in her presence. Hopefully embracing her will help me to gain control *of* her rather than being controlled *by* her.

I should be able to tell whether or not Jennifer Fitzgibbons completed last night's reading based on her multiple choice answers, but instead, I can give a detailed account of the way Dexter Belanger's arm muscles tug on the fabric of his dark blue shirt as he uses gestures to emphasize the importance of analysis and argument in writing.

Who knew talk of thorough and unbiased research could be so hot? Don't you worry, Dr. Belanger. I'd research every square inch of your body as thoroughly as possible. You won't find gaps or room for further argument when I'm done with you.

I'm chewing on my pen, eyes glued to him, when he looks my way and locks eyes with me. *Shoot me. I've been caught, again.* The last three times he caught me watching he didn't acknowledge my stares, instead reverting his gaze back to the class and continuing with his lecture. This time, however, he keeps his eyes on me and smirks before returning his attention to the students.

If only he had winked, last week's fantasy would have become reality. You'd think the consequences of said fantasy would deter me from allowing my thoughts to drift in that direction, but no. The longer I stay in this classroom watching him teach, the more I succumb to my attraction to him.

It's not like I'm the only female in this classroom checking him out. I bet the majority of the women in this class have no idea what he's even talking about because their eyes are glazed over with lust and their thoughts are a million miles away from the topic at hand.

"That's it for today. Don't forget to complete tonight's reading and we'll see you in class tomorrow morning." Just as Dexter returns to the lectern to close his laptop and gather his items to leave, four female students crowd around, asking him God only knows what in an attempt to capture even a second of his undivided attention.

Who am I kidding? I'm nearly as pathetic as they are. While I know I should pack up my stuff and leave, I instead find myself continuing the grading charade in hopes that I'll get a second alone with him when those girls finally leave. I just want to compliment him on his lecture, and maybe thank him for covering this section so I could catch up on grading and not have to take work home with me tonight. *If only I had actually graded while he taught instead of losing myself in his voice the entire time.*

Dammit to hell. I'm going to be up until midnight finishing these quizzes and I have no one to blame but myself.

"I never knew choosing a research topic could be so difficult! Do you have any time tomorrow to help me narrow it down, Dr. Belanger? Maybe during the lunch break?" I choke back a laugh (okay, fine, we both know it was a snort) at the girl's not-so-subtle come-on. I know he heard me, and there's no way I'll own up to it, so I keep my eyes fixed on the quiz before me and try my best to drown out the sounds of young twenty-somethings flirting with their professor. Dexter doesn't strike me as the cradle-robbing type.

I continue grading through two more quizzes when I'm interrupted by a masculine index finger tapping my desk. I look up and see Dexter smiling down at me, eyebrow raised in amusement. "Enjoying yourself back here, Miss Gilmore?"

I push my glasses back up my nose and reply, "Quiz grading *is* riveting."

"Is that so? It looked to me like you were more interested in Daphne's research topic struggles than the quizzes." Dammit, I knew he heard me. "Either that or you were honing your pig impersonation. Five stars, by the way. That was a solid snort if I've ever heard one." *Kill me now.*

"No idea what you're talking about. Which one is Daphne?" I feign ignorance, picking up the stack of graded quizzes and tapping them on the desk to align the papers before setting down the stack and thumbing through the ones I have left.

Dexter snickers and asks, "Need some help finishing up?" *Yes, please.*

"I'm good. I'll just take them home and finish up there." Staying in this room with him for one second longer is not a good idea. I can hardly pay attention to what I'm supposed to be doing when he's in the same room, not paying attention to me and surrounded by fifty-something students.

"Nonsense. I finished class more than an hour early." Dexter raps his index knuckle on the desk twice to pull my attention from the papers and back to him. "Let's order a pizza and knock these out before closing up shop for the night."

I look up to tell him that won't be necessary, but the second our eyes meet my brain short circuits and my mouth betrays me. "Sure. Yeah. Okay." *Watch out, Lin Manuel Miranda. Master wordsmith Alis Gilmore comin' at ya.*

"Great," Dexter smiles down at me and picks up the stack of not-yet-graded quizzes. He takes a step back and nods toward the door. "Let's head to my office. We'll drop off our stuff and walk over to Nico's."

We're almost to his office building, comfortably chatting about the upcoming topics for the class, when a thought slaps me upside the head.

Hold up. Dinner and then work? I thought we were dinnering while working. As in, simultaneously. Is dinnering even a word? My mental Word document doesn't show any red squiggles, so I'm pretty sure it's a word. Interesting.

Dexter is still talking about the strengths and weaknesses he saw in the students based on their interactions in class today. He doesn't seem to notice my mental hyperventilation.

I need a few minutes to clear my brain fog before I can do anything alongside this man, so I cut him off mid-sentence and ask, "Would it be okay if I get to work on these quizzes while you grab the food?" I don't know if it's weird to ask him to leave me in his office, alone, but the words are out of my mouth before I consider anything outside of my need for space.

"Not a problem," he says, smiling down at me as he opens the building door for me to enter. The dim hallway lights are our only guide to his pod, offices and lobbies alike dark without their usual inhabitants busy at work.

It's nearly seven thirty and most people leave for the day at five, so the dark offices don't surprise me. However, I had hoped the cleaning crew would still be working on this building so we wouldn't be *completely* alone.

No such luck.

The second I step foot into his office I'm enveloped by his scent. God, he smells *so good.*

I make myself at home in his sitting area, retrieving the quizzes and my red pen from my bag. Dexter, thankfully, reads the room and sets his bag down before saying, "I'll be back in a bit."

"Thanks," I say, not looking up from the quizzes. I don't want to be rude; I'm just overwhelmed with everything right now and I need a few minutes to sort through all these thoughts and emotions before I interact with him again.

Actually, no. I don't need to sort through my emotions right now because that will just bring them to the forefront of my mind and distract me, once again, from finishing these quizzes. I finish grading another quiz and then pull out my phone to inform Skye about tonight's schedule change.

> Alis: Class ended early but I have some grading to knock out so I'm going to do that here before I head home.

> Skye: Ok. Hiding out in the library?

> Alis: I wish. I'm in L&L.

> Skye: … you don't have an office in L&L.

> Skye: OMG ARE YOU WITH DEXTER?!

> Alis: It's not a big deal. He offered to help me finish grading so I wouldn't have to take it home.

> Skye: *smirking face emoji*

> Alis: I'll be home in a few hours. I don't think I'll be late, but I wanted to touch base with you just in case.

> Skye: Just in case you get carried away with Sexy Dexy and try to sneak in around 1 a.m.?

> Alis: *face palm emoji* No. Just in case I'm a little late coming home since we're going to grade all the quizzes here.

Skye: "grade all the quizzes" is a euphemism for
"have all the sex"

Alis: How are we friends?!

Skye: "Talk nerdy to me, Dexter!"

Alis: Don't let Sunny stay up past nine.

I swear, that woman could turn a conversation about pre-teen acne into something sexual. I tried to get into her headspace once — imagined what it's like to twist any and every thought into a sex joke. Couldn't do it. I tried for maybe an hour before the headache set in. And by "tried" I mean it took a ridiculous amount of effort to force my thoughts in a perverted direction.

Just one more thing we don't have in common, yet, somehow, she's my best friend — she and Tori, whom I haven't heard from in weeks. Skye spends at least every other weekend visiting her in Moraine, but I haven't yet traveled home since we moved. Maybe next time we'll tag along with Skye and spend the weekend with my parents.

I thought I'd be more homesick after moving, but I haven't felt a longing for my parents until recently. After living under the same roof my entire life, save my few years in Ft. Ulysses, I needed the space. My parents have never been overbearing, and returning to my childhood home after living on my own for a few years wasn't *that* difficult, but I'm happy to be the head of my own household for once.

Some may find it strange that I chose to remain at my parents' home instead of getting a place for Sunny and me while we still lived in Moraine, but it worked well for us. At first it was necessary — what with being a twenty-one-year-old insta-parent while mourning my sister and brother-in-law — but by the time Sunny turned four we had a rhythm, a routine. We weren't a burden on my parents, nor were they on us. We were simply a family.

If we hadn't lived with my parents the past nine years, my savings account wouldn't be anywhere close to what it is now and I'd have to work another job to keep the bills paid. I can't imagine working full-time hours in addition to school, working with Dr. Matthews, and parenting. So, even though I hadn't intentionally saved on rent for nearly a decade to prepare for returning to school, I'm thankful things worked out the way they have.

The smell of pizza coming toward this office alerts me to Dexter's arrival, and I look up just in time to watch him walk through the office door with a giant pie in hand and a plastic bag with what looks to be bottled water, plates, and napkins.

"Holy cow! You don't expect us to eat all that, do you?!" My eyes are wide open in shock. That thing could feed four adults a complete meal, at least.

Dexter grins as he sets the pizza onto the coffee table in his office sitting area. "You forget I've shared a pizza with you before. I'm privy to your gluttonous obsession with the food."

I glare at him and set the quizzes aside, taking the bottled water Dexter offers to me. I uncap it to take a drink before responding. "You're one to talk. I've seen you inhale one or twenty slices of pizza these past few months."

"I'm not the one complaining about having too much of a good thing. That's you." He winks at me before opening the box and handing me a slice.

We've kept our weekly meetings professional, but I'd be remiss not to acknowledge the comfortable somewhat friendship we've developed by sharing lunch during those meetings. Our level of comfort with each other has increased since the day he stopped by my apartment and I told him about losing my sister and becoming Sunny's mother. Couple comfort with my increasingly lustful thoughts of him and I'm not sure how much longer I can withstand his charm.

Dexter

"I'm not complaining!" she laughs, mid-bite, cheese stringing from the slice to her teeth. She tries to hide her food-laugh fumble behind her other hand, but it's not working.

My God, she's stunning.

Teaching with Alis in close proximity is nearly impossible, yet I've managed these last few days. I want her in so many ways. Not just physically but emotionally, intellectually, the works. I want to know what she's thinking when I catch her watching me lecture, when her brow furrows while grading papers, when she laughs then suddenly stops, forcing herself back into professional mode when she catches herself letting go of formality in my presence. Like now. She's carefree and laughing while we talk and share dinner.

I could have sat in one of the club chairs, but my ever-growing need to be near her had me opting for the couch instead. We have space between us, but I wouldn't have to reach far to touch her. I can smell her perfume in this proximity, and I'm becoming more of an addict by the second.

"So, how's Sunny?" I ask, hoping she doesn't clam up at the mention of her personal life. She holds up a finger while she finishes chewing, then, thankfully, responds without hesitation.

"Great, actually," the smile on her face lights up the room. "She's making friends at school, loves her teacher. She and Skye have always been close, so having her live with us has been wonderful. I'm sure right now they're sitting on the couch, probably eating ice cream for dinner, and watching the Kardashians or some other dumb reality show." She finishes that last sentence with a laugh and an eye roll.

"I only met her the one time, but none of what you just said surprises me. That kid is a firecracker. And your friend," I shake my head and laugh, "she's something else."

Alis laughs along and rolls her eyes once more, "You have *no* idea. The two of them together is often overwhelming. Who knew two people could make so much noise?!"

"I figured you'd be used to constant noise, having a kid."

"I mean, yes. And also no," she says. "I love that my house is full of laughter and sarcastic comments, but Sunny is so much like her mom, who was the total opposite of me. Belle was always full steam ahead, and Sunny is the same way. I swear that kid never runs out of energy. I love to be around people, but I'm easily overwhelmed and need space and quiet to recharge. It's hard to find that, living with two extroverts in a 1,000-square-foot apartment."

She doesn't often talk about her sister, so I take the opportunity to prod a bit deeper. "You've mentioned your sister before. How was she different from you?"

A soft smile graces Alis's face and she looks out my office window as she answers. "Belle was ... she was amazing in every way."

"Doesn't sound any different from you yet," I interject. Her cheeks flush at my comment.

She looks back to me and continues. "Belle had a never-ending supply of positive energy. She was the life of the party, but not in an arrogant way. She didn't cause a scene to make herself the center of attention; people just couldn't help but be drawn to her. She was snarky and sarcastic without being rude. She was beautiful and popular, but not in a Mean Girls kind of way. She had this way of making you feel like the most important person in the world when in a conversation. Like, um, how do I explain it ..." she pauses, trying to put words to her thoughts.

"She focused her attention on the person she was speaking with instead of multitasking?" I ask.

Alis snaps her fingers and points in confirmation. "Yes! Exactly!" The smile on her face as she continues gushing about her sister is incredible. I've seen her happy plenty of times over the last few months, but I've never seen her light up quite this much.

"She was my very best friend. And I don't just say that because she's gone and I only think about the good times. She truly was my very best friend. Never treated me like a nuisance or a child. Never made me feel insecure or awkward about my introverted personality. I mean, she definitely pushed me to live outside my comfort zone, but not in a way that made me feel pressured or like something was wrong with me."

"What do you mean by that?" I ask. "Why would you ever think there was something wrong with you?"

"Poor word choice. What I meant was that Belle never made me feel awkward for being introverted or for living in my own comfort bubble. She wanted me to go on adventures with her and she certainly talked me into doing a lot of crazy stuff I'd never have had the nerve to do on my own, but she was encouraging about it. Not demeaning. Does that make sense?"

I nod, and she continues.

She pauses again and laughs, shaking her head and looking down at the empty paper plate she's fidgeting with on her lap. "She took risks — ran off to Ireland for a semester abroad, fell in love at first sight, and eloped with her husband two weeks later. I thought mom was going to have a stroke when Belle called and said, 'I'm a Donnelly!'"

Alis is now using her entire upper body to tell the story and it's mesmerizing to watch her light up this way.

"At first my mom thought a Donnelly was some sort of Irish slang, and when she asked for clarification Belle squealed, 'I'm married! Alex and I eloped!' I laughed so hard at the expression on her face. She froze for a few seconds until Belle said, 'Mom?' and then she snapped out of it and yelled for my dad to get his ass in the kitchen before she strangled their oldest through the phone."

"Damn," I laugh.

"Seriously. I thought my dad would take mom's side and say she was crazy for eloping after only knowing the guy for two weeks, but he didn't. He asked her if he was a good man, and she said yes. He asked if she was in love, and she said yes. Then he asked to talk to Alex and she handed over the phone to him. Dad asked him the same questions and then said, 'Alright. I don't know you, but I know my daughter and I trust that she wouldn't have hitched herself to you if she wasn't certain you are what she wants. Be good to her. Make sure you bring her back at the end of the semester, and we'll be good. Try to keep her in Ireland, and I'll gut you.'" At this point, Alis can barely talk through her laughter. Her dad sounds great, and also terrifying.

"How did Alex react to that?" I ask.

"He said, 'Yes, sir. We'll see you in December.' And then they got off the phone." She shrugs her shoulders as if to say *the end*.

Alis calms her laughter and then lets out a wistful sigh. "They flew home at the end of the semester and built their life in Moraine. You'd think the extroverted sister would want to spend her life traveling the world and living all over the place, but Belle was always certain that she wanted a family, and she wanted to raise that family in Moraine. I, on the other hand, never imagined I'd live there again once I left for college. It took me a while to adjust to living back home after she passed."

"I can see how much you loved her," I say, laying my hand on her intertwined fingers now resting on her lap. Her breath hitches at the contact but she doesn't pull away from my touch; instead, she looks up into my eyes, slowly, and breathes out, "Yeah. I did. I really, really did."

I tempt fate and leave my hand where it lay, stroking my thumb over hers. "You're more like her than you think," I say quietly, looking up from our hands and into her eyes.

Alis scrunches her brow. "How can you say that when you didn't know her?" she asks, not in a snarky way but as if she's genuinely wondering how I came to this conclusion.

"You're right. I didn't know her. But I know you, and I know everything you've told me about her. I haven't heard a single thing about Belle that couldn't be said about you as well."

I pause, tilting my head to the side a bit, and I squeeze her hand as I jest, "Well, except for enjoying being the center of attention and eloping after knowing someone for only two weeks. You seem the type to be more keen on sleeping in the Parisian catacombs than having a spotlight pointed at you."

Alis responds by chuckling and rolling her eyes. "I don't know that I'd go that far, but you're right that being singled out in a group of people is pretty much my worst nightmare."

"I think teaching is your exception," I comment. She looks down at our hands, still one on top of the other, and blushes.

"Thank you," she says, and then calmly and slowly slides her hands from under mine. Sliding her gaze from our hands to the stack of papers on the table, Alis takes the opportunity to venture out of personal conversation territory and back to the task at hand.

She nods her head toward the coffee table and says, "We should grade."

TWENTY-TWO

Alis

UMPH. "WHAT THE?!" I bolt upright in bed and look to my left, then to my right, before realizing my sleep mask is still on and I can't see a darn thing. Someone launched themselves onto my full-sized bed, waking me before my alarm. Pulling my eye mask down to my neck, I see Skye perched on her elbow, smirking at me like she knows something.

"What the hell are you doing in my bed?" I ask, frustration evident in my tone.

"Can't a girl greet her bestie in the morning?" She gives me doe eyes as if she's innocent. Fat chance.

I grab my phone and check the time. "It's 4:30 a.m. Unless you are dying, I'm going back to sleep."

Before I can mask up and fall back into my wonderful, dreamless sleep, Skye grabs my wrist and whines, "Nooooooo. You can't go back to sleep! I have to leave for work in twenty minutes but first I have to hear about last night!"

"Last night? What about it?" I'm not awake enough to remember anything right now, much less specifics of my evening activities.

Skye shoves my shoulder. "What happened with Sexy Dexy, obviously!"

"First, don't hit me. Second, nothing happened. We ate pizza and graded quizzes. Then I came home." My matter-of-fact tone leaves nothing to the imagination. Nothing happened. *Except when he held my hand while talking about my sister…* but that doesn't count as *something*.

"I call bullshit." Skye sits up on her knees and bounces, shaking me even more awake than before.

"Not bullshit. Also, stop bouncing!" She can shove me? I can shove her. Right off the side of my bed. Skye catches herself before falling off the bed, face revealing that she still doesn't believe a word I've said.

"If you're serious and nothing happened, you're even more of a prude than I gave you credit for," she scoffs. Seriously? Just because I don't salivate over anything with two legs and a dick doesn't mean I'm a prude.

I rub the sleep from my eyes and sigh, not wanting to have this conversation for the umpteenth time. "Skye, I told you. We work together. He's a professor. I'm his grader. Nothing is going on. I'm not going there."

"But why?! I saw how he looked at you the day he came over. That man wants you. And don't even lie and say you don't want him right back. He's a walking professorgasm, I swear. That man could make me go back to school."

Professorgasm. That's a new one.

"I'm not getting involved with a professor. Period."

"So you don't deny you want him." *Stop pushing me, woman.*

"Skye."

"That's not an answer." *Isn't it, though?*

"It doesn't matter if he wants me or if I want him. It's not happening. Go away. I need sleep." I lay back and lift my mask to cover my eyes, thinking she'll finally leave. Nope. Her next words make my entire body stiffen.

"This is about that douche canoe from Grant, isn't it." *She did not just say that.* I lay silent, hiding behind my mask. If I don't respond, maybe she'll just go on her merry way.

"Alis." Nope. Still not responding.

"I knew it," she says, disappointment heavy in her words. "You're really going to let something that DIDN'T happen a decade ago prevent you from a good thing with a great guy."

I remain silent and unmoving. Please, just leave me alone. Not all of us have the desire to slay our own demons, okay?

"Whatever. It's your life. But as your best friend, I have a responsibility to be honest with you and right now the truth is you're acting like a fucktard." She stands and I feel her weight leave my bed. I hear her walk toward the door and she stops, saying, "I haven't seen you interested in anyone since college, and now that you finally feel sparks with someone you're going to let the ghost of graduate programs past hold you back. Stop being a coward, Alis. You're better than that."

With that, she leaves, slamming my bedroom door and leaving me to wallow in denial and self-pity.

Dexter

We made progress last night. After she let our hands rest on top of one another during our conversation I knew she could no longer deny the chemistry between us. Not that she's ever really denied it, per se, but she's avoided it. I still do not understand why she's so concerned with others' perceptions of our relationship. Sure, Alis prefers to go unnoticed, but she's not insecure or lacking confidence. She also isn't without a backbone. She's strong, intelligent, beautiful, and anyone who has spent even five minutes in her presence knows it. She could never be accused of sleeping her way to the top — *of academia? What a joke!*

I want to pursue her. I also don't want my actions to scare her or push her away. She's made it clear on more than one occasion that my advances are not welcome, but her actions and words contradict each other. I'm not a man with an overly aggressive personality; I'm actually baffled by my dedication to pursuing a romantic relationship with Alis. I've never struggled with gaining a woman's attention, whether for a night or an actual relationship, but Alis is different.

Sure, I've wondered if the thrill of the chase is what keeps me interested, the challenge of it all. But that's not it. The more time I spend with her, the more I want to know her. I like her. Her thoughts. Her ideas. Her words. Her laugh. The spark of mischief in her eyes that she doesn't let out if she's not completely comfortable with present company. She may be introverted, but she's anything but boring. Even if (God, when) she stops resisting this growing connection between us, I know I won't lose interest.

My mind wanders back to the first night we met. I caught her reflection through the bar mirror and felt drawn to her. We slipped into an easy rapport as if we'd already known each other and were two people catching up, reminiscing about times past. I haven't felt a connection like this with a woman in what seems like forever; hell, even with Laura I didn't feel the sense of home I feel when I'm with Alis.

A knock sounds at my door, followed by the sound of Leo letting himself in.

"Yo, Dex!" he shouts. "Patio!" I holler through the open sliding glass door. Now that hockey season is fully underway, Leo and I spend game nights grilling and watching our favorite teams play. Being from Montreal, I'm a Canadiens fan at my core, while Leo pulls for the Hurricanes.

"Beer?" Leo asks as he opens my fridge to grab himself something to drink before stepping outside. "I'm good. Thanks."

He walks out and sits in the patio chair not facing the setting sun and takes a swig from his bottle. "How goes it?" he asks.

"Good. Just trying not to burn the meat. You?" We're a talkative pair, I tell ya.

Leo sets his beer on the table and leans forward on his elbows, hands clasped on the table. "Good."

Silence stretches between us. Leo's had so much shit going on with his ex lately I just expect him to fill in the space with complaining or hockey talk. But, nothing. He just continues to sit, leaning on his elbows, staring at me.

"What?" I ask, eyebrow raised.

"What, what?" he replies. Seriously?

"I'm waiting for your rant. What has Stephanie done this week?" I ask, prodding. If he'll vent about his ex then I can stop thinking about all the ways I could fuck up my relationship with Alis by pursuing her.

"Haven't heard from her. Not since I told her I'm no longer her emotional support animal."

"I bet she took that well," I laugh, imagining Stephanie's rage face coming on full force with Leo's dismissal.

"Wouldn't know. I blocked her number. Figure if something happens with George, Linda can call me with an update." George and Linda are Stephanie's parents. They've been more like actual parents than in-laws for Leo, and even after the divorce, he's remained close with them both.

"Anything new going on with them? George still in treatment?" I ask.

"Yeah," Leo sighs, running a hand over his face. "I haven't seen them in a few weeks, but when I talked to George a few days ago he said after this next round of chemo they'll have a better idea of what comes next."

"Next, as in, remission?" God, I hope so. Losing George would crush Leo.

He shrugs. "Maybe? Yes? I honestly don't know." Leo leans back in his chair and clasps his hands behind his neck. "Everything has been so up and down with this cancer shit. I want to be there for him through every step, but fucking Stephanie is always right there with her idiot husband. Rather than being supportive and mature about things, being near them makes me want to punch a fucking wall."

"Yeah, I can see how that wouldn't be helpful," I smirk.

"Nope. Not at all," he says. "After she called crying about her marriage issues and asking me for advice or whatever I knew I couldn't physically be around her anymore. I hate that it means I can't be with George and Linda as often, but what am I supposed to do? They're her fucking parents, man."

"Rock, meet hard place."

Leo scoffs. "No fucking joke." He pauses and takes another sip of his beer, then says, "What about you? Talk to me about something in your life so I don't have to think about mine."

My life is literally the most uninteresting topic of conversation. I work, watch hockey, read books … that's it.

"Sorry to disappoint, but I've got nothing." I turn back to the grill and flip the steaks.

"What about the grader? You still into her? What's happening there?" I've never gone to Leo for relationship advice — not that I've ever had a relationship to speak of since meeting him — but perhaps he can help me work out of my own rock-and-hard-place situation.

I grab my beer off the tray next to the grill and take a seat at the patio table with Leo. "Yeah, I'm still into her," I say. "And I'm pretty positive she's into me. But she shuts me down at every chance."

Leo laughs. "Why is she shutting you down, again?"

"At first she said it's because she just moved here and needed to find her footing. Then it was because I'm a professor and she's a student, which I'd understand if she was in her early twenties or something but she's thirty. It's not like some old fuck coming onto a kid, eh?" I shake my head in annoyance, taking another swig of my beer.

I continue, "She has a kid." This catches Leo's attention.

"No shit?"

"Yeah. I met her a few weeks ago when I stopped by her apartment when she was out sick."

Leo pauses his bottle mid-lift to his mouth. "You did what?"

Running my hand through my hair, I tip my head back and blow out a breath. "Yeah. She was out sick for a week or something and wasn't responding to emails, so I got her address from Deborah and went over there."

Leo snorts and shakes his head, looking down at his beer. "And how'd that go over?"

I smile, remembering how uncomfortable Alis felt at first, but then how she opened up to me before I left. "Good, man. Really good. At first, she was caught off guard, but I think it was because of her kid. I had no idea she was a mom, but it makes sense given how cagey she'd been. I don't buy the professor/student excuse because she knows she'll never be in one of my classes, but she's clinging to it."

"Have you mentioned any of this to Abigail?" Leo asks.

"No, but that's a thought. Maybe if I clear it with Abigail first I can assuage Alis's fears of crossing this imaginary line she's created. I've been trying to figure out how to move forward with her without disrespecting her boundaries, but I swear, man, her words and her body language say two completely different things."

"Body language?" Leo asks.

"Yeah. Like when we co-taught that fall break intensive for Abigail, I swear I caught her staring at me with fuck-me eyes at least ten times."

"Don't most female students stare at you that way?"

I scoff. "You know what I mean. With her, it's different. It's not like the twenty-year-olds who look at me like they want to suck me off because I'm forbidden fruit. When Alis looks at me it's because she wants *me*, not her professor."

"So he looks at you like Savannah does," Leo smirks right before taking another swig of his beer.

I kick his shin under the table. "Fuck off. You know it's not like that, either."

I stand to check the steaks before he can return the jab, and thankfully Leo doesn't say anything more on the topic. I pull the steaks from the grill and we head inside for an evening of yelling at the television, none of which includes talk about women.

Perhaps Leo is right, and I should talk to Abigail before I try anything further with Alis. Women like it when men take charge of things like this, right?

TWENTY-THREE

Dexter

THE NEXT MORNING I head into my weekly catch-up with Abigail. I have the proposed syllabus for the Ryan intensive ready to go, and I'm hoping for an update on whether or not he'll be joining us.

"Good morning, Amelia," I greet Dr. Matthews' administrative assistant on my way to her office.

"Good morning, Dr. Belanger," she greets. "You can head on in."

I nod my thanks and continue to Abigail's office door, rapping my knuckles twice as I enter.

Abigail Matthews is a powerhouse, a woman to be respected. She's sitting at her desk, glasses on, as she types away on her computer. "Just one moment, Dexter. I'll be with you as soon as I finish this email."

I make my way to the chairs across from her and take a seat, crossing my ankle over my knee as I take in the killer view to my left. I know better than to speak and interrupt her while she's in the middle of something. Let's just say I've been on the receiving end of her death glare a time or twelve.

While I emailed a copy of the syllabus to her this morning before making my way up here, I retrieve the printed copy from my bag while I wait. Glancing over it one last time, I feel confident in what I've put together. I'm open to any tweaks Dr. Matthews recommends, but it would feel fucking fantastic to get her stamp of approval as-is. I've never worked directly with Jonathan Ryan, and for this class to happen would be a dream come true.

"Right. Good morning," Abigail says as she looks up from her computer screen and removes her glasses.

"Good morning," I respond. "I emailed you the proposed syllabus for the Ryan class, and have a printed copy for you here." Dr. Matthews grins in approval as I hand her the printed copy — after all, what English professor doesn't love any opportunity to bust out their trusty red pen. Sure enough, she snags the red sitting on top of her keyboard and removes the cap, using it as a cursor as she reads through the syllabus content.

She makes a few notes in the margins but doesn't cross out entire sections, so I'm feeling optimistic about my proposal.

"You reached out to Ryan's assistant for the lecture series structure, yes?" she asks, not looking up from the papers in front of her.

"I did, yes." I know better than to call her ma'am. I struggled when I first moved here to drop the formality, considering my upbringing required *monsieur* and *madame* when responding to any person of authority. The first time I ever called Abigail madame, she gave me the first of many cutting glares and said, "I don't run a brothel. Dr. Matthews is fine." Considering we were in Montreal at the time, I didn't anticipate her pushing back on a French custom. However, as I said before, Abigail Matthews is a powerhouse and stands her ground, cultural niceties be damned. Upon successful completion of my dissertation defense, she asked me to call her Abigail. I was no longer a student, after all. I was now Dexter Belanger, PhD. I was her peer.

"I like it," she nods and hands the syllabus back to me. "I noted a few changes, but nothing major. What do you think?" Another reason I respect her so very much — she values others' opinions and welcomes push-back.

I read through her notes, nodding along as I silently agree with each one. "I'll make the changes as soon as we're finished here. Do you think he's actually going to say yes?" I ask.

Abigail smiles, the excitement in her eyes a confirmation of her scheming being successful. "I do. I've been emailing with him for the last few weeks, and he wants this, I can tell. If we can send him the finalized syllabus today, we should hear back by the end of the week."

I can't hide the excitement in my response. "This is going to be amazing for our lit program. Are we opening the course to auditors? Prospects?"

"Oh, definitely," she affirms. "We've grown over the last few years, but not enough for the board to take notice. I'm still pissed we didn't get the extra funding this year." I'd say I'm angry, but if we had that funding, Alis wouldn't be my grader and she wouldn't spend an hour lunch meeting with me each week.

"The way I see it," she continues, "if we can draw enough attention to this class to bring in prospects and also get enough under-grads to use an elective spot for the course, we can kill three birds with one stone."

"Three?" I question.

"Three. I know Ryan won't leave Grant anytime soon — the pay is too good and he's got their trustees eating out of his palm. However, if this is successful enough, I bet we could secure him as an adjunct. If nothing more, we can offer this class annually and embed it in the catalog for both English and French Lit tracks. Simply having his name in the course catalog will draw students who couldn't get into his program at Grant."

"Good thinking. I didn't even consider that as a possibility."

"I need to expand this program. I know we aren't ever going to be upper echelon when it comes to lit programs, but we are solid and worth pursuing. If I can get Ryan on as a committed adjunct and have his name officially on our program documents, I'm certain we could expand both our English and French Lit programs by at least fifty percent over the next three years." She's buzzing with excite-ment now, and watching her is intoxicating.

"That's huge. How did you come about those numbers?" Not trying to rain on her parade, but is she spewing facts or fancies?

"This is how I know Ryan wants to say yes to coming this January. We've talked numbers and future possibilities. He provided me with the stats for his applicants and acceptance rates from Grant. Did you know they turn away more than three thousand lit applicants each year? And that's just undergrad. Their acceptance rate for graduate lit studies is nine percent. NINE percent!" She emphasizes that last bit, and my eyes almost bulge out of their sockets.

"When did Grant become Harvard?" I jest. But, damn, that's lower than I realized.

Abigail laughs. "Nine percent is not four percent, but I agree. Ryan is a goddamn celebrity in academia. I'll gladly take his castoffs, assuming they meet our entry requirements. The board can't ignore us if we're growing."

"It's true. Everybody loves Jonathan Ryan. Good thinking, boss," I commend her.

"Thank you, Dexter," she says. "This program means so very much to me, and while we aren't in danger of losing anyone, I want to ensure we reach our full potential and continue to grow."

"You're doing excellent work. I'm proud to be here at Middle Peak, especially under your leadership," I say.

Abigail gives me a wry look and says, "Stop kissing my ass, Belanger. I already gave you the class with him. I don't have anything more to offer at present."

I laugh at her calling me out on my brown-nosing. "So besides finalizing this syllabus and getting it back to you today, what else do you need from me?"

Dr. Matthews taps her pen against her desk a few times before saying, "I need you to continue to keep this quiet for the time being. Assuming everything goes to plan, we'll have Jonathan come for a visit in the next three weeks. Nothing fancy, just two or three days. He's been to the campus before, but it's been years and it'll be good to refamiliarize him with the area. We'll have a dinner party, of course. Bring your charm, and your French. You know he'll love that."

"Can do. I'll wear a suit and even trim my beard, just for you," I offer her my most alluring smile and she rolls her eyes.

"Not for me, boy. For him," she says, playfully. "You already won me over. Now you need to use your skills to convince him to stay beyond the one-time January class. You built the syllabus for this class, now sell him on why it needs continual repeat performances."

"Not a problem at all, Abigail," I assure her.

"Excellent. I don't have anything else to discuss at present; do you?" she asks, not rushing me out of her office as I expect.

I pause for a few seconds, considering whether or not I should heed Leo's advice about talking to Abigail about Alis before saying to hell with it. I'm going for it.

"Actually, yes." I clear my throat and continue, "I'd like to talk with you about the fraternization policy."

This gets her attention. "Go on," she gestures. Fuck me. I don't know if this is the best or worst idea I've ever had.

"I'm considering pursuing a relationship outside work with a woman who is also an employee at Middle Peak, and while I know it's not strictly off limits, I want to ensure this relationship won't be frowned upon by my colleagues."

"I see," Abigail nods. "And is this woman one to cause drama that would result in negative comments from your colleagues or the administration?" Her quirked eyebrow confuses me. She knows I'm never one for drama, so I don't understand why she'd even ask.

"Um, no?" I say. "Why would you think that?"

"I don't think that, but I've also never had a conversation about fraternization with you, Dexter Belanger. I've never known of any romantic relationship in your life — I assume if you are or have been with any woman it's always been separate from the university." I nod, and she continues. "Considering Middle Peak doesn't have a fraternization policy concerning our employees, I don't know why we're having this discussion in the first place."

Of course, she wouldn't. Because she thinks I'm asking about another faculty member.

I rub the back of my neck, not wanting to be cryptic but also not wanting to go into detail out of fear that Alis will hate me for bringing this up to Abigail in the first place. I've come this far, and I'm doing this to ease any worries Alis may have about us 'crossing the line' as she says, so I decide to go all in.

"It's Alis Gilmore." I'm sitting straight and looking directly at Abigail, trying to convey confidence. I expect to see a shocked expression on Abigail's face, but all I see is relief. Relief?

She lets out a breath. "Oh thank God. I thought you were about to say Savannah Martin and then I was going to have to ask what the hell is wrong with you."

That catches me by surprise. "Savannah Martin? Where did that come from?!"

"Oh, please, Dexter." Abigail waves her hand as if to say, *seriously?* "You think everyone hasn't noticed her flirtatious behavior toward you since you arrived? I've never seen a woman touch a man who is not her significant other more than she touches you. She's a smart girl, an incredible political science professor, but she's not subtle about wanting you. That woman couldn't play coy if her life depended on it."

I laugh, "She is definitely forward."

"I respect that," Abigail says. "But I also think a woman should know when to accept defeat. Here I was thinking you had finally caved to her advances. I never thought I'd see the day."

"That will never happen," I affirm. "The only woman I'm interested in pursuing is Alis."

Abigail smiles, "Alis. She's such a lovely young woman. You two would be beautiful together. I assume the interest is reciprocated?"

"I believe so, yes," I nod. "But she's adamant about not crossing the professor/student line. I've explained to her that it won't be an issue because she isn't my student, nor is she my employee. Sure, she grades for me, but that's it. She doesn't report to me, nor will she ever, so this isn't a problem. Also, she's thirty. I'm thirty-six. She acts like our relationship would be something taboo, and her fear is misplaced."

Abigail nods in agreement, then says, "I'm sure she has other reasons for being hesitant to get involved with anyone, not just you."

"You mean Sunny?" I ask. Now Abigail dons the surprised face I expected when I first mentioned Alis's name.

"You know about her daughter?" she asks.

"Yes, I've actually met her. She's hilarious!" I say, thinking back to the day at her apartment.

Abigail's eyes grow even wider. "You've met her? Well, that was unexpected. She rarely ever talks about her daughter. Am I assuming correctly that you know the history there?"

"I do," I nod. "She's been through a lot, and I respect the hell out of her for coming back to finish school almost a decade later. She's inspiring. Makes me want to be with her even more, if I'm honest."

Abigail places an elbow on her desk and leans forward, chin resting on her hand. "You're serious about her? This isn't casual?" she asks.

A smile spreads across my face. "Very serious. I've been captivated by her since the moment I met her, and that hasn't happened with anyone else. I wouldn't play games with a single mother. I want to be with her."

"Have you told her this?"

"Not in so many words. Whenever I've tried to broach the subject of us as more than friends or colleagues, she shuts me down before the conversation even begins."

"And you're sure she wants this?"

"I think so. I really do. I wouldn't be here talking to you if I didn't. I truly believe that the professor/student status is her only hangup, and it's as if she refuses to hear me when I say it won't be an issue. I honestly don't know if I'm ruining my chances by talking to you about her, but nothing else has worked so this is my Hail Mary, if you will."

Abigail smirks and sits back in her chair. "Could go either way. But I commend your effort, nonetheless."

"Thanks?" I laugh. We're silent for a moment, and then Dr. Matthews says, "Well?"

"Well, what?" I ask.

"Are you going to finalize the syllabus so we can get this ball rolling or are you going to sit on your ass and talk to me about your feelings all day?" I know she's poking fun at me, but she's also completely serious.

"Sorry, Abigail," I say as I wipe my hands down my thighs and retrieve my bag from beside the chair before standing. "I'll get right on that and have it to you by lunch."

I turn to leave when Abigail says, "And Dexter?"

I look back at her, waiting to hear whatever pearls of wisdom she has for me.

"Good luck with Alis. She's a great girl, and you both deserve to be happy." The warm expression on her face is more than encouragement from my boss. She truly does care.

"I appreciate it," I say. Then head to my own office to polish off this syllabus.

TWENTY-FOUR

Alis

> Dexter: Tu es libre pour déjeuner aujourd'hui? (Are
> you free for lunch today?)

My phone buzzed earlier during class, but I waited to check it until my lecture was finished. I am free for lunch today, but I've done a stellar job at avoiding Dexter since we basically held hands last week during our evening conversation. A text not responded to is akin to the red notification bubble on my phone screen — that is, nails on a chalkboard — so I have to respond.

I consider texting Skye to ask her opinion, but I already know what she'll say. *Why am I overthinking this? It's just lunch.*

> Alis: Oui, ça me ferait plaisir. (Yes, I'd like that.)

No going back now. I don't have to wait a full minute before he responds.

> Dexter: Merveilleux. On se retrouve à mon bureau à
> midi? (Wonderful. Shall we meet at my office at
> noon?)

At ten to noon I walk into L&L and see Dexter coming out of his office before I even have the chance to greet Deborah. He looks up and smiles when he sees me — a full-on, no-holding-back smile as opposed to his typical half smile.

"Hey," he says. "You hungry?"

His smile is contagious. I can't figure out if my carefully constructed wall of defense is in ruins or temporarily unguarded since I'm willingly here as Alis, the woman, and not Alis, the grader and student. He's Dexter, the man, to me right now, and it's evident from the light in his eyes that he knows it. I haven't seen him this transparent since the night at the bar.

I've spent the last few months fighting my attraction to him, hiding large pieces of myself during every interaction out of fear and self-preservation. My heart feels lighter right now than it has in God only knows how long. I can breathe. I can smile. I can … not stop thinking about touching him and kissing him.

Shit. Good feeling's gone. We're on campus, in L&L, with Deborah not ten feet away. *Oh, Dexter. That megawatt smile is not appropriate for campus use.* My brain drifts off to cartoon land, replacing Dexter's smile with a banana, and I try not to laugh.

What was it Monty Python said about defending oneself from a man with a banana? *Now, it's quite simple to defend yourself against a man armed with a banana. First of all, you force him to drop the banana* — don't think he can drop a mouth attached to his face, but he could dial it back a bit. Bring back the half smile that's only slightly less swoon-worthy. *Then, second, you eat the banana, thus disarming him* — that's a negative, ghost rider. I can't eat his smile. Not in public. Thinking about kissing him is what has me raising my defenses in the first place. *You have now rendered him helpless.*

Oh, but how wrong you are, Monty Python. The only helpless one in this lobby right now is me.

"Alis?" Dexter asks. I blink and return his smile, "Yeah, sorry. I'm ready." I nod my head toward the exit and turn to walk that way, Dexter falling into step beside me.

"What are you hungry for?" His jovial attitude would be contagious if I wasn't so dumbstruck by how beautiful he is.

"I'm fine with whatever." I shrug. "I'm not due anywhere until Sunny gets out of school, so I just need to leave campus around 2:30. Nico's is fine."

Once we exit the building, Dexter starts walking toward the parking lot, as opposed to across campus to the popular pizza joint. "Not Nico's," he says. "Let's go somewhere off campus. Somewhere we can talk."

"Should we take two cars?" I adjust the messenger bag on my shoulder and keep in step with him.

"Not necessary. We won't venture too far," he assures. I nod in assent and Dexter places a hand at the small of my back, steering me toward his car. The black Range Rover is not what I expected Dexter Belanger to drive, especially since it looks brand new.

"You drive a Range Rover?! How do you afford that on a professor's salary?" Please don't tell me he's one of those secret millionaires like the men in romance novels. I swear those unrealistic characters piss me off. Just be a professor, for the love of Pete.

Dexter laughs at my incredulous expression. "Well, for starters, it's about ten years old and I bought it when I moved here three years ago."

"Ten years old?" I'm unapologetically dumbstruck by this revelation. "But it's so *shiny!*"

"What can I say?" he shrugs. "I take care of my things." *Does that mean he'd take care of Sunny and me as well?* Pause. Where did that thought come from? I'm perfectly capable of taking care of myself thankyouverymuch, brain.

Dexter opens the passenger door and I climb in, equally as impressed with the inside.

"I'm surprised your car is this clean on the inside," I say, a hint of mischief in my tone.

"*Oh, la vache.* I told you, I take care of my things." He pulls out of the parking space, heading toward the exit. Heading out of the safe campus bubble where I'm tightly insulated in imaginary bubble wrap, also known as my titles of grader and student.

"From the state of your desk, you could have fooled me." I expect a scoff, but Dexter just chuckles and shakes his head.

"My workspace and my living space are two very different things."

I'm not sure where to take the conversation from here, and Dexter seems to sense my anxiety. Thankfully, he takes the reins.

"I don't want to beat around the bush, and I don't want you to feel uncomfortable if I can help it." Diving right in, then.

"I appreciate that," I say, looking over at him. He looks so handsome right now. So confident. I've never understood how he can be so comfortable engaging with me in a non-student/professor relationship, but from the day we 'met' in his office he's never been anyone other than the same man I met at the bar a few days before — albeit the professional version.

"I'm not going to put you on the spot and ask why you agreed to have lunch with me today, knowing full well it isn't for our weekly meeting. You aren't ignorant about my attraction to you, and I've given a solid effort to maintaining a professional relationship with you these past few months."

I nod in agreement, giving him the words I know he wants as affirmation. "You have." I feel like I should offer more in the way of encouragement, but I'm too curious about his obviously planned monologue to interrupt.

"Last week, in my office, am I wrong to think something shifted between us? You let me touch you, didn't pull away. You didn't even flinch but instead seemed to relax more as I held your hand."

I can't deny what he's saying is true, but I also don't want to sound like a child offering single and double-word answers to his questions. Instead of verbalizing my affirmation, I rest my forearm up against his on the center console. Dexter takes my cue and continues.

"The more time I spend with you, the more confident I am that we could be great together — not just as colleagues or as friends. You're smart, funny, witty — not to mention fucking beautiful." Dexter glances my way and smiles as he says this, clearly anticipating the blush that creeps onto my face at his compliments. "I haven't been attracted to anyone so fully in my entire life, and I'd be an idiot not to tell you exactly how I feel. I'm not trying to pressure you, and I wouldn't have even brought this up if I didn't sense a natural progression toward more in our relationship. But, Alis, I want to be with you. And I honestly believe you want to be with me, as well."

We're at a stop light now and he doesn't end on a question, rather, a statement. As if he sees my walls for the bullshit they are and refuses to let me hide behind them a moment longer. Some could argue his insistence is the opposite of respecting my boundaries, but I don't feel that way. I know he respects me as a person, as a professional, as a friend. He's simply less willing to hide and pretend the pull between us doesn't exist.

Am I ready to stop pretending? Not necessarily. But why? Why am I so afraid of this? Why can't I simply give in to how I feel, free of worry?

Simply put, I don't like surprises. Good or bad. I like to see what's ahead, to plan my steps in advance. I like to analyze every possible outcome and make decisions based on what best aligns with my goals and priorities and Sunny. Could I analyze my relationship with Dexter and a potential future between us? Sure. But I haven't yet let myself venture down that path because I'm terrified I will get my hopes up, feel alive for the first time in nearly a decade, and then have it all ripped away from me once again.

God, I miss my sister. She knew how to live, to love. She knew how to let loose and encouraged me to do the same. I didn't just lose my best friend the day she died — I lost a piece of myself. The piece that felt safe enough to step out of bounds and try new things. The piece that threw caution to the wind because I knew if I stumbled or fell, Belle would be there to help me back up again.

I don't notice I'm crying, or that I've been lost in my thoughts for who knows how long, until I feel Dexter's thumb swipe away a tear from my cheek. "Are you okay?" he asks.

I didn't realize I was crying. This isn't the first time it's happened. I'm often sucked into my thoughts, my memories, my emotions, only resurfacing when someone or something intentionally forces my attention back to reality.

I wipe underneath my eyes, careful not to smear my mascara. "I'm fine. I'm sorry. I was just... just... remembering," I say.

"Remembering? What? Who?" Dexter sounds genuinely curious and interested in what I have to say, not defensive or jealous as if he assumes I'm thinking about another man, someone from my past. *Only one is worth remembering, and those memories are contained to a week in the Caribbean.*

I let out a breath, resolving to be honest with him about my fears. "I was trying to figure out why I'm so afraid of this. Of you." I bat my hands in the air, waving about as if they can erase the words I just said. "Not of *you*. But of *this*. Of us. Of... more."

I turn to look at him and realize we're in the restaurant parking lot. I don't even remember moving on from the red light. How long was I lost in my thoughts?

"We're here?" I ask, looking around as if we've been transported into another dimension rather than having arrived at our intended destination.

"We're here," he replies. "But we don't have to go inside if you don't want to. We can stay here and talk. I should have considered how uncomfortable this conversation would make you feel, and it was a dick move to assume you'd be obliged to have this conversation in public."

I wave him off. Even I couldn't have foreseen this level of emotional reaction to him speaking the truth of our situation. It's not like I've been oblivious to what's happening between us. In denial? Definitely. But not oblivious.

"You didn't do anything wrong. I'm fine, truly. And I need to have this conversation with you. Burying and ignoring my feelings for you isn't getting any easier — believe me, I've tried for months and all they do is grow stronger. Assholes." I grumble that last part and Dexter laughs at my irritation.

"So you like me, eh?" He's wielding that sexy, cocky smirk of his and I can't help but melt. I want to slap his arm, to play off my feelings as nothing more than a crush, but I've already decided to be honest. I decide not to quip back, and offer him the truth.

"I really do." *Well, that came out much more breathy than I anticipated.* I cough and continue, "I do. And I have since the night we met. It's never been about whether or not I like you. My hesitations are just … complicated." I shrug as if to convey, *what can you do?*

"Complicated," Dexter states. Again, not a question, not an affirmation. A statement. I nod, not sure where to go from here. Considering I cracked open Pandora's box of unresolved feelings not five minutes ago and started crying, I don't know that I can offer him any more truths right now. I need space to process them on my own, privately.

"I…" I begin, but pause, looking down at my lap and picking at my nails. "I don't know how to do this."

"Do what?" he asks. He's not annoyed. He's gentle, calmly prompting me to expound further without pushing too hard.

"Us. I don't know how to do 'us' or be an 'us' or even begin to think through what my life looks like with a man in it." I can feel the words welling up in my chest, and before I can regain any semblance of self-control, the word vomit begins. "I told you, before that night at the bar I hadn't even made out with a man since before my sister died. I went on a few dates, but they didn't mean anything. I literally only went on dates when Skye's nagging about revirginizing myself got too annoying and I wanted to shut her up. I'd acquiesce, she'd set me up with someone, we'd go out once or twice, and then I'd tell Skye I wasn't interested in the guy and she'd leave me alone for a while. Before that, when I was in school, I had a boyfriend for about a year? Maybe longer? I honestly don't remember. We were together, but it never felt deep or serious. I never felt drawn to him. He was nice. NICE. That's literally the only word I can think to describe him. I didn't fantasize about him in class. I didn't touch myself to thoughts of him. I didn't crave him. I didn't neglect work because I was too busy watching him lecture and wondering if I could undo the buttons on his vest with my teeth. I..." *Well, fuck.*

My eyes are wide as saucers. I did not just say that. Please, God, tell me I did not just confess to masturbating to thoughts of Dexter and neglecting work to fantasize about undressing him with my teeth. *Fuck my life.*

Dexter doesn't seem surprised by my revelation. Rather, his eyes gleam with an excitement only found in confirming one's suspicions. "Your teeth, eh?" He smirks, raking his gaze down my body and back up to my lips. I can tell he's picturing what I've just described. Me, kissing down his neck, sliding my hand down his chest as I slowly sink to my knees in front of him.

I gulp.

"Um, I didn't mean to say that." Truth. I didn't deny that I said it, or thought it, or felt it. But I definitely did not mean to say any of it out loud, and especially not in front of him.

"Please, continue," he says, gesturing that he'd like nothing more than to hear more of my secret fantasies concerning him.

I shake my head. I can't open my mouth again. Who knows what I'd say, what I'd confess?

Dexter leans over the center console, inching closer to my face. His eyes once again fixate on my mouth, and between his invasion of my personal space and the smell of his cologne, I give myself approximately five seconds before I close the gap and kiss him.

Dexter

Putain, alors. I need to kiss her. I need to kiss her more than I need my next breath. She touches herself to thoughts of *me*. Craves *me*. Fantasizes about dropping to her knees in front of *me*. *Baise-moi.*

"Alis," I beckon, now less than two inches away from her. I scan over her expression. Her eyes are locked on my lips, her breaths grow heavier. Every few seconds she closes her eyes, tightly, and then reopens them as if to shake herself out of the haze of lust she's currently swimming in.

She doesn't respond to my saying her name, so I lift my pointer finger to her chin and tilt her face to meet my eyes. "Alis," I repeat, even more softly than before. I can't remember a time in my life when I've wanted to kiss a woman more than I do right now.

"Dexter," she breathes out. A whisper filled with longing and the acquiescence I've craved for months. I guide her lips to mine, finger still under her chin, and press my mouth against hers. She's soft, supple. Her kiss feels like a sigh of relief, as if she's letting go of all the pent-up tension she's held onto since August and is relaxing into the fulfillment of her desires.

Sliding my hand along her jawline, I deepen the kiss, holding her to me in a way that is still gentle, but undoubtedly possessive. Her lips part and our tongues meet, and just like the night in the bar, I'm overcome with a sense of belonging, of home. I know our potential for passion is exponential and will combust in the right environment, but right now kissing Alis feels like being wrapped in a warm blanket, like sinking into my favorite armchair after a long day, like opening the cover to my favorite book and reveling in it once again, even knowing every detail of the story.

Alis's hand slides up my forearm to my wrist and she holds on tightly, possessively, letting me know she doesn't want me to pull away. Just when I consider pulling back, Alis places her other hand on the back of my neck and weaves her fingers into my hair, gripping tightly and pressing my mouth more firmly against hers.

Holy shit. What is this woman doing to me? And who knew quiet, private Alis had a dominant streak in her. She lets go of my wrist, tangling that hand into my hair as well. She's laying her claim on me. Owning me. I can feel every ounce of her suppressed feelings tearing free from their confines and pouring into this kiss.

Thank God I was right. Thank God I didn't misinterpret this pull, this magnetism between us. And thank, fucking, God I took her off campus. There's no way she'd kiss me like this had we stayed in the faculty parking lot.

I need air. I need more of Alis — so much fucking more of Alis, but reluctantly I peel my lips off hers and inhale the scent of her surrounding me, infiltrating my car. I press my forehead to hers, taking deep breaths as I try to calm my racing heart and raging erection. No words can describe how badly I want to take her home, remove every stitch of clothing from her body, and kiss her everywhere.

"I'm sorry," she whispers, and I'm momentarily torn from my fantasy of Alis laid out on my bed. "Sorry?" I ask. "For what? You did nothing wrong."

We're still whispering, as if speaking any louder will shatter the moment. Alis pulls her forehead from mine and meets my gaze, unguarded affection like I haven't seen since the first night we met shining in her eyes. Then, she snorts.

She. Snorts. And laughs, mind you. But after the initial snort, she's lost all sense of decorum and falls back into her seat, cracking up.

I am so confused right now. How did we go from whispers and intimacy to Alis Gilmore falling into a fit of snort giggles in my passenger seat. I don't say anything — don't know that I could say anything at present. Eventually, she takes in a deep breath, wiping tears from her eyes as she comes down from whatever is going on inside her mind.

Still laughing, albeit sans snorting, Alis replies, "I'm sorry I deprived myself of kissing you for so long. I mean, my God, Dexter. That was…"

My smile is so big, my chest tight with anticipation. "That was. It definitely was."

"Five stars. First class. Ten/ten recommend to anyone considering," she exclaims. "Well, scratch that last one."

"You wouldn't recommend kissing me to anyone else?" I tease. I know what she's *not* saying, what she said so clearly with her hands fisted in my hair while we kissed. But I want her to say it. I want her to use words and tell me she wants this. More than just "I like you" or "I have feelings for you." I want to be hers, and for her to be mine. Only hers. Only mine.

"No, I would not recommend anyone else kiss you," she states, still skirting what I want from her.

"And, pray tell, why not?" I mock offense, and add, "You can't tell me you didn't enjoy kissing me. At my lips' touch you blossomed for me like a flower and the incarnation was complete."

"Well, Gatsby, suffice it to say I don't share. You look at me like all women want to be looked at by a man, and I can't stomach the thought of you sharing those gazes and kisses with anyone else."

I lean toward her once again and place a soft kiss on her lips. "You make me feel uncivilized, Alis. No one else has ever made me feel this way."

She smiles up at me, happiness and hopefulness gleaming in her eyes. "As much as I'd love to continue bantering Fitzgerald back and forth, I think we need to eat, and talk. We really, really need to talk."

She is right. I know she's right. My dick, however, has zero interest in going inside that restaurant and having a conversation that could very possibly lead to Alis overthinking and overcomplicating *us*.

"Let's do that. But, Alis," I start.

I wait to continue, needing her to hear my next words loud and clear. "Yes?" she prompts.

"Don't be afraid of this. Of us. Okay? And don't regret taking the time you needed to get to this point. Let's just let things take their course, and never be sorry."

She offers an unbridled smile my way, "Never be sorry."

TWENTY-FIVE

Alis

"SO, we're doing this. I want this — us." I gesture between us with my fork, as if 'us' requires defining. "However," I start, "I need rules."

"Rules?" Dexter repeats. "What kinds of rules?" He continues eating, and I'm thankful he doesn't plan to interject while I explain myself.

"Well, first, we can't be 'together' on campus." I'm surprised he doesn't shoot me an annoyed look; he simply nods, finishes his bite, and asks, "By together you mean we can't act like a couple, correct? Because it's kind of difficult to never be together when you're my grader. And before you say it — don't even think about stopping our weekly lunch meetings."

I roll my eyes at his assertiveness. "That's not what I was going to say. Yes, I mean we cannot act like a couple on campus. And no, I don't plan on canceling our weekly lunch meetings. But I don't want to meet alone in your office."

This perplexes him. "We meet alone in my office all the time."

"This is true, but all of those meetings took place *before* us." Flashbacks of Margaret opening Dr. Ryan's office door, seeing me at my lowest point. The things she insinuated and the insults she attacked me with that day will forever haunt me. A shiver runs down my spine. Loathing and bitterness and anger I've buried so deeply for so long. I try to keep a lid on it, but my next words are sharp — too sharp.

"It's non-negotiable, Dexter. I'm serious. I will not meet with you alone in your office *ever* again. We can discuss whatever we need to discuss in your pod conference room, at a picnic table on campus, or even at Nico's. But not in your office. Never again in your office."

Dexter never resumed eating once I made this my hill to die on, and he can't hide the hurt on his face. "You don't actually think I'd try anything with you in my office, do you?"

Way to go, Alis. You're off to a great start with this relationship thing.

"It's not that, exactly," I begin. "It's just …" I pause, not wanting to rehash the past. Not wanting to make a mountain out of a mole-hill. Not wanting to explain to Dexter something that never actually happened in the first place. "It's not that I don't trust you, honestly. The need to remain strictly professional while on campus is impor-tant to me, okay? I'm not trying to hide from anyone, but I, person-ally, need the separation. I won't clam up and push you away if and when someone from MPU sees us out to dinner or somewhere else, but on campus, I need for you to be Dr. Belanger and for me to be Alis, your grader. When it inevitably gets out that we're together, I don't want there to be any question about our working relationship and whether or not we've done anything inappropriate. I can't have my professional integrity called into question. Or yours."

"Speaking of," I continue, but Dexter does interject this time.

"I already spoke with Abigail about us." I freeze. *What did he just say?!*

"You did what?" I ask, once again failing miserably at holding back the sharpness in my tone. "When? And for fuck's sake, Dexter, why?!" I don't lose my cool like this. Not ever. It's as if making the decision to succumb to my feelings for Dexter and then kissing him senseless in the car has snapped every bit of self-control I once possessed. I am now a loose canon, full of emotions, without walls to keep everything carefully contained within.

I can't do this. *Feel* all of — of *this*. Everything. All of it. The feelings. All of them. I can't even form complete thoughts right now. When the hell did my internal monologue derail itself and crash into a forest of stuttering trees?!

I can feel my heart rate rise in my chest. The tension. The panic. What is happening to me right now?! I don't panic. I don't worry. I don't take control of kisses with men and devour them. I don't fantasize about removing their clothing with my teeth. A PROFESSOR'S CLOTHING. WITH. MY. TEETH.

I feel the bench cushion shift, and then Dexter is next to me, his arm wrapped around my shoulder, and he pulls me into his body. "Shhh," he soothes. "Everything is alright. You are alright. We are alright. Just breathe, Alis."

Feeling him pull me close, the tension begins to seep from my body. The ominous spots dancing at the periphery of my vision retreat, and I draw my first deep breath in seemingly endless minutes. *What just happened?*

"Do you often get panic attacks?" Dexter's voice is tender, his hand tracing comforting paths up and down my arm.

"No," my reply is a whisper, a lingering dizziness and confusion clouding my thoughts, perplexed by this sudden emotional tempest. He holds me firmly, his lips gently kissing my temple, instilling in me a sense of safety that has been absent for years.

"I'm not sure what triggered it," I lie. "Not specifically, I mean." My mind races — so many bags to unpack. Bags I didn't even realize were in my possession. These emotions are too complex to unpack in a one-hour lunch break.

"Do you trust me?" Dexter's question hangs in the air, his arm steadfast around me, yet he pulls back just enough to allow our eyes to meet. My response is as candid as my tangled emotions allow, "I don't know. I want to. I mean, I do. I..."

He interrupts gently, "It's okay, Alis. There's no need for a definitive answer right now. Trust is a journey; it takes time. I know you trust me; you just haven't realized it yet." My brows knit together at his calm confidence, particularly because I don't understand how he can be so calm, so sure, when I feel anything but.

"May I explain why I spoke with Abigail concerning my feelings for you?" he asks. Had he worded the revelation this way the first time I probably wouldn't have reacted so harshly.

"Please," I nod for him to continue.

"You aren't the only person who has struggled with keeping their feelings at bay. I haven't felt a connection like this with any woman, ever, and before I threw caution to the wind and began a true pursuit of you, I needed to know that I wouldn't jeopardize your future in the process." Alis remains close to me, her maintained eye contact provides the assurance I need to continue.

"I may have seemed reckless and even overstepped when I came to your apartment uninvited and when I held your hand the other night, but I'm navigating uncharted waters here. You've shared enough pieces of yourself with me that I know what, and who, is most important to you, and all of those things are important to me as well. I can't regret the time you spent keeping me at arm's length because those months provided me the time I needed to decide that I want this — us — you. And not just you, but Sunny. I want a life together. I want to support you in your dreams and do everything in my power to help you succeed. I want to learn how to be the partner you need, the man you want. I want to know Sunny and bond with her. I want to take walks together in my neighborhood. I want it to be *our* neighborhood. *Our* home. *Our* life. *Our* family. *Our* future."

Is he insane? That's the only logical explanation for what he just said. "You've known me for a little more than three months, and you're saying you want to, what, marry me?" The incredulity in my tone cannot be missed.

"That's exactly what I'm saying." His gaze doesn't waver, nor does his resolve. "I would never risk your future or your integrity for anything, Alis. I didn't talk with Abigail about my feelings for you because I needed reassurance that this is right. I went to her because I know you, and I knew that without absolute certainty that us being together is not violating any school rules or code of ethics, you would never even consider being with me."

Tears well in my eyes, precariously close to spilling, and my lower lip quivers involuntarily. This. This is the embodiment of being truly known. Of being meticulously studied. It transcends being merely noticed, even beyond being considered; it's being genuinely seen, authentically understood. At this moment, two revelations crystallize within me: 1) The day my sister passed marked my inaugural journey into deep, inescapable loneliness, and 2) For the first time since that heart-shattering day, the oppressive weight of loneliness gently lifts.

"First you say we should let things take their course, then you say you want to marry me."

"Yes," he responds, not seeing his own contradiction.

"Do you not see the juxtaposition of those two statements?"

That panty-dropping half-smile appears on his face, accompanied by a glint of humor in his eyes. Pulling me once again closer to him, Dexter buries his face into my hair and whispers, "Do not take Fitzgerald's words out of context. You and I both know Lois said those words to herself as she penned that telegram to Howard, confirming their elopement. Letting things take their course doesn't necessitate taking things slowly. If anything, it's a call to relinquish control. To surrender to fate. To stop fighting against the inevitable."

He's right, of course. I mumble, "If cowardice is all that's been holding me back there won't be any more holding back."

I can feel his smile against the side of my head. He chuckles, "Thank God."

Pulling back once again, Dexter asks, "Any more rules?"

"I won't sit here and pretend to know anything about being in a relationship. Nor will I sit here and attempt to make sense of the tangle of thoughts and emotions fighting for dominance inside me. I just need space to work through it all. No more rules, though."

"Glad to hear it," he says, lifting his arm from around me to pull his wallet from his back pocket. Dexter signals for the server, handing him cash to cover both the meal and a tip when he arrives with our bill.

"Ready to head back?" he asks, and all I can think about is how badly I need a nap after feeling so much in a short amount of time.

"Sure thing." Sliding out of the booth, Dexter grasps my hand as we walk toward the exit and back to his Range Rover. He's opened the passenger door and I'm about to climb in when I stop, turn to him, and gently kiss him on the lips.

"Dexter," I say, "thank you." He smiles sweetly down at me, pressing another kiss to my mouth. "And be patient with me. I sound like a broken record, but I truly have no idea how to navigate any of this. I've only ever had one true partner in my life, and she died. I don't think I realized how deeply her passing affected my ability to connect with people because until moving here, until meeting you, everyone close to me had always been there. They knew Belle, they knew me, and they knew the depth of the bond we shared. They never pushed me to work through my grief because they were all too busy carrying their own. Not only that, but then even as time passed and life moved forward, they didn't know I *needed* pushing. Belle was always the person encouraging me to take risks and live outside the safety of my own thoughts, but she did it so subtly that I don't think anyone truly grasped the weight of her role in my life. I'm not saying I feel incomplete without her or that I'm incapable of loving someone because I'm irreparably broken, but with you, Dexter, I'm so far outside my wheelhouse I can't even think straight.

"You're a chapter that began in a life that Belle will never be a part of, and while that reality terrifies me, the truth is that this isn't the first chapter she's missed. I just didn't realize time continued moving forward until I made the decision to take an intentional step forward with my life. It's easy to ignore the progression of time when you're surrounded by the familiar."

"You might be the most self-aware person I've ever known." Did he not hear a single word I said?

"I just told you I don't know my left from my right, and you say I'm self-aware?"

"Let's go," Dexter says, helping me into my seat before closing the door and walking around to his side of the vehicle.

We're quiet during the drive back to campus. Dexter holds my hand and strokes his thumb over my knuckles. His touch quiets the chaos inside me, and the reprieve is heavenly.

He stops in front of my car and lifts my hand to his mouth, pressing a gentle kiss to my fingers.

"Awareness and understanding are two very different things, Alis. Awareness is the first step; understanding comes with time, research, and a hell of a lot of hard work."

I let out an exasperated sigh and wave my other hand around my head, saying, "I believe understanding any of this is impossible."

He smiles, a hint of both mischief and determination in his eyes. "Why, Alis, sometimes, I've believed as many as six impossible things before breakfast."

Pulling my hand from his, I swat his arm and laugh. "Smart ass," I quip.

Dexter feigns offense. "Who? Me, or Lewis Carroll?"

"Both," I say. He concedes. "You aren't wrong."

"I'll see you tomorrow?" I ask as I gather my purse and step out of the car.

"Tomorrow," he nods, smile wide, eyes happy, body relaxed.

I haven't felt this warm, this hopeful, in a very, very long time.

TWENTY-SIX

Dexter

ALIS and I have spent the last two weeks getting to know each other freely, stealing away from campus each day for lunch, talking honestly and openly about our hopes, dreams, families, and friends; making out in my Range Rover like two horny teenagers with a curfew. I've never met a woman so smart, so driven, so... warm. At first hearing she hasn't truly dated since college and hadn't even kissed a man in the last nine years, I worried Alis would be detached and distant, only supplying as much information as is necessary. I worried that, despite her saying she didn't want to hide our relationship, she'd be stiff and shy away from public displays of affection.

Thankfully, my worries were for naught. Despite her fears, overthinking, and obvious emotional scar tissue, Alis blossoms when we're together. She's the woman I met at the bar — flirty, intelligent, quick-witted. She speaks of Belle with such reverence and love, and while I admire her affection for her sister I often wonder if Alis uses her memory as an excuse not to embrace her true self. Belle was bold, brave, passionate — the embodiment of everything Alis feels she lacks. I wish she could see herself the way I see her. She is both gentle and bold, careful and brave, logical and passionate. Despite the wealth of literary knowledge stored in her mind, tales of love and laughter and the complexity of the human mind and heart, Alis doesn't seem to apply the universal truths revealed through centuries of writing to herself.

I've found myself prompting her to consider the parallels of life and literature to herself on more than one occasion, and I know she hears me, but there's still something deep inside her that refuses to let go and embrace the freedom that comes with loving someone fully. That 'someone' being herself.

I promised her patience, and, truly, helping her work through her thoughts and feelings is no burden to me. She makes me feel alive, and I can tell I do the same for her.

Today is the first time Alis will come to my home, and she's bringing Sunny with her. Perhaps I should be nervous, but I'm not. More than anything I'm excited to spend time with the kid and get to know her better. Our first meeting was unexpected but delightful all the same. She's a firecracker, no doubt. Alis speaks of Sunny with the same affection and awe bestowed upon her sister, and while, yes, from my limited interaction with Sunny I can see so much of what Alis has told me about Belle in her. However, I see in Sunny all the qualities and strengths Alis refuses to attribute to herself.

The doorbell rings and Otis, my Australian shepherd, barks and runs to greet our visitors. Not many people come to my house, aside from Leo, so I'm curious to see how Otis handles having two females in our space.

"Calm down, buddy," I scratch behind his ears and pat his back, signaling for him to sit while I answer the door.

Upon opening, I find Alis standing with her hands clasped in front of her, picking at her nails — her nervous tell. Before I can offer greeting or invite them inside, Otis pushes his body through my slightly parted legs, causing me to clasp the door for balance, and lunges at Sunny, smushing his nose into her face. She erupts in fits of giggles, hugging and petting Otis and telling him how handsome he is.

"Hi," I say through a laugh, watching my dog and Sunny's instant connection and affection for each other play out on the front porch.

"Yes, you are a handsome boy. The best handsome boy. Give the best kisses, yes you do!" Sunny laps praise on him as he barks and jumps and licks her face. I've never seen Otis interact with children — he's typically too busy chasing other dogs at the park. It's nice to see Sunny isn't overwhelmed by him. He's not a large dog, but he isn't small, either.

"Hi, yourself," Alis says, stepping closer and interlocking her fingers with mine. I'm taken aback by her easy affection in front of Sunny, and she sees the surprise on my face. Laughing, she says, "What? It's not like she doesn't know we're dating. She's nine, not four."

I give her my best half smile, "I know, it's just —" I pause, unsure how to articulate my thoughts.

Alis smiles knowingly, "It's just that you keep expecting me to freak out?"

I rub the back of my neck, chagrin taking over. "Maybe? I don't know. It's more that I haven't wanted to touch and laugh and be close to someone in a long time, and even then, it wasn't like this. I guess I often wonder if I'll overwhelm you, so it's a pleasant surprise when you initiate. It boosts my confidence." I drop my mouth to her ear, lowering my voice so only she can hear, "And, it makes me want to push your back against this door and slide my hand under your skirt."

I pull away before Alis can react, letting out a short whistle to signal Otis that it's time we invite our guests inside. Alis slaps my back in playful frustration, following behind me as both Otis and Sunny run through the open floor plan of my house to the back patio doors.

"Can we go outside?" Sunny asks, Otis standing on his hind legs and pawing at the glass to show his unwavering support and excitement for this request.

"Definitely," I say. "The door's unlocked and the gate is closed. Go crazy out there."

Sunny slides the door open, Otis pushing his way out before it's open wide enough to fit through. She runs out after him, not bothering to close the door behind her.

"Those two are getting on famously," Alis comments.

"You won't hear any argument from me," I say, sliding the door closed once again before backing Alis against the wall next to it and kissing her soundly. I saw her, kissed her, held her just yesterday, but seeing her in my home, in that skirt with those ridiculous blue polka dot tights and bright red Chuck Taylor's does something to me.

She returns my kiss, sliding her tongue against mine and holding me to her with a hand on the back of my neck. Both my hands are braced on the wall, one on either side of her just above her shoulders. I push my body against hers, feeling the length of her pressed against me for the first time. God, I've fantasized about this moment. This feeling. I've wanted to kiss her, touch her, feel every inch of her pressed against my body since the moment I saw her reflection through that bar mirror.

We haven't ventured beyond kissing, what with our liaisons limited to the front seats of my Range Rover, parked inconspicuously in whichever restaurant parking lot we escaped to that day.

Now, with Sunny here, is not the time, but that doesn't stop me from wanting this, wanting her.

"Alis," I groan, pulling out of our kiss but keeping my body firmly in place. I know she can feel the evidence of my need for her against her stomach, and I can see every thread of want and desire reflected back at me in her gaze.

"Dexter," she pants, the rise and fall of her chest no less tempting in her tight sweater than it would be in something more revealing.

I lower my forehead to hers and inhale, her shampoo and perfume working together to create the scent that is Alis Gilmore — the unexpected, beautiful, awkward, nerdy, fucking desirable woman of my dreams. Dreams I never realized I'd had until I met her.

There is no list to compare her to. No fantasy of the perfect woman, my perfect partner, or soul mate. If I've learned anything from the thousands of stories I've read in my lifetime, it's this —

embrace the unexpected, walk in humility, be teachable, and love with abandon. Here I am, heeding the wisdom of writers both past and present.

Many people hold an unconscious bias against fiction, brushing off tales of adventure and love, of conflict and strife, as entertainment instead of truth. I don't know exactly when it happens, but at some point in a person's life, they distort the true meanings of fiction and non-fiction. Fiction becomes fantasy, an unattainable Eden to be used as an escape from real life. They equate 'fiction' and 'fantasy' with 'lie' and 'unattainable', and 'non-fiction' with 'fact' and 'truth'.

The correlation between the words is not wholly incorrect, but to discount the wisdom and truth found in fiction literature is to do a disservice to oneself. This feeling, this desire I have for Alis has provided a deeper understanding, a kinship and a bond between myself and the countless authors I've read who have written about the intangible experience of falling in love.

When Antoine de Saint-Exupéry penned the words, "It is only with the heart that one can see rightly; what is essential is invisible to the eye," he spoke to the desires of the human soul. Fiction, fantasy, none of it is a lie. It's an unfiltered reflection of our truest selves, our deepest longings, and the purest account of the human experience.

This is my experience. This is my fantasy. Not because I set a standard and found a woman who meets my every expectation, but because there never was any list, any expectation, any standard. This is my fantasy because this is honesty. Freedom.

I've heard people discount the love written about in novels, saying that love doesn't work that way, that you don't fall in love at first sight and live happily ever after. That passion and desire dwindle with time, and fighting and disagreeing will eventually tear two people apart.

I don't believe that for one second. I also don't believe that falling in love at first sight is as full of lust and emotion as people assume. I would say I fell in love with Alis at first sight — at first reflection.

Was she beautiful? Absolutely. But her physical beauty, while unde-niable, is not the same as her beauty as a person. Her demeanor, her honesty — that is why I can say I loved her at first sight.

Love cannot be claimed without intimacy. Intimacy, in its purest form, is vulnerability, honesty. When I saw her reflection, I saw her. I saw in her something that cannot be described, explained, or formu-lated. My honest self recognized her honest self. *Nos âmes se connaissent.*

The sound of Sunny and Otis running and playing in the backyard slowly reenters my periphery, but the spell I'm under with this woman is not broken. However, it does serve as a reminder that we are not, in fact, alone. I press a chaste kiss to her mouth and begrudgingly separate my body from hers, adjusting my erection to be less noticeable and praying it softens completely before Sunny returns inside.

I clear my throat and ask, "Would you like a tour?"

"Not right now, thank you," she replies. Who has ever turned down a tour when visiting someone's home? Returning my wandering gaze to hers, I see that her smile is mischievous and tantalizing, a beckoning strangely familiar, though an expression I've never seen from Alis.

"No? You don't want to see the rest of my house?" I ask, perplexed.

"Sure, I do. But if you walk me down that hall, out of sight, and reach from that sliding glass door, neither of us will be able to control ourselves. Not after what just happened against that wall." She nods her head toward where I, not three minutes ago, had her confined. Here I was trying to escape the lust-filled haze over-whelming my senses, and my subconscious was busy scheming against my better judgment.

I exhale a laugh, shaking my head and running a hand through my hair. "You are not wrong," I admit, then turn to the kitchen to start preparing lunch. "Let's make something."

"You're cooking?" Alis asks, curiosity piqued. "*We're* cooking," I correct. "I asked you over to spend time with you and Sunny, to familiarize the two of you with my house, my space, Otis. I want you both to feel at home here. Part of feeling at home is knowing where everything is in the kitchen."

"Sounds great," she says, approaching the counter bar and leaning forward on her elbows. "What are *we* cooking?"

"*We*," I say, emphasizing the word as I rummage through the refrigerator and pull out bacon, butter, and cheddar slices, "are making the best grilled cheese sandwiches you ever tasted."

The sound of Alis's genuine excitement confirms I made the right choice in deciding to spend the day at the house, low key, as if this was any typical Saturday in the home we shared. Pushing off the bar top, Alis walks around the counter and asks, "What can I do?"

———————

It's nearly 5 p.m. when Alis and Sunny prepare to head back to their apartment. Sunny bids farewell to Otis, who whines and licks her cheeks in protest. Today has been everything I'd hoped it would be — relaxing, entertaining, and comfortable. Alis hands off her keys to Sunny and says she'll meet her in the car, and aside from her obvious reluctance to depart from Otis, she tells me goodbye and skips out to the car.

I envelop Alis in my arms, hands rubbing up and down her back. "Thanks for spending the day with me," I murmur into her hair. I feel her smile against my neck, "Thank you for having us." I look down and meet her eyes, her smile soft, content, happy. I kiss her gently, planning to say goodbye but then remembering the upcoming faculty dinner. I've been so wrapped up in playfully bantering back and forth with Alis and Sunny all day that I forgot all about asking her to accompany me.

"Has Abigail mentioned anything to you about a special J-Term class?" I ask, feeling out whether or not Alis is privy to the details I was so clearly instructed to keep to myself.

She thinks for a moment, and says, "No, why? Should I know about it? Does she need help with anything or for me to teach again? I don't have anything special happening over the break so I can help if she needs it."

And that's one more reason why I love this woman. Her first thought is to offer assistance, to lessen someone else's burden if she can be of service.

"Not that I'm aware of," I say, tucking her loose hair behind her ear before kissing her forehead. "I can't go into too much detail because we're still wooing the powers-that-be, but a few guest lecturers are flying in this week to talk details and Abigail is hosting a dinner reception at her place. I'd like for you to accompany me. Not as a student, or as my grader, but as my girlfriend."

Brow creased, Alis considers my request and says, "A faculty dinner."

"Yes," I affirm.

"As your girlfriend."

Again, I nod and say, "Yes. As my girlfriend." For a moment I wonder if she will deny my request, but instead, she asks, "Who will be there?"

As much as I'd love to name-drop and brag about a possible collaboration between MPU and Jonathan Ryan, Abigail has yet to release that information. Not that I think Alis would say anything, but I gave my word. I decide to be honest, but vague.

"A handful of MPU faculty and the visiting potential collaborators for the class. It will be small, I promise."

"And when is it?"

"Friday evening at 7. I'll pick you up and we can ride together," I say as I slide my hands down her back, palms stopping just above her ass as I lean closer and say, "And maybe, if Skye doesn't have to work too early the next morning, you could come home with me afterward?" I can feel the tension building in her body with every whispered word, and her arms tighten around me, holding me to her. Her fingers digging into my back are all the confirmation I need.

We'll attend Abigail's dinner party. I'll introduce Alis to the other L&L faculty and then to Dr. Ryan. We'll shake hands and I'll hope to God he remembers meeting me and helping me when I was a lowly PhD student riddled with writer's block. Not that I need to impress her, but Alis will appreciate the surprise of meeting someone so revered in our field. I'm sure she's heard of him — you can't partake in L&L Academia, particularly the French lit sector, without having heard of and even fawned over Dr. Jonathan Ryan. He'll agree to the lecture series, she'll be high on the thrill of meeting Dr. Ryan, I'll be high on the promise of a dream come true — a collaboration with *the* Jonathan Ryan. Most importantly, we'll both be taught with the anticipation of returning to my house, to my room, to my bed, where I will spend the rest of the night indulging myself in Alis's body.

Friday night is going to be the best night of my life.

TWENTY-SEVEN

Alis

BEFORE I KNEW IT, Friday had arrived and I was standing in front of my floor-length mirror, holding two dresses in front of me, trying to decide which I should wear. It's November, so it's too cold for most of my dresses, however, I have two long-sleeved, knee-length cocktail dresses that would both suit the occasion.

I'm pulling one to the side and replacing it with the other when Skye enters my bedroom. "The blue one," she says. "Definitely go with the blue one."

"And why, my dearest Skye, would I heed your opinion on what to wear to a faculty dinner of all places?" She knows I'm poking fun, and she plays right into my hand, offering an undeniably 'Skye' response with so much conviction, I may acquiesce and choose the blue instead of the green.

"For starters, your boobs look fuck hot in the blue dress. Fuck hot but not skanky hot, you know?" I shake my head and laugh, but she continues. "Second, you are wearing thigh highs, not tights, under that dress and only the blue one provides the opportunity to slip a glimpse of your garter to Dexter at the dinner table."

"Is sex the *only* thing you think about?" I laugh, secretly loving the thought of flashing Dexter a peek at my garter under the table.

"Typically, no. But tonight, when my fuck hot best friend is going to be stripped naked by her equally fuck hot professor boyfriend, most definitely."

"Why are we friends?" I kid, once again replacing the dress in front of me as if I'm still conflicted about which one to choose.

"Because I'm fucking fabulous, that's why." She's not wrong. Skye is definitely an acquired taste — too much for some, but she couldn't care less. She's brash, fierce, and takes the world by storm (fitting that her name is Skye). And I love her more than my own life. It was Skye who literally held me together after Belle and Alex's funeral. Skye, who didn't take a second to consider her options when I decided to attend MPU. Hell, she didn't even wait for the invitation to move with us — just seamlessly traded singular for plural pronouns. I wasn't moving to Grand River — *we* were. I wasn't leaving everyone I know and love to move to a city four hours away where I didn't know a single person — *we* were. I am the least single single parent that ever lived.

I return the green dress to my closet and hang the blue on the back of my bathroom door before stepping in to shower and shave every square inch of my body from the waist down. I may not have had sex in nearly ten years, but I still remember the importance of smooth legs. I got waxed earlier this week, which I hadn't done in at least five years. It's incredible, the things we do to present ourselves as a suitable offering to a lover. I'm not sure many things convey self-lessness as clearly as "I let a stranger smear hot wax all over my vagina and then rip the hairs from the roots, all for your pleasure."

As I step from my bathroom I find Skye still sitting on my bed, perched in the same position I left her in fifteen minutes ago. The pink bag gift bag, however, was not there when I left.

"What's that?" I ask, already knowing it's lingerie by the brand stamped across these alternating light and dark pink stripes.

"You may call me your fairy cuntmother," Skye says melodically, wiggling her fingers over the bag as if depositing fairy dust on its contents.

I palm my forehead. *She did not just say that.* "For the second time, *why* are we friends?!"

"Lookie, lookie! It's lacy!" she squeals, not bothering to wait for me to open the present myself. Skye tosses the pink tissue paper aside and then takes out two black, lacy, incredibly see-through undergarments. I'm standing before her in my towel, hair clipped into a messy bun to keep it dry while I showered, trying desperately to be appalled at what I'm seeing.

Who am I kidding? *I love it.* "It's perfect," I beam, and I know that was the exact response she hoped for when she squeals again in excitement, tossing my both items before reaching into the bag once more to reveal new thigh highs and a matching garter belt.

"You do know I already own something very similar to this, right?" I ask.

"So what if you do? This is a big night! It deserves to be celebrated, and what better way to celebrate the de-revirginizing of your poor, neglected vag."

"Get out," I swat at her with the panties. She stands, laughing at my frustration, and then clasps her hands together under her chin, saying, "My sweet baby girl is finally becoming a woman. I've never been more proud than I am at this very moment."

Swatting her again, I add my foot to the mix, literally kicking her out of my room so I can get dressed.

It's 6:30 when Dexter arrives, his tall, exquisite frame coming into view as I step from my room in my navy blue, velvet cocktail dress and black pumps. I don't wear heels often — the last time was the night I met Dexter and I will never wear those shoes ever again — so I chose a modest-height shoe that still accentuates my calves. My hair hangs over my shoulder in a teased fishtail braid, loose waves framing my face. I decided to forego the glasses in favor of contact lenses, not wanting to feed into the "younger woman" persona any more than my short stature and obvious lack of life experience suggest.

"You look… incredible." My cheeks blush under his praise, and I step closer to him, gently tugging on his tie as I offer my own words of affirmation to him.

"You clean up nicely," I say, smiling up at him. Dexter leans in and kisses me, a chaste hello, and asks, "You ready to go?"

I nod and gesture toward the small overnight bag sitting by the door. "Would you carry that for me?" I ask. Dexter pulls me in for another lingering peck before intertwining our fingers with one hand and securing my bag in the other.

"Y'all have fun now, ya hear?" Skye calls from the hallway. We lucked out when Sunny was invited to a sleepover birthday party for one of her class friends, so I didn't have to even attempt to broach the subject of my staying the night with Dexter. Skye, however, we could never escape.

"You're worse than my parents on prom night," I huff, an accusation she feeds into with ease, offering reminders to 'practice safe sex', 'make wise choices', and 'have her home by curfew!' Dexter takes her pestering in stride, offering every assurance that he respects me and will act like a gentleman. Skye's look of disgust throws him — he doesn't know Skye well enough to know he willingly walked right into her trap.

"You better not," she scoffs.

Dexter, brows furrowed, asks, "Better not, what?" I don't say anything, keeping my face as calm and neutral as possible.

"You better not act like a perfect gentleman or return her home to me before noon tomorrow. I didn't spend $150 on sexy lingerie for her to wear tonight so you could do the gentlemanly thing and offer to sleep on the couch. I expect debauchery, ripped lace, and my friend to be so thoroughly ravaged the next time I see her that there's no question of how satisfying her night was. Do not disappoint me, Mountie."

Skye takes the opportunity to acknowledge her own joke, laughing hysterically as she adds, "Ohmygod ohmygod ohmygod. You're Monty's Mountie. A fucking stallion. A *fucking* stallion. I can't. I just can't." She's crying laughing at this point, and I can't help but snort a laugh or two in response.

"I'm not sure how to respond to any of what you just said, so, we're going to leave. Have a good evening, Skye." Dexter opens the door quicker than I had anticipated, pulling me along behind him as Skye continues cackling from her prostrate position on our hallway floor.

"Where, exactly, did you find that one?" Dexter asks, shaking his head while also laughing at the absurdity that is Skye Kennedy.

"At the pound, obviously," I quip. "She's a rescue."

"I'm not at all surprised."

Dexter

Abigail's home is sleek and modern, the picture of understated elegance — much like the woman herself. I've had the pleasure of attending faculty dinners and holiday parties here previously, but I've never once pulled into her driveway with sweaty palms and an elevated heart rate. Why am I so nervous? It's not Alis. If anything, her presence offers calm reassurance, something I so desperately need right now.

"Are you alright?" Alis asks as I park my Range Rover in the circular drive.

"Of course. Why do you ask?"

"For starters, you're strangling that poor steering wheel and you've popped your knuckles at least ten times since we left my apartment. You only do that when you're stressed about something." Observant, this one.

I loosen my grip on the steering wheel and take a deep breath. "You've never seen me stressed, so I don't know how or when you would have noticed me popping my knuckles —"

She cuts in, "Thirty minutes before teaching your undergrad comp class you start popping your knuckles in anticipation of the stupid questions they'll ask about things they should have learned in high school."

I laugh, she's not wrong. "Ok," I concede. "So you've seen me stressed. I'm not anxious or dreading tonight, I promise. The anticipation is getting to me. I've wanted this for so long, and now it's finally happening. Well, I think it's finally happening. I *hope* it happens."

"Who has you so worked up? Has Dr. Matthews flown in a group of academic celebrities or something?" she asks, equal parts serious and joking, acknowledging the weight of what tonight could mean for my career while also lightening the mood with sarcasm.

Before I can respond Alis's hand grips the back of my neck and she pulls me in for a scorchingly hot kiss. I start to pull away but she digs her fingers into my loose hair, holding me firmly to her and she massages my tongue with hers. Suddenly I'm lost in her, drowning in her touch, her kiss, her scent. Alis slides her hand down my torso to my groin, palming my erection through my trousers. I groan at the contact, pleasure pulsing throughout my body.

More. I need more. Next thing I know my seatbelt is off and I'm leaning over the console, pushing her back into the cool black leather. I slide my hand up her thigh, fingers brushing the tiny metal clamps affixed to her stockings. *Thigh highs? Garters?* Is this woman *trying* to kill me?

"Fuck, Alis," I groan as I palm her leg, digging my fingertips into her flesh possessively. I'm a second away from moving higher when headlights appear in my periphery — a stark reminder that we are not alone. Hell, we're the furthest thing from alone right now. We're in my boss's driveway, surrounded by faculty members, and I'm two seconds away from coming in my pants.

"We need to stop," I say, returning to my seat and adjusting myself while Alis opens the visor mirror to check her makeup.

"Thank goodness I hate lipstick," she says. "Although, I can think of some good uses for it." She winks at me before opening her door, stepping out onto the driveway while I'm stuck in my seat trying to calm an erection she just brought back to life.

Once again presentable, I exit the vehicle and meet Alis around front, clasping her hand in mine before guiding her up the pathway to Abigail's front door. The elegance is not lost on Alis — she looks around the foyer in awe, admiring the clean lines and simple design of the space.

"Dexter, Alis, so glad you could make it," Abigail welcomes us, pressing her cheek to each of us in greeting.

"Thank you for having us," Alis replies, ever the gracious guest. "Your home is beautiful," she compliments, once again offering her appreciative gaze to the room.

"Thank you! And I must say, that dress is simply stunning."

While the women volley compliments at each other, I take the opportunity to survey the crowd, looking for Jonathan Ryan. We lock eyes from across the room and he nods in recognition and acknowledgment, offering his excuses to whoever he is talking to before heading in our direction.

My hand rests on Alis's hip, and I offer a gentle squeeze, beckoning her attention. "I have someone I'd like you to meet," I say close to her ear. She turns and smiles up at me — *my God, she's beautiful* — and just as she asks, "Oh? Who?" another voice cuts in.

"Dexter, my boy. Such a pleasure to see you again!"

Before I can tear my gaze away from her, Alis's face freezes. Tension coils throughout her body, fingers digging into my biceps like a vice grip. It feels like minutes, but I know only a second passes before the voice continues, "And Alis Gilmore! What has it been, eight? Ten years?"

They know each other?

TWENTY-EIGHT

Alis

THAT VOICE. That man. It should have at least crossed my mind that Jonathan Ryan would be worth wooing for a special, collaborative teaching opportunity at MPU. That Dexter would know him, would aspire to work with him. I'm suddenly all too aware of the extent to which my blinders have shielded me from dealing with my past.

But nothing happened.

Seriously. Nothing. It was a misunderstanding. A fluke. An insecure, neurotic woman spreading lies and gossip because hurting other people was preferable to dealing with her own issues.

But he didn't protect me. Defend me. Support me. Nothing. I trusted him; he was my mentor, my professor. Five years I studied under him, two of which I worked as his teaching assistant.

He never even reached out to check on me after what happened. Never emailed. Never called. Nothing. My entire world came crashing down around me, punctuated by the fact that his wife — his infuriating bitch of a wife — accused me of trying to *seduce* him.

This is not happening.

Oh, but it is.

I tear my gaze from Dexter and plaster on the best smile I can muster at present. I know Dexter can feel the anxiety radiating off me, and I can sense his obvious confusion at my prior acquaintance with Dr. Ryan.

"Jonathan," I offer — I'm not a twenty-one-year-old girl any longer, asshole — and extend my hand to him. He grasps it and pulls me in for a quick hug, stepping back with his hand still grasping my arm as he gives me a once over and says, "It has been way, way too long, my dear."

My dear? I don't know what to say, how to respond, so I nod in acknowledgment, fake smile still plastered to my face.

"You two know each other?" Dexter inquires, looking between the two of us, possessive arm still resting against my back.

"Of course! She didn't tell you?" Dr. Ryan looks at me, baffled. As if he cannot fathom why I wouldn't shout from the rooftops that I was one under his tutelage.

"Must have slipped my mind," I offer. Wanting to run away but knowing I cannot. This is the partnership Dexter has been so excited about. This is the opportunity he's been waiting for. I cannot ruin this moment for him because of something that *didn't* happen nine years ago.

"So modest, this one," Dr. Ryan jests. "Alis was my protege. My star student. I always knew you were destined for great things. It was too bad I had to lose you after your sister's passing. How is your family? Are your parents still living in Moraine?"

Does he honestly not remember why I left? Was the *incident* that *didn't* happen so minor to him that he brushed it off as nothing? Impossible.

"So happy to see you found your way back into the fold, and on the arm of a rising star. She's always had a knack for making these types of important and strategic connections."

Aaaaaaand I've had enough.

I tear my gaze away from the asshole spewing bullshit all over the place, looking instead toward a still very confused Dexter. "If you'll excuse me, I need to find the washroom." Detaching myself from Dexter, I use every last bit of my self-control to walk, not sprint, from the room. From that man. From his distorted, revisionist history and backhanded compliments.

I find the bathroom, washing my hands — *I can't believe he had the audacity to touch me* — and then press my clean, cold palms to my cheeks.

Calm down, Alis. Nothing happened. The rumors were just that — rumors. You never touched the man. He never touched you. You left. You didn't even have to suffer through the gawking and staring around campus. He probably didn't mean it as it sounded. It was a compliment. You are a strategic thinker. You do make great connections. You're a go-getter, a goal-chaser. You are not a whore. I repeat, you are not a whore.

Self-control adequately, if shakily, reestablished, I smooth out my dress, check my hair and makeup, and return to the party. At least, that was my plan, until the only other person who could possibly transform this party from a dumpster fire to a nuclear explosion turns the corner at the same moment I step foot into the living room. We collide, and red wine spills down the front of my dress, my legs, and into my shoes. Abigail's silver and white — yes, *white* — abstract area rug now resembles a bloody Jackson Pollock, and just as I think I've hit rock bottom I hear it.

"You!"

Somebody, please. Just kill me. Kill me now.

Dexter

Considering this dinner party started no more than thirty minutes ago, the rollercoaster of emotions I have both felt and witnessed from Alis in that short amount of time is astounding.

"She's still as beautiful as ever, I see," Dr. Ryan comments as Alis walks away. His declaration seems inappropriate, especially considering she was his student, but he doesn't watch her long enough for me to assess the intent behind his words. "How long have you two been together?" he asks.

"Not long. It's new," I say, still not certain whether Alis's omission of anything pertaining to her acquaintance with Dr. Ryan was out of humility or something else.

"Is she yours?" he continues, lifting his drink toward the hall where Alis disappeared.

"My, what?" Alis isn't property. She's not an animal. Is she my girlfriend, yes. Is she the most beautiful woman in this house, most definitely. Is she mine? I want to lay claim to her, to make her mine in every sense of the word, but those desires are mine alone to share with Alis — not fodder for conversation at a faculty dinner party.

"Your student." Of course. What is wrong with me? Why am I suddenly so wary of this man? This man who is well respected, admired, even celebrated in academia? *Get it together, Dex. There's nothing wrong. Alis will explain her connection to Ryan later. Focus on the conversation. Focus on the seminar.*

I laugh, "Oh. Of course not. I believe dating your students is frowned upon, even in the most liberal and casual academic circles. And we both know Abigail Matthews would never condone such behavior."

He lifts his glass in acknowledgment. "She certainly would not," he laughs.

I'm beginning to wonder why Alis has yet to return from the washroom when a commotion stirs in the living room beside us.

"Oh, my goodness. I'm so sorry," I hear Alis exclaim. She's covered in red wine, crouching down to retrieve the other woman's now empty wine glass from the carpet. She stands and looks around for somewhere to set the glass. I cannot tell if she's unaware of the wine literally dripping down her leg and into her shoe, or if she's intentionally ignoring her own dilemma in lieu of making sure Abigail's area rug isn't ruined.

"*You!*" The woman who spilled her wine all over Alis and the floor shrieks. For the second time in less than an hour, Alis's entire body goes taught. Before she can say another word, Abigail sweeps into the room, laden with paper towels and promises to Alis that everything is fine, she shouldn't apologize, and the rug is not important.

The other woman is still standing there, glaring daggers at Alis. Had her voice not revealed her displeasure with Alis, her eyes would leave no doubt to the fury within.

Dr. Ryan scurries into the room, approaching the offended woman and wrapping an arm around her waist. He pulls her closer to him and whispers something in her ear, and if I thought this woman hated Alis, it has nothing on the rage she directs at Jonathan Ryan. Thankfully, whoever this woman is — his wife, I assume — has been instructed to stand down. From what? I cannot be certain, but I'd bet my salary this has to do with much, much more than an accidental collision and spilled pinot.

I quietly follow after Alis as she returns to the washroom, where I find her sitting on the floor with her back against the tub. "Alis, are you okay?"

Her face is buried in her hands, her back shaking. She's crying.

I sink to the floor beside her and envelope her in my arms. "Sh, baby, it's alright. Who was that woman? Do you know her?" Alis doesn't answer, but continues to cry, removing her hands from her face to clean the smeared makeup from under her eyes.

"I'm ok," she sniffs. "Promise. I'm fine. Just… I'm just embarrassed." Embarrassed?

"You heard Abigail — it's just a rug. And it's not like you did anything on purpose. All you did was exit the hallway." I try to lighten the mood, to no avail.

"Yeah," she huffs. "That's all. No biggie. Nothing to see here, folks. Just a woman, minding her own business, carrying on with her life, moving FORWARD and not BACKWARD." I know if I interject, even to ask for clarification, she'll stop talking. What has her so shaken by seeing Dr. Ryan? She's never alluded to anything besides her sister's death and becoming Sunny's guardian, drawing her away from school. Is there more to the story?

Surely, there has to be a logical explanation for why Alis never mentioned him. Perhaps they weren't as close as Ryan let on, and he was trying to make her feel seen, feel important. He greeted me as if I was a long-lost friend, when in reality, I met him at a conference and had one conversation with him. He probably didn't even tie the face to the name until Abigail sent him my credentials and explained that I would be the one to co-teach the seminar with him.

Alis hasn't offered any more information, and I've now convinced myself that I'm overthinking the entire situation and need to let it be. "I need to go home. I'm so sorry, but I cannot be here."

"Of course, baby. Let's go." I stand and offer Alis my hand, helping her from the floor. I'm sure she feels worse than she looks, but I'd never ask her to stay after the clear toll this night has already taken on her. Alis checks her reflection, removing the last of her smudged mascara from underneath her eyes, and takes a steadying breath.

"You should stay," she says, catching me off guard once again.

"What? No," I retort. "We arrived together; we will leave together. Besides, I drove us here. I'll make our apologies and then we can leave. We can go to my place, you can take a bath and decompress, and then I'll hold you until you fall asleep."

"No. I am going home. You are staying here." Her tone is firm, her words sharp.

"Alis —" I start, but she cuts me off, shaking her head adamantly.

"No, Dexter. I'm covered in wine, the only change of clothing I have in your car is a pair of gym shorts and an oversized hoodie. This dinner is important. Not just for you, but for Abigail. For MPU. I know Jonathan Ryan. I know the influence he has in the academy. I, probably better than anyone else you know, understand the magnitude of what this opportunity could mean for your career. You are not leaving this party with me."

So she really does know him? Were they close? Why hasn't she, even once, mentioned him?

"Why...?" I start, "How—?" Once again, Alis refuses to let me finish speaking.

"I will explain everything to you later, but not right now. I'm overwhelmed, exhausted, sticky, and I need to leave. I already called for a cab." She glances down at her phone, saying, "Actually, he's here."

"When the hell did you call a car? And *why* would you call an Uber when I fucking drove us here?" Now I'm getting angry, and while I don't mean to yell at her my words come out in an undoubtedly accusatory way.

"I called the cab the second I got in here." I scoff, no longer capable of controlling my frustration at the situation. This night was supposed to be the start of everything I've ever wanted. I was supposed to secure this partnership with Jonathan Ryan and end my night lost in the throws of passion with Alis moaning my name. Instead, I'm arguing with my girlfriend in my boss's washroom — my girlfriend who, might I add, already knows Jonathan Ryan and never mentioned him once in any of our conversations during the last four months — and now she's bolting, without me, before the dinner has even begun, and acts as if this isn't a big deal. She just needs to go home. To *her* home. Her apartment. Without me.

Before I can say anything more, Alis steps toward me, presses a kiss to my cheek, and says, "I have to go. Good luck tonight. You're going to be great. He's a fool if he says no to you." Then she straightens my tie and brushes a hand through my hair — no doubt smoothing where I've pulled on it in frustration. She offers me a soft smile, a reassuring smile that communicates everything will be alright and I'll talk to her in the morning.

The moment she's gone I know everything will not, in fact, be alright. She didn't say anything, but I'm certain Alis just lied to me for the first time. She may have withheld information about her past and cut off conversation when it veered into uncomfortable topics, but she's never straight-up lied to me until tonight.

Her kiss. Her smile. The affectionate way she adjusted my tie and smoothed down my hair. Those were the lies. And I fell for them.

TWENTY-NINE

Dexter

EIGHT DAYS. I haven't heard from Alis in eight. fucking. days. The dinner party continued without a hitch after Alis left, no one acknowledging her disappearing act or the shrieking woman from the living room's overreaction to what was clearly an accident.

I sat next to Dr. Ryan at dinner and he didn't mention Alis again, nor did I, instead diving deep into conversation surrounding the upcoming seminar, his lecture series, and future opportunities for collaboration. I should be ecstatic, but instead of reveling in the bliss of knowing my academic dreams are coming true I'm sitting in my recliner, in my pajamas, watching playbacks of this week's hockey matchups and wondering why the fuck my girlfriend refuses to answer my calls, ignores my text messages, and has all but fallen off the face of the earth since the second she rode away in the cab. Even Otis can feel my misery. He's curled up on his bed near the fireplace, staring at me with so much pity I want to throw something in his direction just to make it stop.

It's Thanksgiving break, so she has no reason to be on campus. She's caught up on grading, so I can't use that as an excuse to make her talk to me. I'm considering opening my third beer of the day —

it's 11 a.m. — when a knock sounds at my door. Fucking Leo. He sent me a text earlier this morning saying he was coming over to grill and watch hockey and I told him to fuck off. I don't want him here. I don't want anyone here — well, except Alis.

"Leo, *je t'ai dit de ne pas putain venir. Va-t'en!*" I shout at the door, hoping the severity of my disdain is conveyed in the words I know he does not understand.

I assume he's left, when I hear a voice through the door. And not just any voice — a pissed-off, hot-headed, distinctly female voice. "I don't know what the fuck you just said, Mountie, but if you don't open this goddamn door right now I'm going to slice the tires on your pretty little Rover and shatter the windows with a hammer."

I open the door — fuck, it's bright outside — and find Skye, all five feet of her, staring up at me like *I'm* the problem. Not her, the one threatening to slash tires and shatter windows.

"Why are you here?" I ask, still shielding my eyes from the sun.

"I'm here because you are fucking stupid and need to get your head out of your ass." Excuse me?

"Excuse me? My head is in my ass?" I ask, genuinely curious about her accusation.

"Did I stutter?" Skye pushes past me into the house, her purple hair flopping around as she stomps like a toddler into the living area.

"Please, come in."

"What the hell happened?" Skye leans against the back of my couch, one black combat boot propped against the fabric.

Propping my hands on my hips, I let out an exasperated breath, staring up at the ceiling. When I don't respond quickly enough, she stomps her boot on my hardwood floor—again, like a toddler. "Well?!" she demands.

"I don't know what the hell happened!" I yell, throwing my arms out to the side in frustration. "Have you asked Alis? I've tried to call her, text her, email her for the last eight days. Hell, I drove to your apartment, but I couldn't get anyone to open the door to your damn building. I sat in my car for two hours waiting to see if she'd pull up or if someone would come out, and nothing. I haven't seen her, I haven't spoken to her, and I don't know what is going on. The last time I spoke to Alis, she acted like everything was fine. She was over-tired and embarrassed about the wine spilling down her dress, and she booked a cab without even consulting me, demanded I stay at the party to kiss Ryan's ass, and then she left."

Skye's stance is no less defensive than it was a minute ago. Does she not believe me? Her face is scrunched up in confusion. She's just as confused as I am.

"Wine? Tired? Why the heck was she embarrassed? And what is this about a cab? She went home with you that night, didn't she?"

Now I'm freaking lost.

"No. She did not come home with me after the party on Friday. She left in a cab—a cab I had no idea she summoned—and gave me some bullshit excuse about being tired and overwhelmed. I still don't see why she was so embarrassed about it. It wasn't her wine that spilled all over the rug. That other woman wasn't watching where the hell she was going."

"What other woman?"

"The woman who spilled wine all over Alis and on Abigail's rug."

"I'm going to need you to start from the beginning."

"Before I say anything more, why the hell did you show up at my house banging at my door, call me stupid, and demand to know what I did wrong? I did nothing wrong. She was fine, and then things got awkward when I introduced her to Ryan, whom she apparently already knew, and then—"

"STOP." Skye stands stock still, her face frozen in terror. "Who did she already know?"

"Jonathan Ryan."

If I thought I'd seen rage in a woman's eyes before, I was damn wrong. Terribly, terribly wrong. Because the look Skye has aimed at me right now promises slow, painful death by her hands.

"Let me get this straight," she says, teeth clenched together, her voice a dangerous whisper. "You showed up at our damn apart-ment, picked up my roommate—my kind, loving, way too fucking out of your league roommate—and took her to a dinner party. A dinner party where you 'introduced' her to Jonathan. Freaking. Ryan."

It's not a question, but I offer an affirmative nod. "Apparently they already know each other?" I'm hoping the uncertainty laced throughout that statement prompts some sort of explanation about why Alis never mentioned him.

"Yeah. She knows him."

"That's it? That's all you're going to say? Your roommate, your kind, loving, and most definitely way too out of my league roommate, who also happens to be my girlfriend, comes with me to a party, gets reintroduced to someone from her past, collides with a woman on her way back from the washroom, and is suddenly so overwhelmed by spilled pinot that she sleuths out of the party and ghosts me for eight freaking days. And 'yeah, she knows him' is all you have to say about it?!"

"It's not my damn story to tell, so yeah. That's all I have to say."

You have got to be kidding me. "You show up at my house, bang on my door, threaten to slice my tires, and that's all you have to say. No. That's not happening. I get that you're mad and you want answers, but damn it, so do I. The woman I love hasn't spoken to me in eight days, and if I hadn't known she and Sunny were leaving for Moraine last Saturday, I probably would have thought she was dead in a ditch somewhere. Talk, woman. You owe me more than 'yeah, she knows him.' What the hell is going on?"

Skye crosses her arms over her chest. Her rage still present, but now it's accompanied by worry.

"You love her?" she asks. "Truly? You love Alis."

"Yes."

"And does she know this?"

That's an excellent question—one to which I do not know the answer. "If you're asking if I've said the words to her, no, I have not. I had planned to tell her Friday after the party, but I never had the chance."

"I see," she says, drifting off into who knows where inside her head.

"Skye. Focus. What happened Saturday?"

"Right, right, right," she continues. "So, Saturday. I left that morning around five to head toward Moraine. We had talked about riding together, but I had some things to take care of that week and didn't want to be stuck driving my dad's truck, plus I had to be back in Grand River for work on Monday so I went ahead and drove myself. I expected to meet Alis for drinks with Tori that night after dinner, but when she didn't show up I texted her to where she was. She texted me back saying she was wiped from the drive and wanted to turn in early. I didn't think anything of it. You know Alis—she needs her own space. I wanted a night hearing all about the orgasms you gave her, but I wasn't going to push her to come out if she needed sleep. I figured staying up all night with you and then driving four hours home was a good enough reason to skip girls' night for once."

She pauses, and I gesture for her to continue.

"I didn't talk to her Sunday because I was helping Tori with some stuff, and I drove back Sunday night because I had to work this week. Alis didn't text me, which, again, isn't out of character for her. She hasn't been home since we moved here, and she's close with her folks, so I assumed she was fine and went about my week. I drove back to Moraine on Wednesday after my shift and went straight to the G's place—"

I interrupt. "G's place?"

Skye backtracks, waving her hand around. "The Gilmores'. Alis's parents," she clarifies.

"Right, so then what happened?"

"She wasn't there," she says, propping her hand on her hip and looking at me like I should already know she wasn't at her parents' house. Well, of course, I should know.

"And?" I prompt, once again signaling for her to get on with her story. "Did you find her?"

"Eventually, yes. Her parents didn't know where she was. Sunny was at a friend's house. Tori hadn't heard from her, not that she would even check her phone when she's dealing with Chase and his crap. I swear, sometimes I just want to walk up to that man and punch him in the throat. Who the hell does he think he is? God? The Pope? Henry Cavill?"

"Skye. You're getting off topic."

"Sorry, sorry. It's been a long week, okay? Alis. I found Alis at the cemetery, talking to her sister."

My heart sinks at this revelation. "Is that something she normally does on a Wednesday?" I ask, trying to sound more curious than upset.

"I mean, maybe? For the first year or so after Belle died, Alis spent a lot of time at her grave. We're close—I mean, we're best friends. Have been since we were kids. But Belle was her person, ya know?"

I nod in understanding. "She's told me about their relationship. They were more than sisters."

Skye snaps her fingers at me, nodding enthusiastically. "Exactly. So it wasn't weird or anything that she'd spend time there. She slowed down over the years, and eventually only went on her birthday, Belle and Alex's anniversary, Sunny's birthday—you know, the important days."

Skye has been talking for what feels like thirty minutes, and I'm still not one step closer to finding out what's wrong with my girlfriend. "Look, Skye, I'm not trying to be an asshole, but can you please get to the point? What is going on with Alis? What happened between her and Jonathan Ryan, and why does she intentionally omit him from her personal and academic history? Don't tell me it's not your story to tell because right now I'm making it your story. Give me the bullet points, not the entire backstory. Where is she?"

Skye still doesn't look convinced that I haven't done anything wrong, but mentioning Dr. Ryan has changed the tide. "Fine," she huffs. "Alis is at the apartment. She's back from Moraine, but she won't leave her room. She tried to act like nothing was wrong while we were at her parents', but I knew from the second I saw her crying her eyes out at Belle's grave that it was more than a standard visit. She's refusing to talk to me about it; keeps brushing things off like she's fine and you guys just aren't going to work out. Problem is, I've known her since we were in preschool. She has a tell—"

"Picking at her cuticles," I interject.

Skye doesn't complete her story, suddenly softening her gaze toward me, seeming to fully embrace what I've told her more than once since she arrived — I'm in love with Alis, and I would never intentionally hurt her.

"You really do love her," she whispers.

"Yes," I exhale. I'm done with this conversation; I need to see Alis.

"And now, I'm going to go see her. You are going to drive back to your apartment and you are not going to call her to give her any warning that I'm with you. I will follow you. You will let me into the building and into your apartment, and then you will leave."

My tone warrants no pushback, and thankfully, Skye's fury has temporarily subsided — at least, I believe so.

"Sure. Yeah. Whatever." Skye walks over to her cracked phone and picks it up off the floor, mumbling "fucking Jonathan Ryan" under her breath as she walks past me and out the front door to her car.

"Are you going to at least give me a heads up about what happened between the two of them?" I ask, unlocking my Range Rover and opening the driver-side door.

"I told you," Skye says, lowering her sunglasses over her eyes. "It's not my story to tell. But she won't talk to me, and she's ignoring you. Tori's going through too much of her own shit to drive down here and pry the truth from her. I've never been in this situation with Alis before — her being so shaken up by something that she won't talk to me. But I've seen her with you these last few months. She's happy — really, truly happy for the first time since before the accident — so I figure what the hell. Let's see if you can bring her back to life again."

With that revelation, Skye sinks into her driver's seat, pulls her door shut, and backs out of my driveway.

THIRTY

THERE'S a reason why I don't put myself out there; a reason I don't make a habit of connecting with people. I'm not bitter; I'm not broken. I'm just ... lost, right now. My reason for not connecting with people isn't just because, until recently, I lacked the opportunity. It's mainly because I've never met anyone who understands me the way Belle always did, and I knew at my core that trying to find that connection with anyone else would be lackluster.

I didn't realize I was refusing to let go of her. Honestly, I never understood why so many people write about letting go of the people they lost. Why would I ever let her go? It's not like my holding her memory close to my heart is affecting anyone else. It's not like my needing her has hindered her from passing on or resting in peace.

Holding onto Belle has kept me steady. Grounded. I wouldn't have had the courage to go back to school if I hadn't been holding onto her.

I used to talk to her. Used to ask for her advice and conjure up in my mind what she would say. Draw courage from her influence. I could practically hear her voice in my head sometimes, and it gave me peace, courage, and whatever else I lacked. She was so... so... everything to me.

I thought the worst pain I'd ever felt in my life was the day she died — I was wrong. The worst pain I've ever felt in my life was last Saturday when, after fleeing that God-awful dinner party, taking a giant dose of melatonin, and driving home to Moraine in record time, I went to my sister's grave to talk to her after having not been to see her since August and realized I cannot remember the sound of her voice.

Since moving to Grand River, going back to school, and meeting Dexter, I've found myself talking to her less and less frequently. I would randomly think to myself that I hadn't sought Belle's advice in a while, but the complete and utter loneliness I felt sitting at her grave, not able to feel her or hear her, was debilitating. Had I let her go and not realized it? If so, when did it happen? Did she leave, or did I push her out of my mind, my thoughts?

Thinking back over the last few months, I realized I would talk about Belle to Dexter in lieu of talking to Belle inside myself. I know on an intellectual level that no longer talking to my dead sister in my mind isn't an act of betrayal, but it doesn't change how I feel.

Alone. Terrified. Unsure. When I would talk to her and could feel her, hear her in my heart, it didn't matter that I ever felt any of those things because Belle balanced them out. She made me feel less alone. She gave me courage. She gave me confidence.

And now — now I'm a thirty-year-old woman who recently came face-to-face with the two people whom I have successfully avoided for nearly a decade. I am now having to confront the truth that I buried Hurricane Margaret deep in a mental file labeled 'nothing happened', treated it as such, and went about my life grieving my sister and raising her daughter, only to have the 'nothing' reveal itself to be 'something'.

If nothing happened, then I had nothing to work through. If nothing happened, then I didn't have to think about it ever again. If nothing happened, I didn't need to talk to anyone about the details of the day Margaret Ryan walked into her husband's office and accused me of trying to seduce him, all the while her husband, my mentor, and who I considered a close confidant and friend, stood by and did absolutely nothing to protect me.

Something did happen. In the midst of losing my sister and my brother-in-law, in the midst of finding out I was now the legal guardian of an infant — something else, something not as earth-shattering as losing Belle but still heartbreaking and painful, happened. I was falsely accused of lying, manipulating, and having adulterous intentions by an obviously mentally unstable woman. I was betrayed by a man I trusted, respected, and dedicated more than five years of my life to following.

I didn't just lose my sister and brother-in-law that week. I lost a substantial piece of myself. I was wounded, personally, and I let that wound fester for nine years. I can't say it was intentional avoidance; it was simply overshadowed by a bigger loss — a lifelong love and connection with another person that was more important to me than my own hopes and dreams.

I'm lying in my bed, staring at the ceiling, when a knock sounds on my bedroom door. I've been so lost in my thoughts that I didn't hear Skye return from wherever she stormed off to earlier when I refused to let her into my room, claiming a migraine. Sunny is staying the night with a friend again for their last night of break, and I couldn't be happier to have the apartment to myself. I need space. I need the quiet. I need Skye to stop knocking on my bedroom door.

My door is locked, so I'm not worried about her coming in. I can pretend to be asleep, and she'll go back to minding her own business. At least, I think that's how this will play out until I hear a click and watch the door handle turn.

What the hell?

I throw my arm over my eyes and groan, "I still have a headache. Go away." I don't know how she unlocked my door, but I'll find out later when I'm done sulking. If I'm ever done sulking.

The mattress dips and I feel her start to climb into bed beside me. I'm not in the mood, and I'm about to, once again, tell her to leave, when strong arms envelop me and I'm rolled and pulled into a firm chest. Strong, not very feminine arms and a firm, definitely not female chest.

I know this smell. I know these arms. Suddenly, I no longer feel alone. I'm no longer afraid. I feel… calm. Warm. Home.

Dexter holds me tightly to him and kisses the top of my head. He doesn't say anything — doesn't need to. We haven't spoken since I said goodbye to him Friday night, and he should be furious with me, but instead, he's holding me.

I, too, don't offer any words. I have none. Instead, I wrap my arms around his body and pull myself tighter to him. I nuzzle my face into his chest and cry.

———

IT'S afternoon when I wake in Dexter's embrace. His fingers run through my hair, and I sigh at how good it feels.

"You're here," I say, not yet allowing my gaze to meet his. For now, I'll stay exactly where I am — nose buried in his chest, smelling the delicious scent that is Dexter Belanger.

"I'm here," he replies, once again placing a kiss on my head and leaving his nose buried in my hair. We're quiet; I don't know that either of us knows what to say next. Finally, thankfully, he speaks.

"I don't want to push you, but I need to know what happened. I've been going out of my fucking mind this last week wondering why you disappeared. If I hadn't known you'd be at your parents' for the week, I would have thought something had happened to you."

He's right. I know he's right, but that doesn't make explaining this any easier. I push back from his chest and meet his eyes. I've never seen him like this before — relaxed, hair loose, wearing an old college tee and sweats. This is how I imagined waking up to him last Saturday, had the night before not gone to shit.

"I'm sorry I disappeared. I was overwhelmed and — no, that's not it. I don't even know where to begin." I sit up, running my fingers through my hair to somewhat tame my bedhead, and let out a deep breath.

Dexter turns fully onto his side, leans on his elbow, and props his head on his hand. "Do you want me to suggest starting at the beginning, or should I be quiet?" he asks, unleashing that intoxicating half-smile on me.

I swat his arm and laugh, thankful for levity when what I'm about to reveal is anything but light. "How about you start with how you know Jonathan Ryan."

Now I'm sitting next to him, legs crossed. I fold my hands in my lap and pick at my cuticles, trying to find the words to begin.

"Right. Dr. Ryan. I attended a lecture of his while I was still in high school, and knew immediately I wanted to study under him at Grant. School was never difficult for me, so I didn't have trouble getting a scholarship or into the English lit program. I spent my undergraduate years preparing myself to be one of his select graduate students."

"Impressive," Dexter says, adoration and respect gleaming in his eyes.

My cheeks pink at his praise. I'm not typically shy about my accomplishments or academic prowess, but I know Dexter understands the weight of what it means to study under Jonathan Ryan.

"Thank you. I assume you gathered from the party that my work paid off, and I secured a spot in his grad program, and then eventually I became his TA. I had about a year left when the accident happened..." I drift off, not sure how to explain the next part because I'm still coming to terms with the situation myself.

"You're tensing up again. When you saw Jonathan at the party Friday, your body reacted the same way. What happened?"

"I... I..."

"Look at me, Alis." I look in his eyes, so full of comfort and understanding. I know that no matter what comes out of my mouth next, even if it doesn't make sense to me, he'll know how to help me through it.

"I went to Dr. Ryan's office to talk with him about adjusting my schedule so I could become a commuter student. I had already decided to sublet my apartment until my lease was up and move home so I could raise Sunny with my parents. It was just a few days after the funeral, and I was a wreck. My emotions were everywhere, I hadn't slept well in days." I rub my forehead, trying to remember the details of that day as best I can.

"Dr. Ryan was incredible that day. He sat with me for probably an hour, reworking my schedule so I could stay in school and also still work as his TA. Instead of handing off my position to someone else, he was going to let me cut back and take on another student to fill in the gaps. I don't know if it was his generosity or something else that set me off, but I started sobbing. I couldn't stop crying, and he held me while I fell apart. I knew I looked up to him and respected him; I knew there was a reason why people loved him so much, but his sitting with me and reworking everything to accommodate me wasn't anything I expected. I guess I was overwhelmed," I shrug, stare up at the ceiling, and prepare to tell him the rest. I take a few seconds to gather my thoughts, and I'm thankful that Dexter doesn't interrupt or prompt me to continue. He knows I'll finish the story; I just need a moment.

"I honestly don't know any of the context for what happened next. It happened so fast, and I was already overwhelmed and overstimulated from everything that had taken place that week. All I remember is that Dr. Ryan was telling me everything was going to be alright, and then his office door opened, and his wife, Margaret, started shooting accusations at me, at him. I think she accused him of favoring me because he spoke of me at home. She insinuated that his working late had something to do with me. She seemed to start in the middle of an ongoing argument, and I had no context for what she was saying. At first, Dr. Ryan tried to calm her down and tell her she misunderstood what she walked in on, but she wouldn't stop. I tried to protect him by interjecting, but all that did was turn her ire on me. She accused me of trying to seduce him, of worshiping the ground he walks on... I don't remember everything she said. I tried to offer an explanation for why he was hugging me, even telling her that my sister had just died. She wouldn't listen. I think she even accused me of using my sister's death as a way to further manipulate her husband into my bed or something? I don't know. Like I said, it's a bit of a blur."

As the severity of my story grew, Dexter sat up from his position and sat back against the headboard, legs stretched in front of him. He's fisting my sheets on either side of him, visibly upset by what I've revealed.

"And Jonathan?" he asks.

"He just stood there. At first, he defended himself, but it's like once she really started going off, he cowered back and didn't say anything."

"Let me get this straight," Dexter says. "You were distraught and had just gone through the worst week of your life. He knew this, and when his wife burst in and started verbally attacking you, he did nothing?"

"Correct," I nod.

Dexter runs his hands through his hair, pulling at the roots. I can see he's trying to calm himself, trying not to fly off the handle at what I've just revealed. Eventually, albeit through clenched teeth, he asks, "Is there more?"

"More? Not really, no. Once I realized he wasn't going to defend me, protect me, whatever, I left. I remember hearing them yell at each other through the door as I left the offices, but I don't know what they were saying. I never went back."

"You just walked away?" I cannot tell if he's annoyed that I walked away or if he's simply trying to understand, but even if he is annoyed with my choice, I refuse to feel ashamed of my choice to leave that day.

"I did. It was all too much, and the moment I realized he wasn't going to bat for me, wasn't defending me or protecting me after I put myself in the line of fire to protect him, I was done. I hadn't done anything wrong — neither had he, really. He never touched me, never came onto me, nothing. Jonathan Ryan's only fault in all of this is being a spineless coward."

THIRTY-ONE

I AM STUNNED by what Alis has just revealed about her past with Dr. Ryan. Spineless coward is giving him too much credit, in my opinion, but I'm not here to perpetuate the problem or stoke her pain. I wish I knew what to say at this moment; wish I knew how to direct the anger I feel boiling up inside me. My frustration must be evident from my facial expression because Alis looks like she's trying to decipher my mood but can't. That makes two of us.

In the absence of any words to rectify the situation, I lean forward and grasp her hand in mine, beckoning her closer, and pulling her into my lap. I may not have words, but I can hold her.

I brush an errant hair from her eye and tuck it behind her ear, pulling her closer by the back of her neck and pressing my forehead to hers.

"I'm so sorry that happened," I whisper. And I am. I am torn apart that someone so hardworking, beautiful, and kind could be accused of something so disgusting and out-of-character.

"Thank you," she whispers in response. "I'm sorry I disappeared. You didn't do anything wrong. Seeing him was a shock, and then I got stuck in my head reading in between the lines of everything he said about me." I remember thinking the same thing about his comments — they conveyed a double meaning I couldn't quite grasp. Now I see his words for what they were — sharp jabs, carefully placed to slice through Alis's insecurities. What I don't understand is why he would attack her at all, no matter how subtly.

"I don't think anyone can be expected to consider anyone else's feelings when that type of emotional storm is raging inside," I try to offer words of comfort to let her know I am not angry or upset with her, not now that I understand their history.

One thing I still need confirmed, however, is the woman in the living room. "The woman who spilled her wine — was that his wife?" Alis is nodding before I've finished my sentence.

"Yes. I didn't realize it was her I had collided with until she shrieked 'you!' like I was some kind of harlot. Hearing her voice, laced with so much disgust and accusation even nine years later… It was too much. I think I went into self-preservation mode. It was so similar to how I felt when the accident happened and everything exploded around me. Maybe it was shock — I don't know. I just knew I had to get out of there as quickly as possible, so I called a cab and planned my escape."

"And with everything happening, you still tried to prioritize my career over your emotional well-being?" I ask, now, more than ever, certain this is the woman I want to spend the rest of my life loving. Her scrunched-up face is so adorable to look at right now. She's looking at me like I'm the daft one — questioning her commitment to seeing my hopes and dreams come to fruition.

"You couldn't lose this opportunity because your girlfriend got upset about something that happened nine years ago. In what world is that fair?" I let out a soft laugh and shake my head, sliding my hands to either side of her neck and pulling her mouth to mine — effectively cutting off her rant.

The kiss is short but effective. Alis smiles against my lips and I know this is what we needed. To talk, to touch, to start working through her pain together.

I pull back slightly, just enough to meet her gaze so I can tell her what I've been yearning to tell her for weeks now. "I love you, Alis," I say. My thumbs slide over her dimples as her smile lights up her face, eyes sparkling with joy at those few simple words.

"I love you, Dexter," she replies and takes my mouth with hers again. Alis slides her fingers into my hair and grips tightly, deepening our kiss and pressing her chest into me.

Alis wastes no time; in a matter of seconds she has readjusted her body to straddle my lap, her core pressing into my growing erection. We're kissing, grasping at clothing and writhing against each other. I break the kiss to lift her sleep tank over her head and I'm greeted by the sight of her bare chest. My God, she's breathtaking.

I trace my fingertips up her ribcage to the sides of her breasts, my thumbs tracing the crease underneath and up around the sides of each mound. I haven't touched anywhere near her nipples, but they are already puckered in anticipation.

Alis breathes heavily, her chest rising and falling rapidly as I take my time tracing the contours of her chest and up to her neck. It's when I'm tracing her collarbone that I see it — a cluster of freckles on her left clavicle. I'm suddenly hit with a sense of deja vu, as if I've done this before. Touched her before.

Rory? But, no, that doesn't make any sense. Rory was in college, on spring break with her friends. I'm stuck on the patch of freckles, unable to tear away my focus from them as I sift through memories from, what, twelve, thirteen years ago? It was a week — an incredible week, but a fleeting moment. A blip on the radar of my life.

"Dexter?" Alis asks, worry lacing her tone. "What is it?" she asks.

I clear my throat and shake my head to clear it. There's no way. The math doesn't add up. "It's nothing," I say, and I drop a kiss to the patch of freckles. It's when I'm pulling away and giving them one last glance before continuing my exploration of her body that I see it — the constellation.

"Andromeda," I breathe.

"What?" she asks. Does she not know her freckles are a constellation or did she not hear what I said?

"Andromeda," I say louder, looking up to her face to watch her reaction. She smiles, laughing lightly, and confirms what I've said. "You're only the third person to notice that. My grandmother taught me about constellations when I was a kid and she showed me how my birthmark makes the constellation Andromeda. One other person pointed it out once, but that's it."

I'm certain that Alis and Rory are one and the same, but I need her to realize who I am without my telling her. I don't know why, but it's important that she makes the connection herself. I decide to prompt her on this unexpected journey to reunification, teasing, "For anyone to notice a constellation of freckles on your collarbone they'd have to be pretty intimately acquainted with that area, no?" Alis blushes, my insinuation and her reluctance to confirm my suspicions clear in her expression.

She's not going to offer any more explanation, whether out of embarrassment or in an attempt to spare me thoughts of her with another man. She needs more prompting, for me to tug on the leash of her memories. I know she's fighting internally to stay in this moment and not veer off into thoughts of someone else, but I need her there.

"Tell me about him," I say, kissing up the side of her neck. My hands continue their exploration of her bare skin. Alis is breathless when she asks, "You want me to tell you about another man while I'm half-naked on your lap?"

"Tell. Me," I assert, nipping at her ear before continuing with languid kisses down her neck and back to her freckles.

Alis presses her core more firmly against me and starts to rock her hips, rubbing her clit up and down my shaft through our shorts. "Dexter," she pants, speeding the motion of her hips in an attempt to distract me from pressing for more details.

I grip her hips and hold her firm, removing my mouth from her shoulder where I was poised to continue tasting down her arm.

"I want to hear it," I say.

"Why? What if I don't want to share that with you?"

"Why wouldn't you want to share anything with me? Afraid I'll get jealous at the thought of you with someone else?" I smirk, letting my confidence and, let's be honest, cockiness shine through.

Alis huffs, "No. That story is just... it's awkward." Awkward? That week was anything *but* awkward for me.

"Why was it awkward?" I inquire. "Now I'm even more curious. Now you *have to* tell me." I'm teasing and she knows it, still, that signature shy expression appears on her face and I see her clearly. Twelve years younger, blue sundress blowing in the wind, laughing at something one of the other guys in our group said while recounting tales of frat parties past. I remember watching her, thinking she was the most beautiful girl I'd ever seen. Wide open, carefree, overflowing with happiness and joy. And her sister, oh my God, I remember Belle.

Before I can think deeper into how incredible a coincidence we've found ourselves in, Alis says, "I met him on a cruise during spring break of my senior year." Senior year? Wait. I do the math — holy shit, she was *eighteen*. I was twenty-two? No. Twenty-three.

"I met this guy, and we spent the week together. I didn't even tell him my name. Well, that's not entirely true. I went to introduce myself to him and Belle cut in telling him my name was Rory. Not technically a lie, but like I said that day in your office, I've never gone by Rory because I didn't want to make people think of Gilmore Girls."

I vaguely remember mention of this from when Abigail introduced us at the beginning of the school year. Alis continues, "Belle told me that I didn't have to feel self-conscious because Rory could be anyone she wanted to be. She knew I needed to let loose and enjoy myself, and, I don't know, I liked being able to recreate myself that week."

Before I realize what I'm doing, I say, "You didn't have to recreate yourself. You were your truest self that week."

My hands tense on her hips, but Alis is too busy brushing off my comment to notice. "Whatever. How would you know? You weren't there." She swats at my chest, "Do you want to hear the story or not?"

I swallow. I know what happens next. And I'm dying to hear it told from her perspective.

Alis

Dexter grows impossibly more stiff underneath me as I recount details of a week I spent with another man. I'm confused by his insistence that I tell him, and also by his reaction. I don't want to think of anyone else while I'm with him, nor would I ever want to hear about him with another woman, so I skim over the finer details and only share what I know he wants to hear.

"So the group of us girls met a group of college guys from the East Coast, and I hit it off with one of them. We had a really great week together, and I hadn't felt that easy of a connection with anyone before, so I took the plunge and slept with him the last night of the cruise."

"Took the plunge?" Dexter laughs, "Who says that?"

"Stop it," I chastise. "You're the one who wanted to hear all about how I lost my virginity to Andromeda man."

He freezes under me. "I was your first?" he whispers, eyes wide with shock.

"*He* was my first," I clarify.

"DJ," Dexter says.

"Yes, D— wait." I freeze. I never mentioned his name. How did he…?

Dexter locks his eyes with mine and unleashes that half-smile I adore so much. "I can say that you were your truest self that week because I was there, Rory." The way he says that name, *Rory*.

"Wh-what? How?" I ask, unable to grasp what he's saying.

"I realized it when I saw your birthmark," he says, leaning down and pressing his lips to my collarbone once more. "You confirmed it when you mentioned your grandmother, and, I must say, hearing that

I am the only other person to catalog this detail about you is every-thing to me right now."

"But, your hair. And your beard. And ..." I place my hands on either side of his face, searching his features for the much younger man I met so many years ago. His eyes. His smile. "Oh my God," I breathe. It's amazing how different a person can look with a few simple changes. But it is him. Dexter. DJ. One and the same.

The happiness welling up inside me at the confirmation that the man I love is the same man my sister encouraged me to let go and be free with is intoxicating. I slam my mouth against his, needing to be as close to him as possible.

Dexter wraps his arms around my back and holds me flush against him, our tongues dueling and bodies writhing against each other. I tear my mouth away from his and tug up his t-shirt roughly, needing to be skin-to-skin with him. He helps me to remove the shirt and tosses it to the side, sliding his hand to the back of my neck and pulling my mouth back to his.

I can feel him beneath me, hard as granite and lighting a fire in my core. I rock my hips against his, pressing myself down on his erection. It's not enough. I need more. I need to be fully connected to him. I need him inside me. Now.

"I need you," I moan against his mouth, pressing my core into him more insistently to convey my eagerness and impatience. Dexter grunts before gripping my hips and flipping us over so he's pressing me into the mattress.

"*J'ai besoin de toi*," he says gruffly, kissing down my neck, nipping at my collar bone before continuing to trail open mouth kisses down my chest to my breasts. "*Mon dieu, tu es délicieuse. Je vais te dévorer.*"

I'm about to combust from his words alone when he thrusts his pelvis into me, grinding his erection against my clit. At the same moment, he sucks my nipple into his mouth and bites down, tugging gently with his teeth while his hand roughly kneads my other breast.

Overwhelmed with sensation, I explode, tangling my fingers in his hair to keep his mouth exactly where I want him. Head thrown back, mouth open in a silent scream, I arch myself into him as I shudder beneath him. I have no words to describe the release I just felt with this man. It's as if the orgasm that rippled through my body went beyond the physical and into my very being. A complete surrender of oneself to another.

I'm still basking in the bliss of my orgasm when Dexter pulls his mouth from my breast and asks, "Do we need something?" A condom. Why didn't I think of that? I shake my head, panting, and say, "I'm on the pill."

"I'm clean," he states, trailing kisses back up my chest to my neck and to my ear. "Do you have any fucking idea how often I've fantasized about sinking myself inside you?"

I tremble at his words, unable to respond. The next thing I know Dexter is tearing my shorts and underwear down my legs. He shoves his shorts and boxer briefs down his thighs, not bothering to completely remove them before gripping me underneath my thigh to hike my leg up and around his waist.

He doesn't pause to ask if I'm ok like he did in the library so many years ago — I'm not the timid eighteen-year-old girl I was then. He knows I'm just as lost to him as he is to me at this moment. Leg now secured around his hips, Dexter reaches one hand up to my headboard and thrusts his hips forward, filling me in one stroke.

"Dexter!" I shout at the same time he grunts and exclaims through clenched teeth, "My God you're so fucking tight."

Sex, for me, has never been this raw, passionate, and unhinged. Dexter slams into me again and again, one hand braced against the headboard while the other grips my thigh. He slides that hand to my ass, tilting my hips and opening my leg wider for a better angle. My eyes roll into the back of my head as his next thrust rubs against my g-spot inside while his pelvis grinds against my clit.

"Dex," I pant, trying and failing to utter a complete sentence. "I… I'm going to…"

Dexter drops his mouth to mine, silencing my futile attempts at communicating. He kisses me once before pulling back slightly and whispering, *"Lâche prise, ma chérie. Lâche prise."*

Once again, I combust. I clench around him, my core pulsing, pulling him deeper into me. "Fuck, Alis," he groans, pressing his forehead against mine as my release triggers his own. We remain in this position for half a minute longer, breathing heavily, spent, slick with sweat. Eventually, Dexter opens his eyes and meets mine. He traces my cheekbone with the pad of his thumb and whispers, "I love you," before pressing a gentle kiss to my lips and carefully pulling out.

I lie there, completely relaxed and grinning like an idiot, while Dexter stands and walks to the bathroom to retrieve a towel for cleanup. I watch him walk across the room in all his naked glory, and I couldn't wipe the smile off my face if I tried. He soon returns and helps to clean me up, then climbs back into the bed and pulls me close to him.

I'm just about to drift off to sleep once more when he says, "We still need to talk about how you deceived me into thinking you were in college and then tricked me into taking your virginity."

I laugh into his chest and say, "I didn't lie; you assumed. On both fronts."

Dexter lets out a scoff and says, "*T'es un p'tit cave, mais je t'aime.*"

I snuggle closer into him, kissing his chest. "*Je t'aime,*" I whisper, and fall asleep in his arms.

EPILOGUE

Alis

LIFE CAN CHANGE SO MUCH in so short a time. I never could have imagined after less than a year in Grand River I'd be happily engaged to a professor at MPU and packing to move in with him. I can't decide who is most excited about our transition from apartment to house — Sunny or Otis. I never had pets while growing up, so I wasn't aware that the bond between a child and her dog could be so strong. And that's exactly what Otis is — hers.

Dexter and I are still learning to navigate the idiosyncrasies of co-parenting. He doesn't want to overstep but also knows it's his responsibility to be a father to Sunny. Some days are smooth, some aren't, but with open communication and a lot of love and grace, we're figuring it out, day by day.

Jonathan Ryan accepted Dr. Matthews' invitation to teach his lecture series as a seminar for MPU students. Dexter and I had numerous conversations about whether or not we should reveal what happened all those years ago to Abigail, and, while we still don't fully agree, Dexter respects that it's ultimately my decision to confront Jonathan about the past and to tell anyone else.

Perhaps I made the cowardly choice to not confront him or Margaret, to expose what happened so others could see the truth of the Ryans' marital dysfunction and how their toxicity can hurt the people around them. It's possible — nay, probable — I'm not the only person who has been the victim of Margaret's deeply-rooted insecurities. However, I refuse to take on the burden of responsibility for someone else's issues. It's not my responsibility to force another person to deal with their own problems. Hell, I'm still working on my own.

I'd never refuse support to someone who went through something similar, nor would I ever lie to keep my past hurts buried. I do, however, have a right to my own privacy. I don't owe the world my story. This isn't some novel where the characters complete their respective growth cycles with an epiphany that instantly corrects every wrong choice they have ever made or heals deeply-seeded wounds.

I am a whole person, scars and all, and I will struggle through my past one day at a time. I'll marry Dexter Belanger while still battling my insecurities about not being strong enough or confident enough without a support system, without my sister. Not having every question answered or insecurity dealt with before partnering with someone else doesn't make me codependent or incapable of standing on my own two feet.

We aren't walking into happily ever after — we're continuing our walk through life, one step, one chapter at a time. The difference is that now we're walking together, hand in hand with the person we love and trust to help us avoid potholes and climb over boulders in our path. We'll laugh, cry, fight, disagree, disappoint, make mistakes, act selfishly, act lovingly, forgive, support, and learn from each other. And isn't that what makes life worth living? Not reaching a destination or state of perfection, but growing with the people you love.

"Alis?" Dexter's voice cuts through my inner monologue. "What's up?" I ask, still folding the same sheet I grabbed twenty minutes ago.

He laughs, "Having trouble there?" I swat his arm and tell him to hush, then give up on the sheet, folding and crumpling it into a ball before shoving it into the box in front of me. We're packing up the final few boxes to move to Dexter's home — our home.

When he asked Sunny and me to move in, I was unsure how we'd accomplish that with nearly half a year left on our apartment lease. Little did I know Skye would be relieved when I sat down to talk with her about it — apparently she has a friend in need of a place to stay, and now she can move in here and split the rent costs.

I haven't met this friend, and Skye has been tight-lipped about her; only revealing that she's in a tight situation and has been looking for a new roommate.

I'm taping up the last box when I hear the front door open and Skye's voice calling, "Honey, we're home!" *We?*

I stand and lift the box of linens to carry to the living room, nearly tripping over a pile of shoes in the hallway. "Sunny! Why aren't your shoes in a box already?" I call out to her before continuing into the living room. I thought her room was completely packed and ready to load into the Rover, but apparently that's not the case.

"Hey," I say to Skye as I walk into the living room and set the box down with the others. Dexter and Leo have been carrying them from the apartment to their vehicles, trying to fit the rest into my car, Dexter's Range Rover, and Leo's truck to make this our last trip.

I'm about to ask what she meant by 'we' when the last person I expected to see walks through the door, two suitcases in tow.

"Tori?!" I question, not sure why she's here. She sets down her suitcases off to the side and steps closer to wrap me in a hug. "Hey, babe," she says, squeezing me tightly and holding on for longer than a greeting hug warrants.

I pull back, keeping my hands on her arms as I study her. "What are you doing here?" I ask, then add, "I mean, holy crap am I happy to see you. I just wasn't expecting it. And what's with all the baggage?"

Tori smiles softly and meets my gaze, and that's when I see it — the dark circles under her eyes, the sheer exhaustion on her face.

"Are you okay?" I whisper, suddenly overwhelmed with concern for my best friend.

"Yeah," she says. "Or, at least, I will be." She shrugs and turns to look at Skye.

"You didn't tell her?" Tori asks. Skye shakes her head as I ask, "Tell me what?"

I look back to Tori, who now has a nervous expression on her face when Skye says, "Say hello to my new roomie!"

ABOUT THE AUTHOR

B.J. Hill wants to live in a world where it doesn't matter if you're a square peg or a round hole; where 'round' is a perfectly-acceptable goal for getting 'in shape'; and where unfiltered and messy life is not only welcomed, but celebrated.

Her books—edgy and heartfelt narratives—explore the depths of human connection, the bittersweet taste of life, the redemptive power of love, and the belief that true strength is often found in vulnerability. They are important to her because they offer a space where passion meets purpose, where characters break and mend, and where readers can find solace in the shared experience of resilience and hope.

She is the sunshine to her grumpy-ish college sweetheart, mom to the three coolest offspring in the world, and devoted subject to her feline royal majesties, Belle and Lucy. When she's not writing stories about her imaginary friends, you can find her reading, using her outside voice at inopportune moments, or being generally awkward (I mean, awesome. Totally awesome).

BUT WAIT, THERE'S MORE!

B.J. is also the innovative founder and CEO of JibblyBitz, a company that embraces the vibrancy and authenticity of storytelling. Through JibblyBitz, she aims to extend that connection, crafting a community where stories uplift, challenge, and transform.

Find JibblyBitz at an author signing event near you or at:

JibblyBitz Website
Instagram
TikTok
Facebook

www.ingramcontent.com/pod-product-compliance
Lightning Source LLC
Chambersburg PA
CBHW070441300726
48975CB00007B/1995